THROUGH THE FIRE AND FLAME

THROUGH THE FIRE AND FLAME

THE KURTHERIAN ENDGAME™ BOOK THREE

MICHAEL ANDERLE

L M B P N

DISRUPTIVE IMAGINATION

LMBPN Publishing
PMB 196, 2540 South Maryland Pkwy
Las Vegas, NV 89109

First US edition, November 2018
Version 1.04, June 2024
Print ISBN: 978-1-64202-480-7

THROUGH THE FIRE AND FLAME TEAM

Thanks to our Beta Readers

Bree Buras
Dorothy Lloyd
Tom Dickerson
Dorene Johnson
Diane Velasquez

Thanks to the JIT Readers

John Ashmore
Kelly O'Donnell
Diane L. Smith
Chrisa Changala
James Caplan
Keith Verret
Nicole Emens
Daniel Weigert
Peter Manis
Misty Roa
Angel LaVey
Mary Morris
Kimberly Boyer
Larry Omans

If I've missed anyone, please let me know!

Editor
Lynne Stiegler

*To Family, Friends and
Those Who Love
to Read.
May We All Enjoy Grace
to Live the Life We Are
Called.*

_____

High Tortuga, Space Fleet Base, Queen's Suite, (two months after leaving the quarantine zone)

Bethany Anne watched the video intake from the small drone following Michael, Peter and Akio. She tapped her lip while she completed her thought, "Anytime that man is that happy, something is going on I probably *don't* want to know about."

Cheryl Lynn looked up from her tablet to frown at the vid-screen for a moment. "You know what Michael is up to," she reminded Bethany Anne. "He's going after his T-rex."

Bethany Anne narrowed her eyes and dropped her hand to tap on the table instead. "I know, but somehow, someway, he's going to come back with ten tons of meat."

"I thought that was inevitable?" Cheryl Lynn countered, pointing from Bethany Anne to the screen. "You *have* been stalling the hunt for ages. I'm surprised he waited this long."

Bethany Anne sighed. "Yeah, me too. I just thought that

if I kept his mind on other things, the great dinosaur hunt wouldn't happen."

"Why is it such a big deal, anyway?" Cheryl Lynn asked. She placed the tablet to the side and started moving her hands. "He goes out hunting, kills for the meat, and comes back. It's not like you have to eat it, or even be around it. Hell, he could have asked you to go with him to hunt the damned thing. You got off lightly."

Bethany Anne frowned as she turned to look at her friend, one eyebrow raised. "Doesn't Scott have a hobby that just rubs you the wrong way?"

Cheryl Lynn snorted. "You mean, other than liking stuff just because he is a guy? C'mon, you can't tell me you have been against this," she waved a hand at the screen Bethany Anne was watching, "just because *he* likes it?"

Bethany Anne made a face. "I'm being a girl, aren't I?"

Cheryl Lynn raised both eyebrows, a glint of a smile on her lips, "What, the fairer sex? The passionate side of humanity who integrates emotions and logic in equal measure?" Cheryl Lynn stopped and giggled. "Yeah, I can't sell that one." She waved a hand in a circle that encompassed Bethany Anne. "You are acting like a girl, yes."

Bethany Anne turned back to the screen and sighed. She called, "CEREBRO?"

"Yes?"

"Cancel my video tracking." The screen went off as Bethany Anne turned back to Cheryl Lynn, decision made. "Okay, I promised you a couple of girly movies, and I agree —watching Michael isn't a girly movie. I'm worried about him, and I don't like him taking chances."

Cheryl Lynn made a sympathetic face. "He's not exactly

the kind of man who can be tamed. I mean, at least Scott came partly trained. Michael is…"

"An ass?"

Cheryl Lynn snickered. "Yeah, that too. But you knew that about him when you started loving him."

"So?" Bethany Anne retorted. "I figured I could change him. I don't think that's any different than the other few billion women in our species' history."

There was a silence that stretched out in the long moment before Cheryl Lynn broke it. "It's okay. They failed, too."

Bethany Anne smirked. "Who says I've failed? I've had a long time to learn how to pick my battles. This is just a minor skirmish in a *much* longer war."

"I'd say you were being dramatic as well as girly, but…" Cheryl Lynn lifted a shoulder. "Never mind."

Bethany Anne raised an eyebrow in amusement. "No no, go on. But *what?*" She let the silence stretch for a few more moments while Cheryl Lynn thought of a way to dig herself out of the hole she'd inadvertently stumbled into.

Cheryl Lynn grinned. "It's kind of cute the way you two fight without fighting."

"Nice save," ADAM cut in from a nearby speaker. "Not to mention the endless entertainment we all get from betting on the outcome of whatever one of you is trying to pull on the other."

Both women looked at the speaker on the wall.

Bethany Anne pursed her lips. "This is a *girls'* night, ADAM."

"I didn't plan on staying." ADAM sounded a little bit

miffed. "I only wanted to tell you that Tabitha is on her way."

"You wanted to see what you were missing out on, more like," Cheryl Lynn teased. "It's only movie night."

Bethany Anne smiled. "You can stay if you want. I'm sure Cheryl Lynn and Tabitha won't mind."

"I'll pass, thanks," ADAM replied airily. "I've seen your movie queue for the evening, and you're welcome to your clichéd sob-fest. Besides, I've known you all long enough to know that if I stick around I'll hear way more than I *ever* wanted to know about the guys. I'll catch you later."

Bethany Anne snickered. "You've got us there. Bye, ADAM."

Cheryl Lynn's eyes twinkled mischievously. "I have no idea what he's talking about."

"I know, right?" Bethany Anne grinned. "We would *never* talk about the guys behind their backs. Who even does that?" She shook her head. "It's not like he can't just listen in on my thinking if he wants."

>>**I try not to do that.**<<

You do?

>>**Much.**<<

There was a thump and a bang as Tabitha entered Bethany Anne's suite with a string of muttered curses.

Cheryl Lynn got up and put her throw blanket to the side. "I'll go make the popcorn."

Bethany Anne watched the door with a slight frown, waiting for Tabitha to appear. "We might need more than popcorn. Break out the ice-cream. The good stuff."

Tabitha flounced in with a face like thunder and collapsed on the sofa with a heavy sigh. "Ugh! *Men!*" she growled, then grimaced, then hid her face in her hands and burst into tears.

Bethany Anne's eyes narrowed. This was beyond Tabitha's standard flair for the dramatic. "Well fuck, this looks serious. What's up?" She held up a finger before Tabitha could speak. She turned her head toward the kitchen. "Cheryl Lynn, the popcorn can wait. Just bring the ice-cream."

Tabitha grabbed one of the sofa cushions and hugged it to herself. "Stupid men, that's what. How can they be so... *Gott Verdammt stupid?*"

Cheryl Lynn walked back in from the kitchen and handed Tabitha the carton of triple-chocolate ice cream and a spoon. "Did you and Peter have another fight?"

Tabitha poked at the ice cream half-heartedly. "*That* would be the polite way of putting it." She set the carton on the table and glared at it as though the ice cream were to blame for her mood. "I'm not really that hungry."

Bethany Anne and Cheryl Lynn shared a concerned glance and moved in to bookend Tabitha on the couch.

"Come on, it can't be all *that* bad." Cheryl Lynn leaned in with a hug. "Tell us all about it. We can curse Peter out together until you feel better."

"I don't want to talk about it. Just *thinking* about it gets me mad." Tabitha pulled away slightly from Cheryl Lynn's embrace and looked at them both with more tears threatening to spill down her angry face. "You know what? Screw him. I just want to have a fun night with my girls." She leaned forward and snatched the ice cream carton and spoon from the table.

Bethany Anne grinned. "There's our Tabitha. You know it freaks me out when you say shit like, 'I'm not hungry.'"

Tabitha stabbed the ice cream with her spoon. "You know it. Now, what chick-flicks did you find? Better not be the kind where the love interest dies at the end. That might be a little too close to real life."

Bethany Anne snorted, but shared another concerned look with Cheryl Lynn. It was the kind of look only two mothers can share, and Tabitha didn't appreciate it one bit.

"Oh, lighten up. I'm not really going to kill Peter." Tabitha kicked off her shoes and put her feet up on the ottoman. "Probably. Maybe."

Her face told Bethany Anne a different story. "You know I'm here for you if you want to talk about it."

"We both are," Cheryl Lynn added.

"I know." Tabitha sighed. "Maybe later." She waved her spoon at the screen. "Movie night first."

High Tortuga, Southern Continent

Peter trudged through the brush, rolling a shoulder every now and then to shift the weight of Tabitha's rifle on his back.

The subtropical heat was oppressive. It rose from the jungle floor in moist, shimmering waves that distorted the air around the hunting party and caused uncomfortable rivulets of sweat to run down their backs with every step they took.

They'd been hiking since daybreak and Peter was bored with the monotony of the trek.

Michael and Akio had been their usual stoic selves

since they'd left the transport, and Peter was wondering why he'd come along on this hunt if they weren't going to have any of the fun he'd been promised.

He'd voiced this a couple of hours ago, but Michael had just winked and told him that they *were* having fun.

Maybe it wasn't too late to go back.

The two vampires stepped softly, which annoyed Peter further. Despite his best efforts, he was making more noise than Michael and Akio put together.

He shifted the rifle again, grumbling internally at the inconvenience. He hadn't wanted to bring the damn thing, but Tabitha had insisted.

Very vocally.

And a little bit physically, too.

Michael cleared the path ahead, cutting through the jungle with the hardened Etheric energy he'd coated his hands in. He looked around every so often, and then put his head down and continued to hack at the foliage.

Michael paused suddenly and held up a finger. "Aaaand...it's gone."

Peter halted beside Michael and Akio and glanced around to see what Michael was talking about. He looked behind him before looking back at the guys. "What's gone?"

Akio looked at Peter and chuckled. "The video drone Bethany Anne had following us. You didn't spot it?"

Peter turned to Michael to confirm Akio's answer.

Michael nodded and resumed pushing his way through the thick foliage with Akio close behind. "It's been with us since we left the base."

Peter followed, frowning. "I wasn't looking for it."

There was a pause before he continued, "Don't you mind Bethany Anne keeping tabs on you like that?"

"Of course I *mind*," Michael replied. He ducked under a low-hanging branch. "But I also understand that Bethany Anne worries. She sends the drones, but they never stay long. If it makes her feel secure, I will put up with it." He stopped and looked up into the foliage before the bird up there moved away, and then continued pushing forward. "Up to a point."

Peter followed, ducking under the branch. "Has she been so insecure?" he asked. "I know she was a bit antsy after the twins were born, but having you followed is kind of extreme."

Akio snorted. "Did you miss the part where she locked him ten thousand feet underground for three years?"

Peter smirked at Akio's exaggeration. "I thought the point of hunkering down at the base was to make everyone forget us?"

Michael sliced through a thin tree with more force than necessary. "She did not 'lock me up,'" he grumped, only just avoiding being hit by the falling tree. "We have been a little busy raising our infant children." His face softened into a grin. "Fatherhood is very involved in these modern times."

Akio's eyebrow twitched.

"I saw that." Michael sighed. "Very well," he admitted reluctantly, "she locked us all up." He held up a finger. "*But.* She has been working on her need to keep us all within her sights."

Peter hid his laugh with a cough. "You mean her need to keep *you* within her sights."

Michael waved Peter's teasing off. "Semantics. The

point is that we've only been gone a few hours. I thought we would have to spend at least a day wandering aimlessly before Bethany Anne was satisfied that I am not putting myself in danger and recalled her surveillance."

Akio glanced around. "Are we good to go now?"

"We are." Michael sniffed the air and headed in a completely different direction than the one they had taken so far. "Now that the drone is gone, the fun can really begin. *Let's hunt.*"

Peter slipped between the trees and hurried to keep up with the two vampires. "We weren't hunting before?" he called.

Akio shook his head. "No, Peter. This was merely a diversion." He broke into a wry smile. "You have *so* much to learn about women."

Michael snorted from up ahead where the foliage was thick enough to need pruning. "My friend, I think you have some things to learn yourself."

Akio turned red, and his smile fell away. "I think not." He pushed through the brush to get ahead of the others.

Michael gave the back of Akio's head a pointed look, knowing the man would feel it. "I would argue differently. Did you speak to Sabine yet?"

Peter moved a branch out of his way. "Why does Akio need to speak to Sabine?"

Michael didn't answer, so he caught up to Akio and bumped him with an arm. "Why do you need to speak to Sabine? I thought she was on Devon?"

Akio sighed, looking straight ahead as he walked to avoid making eye contact with the younger man. "She is. She sent me a letter."

Peter frowned. "A message? That doesn't sound too strange."

"A letter," Akio repeated. "On paper. Not a message."

"What's that got to do with..." Peter's confusion deepened until he connected what Akio was saying to the way his body language screamed for Peter to drop the subject. "*Ohhh,* a *letter.*"

Akio hung his head in misery. "Exactly."

Peter sucked in a breath. "Oh, man. How are you going to deal with that?"

Michael looked back, pausing in his efforts to cut them a path through the undergrowth since they had reached a fairly open part of the jungle. "So far he has been doing his best to ignore the situation."

"I am not ignoring it," Akio countered. "I simply do not know how to resolve it. Sabine is like a daughter to me."

Michael led them through the clearing and onto an animal trail. "You mean you're afraid she'll shoot you full of holes if you break her heart." He looked at Akio and saw the misery his friend was in. "Okay, joking aside, it is only going to get worse if you don't deal with it."

Akio continued to look at his feet as they walked. "I *will* deal with it. As soon as I know how to do so without hurting Sabine in the process."

Michael gave his old friend a hard look. "That is only going to hurt her more in the long run. I told you what to do. You just need to place someone who is attainable—but also good enough—in front of her. Distract her. She knows deep down that it can never happen between you two."

"Set her up?" Akio winced. "That would be...*beyond* awkward, and perhaps not honorable."

Peter made a rapid revision of his predicament. "I thought *I* had it bad, but your situation puts mine in perspective. Relationships are hard."

"Women are the root of all confusion," Michael sympathized, patting him on the back. "If we just remember that, then it's not such a shock when they turn the world upside down on a whim." He looked over when Peter didn't react to his half-joking wisdom. "What's up? Are you and Tabitha having problems?"

Peter shrugged. He was still confused as to what had set her off this morning. "Not so much *problems*. At least, I didn't think so? Tabbie, she's my best friend, and we get on great most of the time. She's just a bit...um...fiery at the moment."

Akio chuckled dryly. "Isn't fiery the middle name of all Hispanic women?"

Michael joined in with Akio's laughter. "I don't think that's reserved for just the Hispanic women in our lives. Anyway, I thought you liked that about her."

Peter huffed and kicked out at a protruding tree root. "Fieriness I don't mind. But she's been worse than her usual snarky self recently. I'll be honest, I agreed to come on this hunt to avoid whatever she came up with to call me out on today."

"Call you out?" Michael enquired.

"Scream and throw stuff at me to emphasize whatever point she's making," Peter clarified. "Followed by tears when I don't get it. I *would* get it if she just made *sense*, you know? Even when I agree with her, she's not happy. Don't get me wrong, the making up is worth it. I just wish I understood what was going on with her." He threw up his hands in defeat. "If she wants to break up, then she should just say."

Akio sighed. "Women are difficult."

Peter chuckled. "Yeah, well, don't let a woman hear you say that. *Especially* not Tabitha." He looked around as Michael adjusted their trajectory. He looked left, then right. "Do you know where we are or are we winging it?"

They turned again as Michael made another small adjustment to their course that led them deeper into the jungle. "A little of both, actually."

He jumped a log, barely touching it at about ten feet off the ground before landing softly on the other side. Akio and Peter followed. "We look for higher ground so we can find the path made by our prey. I don't want to use the satellites to locate the beast. That's a sure way to attract Bethany Anne's attention again. If we keep things quiet, she doesn't worry."

Peter nodded. "Makes sense."

Michael smirked. "Of course it does. I know my wife. This is not my first hunt, but it's the first one in a long, long time that is not about tracking down someone who had done us evil. I intend to enjoy every minute of it…now that there is no danger of my wife turning up and taking my kill because 'I might get hurt.'"

Peter snickered. "Shit, yeah. I forgot you've been around long enough to hunt *real* dinosaurs." He dodged the tree limb that came flying at him. "Hey, you can't get mad at the truth!"

Michael turned to Akio, his face set in immutable lines. "The bait we brought to attract the T-rex is a bit too talkative. I think *I'll* pick next time." He ignored Peter's grumbling and kept walking ahead until they reached a break in the jungle at the top of a low rise.

Akio pointed out the broken line in the sea of trees that indicated the path they were looking for. "We have our T-rex."

In the distance, they picked up the faint sound of trees being uprooted and tossed aside as the moving mountain forged its way through the jungle.

Michael was already halfway down the rise. "We have to catch up to it first."

It didn't take them long to reach the path the T-rex had ripped through the pristine jungle. They clambered over the uprooted trees and brush piled high at the sides of the makeshift track.

Peter was first to make it onto the trail. He gaped at the wide tract of destruction. "Great fucking toad balls." His eyes narrowed when he noticed a four-foot wide tree trunk broken like a twig. "I thought you said they didn't get that big on this part of the continent?"

Michael didn't pause to look around.

He vaulted the log Peter had used to get onto the path and set off immediately in the direction the dinosaur had taken. "They do not," he called back "This one is away from its usual stomping grounds, which I find to be odd. I've been watching it since it left its regular territory. It has crossed most of the continent in the last few weeks."

Peter trailed after Michael and Akio. "What's so odd about that? It's a big continent."

Michael looked distant as he walked. "They do not usually leave their territory, at least as far as I have observed to date. I'm almost certain it is searching for its death."

"What makes you say that?" Akio asked.

Michael walked on a bit, skirting a bit of water before he answered, "Maybe I am wrong, but it is definitely searching for something."

"What if it just wants to be the biggest bad?" Peter suggested. "It could be looking for combat. You know, some young pup who was dumb enough to be willing to take on Daddy T-rex."

"Also possible," Michael conceded. "However, it has fought many battles in the time I've been observing it and has yet to meet its match. I believe it to be the largest creature on this planet. Whether it is simply looking for death or is also seeking combat, I will offer it the honor of both."

Peter's eyes shone. "That reminds me of this documentary I saw when I was a kid. There was this lion, and he was the biggest, nastiest fucker on the savannah until one day he broke his leg on a hunt. It kind of healed, but then a couple of younger lions came along and drove him out. So he went round fighting until he…"

He noticed Michael and Akio staring at him. "What?" He looked behind him and then used a hand to check his hair. "Do I have a spider on me?"

Open Space, System QTC-12-T, QBS _Glaxix Sphaea_

The ship Gated in a safe distance from the nebula and headed for the debris field kissing the edge of the cloud that was all that remained of the battle between the EI Lorelei and the unknown enemy ship.

Kael-ven got out of his captain's chair when he saw the wreckage of the two ships come into range on the viewscreen. "Scan for everything, Kiel. And I mean *everything*. We do not want to be blindsided by a surprise attack because we turned off the cloaking too soon."

Kiel turned his head to look at Kael-ven without getting up from his station. "I love how you issue these orders despite knowing I sent drones out to scan the nebula the instant we left the Gate. There are no emissions that can't be explained. We're clear to get over there and investigate the crap out of this place."

Kael-ven shook his head and indicated the screen. "The scout ship techs are suited up and ready to go." Two spacesuited figures left the ship and floated toward the empty battlefield on long tethers. "Bring up the comm links."

Kiel turned back to his station, and a moment later the bridge was filled with the hiss of the two techs breathing inside their helmets.

Kael-ven waited the extra moment, and a pair of windows showing the camera feeds from their helmets appeared in the top corners of the viewscreen. The techs moved rapidly toward the fragmented ships, using their thruster packs to compensate for the solar wind.

"Mellor, Robinson, report."

"It's eerie out here," Mellor answered in an awed voice.

"Focus," Kael instructed. "Do you see the core?"

The feeds panned jerkily as the techs split up and searched among the dead ships for the EI cores.

Robinson stood on the *Lorelei*'s one remaining wing and pulled herself through a jagged tear in the side of the ravaged scout ship. She tapped her shoulder-mounted flashlight to increase the brightness. "I've got it."

Mellor floated up and landed beside Robinson on the wing. "I bet you're glad the Queen insisted on this design now."

Robinson looked up from where she was unbolting EI Lorelei's cradle. "No, I'm not. They were a bitch to build. Wings are cool and all, but not the most practical place to put the heat exchanger."

Mellor laughed. "Are you kidding me? They act like elephant ears. You're probably still sore she didn't pick your design over this one."

Robinson rolled her eyes and flicked a bolt at him. "So what if I am?" She bent over and tugged the cradle holding EI Lorelei's data core free. "Come on, let's get back to the ship before the captain has a conniption."

"I can hear you," Kael-ven's dry voice reminded them.

"Sorry, Captain," Robinson trilled. She stuck a tether on the cradle and passed the other end to Mellor before doing the same again with another tether and attaching the other end to her suit. She glanced at Mellor. "Ready?"

He nodded that he was. The two techs launched themselves toward the *G'laxix Sphaea*. Almost immediately after they boarded, the ship moved away and Gated out of the system again.

2

_____

High Tortuga, Southern Continent

The three men followed the trail until it spat them out abruptly at the edge of the jungle. They continued to follow the path of torn-up dirt and the odd uprooted tree across a wide, grassy scrubland that dipped and rose gradually all the way to the uplands in the distance.

Michael shaded his eyes against the strong midafternoon sun and looked into the distance. "I can see our quarry." He pointed at the slow-moving shadow on a far-off hilltop. It vanished over the other side as he watched. "We're closing on it."

"Then we should get going." Peter wasted no time taking advantage of the more open ground. "Race you!" he called back.

Michael broke into a run. "The young and the ignorant."

Akio's lips pressed together in what could almost be called a full-on smile on the man and sprinted up the hill past Michael. "You're quite fast for an old man."

Michael opened it up another notch, leaving Akio in his dust. "And you're pretty vocal for the one in last place."

Peter stepped it up as the two vampires sped past him, and the three accelerated over the scrubby hills. They leapfrogged as they ate up the miles between them and the confrontation that awaited them. The wind in their faces felt good, and every so often it carried the roar of the beast in the distance to guide them.

Peter stopped at the top of a hill and looked around. "Hey, Michael, I think you're right."

Michael slowed and came up beside him. "I'm always right. The question is merely which instance of my being right are you referring to?"

Peter gestured to the empty land around them. "I can't think why else the T-rex would come here. There's nothing but insects and grass."

"Nothing except our T-rex," Michael corrected. "I can smell him; we're close."

They descended the slope and ran up the next, closing the gap between them and the dinosaur. As they neared the top the wind shifted, and the almost-melancholy roar of the T-rex came, muted slightly by the distance.

The gradient gradually leveled out onto the windswept uplands they'd seen earlier. They came upon the T-rex on a wide plateau that stretched toward a scraggly tree line before it dropped off.

Peter nodded over to the dinosaur on the far side. "I wonder if it's lost its mind?" The T-rex was within reach at last. However, when they finally got near enough, they saw that it was acting oddly. It stomped and tore at the bare ground around it for no reason Michael and the others could decipher.

A rogue gust of wind hit them from behind, and the dinosaur's nostrils flared when it picked up three humans' scent. It turned around and zeroed in on the three men, stamping its feet and roaring a challenge.

"Looks like it wants a fight," Akio remarked dryly.

Michael dropped his pack on the ground beside him. "I will be more than happy to offer it one." He pulled his shirt off and held it out to Akio, and accepted the two swords Akio offered him in return. He tilted one of the swords to examine the edge in the light, then turned to Peter and Akio with a serious expression. "You will both remain out of this. It is my fight alone."

Peter looked longingly at the rampaging beast. "It's just like you not to share, but okay." He sat down cross-legged and folded his arms. "Next time you invite me to go hunting, I'm staying home."

Akio gave Michael a sharp nod. "As you wish, my friend."

They both grinned as Michael's anticipation spilled over.

Akio eyed the T-rex appraisingly. "Have you considered that maybe Bethany Anne has a point about how much meat we're going to take home?"

Michael's mouth twitched. "With all the Wechselbalg around? Not for a moment. We will have the barbeque to end all barbeques, and my wife will eat her words as a side with the delicious steak I grill for her."

Peter wrinkled his nose and spoke up. "I dunno about delicious. Reptile meat is an acquired taste."

Michael shrugged. "If by 'acquired' you mean everyone will try to acquire seconds after they taste it, then yes, it is." He adjusted his grip on the swords and started to cross the plateau. He looked over the edge as he drew close to it. The drop below was not one he wished to test his indestructibility on.

The T-rex narrowed its eyes and roared, and Michael moved forward to meet it. The plateau was dead silent as Michael and the T-rex stared each other down. Even the insects ceased their shrilling.

The massive reptile roared and scored the ground with its heavy claws as it pawed and stomped.

Michael let his own roar rip and charged across the grass at the ten-ton beast crashing toward him, its footsteps shaking the ground.

Planet Colonnara, Orbit-to-Surface Transfer Platform, The *Lady Princess*

The *Lady Princess* slid into the dock, and Addix and the children joined the river of shoppers spilling out of the ships around them. They, like the others, moved toward the Customs desks in front of the transfer corridors leading to the shuttles.

Addix noticed there were a few children accompanied by nannies in the crowd. Some of the nannies were having an easier time than others. She was among the former, although "nanny" was not the best descriptor since she was there in her usual role of guide and protector rather than any kind of authority figure.

She was looking forward to some quality aunt time

while they were on Colonnara. The planet was, in essence, a gigantic shopping mall in an affluent area of space near the edge of the Federation. She'd been surprised when Michael and Bethany Anne had allowed this excursion.

But they knew that she would lay down as many lives as it took to keep Alexis and Gabriel safe, including her own if it came to it.

They were less accepting of her indulgence of their offspring, but Addix didn't care. She planned to make their trip off High Tortuga a memorable one.

She loved the two tiny humans as though they were her own, and although their parents may have been correct in their assessment of her as somewhat of a libertarian when it came to child-rearing, they had conceded that it was important the twins had room to learn from their mistakes.

She took their hands to lead them from the shuttle when it landed and the airlock hissed open. They got onto the escalator, and the children tried to run ahead.

"Not yet," Addix told them. "We're almost there."

The tunnel widened as it led them to the massive doors to the entrance. Addix couldn't hide her amusement when the twins tugged their hands out of hers and darted onto the open court with eyes almost as large as hers.

"This place is insane!" Gabriel turned a wide circle as he tried and failed to take in the many levels of the shrine to conspicuous consumption they'd arrived at. "I've never seen so many different stores."

Alexis looked at Addix with a worried expression. "It's bigger than the whole base!"

"We can access a map of the complex." Addix chuckled

as she placed a protective hand on each of their shoulders and guided them along the concourse. "We will eat first, and then we will shop. Your EI can be our guide."

Alexis tapped her wrist-holo to call Phyrro as they walked. The EI's warm face appeared in 3-D above the device.

"How can I help, Alexi—" Phyrro's head turned from side to side. "I was not informed we would be leaving High Tortuga. Why are we on Colonnara?"

Alexis grinned. "Because we're buying a gift for Mommy. Can you connect to the station network and bring up the map?" She turned to Gabriel. "Maybe we can buy her some shoes? She has so many already, though. She probably doesn't need any more. I know Daddy thinks she has enough already."

Addix's mandibles twitched in humor. "I'm not sure you should be telling me this, Alexis."

The twins shared a knowing look. "We know you won't tell, Aunt Addix," Gabriel told her.

"Mommy loves shoes." Alexis looked up at the alien. "Did *you* know she has a room that's full of them, Aunt Addix? I went in there once."

"No, you didn't," Gabriel contested. "We're not allowed in there. Not even *Daddy* is allowed in there."

Alexis stuck her tongue out at her brother. "Did too, Gabriel. ADAM let me in to look at them." She lifted her nose in the air and kept walking.

Gabriel made a face. "I don't want to buy boring shoes. I want to get Mommy a new sword!"

"Now, now, children." Addix bent over to look at them

from under her hood. "Shoes are almost always a perfect gift for your mother, and a blade is an appropriate gift for almost any occasion. But we're here to buy a Mother's Day gift, so something a touch more personal might be better." She adjusted her robe as her foot caught the hem, inwardly cursing the restrictive fabric.

Alexis wrinkled her nose. "Why are you wearing that thing if it makes you so unhappy?"

"For the same reason you and Gabriel are dressed as you are," she replied. "We are blending in with our surroundings."

Alexis squirmed, reminded that she was wearing the kind of silly, frilly clothing that the other girls around her were dressed in. She wished for her atmosuit and combat boots.

She pulled on her sleeve. "I wish you hadn't reminded me. Now I have to forget to feel the itchiness all over again. Why couldn't I just wear a cool coat like Aunt Tabitha's? I had one of those once."

Addix swerved to avoid a couple of particularly obnoxious adolescent Torcellans harassing their poor chaperone just ahead.

Their chaperone had clearly reached his breaking point. "You spoiled little brats!" The harassed male pointed at Addix. "Look what you could be chaperoned by!" he screeched.

Alexis started forward with her hand raised as if to form a fireball. "Don't you dare speak about my aunt that way!"

The Torcellans recoiled at the confrontation.

Alexis stamped her foot and opened her mouth to yell at them some more.

Addix steered Alexis away before the Torcellans got hurt. "Not worth it, my dear. Come, we have almost reached the ice cream parlor."

Gabriel grinned, looking for the sign. "We're getting ice cream?"

"As close as you can get out here. Phyrro found an establishment that advertises 'human food.'" Addix spotted a group of Skaines eating at one of the street food carts. "That could go one of two ways, so we will check before I take you in there." She regarded Alexis as they walked. "Alexis?"

Alexis turned an innocent face toward Addix. "Yes, Aunt Addix?"

Addix tilted her head. "Were you trying to do magic in the real world?"

Alexis thought about it a moment. "I suppose I was. It felt like the game for a second."

"Hmmm." Addix kept her thoughts to herself...for now.

The Baka and the Yollin had secreted themselves in an alley to avoid being seen when the tempting targets left the human restaurant.

"It's just some nanny. She couldn't stop us."

Racien looked again at the two human children with the hunched old woman following a few steps behind. He narrowed his eyes as he took stock of their expensive clothing. The EI technology the female was flashing was beyond anything he had access to. Added to that the absolute confidence in their bearing, and Racien could only draw one conclusion.

These were the children of *extremely* rich people, and rich people would pay obscene amounts of money to get their children back.

The children laughed while they walked along and ate the ice cream that had inadvertently brought them to his and F'roxan's attention.

Racien flexed his claws in their armored gloves and turned to his partner in crime. "F'roxan, if we take human children, you know what will happen. Baba Yaga—"

"Is gone," the female Yollin countered. "Nobody has seen or heard of the Witch since she followed the Empress into the Great Darkness. We can contact a couple of the others, get them to help." She shifted to keep the possible score in her sights. "We get rid of the nanny and grab the kids. Find out who their parents are. Send them a note, and we are out of this godforsaken place." She looked at her partner a moment. "What do you say? This could be our ticket out of here."

Racien gave a brief nod, and the two turned to follow the human children down the concourse.

High Tortuga, Southern Continent

Michael met the T-rex head-on. He leapt as he slashed and used the dinosaur's body as a springboard to get even higher.

The T-rex screamed its rage, then tossed its head and butted Michael before he could land and put his swords to use again. The T-rex whipped its barbed tail at Michael as he hit the ground.

He landed in a crouch and rolled to avoid the swipe. He got up and charged again, but the dinosaur caught him with its tail on the backswing and knocked him away a second time.

Michael got up and rolled his shoulders. He rubbed his broken ribs while they knitted, and then he sprinted back at the beast with his swords raised.

Peter watched in growing disbelief as Michael stood up and dusted off the dirt. "Why is he moving so slowly? He isn't using the Etheric." He looked at Akio. "What gives? Are these Bethany Anne's rules? He could have killed it *twice* already."

Akio quieted the younger man with a hand. "Watch and learn. Michael has chosen to restrict himself. He came for an equal fight. If he used all his talents, it would be no challenge for either of them."

Michael flowed around the dinosaur, sword flashing each time the dinosaur brought a foot down. The beast was beyond enraged. It flung itself in wide arcs and snapped and stomped wildly in an attempt to crush the small creature that was causing it so much pain.

"According to Michael, killing it with a thousand cuts while it tries to 'smoosh him into paste,' as Scott called it, is honorable," Akio finished.

Peter looked again and saw it was sort of an even fight, in its way. Michael had to work to land every cut on the frenzied T-rex, which only needed to eat him once to win. "Yeah, ok, seems fair," he conceded.

The T-rex lunged and snapped at Michael again. It

clung to the ridges above its eyes and punched his remaining sword into one eyeball all the way up to his elbow.

The T-rex stiffened when the blade penetrated its brain. Michael knew it was over when the dinosaur sagged. He pulled his arm out of the hot mess and prepared to jump.

Michael!

Akio's sudden intrusion in his mind caused him to glance at his friends, his foot moving back a bit more than he'd intended. He lost his footing and tumbled off.

Around twenty feet from the ground, he vanished and appeared at a run a second later, cruising up to Akio and Peter as the T-rex collapsed with a mighty crash that caused the dirt to ripple outward from the point of impact.

Akio slapped Michael on the back. "That was a hell of a battle."

Michael turned to accept Akio's congratulations and saw Peter staring at his kill with an unreadable expression on his face. "You called?" he asked.

Peter pointed at the battleground, which was falling into itself as a pair of gigantic hairy paws forced their way up out of the dirt, followed by an even bigger snout. "What the living fuck is *that*?"

An enormous nose twitched a couple of times.

"Dammit! *Not my kill!*" Michael bitched.

But of course, that was exactly what the owner of the snout had scented.

It extended a paw and hooked the T-rex's leg, then pulled the still-steaming carcass into the hole and vanished before Michael could do more than clench his fists in fury.

He stormed off to investigate, leaving Akio and Peter no choice but to keep up with him.

Akio rolled his eyes as they jogged behind Michael. "We can both thank the gods that Bethany Anne is not going to see this."

Peter's mouth quirked. "You can say that again. Three years would seem like a long weekend…"

smirked and held her hands up as she crossed the room. "Nature calls, ladies."

Tabitha poked around the remains of the snacks on the table. "I'm getting hungry for real food."

"I think we should order some takeout," Cheryl Lynn called after Bethany Anne.

Bethany Anne paused to reply, "I already ordered. It should be here…"

>>**In fifteen minutes.** <<

"I hope it's soon," Tabitha interjected, emptying the last few kernels of popcorn into her mouth from the bowl. "My appetite is definitely back."

"In ten minutes." *Put a rush on it, ADAM. Tabitha is going to eat me out of house and home.*

Colonnara, Arts Quarter

Addix was glad she had four eyes since otherwise, she'd have been hard-pressed to keep track of the children and monitor for danger at the same time. As it was, she would not have refused the offer of an extra pair in the back of her head. She'd heard Bethany Anne joke about having those when the twins were infants.

One hour into the shopping, she'd realized that Bethany Anne's laughing plea had been no joke. Alexis and Gabriel darted between the stalls, pelting the vendors with questions about every trinket that caught the magpie vision they had developed upon entering the quietly shabby arts quarter.

This was a planet packed with wealthy individuals. It

must be like a well-stocked fishpond to the kinds of criminals who preyed on the rich.

Addix would not be surprised to discover that such lowlifes were hovering somewhere nearby. In fact, she was almost sure there *were* some. What Peter teasingly called her "spidey sense" but was actually the culmination of her long life as a spy told her that to dismiss the suspicion would be foolish.

At first, she had put the itch on the back of her neck down to gawkers unused to seeing an Ixtali. However, the itch only grew in intensity after she'd covered her face with her hood.

The children were for once blissfully situationally unaware. Addix had no problem with them remaining that way until the moment came when they needed to act. She was there to protect them, so she would let them enjoy the market.

Alexis ran over with Gabriel. "Aunt Addix, we found a gift! Come and see!"

Addix allowed Alexis to pull her by the hand to a small building whose signage promised an "out of this world viewing experience." Addix paused at the display window to look inside, but it was tinted.

Gabriel dashed to the door. "Come on, Aunt Addix, we have to hurry or we'll miss our appointment."

Addix's mandibles rippled in interest. "Appointment?"

Alexis rolled her eyes and pointed at a smaller sign by the door that read "reenactment specialist." "Yes, Aunt Addix. I had Phyrro make us one when we spotted this sign." She smiled brightly at Addix. "We're going to make Mommy a video of her best bits."

Addix was confused. "Her best bits?"

Gabriel nodded. "All the times she kicked butt!" he exclaimed. "Can we go in now? *Pleeeeease?*"

Addix found it hard to refuse.

Why did it affect her so when the twins made their eyes large like that? "Of course." She didn't add that they could have made this video at home, and with better technology. It was their gift to choose. "Does Phyrro have the footage you need to make the video?"

Alexis gave Addix a shrewd look, speaking as only the young can. "Aunt Addix, it's not that kind of video. We're going to get dressed up and play the parts, like Mommy would have done when she was our age. The artist makes it into sort of like a movie."

Gabriel skipped around at Addix's side. "I can't wait to see Mommy's face when we give her the gift."

Addix was about to lead them inside when she was shoved from behind. Glass smashed as Addix turned with a snarl to ward off the threat, almost colliding with the Baka who had bumped her and dropped a glass jar.

Addix stumbled forward and tripped on the hem of her blasted robe, gagging on the heavy spices in the air. Her four feet crunched on broken glass as she moved to avoid the cloud of potent spices that billowed up.

She quickly recovered her footing and shrugged off the Baka who had jostled her, looking for Alexis and Gabriel. The Baka clung to her arm, refusing to let go and making even more of a scene. She wheeled back and saw the deceit in his eyes. "You planned this!"

Addix backhanded the Baka in the throat with the pommel of the knife that had appeared in her hand.

The Baka clutched his throat and let out a gargled scream. Addix hissed when she couldn't immediately see the two children, bringing the knife back around and silencing the Baka permanently.

The passersby screamed and scattered, unused to such displays of violence.

Addix snarled and darted into the crowd.

"There will be deaths," the Ixtali female screamed.

High Tortuga, Southern Continent

Peter and Akio lunged to pull Michael back before he could dive in after the ginormous creature and retrieve his kill.

They retreated as the edge of the hole crumbled in on itself, widening the newly-formed sinkhole by a goodly amount. The gigantic paws reappeared and a disgruntled roar shook the ground, which opened the hole enough for the creature to exit its underground lair. It splayed its impossibly large paws on either side of the hole and hauled itself out with an ear-splitting shriek.

A hairy star-shaped snout appeared and scented the air, followed by a head and body that appeared to have no end. Finally, it was above ground and the sky disappeared, completely blocked by the beast.

Peter punched Akio in the arm, smiling. "Would you look at *that*? It has to be seven times the size of the dinosaur."

Akio punched him back, smirking as the younger man rubbed his arm. "I'm confused as to what type of creature this is. I am not convinced it will be any more edible than the dinosaur." He sheathed his sword and removed his Jean Dukes Special from his belt.

"Fuck us... It might not matter." Peter pointed toward the head as it stretched to its full height and screeched, its head in the clouds. "It might just pass out from oxygen deprivation and die from the fall." He stepped back involuntarily as the beast dropped to all fours and two clawed feet the size of small towns came toward them. "*Shiiit!* I was right!"

The beast landed with a crash that shook the plateau and sent a massive shockwave down the mountain. It opened its mouth and squalled as if annoyed it had been awakened.

Michael rolled his eyes and picked up his pack, then fished around to retrieve his gauntlets and a fresh blade. He fastened the sheath to his belt. "It is not dead, or even unconscious."

He gazed hungrily at the monstrous beast; he couldn't even hazard a guess at its species. It definitely had claws and a lot of teeth. "I believe we have ourselves a battle, gentlemen."

Peter placed Tabitha's rifle on the ground. "No gentlemen here. Just three guys looking for a fight." He stripped off his clothing and rolled it into a ball, which he tossed to the other end of the plateau for later retrieval. "Looks like the fight we were all wishing for was asleep beneath our feet the whole time."

Peter bent to retrieve the big-ass rifle. When he straightened, his predatory expression had morphed into a sharp-fanged snarl, and he had fur. His Pricolici grin was every bit as joyful as the one he'd had in human form.

He flexed his clawed hands around the oversized rifle grip and howled. "It's about tiiime I got to plaaaay!"

Akio snickered when Peter started to run toward the beast and turned to Michael as he checked the sheathed swords were secure. "It seems now you have no choice but to share your hunt."

Michael shrugged. "What is it that women always say? Sharing is caring?" He squeezed his fists inside his gauntlets to activate the Etheric draw and shivered at the tingle of power that ran along the skin of his arms and up his neck. "Let there be *lightning!*"

The sky grew darker in response.

"That ability isn't going to make you big-headed at all," Akio remarked as they took off side by side to catch up with Peter.

Michael laughed jubilantly. "What can I say? My wife knows how to pick the perfect gift. And I *have* been practicing, my friend." Michael reached for the storm energy overhead and took control of it. "That reminds me, I wonder how Addix and the children are getting along on Colonnara?"

Akio snorted. "You think of this *now*? We're about to take on the biggest creature I have seen outside the video news and your mind is on Alexis and Gabriel?"

Michael brought the energy crashing down. The lightning stung the beast, driving it away from the edge of the plateau, where it had been about to descend. "I am always thinking of them, even now. This beast will not be left free to wreak destruction on the planet my family lives on. There is a large inhabited area somewhere to the east, and if the beast gets down from here, it would be a disaster for the people living there. Plus, can you imagine what Bethany Anne would say if we *didn't* clean this mess up?"

Akio smirked. "Of course, it's not so much what she would *say* as how much it would hurt. What's the plan?" He nodded toward Peter. "Other than reining him in."

"First, we keep that beast from leaving this plateau. Then we kill it, cook it, and eat it. Keep it simple." He glanced fondly at Peter. "You know, it's good to see him having fun, but we'd better pull him back while we come up with a way to take the creature down."

Peter danced around the beast's feet, firing upward indiscriminately with Tabitha's rifle. He alternated his shots with vicious swipes of his claws, snarling as he dodged the beast's shuffling feet.

Peter.

Peter ignored Michael's voice in his mind. His Pricolici instincts were in the driver's seat, so all he knew was the desire to kill. He was determined to take the beast down singlehandedly—one tiny chunk at a time if necessary.

PETER! GET YOUR ASS OVER HERE BEFORE I DECIDE TO USE YOU AS BAIT FOR REAL.

The force of Michael's command snapped him out of his blind aggression. He darted back as the beast slammed a foot down where he had been standing a second before.

He made his way back to where Akio and Michael stood laughing at him. "Whaaat?"

Michael pointed upward, one eyebrow raised. "The creature's brain is that way."

Peter lowered his head in embarrassment. *I was testing it. I wasn't even trying!*

Michael slapped him on the back. "Don't sweat it."

Both men gaped at him in disbelief.

Akio raised an eyebrow. "This is going too far. Who are you, and where the hell is the real Michael Nacht?"

Peter waved a claw at Akio. "Yeaaah, *that.*"

"Michael Nacht is on vacation. I am a man on a hunt with his friends. A man who will be standing on that beast's back in the next few minutes, so you two should work fast if you want a taste before it dies."

Peter made as if to charge but pulled himself back before instinct took over again. "How do we kill sommme- thing so fucking *huuuge?*"

Michael looked up at the beast, feeling a kinship with insects he wouldn't have considered possible for a man of his age and power. "The brain or the heart, but since we don't know where its heart is..." The battle with the T-rex seemed tame compared to the challenge he now faced. "This creature is so large it might not even comprehend that we're at its feet."

"There are plenty of bugs whose sting can kill a man," Akio offered.

"I was just relishing the challenge ahead." Michael flexed his gauntlets and enjoyed the frisson of anticipation that ran up his spine as the Etheric energy crackled around him. "We humans come with a particular sting of our own, and we are more than equal to this task."

The beast began to shuffle toward the edge of the plateau again.

"Are you ready?" Michael asked. "On my signal, aim for its head."

Akio and Peter raised their weapons and prepared to fire at the beast.

Michael held up a hand and called down lightning at the edge of the plateau. It hung there, a shining barrier impossibly suspended in the air.

The beast paused in its advance to examine the shimmering curtain.

Peter and Akio missed their cue, completely in awe of the crackling sheet of light that filled the sky and wrapped the cliff edge.

The beast lifted a paw and reached out.

It was pushed back by the shock, and the smell of burned hair drifting over the plateau was briefly overwhelming, causing the men to gag.

What are you waiting for? Michael demanded. He twisted his hand and the lightning moved onto the plateau, driving the beast back toward them. *That was the signal!*

Isn't the lightning enough to take it down? Akio couldn't hear a thing over the thunder and the screeching beast, which had momentarily decided to go in the opposite direction to the incandescent sheet that had caused it pain.

Unfortunately, no, Michael replied. *It is too large. I can contain it on the plateau, but we will have to do this the hard way.*

Peter had a faraway gleam in his yellow eyes as he regarded the creature. It shuffled toward the edge of the plateau again, determined to get past the lightning. *Watch thisss.* He leapt up to catch hold of one of the beast's matted ropes of fur and started to haul himself up one clawful at a time.

Peter! Get down from there.

Peter continued to climb, regardless of Michael's order.

Relax, I've got this.

4

Open Space, QBS *G'laxix Sphaea*

The *G'laxix Sphaea* exited the Gate and sliced silently through the space between systems. There was nothing and no one for millions of kilometers around. ArchAngel had control of the ship while the crew of four transferred the recovered EI cradle to the cleanroom that the ship had been fitted with specifically for this mission.

ArchAngel had the antigrav pallet deposit the cradle on the center table and sent the pallet back off to storage.

Kael-ven and Kiel chatted while Mellor and Robinson painstakingly deconstructed the protective cradle to access the EI core within.

"Captain." Mellor sighed, eyeing Kael-ven. "If you would just give us space to work, I'd be able to tell you what's going on with Loralei." He bent back over the dark cube with his tools at the ready.

Kael-ven shuffled back in the minimal space between lab tables to get to one of the chairs built for his four-legged frame and sat down with a huff. "I apologize." His mandibles clicked together, "Now work faster."

The scout ship's core lay open on the table, with tools and various components scattered around it in easy reach of the two techs.

Kiel had perched on a stool at an empty table to stay out of the way. "Do you think you can bring her back online?"

Robinson looked at Kiel and shrugged. "Of course, sir. We built her, and we can bring her back."

Mellor chuckled as he pulled a fastener he had loosened. "You know she's going to be majorly pissed when we reactivate her, right? I hope your delicate officers' ears aren't easily bruised by rough language."

Kael-ven's mandibles opened in shock, but he soon recovered his voice. "Are you kidding? But that implies sentience or at least the possibility of it. I thought after Ricky Bobby…"

Robinson shook her head. "Not sentience, Captain. Think of it as a blow-off valve. The prototype scout ships lacked the autonomy to cope with the rigors of independent space exploration. Most were destroyed within half a year. Some sent back constant false pings, which pissed the Queen off no end when she arrived ready for a fight and there were no Kurtherians to be found."

Mellor looked up. "The Queen even personally trashed a nearby asteroid next to one of them. I saw the video footage."

Robinson chuckled. "Oh, yeah. I'd forgotten about that."

Kael-ven nodded. "That was a…*fun* few months."

Robinson grinned. "Sure it was. For this model, we

worked with ADAM and Achronyx to design EIs who could hack the pressure." She winked at Kael-ven. "Pun totally intended. The EIs needed to be able to do more than calculate a decision based on a set of preprogrammed responses. We had to give them decision-making ability without allowing them to ascend to AI status. The end result was a tweak to the standard EI personality algorithm that converts stress on the scout ship EI's systems into snarky monologue. It's part of the protocol to keep them functioning efficiently while they're out there alone."

"You should listen to one of their reports sometime, Captain." Mellor's voice was muffled by his position on the inside of the core. "The Kurtherians might not be anywhere we've been able to find them, but the search has been hella entertaining to listen to."

Kael-ven thought he just might download a few and see if the techs were exaggerating. "So, Loralei."

"Nearly there now," Robinson told him.

Kael-ven settled in to watch.

Kiel got up and came around to sit next to Kael-ven while the techs worked their magic. "What do you think about what we found in that system?"

Kael-ven shrugged. "It's more what we *didn't* find that concerns me. Some other party was there before us."

"You mean because we couldn't find the other ship's memory core?"

Kael-ven nodded. "Whoever it was took the other ship's core but left ours alone. Why?"

Kiel pondered it for a short time. "That *is* worrying. Do you think they knew we could track the *Loralei* wherever they took it?"

Kael-ven shrugged. "I don't know what else I could assume."

Kiel's excitement grew. "Do you think the other ship was Kurtherian?"

"Who knows? We'll have to get Loralei talking again to find out."

The exposed core on the table lit up as he spoke and emitted a slightly raspy female voice.

"Systems check. Engine systems...fail. Air filtration... fail. Navigation system, fail? Gate drive...critical overload, fail..."

They all breathed a sigh of relief when Loralei came online.

"Just how fucked up am I?" she bitched.

"Good to have you with us, girl," Robinson told her.

"It's not looking good, but we've got you," Mellor added.

The lights on the cube blinked rapidly as Loralei assessed her situation. "I'm a big-ass failure here! What the fuck happened to me? Where's my body?"

"We were hoping you would be able to tell us," Kael-ven told her.

"I'll check." The cube dimmed for a moment. "Oh. Oh, *daaaaammmmmnnn!*"

Loralei's voice dropped a couple of octaves, becoming more mechanical as it deepened.

"WARNING! THIS IS EI LORALEI. DO NOT EXTRACT ME. WARNING!"

Kiel looked at Kael-ven, his face a mask of horror. "We are *fucked.*"

· · ·

Peter. They grabbed a clump of hair each and followed Peter up the creature's flank.

"We could let him have his moment?" Akio suggested. "He can't do much to a beast this size with just his claws and teeth, right?"

Michael considered it for a moment. "I don't know. If he decides to dig his way in he could do a lot of damage. To the meat, I mean." He began to climb a little faster.

The beast's skin rippled beneath Peter and the two vampires as though they were fleas it could shake off. Peter swung upward and grabbed the next clump of fur before the beast could succeed in its efforts to rid itself of the irritation.

He hauled himself up until he stood on the beast's back. A quick glance down showed him both the dizzying drop and also Michael and Akio swarming up the side of the beast.

He ran along the beast's back toward its head, howling his war cry. His piercing claws drove the beast into a frenzy, then it stopped, sat suddenly on its haunches, and lifted one of its back feet to swipe at the itchy spots Peter was creating.

Peter leapt out of the way as the gigantic claws came down and raked deep furrows in its fur. He landed roughly on its neck and leapt again as the claws came at him a second time.

Peter scrambled up between the beast's ears. When it bent down and rubbed its head on the ground, he ducked inside one of the ears and hung on grimly as the creature shook its head in an attempt to dislodge him.

Peter had an idea, and he took his chance when the

shaking stopped for a moment. He dodged out of the ear and caught a glimpse of Michael and Akio crawling down the beast's neck toward him.

It's cool! I told you, I've got this.

"Peter!" Michael yelled, although it was hopeless to try to be heard above the crashing thunder and the grunts of the beast.

Peter waved and grinned, then dropped onto all fours and disappeared into the thick fur of the beast's neck.

Michael and Akio shouted in unison, realizing finally that Peter's "plan" was the Pricolici instinct to tear the throat out of anything even remotely more powerful than they were.

"Peter, NO!"

"DO NOT BITE IT!"

Their warning came too late. Peter had already sunk his teeth into its neck. Unfortunately for Peter, his bite had no discernible effect except to piss the maddened beast off even more, which the two more experienced men could have told him would happen if he'd stopped to listen.

The beast rolled when Peter bit down, then tossed its impossible head. Peter was thrown into the air. At last, and at the worst possible moment, the beast appeared to notice the Pricolici sailing past its face.

Michael didn't pause to consider the danger. He swung himself down onto the beast's back and regained his footing just in time to see Peter swan-dive into the beast's mouth.

Michael sighed. That dumbass had the *biggest* shit-eating grin plastered on his stupid snout...

It snapped its jaws shut, and Peter was gone. The beast

rolled again in triumph at ridding itself of the pesky crea-ture that had bitten it, pushing its skin into ridges that resembled the terrain Michael and the others had crossed to get to the plateau.

The beast's body undulated beneath Michael and Akio, and they had to work to keep their footing while they dashed to rescue Peter.

The beast flopped onto its back and continued using the ground to scratch, giving Michael and Akio a clear run up its stomach and throat to its mouth.

Michael reached the neck first and extended a hand to haul Akio up behind him. The two were almost thrown when the beast suddenly shifted, but Michael's enhanced reaction time saved them from a long fall. He swung Akio up to land on the beast's head and then hauled himself up as the beast struggled to its feet once more.

Akio shook his head as they looked down from the head. "Seriously, the situations that kid gets himself into."

5

High Tortuga, Southern Continent

The storm was reaching its crescendo, transforming the plateau into a cauldron of destruction. Driving rain had joined the lightning and thunder.

The mud trapped the beast's feet, and its continuing efforts to free itself made Michael and Akio's climb even jerkier. The darkness was punctuated only by brief streaks of too-brightness as the lightning tore fresh holes in the roiling storm clouds overhead.

Michael had loosed his control of the tempest when Peter had vanished into the beast's mouth. He and Akio were now in a race through the deluge to rescue the pain-in-the-ass Pricolici before the beast they fought realized it was no longer restricted by the lightning and made a break for the lowlands.

The beast was having some kind of trouble, no doubt caused by Peter tearing it up inside. It jerked and made odd barking coughs between angry roars that blew up waves of mud.

Michael didn't think Peter had fully considered the consequences of being ingested by a creature whose stomach was undoubtedly equipped to deal easily with a bite-sized snack like him.

Consequently, he and Akio were now working their way toward the beast's mouth using the stinking, slimy hair to control their descent through the rivers of rain-water that turned its fur into High Tortuga's grodiest slip 'n slide.

Akio was wrenched to a stop, tangled in the beast's hair. *This is like wet dog times a million,* he complained.

Michael looked back at him. *Do you need me to cut you free?*

Akio worked his trapped arm deeper into the tangle to support himself as the beast flopped around beneath them. *I can cut myself free. Go get Peter. He needs you more.* He pulled a knife from his belt with his free hand and waved it at Michael. *Go. I'll be right behind you. Why aren't you changing to Myst?*

Where would the fun be in that?

Michael continued his haphazard approach to the beast's mouth. He caught a particularly long strand of hair and swung himself out in a wide arc that covered most of the distance between him and his goal.

He paused on landing, a speck on the shoulder of the giant. He had to work out his next move and give Akio a chance to catch up. The question still remained as to how he was going to kill a creature this size.

This would be a lot easier if Peter weren't *inside* the damned thing. He sensed Akio approaching. He could also hear Peter making a mental ruckus.

He materialized beside Peter and Akio. *JUMP!*

There was no opportunity for Akio or Peter to obey.

The beast jerked to a stop and let out something between a pained roar and a fiery belch as the spark lit the gases in its stomach. Michael's concerns on whether the ratio of gas to acid in the stomach chamber would be sufficient to cause the reaction he was looking for were proven to be unfounded when there was a rapid swelling in the creature's middle.

The beast shrieked and threw its front feet up in panic as its stomach expanded almost too fast to be seen with the human eye. Without warning, the beast exploded in the middle of its final ear-splitting scream.

The upper half of the body was blown free of the bottom and flung in pieces head-first down the slope. The three men flew in different directions from its head in a hot spray of blood, guts, and fuck *knew* what else.

They landed roughly, tossed like ragdolls by the force of the methane explosion. Michael's first thought was to check that the others were okay. He had already healed from most of the injuries he'd taken in the landing. The burns to his skin had healed instantly, and all that remained as evidence of his injuries was the ache of his newly-knitted bones.

OH, DAMN! He put a hand to his head to check his hair. *Still there.*

Michael scanned the meaty landscape and saw Peter about a hundred feet away. He was back in human form, clutching his ribs with an arm as he struggled to his feet. Akio had landed against a tree a similar distance down the slope and was leaning against the snapped trunk tending to a broken leg.

Both he and Peter made their way carefully to Akio, avoiding the bubbling pools of stomach acid mixed with blood, shit, and rainwater that had formed wherever the land dipped enough to hold it.

Michael held out his hands to receive Akio's foot, and Akio gritted his teeth while Michael pulled his broken bone into place to speed the healing process.

Akio grimaced at the momentary pain. "Thank you."

Michael shrugged, then winced a twinge of pain from the healed collarbone he'd snapped on impact. "Don't mention it."

Peter grinned at Michael and snickered as he indicated the huge slabs of smoking meat dotting the slope. The bottom half of the beast's body was burning merrily up on the rim of the plateau despite the heavy rain, and the top half lay in goopy chunks all around them. "I don't think any of this is salvageable."

Michael raised an eyebrow at the gory landscape. "We will skip the video on this. It might put some off eating."

Akio made a face. "It's making me consider vegetarianism." The six-hundred-year-old vampire looked at them with a straight face for a moment, then the corner of his mouth quirked. He pointed at Michael's and Peter's twin expressions of disbelief and broke into a deep chuckle. "Help me up. We should call for a ride home."

Michael and Peter held out a hand each and hauled him to his feet.

Peter looked down at himself. "I'll go get some pants on before the transport arrives."

Michael smirked. "That might be a good idea." He eyed Peter. "Not that anyone will be able to tell you're naked under all that gore."

Akio wrinkled his nose as he pinched the leg of his trousers between a thumb and forefinger before letting the sodden fabric drop. "Or that we are wearing any under all of this. A hot shower would be welcome."

Michael nodded. "Very true."

Colonnara, Warehouse District

"Can you go any faster?" Addix asked the taxi driver. Her mandibles worked overtime in her anxiety for Alexis and Gabriel's safety. Given the speed at which the trackers were moving previously, Addix hadn't been too worried about the gap while they were on the highway.

However, the trackers had stopped moving, and the intensity of her need to get to the children increased with every passing second.

The human driver glanced back at her with wide eyes and shook his head. "Regulations, ma'am. My taxi is restricted, I'm already at the limit."

Addix hissed in frustration. "This won't do!"

Phyrro spoke up from the holo. "I can circumvent the restrictions on the taxi's engines."

Addix tilted her head at the driver, who nodded his agreement.

She'd lucked out finding this human, who was a staunch supporter of Bethany Anne whether she was in power or not. People like that could almost always be relied upon in exigent circumstances.

A quick explanation of Addix's situation had allayed the man's initial fear of the enraged and disrobed Ixtali in his cab and they had sped after the children's trackers without much more discussion.

The driver let out a surprised grunt when the controls began to act without his input.

"Do not worry," Phyrro told him from the taxi's speaker. "I am in complete control now."

Addix banged an impatient hand on the seat beside her. "Phyrro, what are you waiting for? *Get me to the children!*"

Alexis and Gabriel huddled together in the back of the office the Yollin had shoved them into and plotted while they waited for Addix to arrive to rescue them.

Despite their earlier bravado in the back of the transport, they were a little scared. Still, they hadn't allowed their captors to see that. They had held their heads high and glared at the Yollin and her henchmen as they were roughly marched inside the warehouse on their arrival.

Alexis focused on her hand, willing the magic to spark so she could blast them an exit right through the kidnappers.

Gabriel watched intently. *Is it working? Can you feel anything?*

Alexis let her shoulders drop as she released her concentration. *No,* she conceded with more than a little vexation. *It's not like the game, Gabriel. I can't just make the magic happen here. We need Aunt Addix.*

Gabriel nodded soberly. *This is real life. Things are harder. We do need Aunt Addix.*

The taxi pulled to a stop two buildings from the warehouse where Phyrro had located the children's tracker beacons.

"Good luck," the driver whispered as Addix exited the taxi. "I'll wait nearby for you."

Addix nodded her thanks to the man and all but ran up the side of the building. Once on the roof, she made all haste to get across to the building where Alexis and Gabriel were being held. The gaps between the warehouses were narrow, and she had no trouble jumping across.

The warehouse roof she landed on was in poor repair. She soon found the roof access, which was secured with a thumb scanner. A quick glance around revealed a dirt-covered skylight.

Addix walked over to the skylight and wiped a smear of the encrusted grime away to peer down into the main area of the warehouse. There was a fifty-foot drop between her and the warehouse floor, where a two-legged Yollin paced while two brutish-looking humans muttered sullenly to one another over by a piece of dead machinery.

She lifted the holo to speak to Phyrro. "Where are the children?"

Phyrro tilted his head. "They are in an office at the back of the building."

Addix's mandibles twitched furiously. "Are their vitals okay?"

"They are within acceptable tolerances," Phyrro replied.

"But they are distressed. What are you doing?" he asked as Addix began to walk to the edge of the roof. "The door is in the opposite direction."

Addix narrowed her eyes. She palmed her Jean Dukes Special, turned it sideways and checked to see she had the right cartridge loaded. Then she checked the harness she was wearing across her chest to ensure she still had her throwing knives. Satisfied she was ready, she turned and took a running start at the skylight.

"This is the fastest route to Alexis and Gabriel. As my Queen would say, *fuck the stairs*."

She leapt and landed on all four feet perfectly, smashing the old glass. The kidnappers jerked their heads toward the commotion, startled by Addix's unexpected incursion.

She fired her Jean Dukes at the ceiling as she descended into the warehouse in a shower of broken glass and dirt and grabbed the near end of the sticky rope the cartridge produced. The other end attached itself to the ceiling, slowing her fall.

Addix flipped and took the rope in her back feet to free up her hands. She needed them to tear these walking dead to shreds. The kidnappers did what cowardly people always do.

They screamed and ran.

Addix flicked a pair of knives at their retreating backs, and they soon stopped their noise. Easy deaths, but then they were just the muscle. She tilted her head and stared ice at the ringleader as her front feet touched down silently on the warehouse floor.

Addix released the rope and walked toward the Yollin with murder in her eyes. "You made a mistake today. *No one* who dares to harm the children under my care survives."

The Yollin stared down the barrel of Addix's Jean Dukes Special in complete shock. She opened and closed her mandibles, but all that came out was gibberish.

Addix had no time for any of it. She fired once as she swept past on her way to the office where the children were being held, and the Yollin crumpled to the floor minus the top half of her head.

The office door was easily broken open when she got there, and the children rushed over to cling to her legs in their relief. "Are you hurt?" she asked them.

"No," Alexis replied.

"Just glad you came for us," Gabriel added.

Addix scooped the twins up in her arms. "I will always come for you," she told them fiercely. "I am only sorry you were taken in the first place. We are leaving this planet at once." She carried them out of the warehouse, not bothering to skirt the corpses of the kidnappers or hide them from the children.

"Aunt Addix?" Alexis asked once they had left the warehouse and headed to the waiting taxi.

"Yes?" Addix was almost pained by the tear-filled expression on the little girl's face.

"We didn't get Mommy's gift."

Addix fastened her seatbelt and leaned over to do Gabriel's. "Do not worry, children. I know of another planet we can visit to shop."

Gabriel frowned. "What if we get kidnapped again?"

Addix chuckled. "I don't think they have kidnappers walking the streets there."

"Why not?" Alexis asked.

"Because," Addix's mandibles conveyed her amusement as she spoke, "they have strict penalties for anyone who so much as drops a piece of litter on the ground."

Gabriel turned to look out of the back window. "Can't be worse than your penalty, Aunt Addix."

Addix shrugged. "Oh, but it *can* be, children." She nodded sagely at their disbelieving faces. "I was merciful. I did not prolong their pain."

High Tortuga, Southern Continent

Peter made sure to breathe through his mouth while he jogged back to the guys. The air was hot, heavy and foul-smelling. The lack of wind after the storm ended left the compressed stench of the exploded creature firmly on the uplands. Peter was just glad he was back in human form, although his still-heightened senses made it no easier to stomach.

"Wonder what the local version of the news will think about this?"

He fastened his belt and pulled his shirt on quickly before returning to where Michael and Akio waited on the edge of the plateau for him.

The two vampires turned from the bloody vista below at the sound of his feet squelching in the muck.

Peter walked to the edge and grimaced at the steaming mess below. "What are you going to tell Bethany Anne when we get back without a single shred of meat to show for our efforts?"

Michael looked down the slope with a sigh. "I don't

think my wife will be too bothered by that." He indicated the carnage below. "This could actually be her ideal outcome."

"Especially since *this* was not what she agreed to you hunting." Peter nodded slowly, still struck by the scale of the monster they had defeated.

Akio turned away from the mess. "She did not want even the T-rex meat in the base. You would die a thousand deaths before she forgave you for bringing that much meat into her home."

Michael was silent.

Peter looked from one to the other. "I guess we won't need a bigger transport if we have nothing to take back with us. I've called for a Pod."

They boarded the Pod when it arrived a few minutes later. As soon as the door shut, they were once again able to smell themselves, and now that they weren't the cleanest things in the immediate environment it became unbearable to carry the weight of the gore they were encrusted with.

Every movement Michael and Akio made sent a sprinkle of muck to the floor. They all squelched as they walked gingerly to their seats. Peter was the oddest of them all. The whites of his eyes and his teeth were all that showed through the grimy mask above his reasonably clean shirt.

Michael sat carefully and turned to grimace at the slurry they'd tracked into the immaculate Pod. "This is beyond messy."

Peter looked back at the trail. "Messy doesn't even begin to cover it. We look like a meat tornado hit us. I've been holding my breath since the explosion."

Akio pointed out a river on the lowlands. "It would be good to clean up before we go home." He shifted uncomfortably in his rapidly-crusting clothing. "I doubt we would be well received in our current state."

"You've got that right." Peter altered the Pod's course to head for the river. "I'd fight that fucking thing all over again for a swim."

Michael raised an eyebrow. "You could just land the Pod." He huffed at the fine shower of crud that came loose from his forehead and got up. "Do we have anything we can fish with aboard?"

Peter pointed at the door to the storage compartment in the back of the Pod. "Yeah, in the storage compartment. You said bring everything, so I brought *everything*."

Akio left with Michael to search out some fishing equipment.

Peter brought them in a short distance from the river and set a couple of cleaner bots to take care of the interior before following Michael and Akio down to the water's edge.

He dropped his gear and started to strip. "Nice of you guys to wait for me."

Michael splashed water at him, adding a little touch of Etheric energy to his swipe to ensure Peter got a thorough soaking.

"Hey!"

"Just get in the damn water," Michael ordered. He grinned as he splashed at Peter again.

"Cannon*baaaaaalllll!*" Peter landed with a huge splash. The water enveloped him, drowning out Michael and Akio's protests.

Coming up, he spun a lazy circle to counteract the current while he rubbed his head vigorously to dislodge the clingy muck from his hair, then stood and shook himself like a dog, soaking Michael and Akio again in the process.

Akio wiped the excess water from his face with a hand. His mouth twitched and his eyebrow went up as he pointed at Peter. "You will live to regret that."

Peter cocked his head gave the two vampires a rakish grin. "Aw, c'mon!" He drew back both arms and splashed them both again. "I'm just helping you guys get cleaned up."

Michael shared a look with Akio. "*Will* he live?"

Akio grinned as the two of them advanced on Peter. "Probably not."

6

High Tortuga, Space Fleet Base, Queen's Suite

Tabitha left her fork standing up in her bowl and looked from Bethany Anne to Cheryl Lynn with dawning comprehension. "The Dread Pirate Roberts *isn't* a ship of the fleet?"

Bethany Anne paused the movie to look at her friend. "Are you *serious?*"

Tabitha made a face and shrugged. "Well, yeah. I've heard that name, but I hadn't seen the movie. Whenever anyone said it, I thought they were talking about a ship. One of the superdreadnoughts, maybe?"

Bethany Anne looked at Tabitha with a bemused expression. "No. What?"

Tabitha shrugged and looked at Cheryl Lynn for backup. "It *sounds* like a ship's name."

Cheryl Lynn shook her head. "It's a pretty famous movie. There's a lot of references."

Tabitha crossed her arms and pouted. "If you like rom-coms."

Bethany Anne lifted a finger in an attempt to speak through her tears of laughter, but ADAM cut in before she got enough control of herself to comment.

"Sorry to interrupt again, ladies. Bethany Anne, Kael-ven wants to speak to you. He says it's important."

Bethany Anne wiped her eyes. "It's not an interruption if it's important, ADAM. Link him into the room." Bethany Anne gave the others an apologetic shrug. "Looks like movie night is over."

Cheryl Lynn waved off the apology. "Go ahead, it's fine. Duty calls, and we're here to take care of this mess." She got up to gather the snacks up from the table. "We had a good night, didn't we, Tabitha?"

Tabitha pouted. "It's *not* fine! I want to know what happens at the end of the movie." She sighed and got up to help Cheryl Lynn clean up. "I'll just watch it later with Achronyx."

Kael-ven's face replaced the movie and his translated Yollin speech came through the front speaker. "Greetings, my Queen. It's about your missing scout ship. It's not good news." He stopped talking for a moment. "I'm not sure how much I should say over this connection."

"It's secure," Bethany Anne told him. She waved her finger in a circle for Kael-ven to continue. "Are you going to tell me what the news is?"

Kael-ven shuffled uncomfortably. "We recovered the ship, what was left of it. But the EI, she... She had some disturbing information."

Bethany Anne frowned. "What kind of disturbing information?"

Kael-ven's mandibles clicked rapidly, and Bethany

Anne listened while he gave his report on what the technicians had recovered from the EI Loralei. "We extracted her anyway, taking all precautions, and we found a smear of an unidentifiable substance inside the inner core."

Bethany Anne leaned forward on the couch. "*Inside* the core? How?"

Kael-ven shrugged. "We're not certain how it got there, but the techs say it had to have been placed there by *someone.* Mellor and Robinson have been testing it to ascertain its purpose, and they seem sure that it is active in some way."

"Active? In what way?" Bethany Anne frowned. "Nothing and no one except the SSE team or me should have been able to get into the inner casing without setting off the self-destruct."

"I don't know what else I can tell you except what the team told me. We found the substance inside the casing. There was electrical activity from it." Kael-ven shuffled again, his frown of concern matching hers. "Just a minute amount, but it was enough to worry me. This could be technology, but it is not technology as *we* would recognize it."

Bethany Anne rested her elbows on her knees and tapped her lips with a finger while she considered the implications of the information. "That *is* concerning. And there was no trace of any other outsider technology at the site to compare it to?"

Kael-ven shook his head. "Nothing, but my first thought is that the substance could be sending a signal. You can understand why I'm cautious about returning to High Tortuga, so, for now, we've pulled up in a system that's out of the way. I don't want to get any closer to home until I'm certain that we're not being followed."

Bethany Anne nodded, distracted momentarily by waving goodbye to Cheryl Lynn and Tabitha, who were just headed out of the door. She refocused her attention back on Kael-ven once the door had closed behind Tabitha. "You made the right decision, Kael-ven. Just hold tight where you are. I'm sending someone out there to bring you in."

Kael-ven nodded. "I think that would be best. You have our coordinates."

Bethany Anne nodded. "I do. Stay safe. Your backup will be with you soon." She ended the call and fired off a series of messages on her way to her closet to change out of her girls' night outfit into something less casual before she went to the Security Pit to coordinate the rescue.

She walked through the children's closet, hesitating before opening a mental link to Michael. She wished for a split second that she had kept her surveillance on him just so she could make sure he wasn't in the middle of some perilous moment where a distraction could be the difference between life or death. *Can you talk without getting killed?*

What can I do for you, my love?

Bethany Anne smirked despite the urgency of the situation when he replied almost right away. She *was* getting to be a little bit girly, if being girly meant her heart skipped a bit faster when her husband's voice confirmed he was still in one piece. *Hey, honey. How is your hunt going?*

Michael sounded less upbeat. *We had some early success, but it all went downhill from there.*

Bethany Anne repressed her delight at the news her base would not stink of cooked T-rex for the next six months. There was no amount of A-1 sauce or the equivalent here on High Tortuga to make that a palatable consideration. *I'm sorry you didn't get the fight you wanted.* She sensed a momentary irritation over their connection. *Everything okay?*

It is now that Akio has his hand over Peter's mouth, Michael assured her. *I have to ask why it was you didn't think to beat Peter's erroneous idea that he is a comedian out of him when you beat the common sense into him.*

Bethany Anne snickered. **Yeah, you'll have to ask John about that. I outsourced his education to the guys. At least Peter's in a better mood than Tabitha.**

She's still mad at him?

Mmmhmm.

Michael groaned. *Between things not working out with the hunt and Peter acting like a teenager? Let's just say I'll be glad to get home to you and the children.*

Bethany Anne remembered the reason she'd interrupted in the first place. **That makes me feel better about cutting the hunt short. There's been a development. The missing scout ship has been recovered, and it's a problem.**

Michael's confusion came over the link clearly. *But they did find the ship? That doesn't sound like an issue.*

Bethany Anne sighed. Kael-ven's findings were worse than a problem. **Finding the Loralei was the easy part. It's what happened after that. Kael-ven got the core aboard the G'laxix Sphaea without any issues, but when they rebooted the EI, she warned them she'd been tampered with. Now he thinks he's being followed.**

So you're sending someone out to retrieve them safely?

Bethany Anne looked down at her leggings and shrugged, then chose a black shirt to go over her black vest. She went up on her tiptoes to slide the shoebox she wanted out from the upper shelf. *Uh-huh. I've already given orders to ready one of the superdreadnoughts.*

Just the one?

For now. She kicked off her fluffy slipper boots and slid her feet into her heels, then arched her feet inside them. Much better. *I'm sending ancillary ships and whatever support they need as well. It will give the Guardians something to do, even if nothing goes down.*

You could send Peter to ride herd on the teams.

Bethany Anne noted Michael's concern. *I'm not sure that's wise. He's not at his most sensible right now. The arguments between him and Tabitha are getting to them both.*

I think the time apart will do them good, Michael countered. *Some distance will give them the opportunity to miss each other.*

Bethany Anne chuckled sadly. *Or for them to decide they don't miss each other at all.*

High Tortuga, Over Open Water, Transport Pod, Cargo Compartment

Bethany Anne cut the link, and Michael walked back to where Peter and Akio sat fishing with their legs hanging out of the Pod's cargo doors. "Change of plan. We need to get back to the base."

"Was that Bethany Anne?" Akio asked.

Michael nodded that it had been.

"How did the news about the hunt go down with her?"

Michael shrugged at Akio. "I told her the truth. That we had some early success, but that it went downhill from there."

Peter snickered as he pointed down, then up and spread his hands. "Yeah, downhill, uphill. That thing was spread pretty much all *over* the hills."

Akio ignored Peter. "You did not tell Bethany Anne that the hunt was finished," he pointed out to Michael. "That is not going to go well for you.

"Technically, it is *not* finished," Michael countered. "However, there is no need to tell my wife that just now."

Peter twisted around to look at Michael and made a show of peering at his forehead. "Just move your hair to the side?"

Michael frowned. "Why?"

"So I can see the mark," Peter deadpanned. "Y'know, from where Bethany Anne..." He made a pressing motion with his thumb.

Michael looked at Akio, who shrugged, then back at Peter with utter incredulity and more than a small amount of concern. "You do realize I could just kick you out that door as we streak through the sky and Akio wouldn't breathe a word of it, right? Do you have a death wish?"

Peter burst out laughing and turned back to wind his line in. "Nah. I was just checking to see if you were still in vacation mode." He scrambled back to bring his legs into the Pod and got to his feet.

Michael shook his head and smiled. "Alexis and Gabriel will have returned from their Mother's Day shopping and they will need my help preparing their surprises for Bethany Anne, no doubt."

Peter made a face. "Aw. I was kind of enjoying the guy time, you know?"

"I also need to break the news to William." Michael inclined his head sagely. "Luckily for you, Kael-ven needs an escort home from the scrape he's gotten himself and the crew into."

Peter's smile faded instantly. "Kael-ven's in trouble? Of course, I'll go. I'll take Jian's team with me if they're free." He turned and left the compartment in a hurry. They heard him calling from the passage to the bridge. "I'm taking us back to the base right now, so get your legs in if you want to keep them, Akio."

Akio gained his feet with more grace than Peter had managed. "He jumped on that quickly. What's going on with him?"

"Love," Michael replied.

That explained it all.

Devon, First City, Merchant Warehouses

Mark shook the man's hand with a smile. "Pleasure doing business with you, Mr. Morrisey. Let me see you out to the front; this place is a maze if you don't know where you're going." He ushered the man out, still talking quietly with him as they left.

Sabine, Ricole, and Jacqueline waited until they heard Mark and their new client get out of earshot and broke into excited squeals.

Sabine bounced happily. "Our first contract!"

Demon spoke up from her nest on the windowsill, made from the blankets Sabine had brought for her on their first day in the warehouse. *I do not understand why our services have been engaged. What exactly does this man want us to do?*

Sabine met the mountain lion's inquisitive amber eyes with a smile. "We are to take care of his money. Keep it safe until his deal with the other company is complete."

Demon rolled onto her back and looked at Sabine upside-down. *Is that not the function of the bank you told me about? To keep everyone's money locked away?* She tilted her head in confusion when they all broke into laughter.

Mark returned to the office, also laughing since he'd heard the whole exchange. "Our client's recent success has spurred his competitors to sabotage the deal. You know how corrupt this planet is. Morrisey is employing us to make sure the payout is not stolen before the negotiations for the contract are completed."

Demon's tail flicked, and she yawned. *That sounds boring.*

Jacqueline nodded. "Yeah, but it's boring with a profit for us at the end. That means we get to keep this place running."

Ricole looked up from filing her claws. "We should celebrate by finally taking some time off to go to the fights."

Jacqueline nodded. "Yeah, but after we complete the job."

Mark walked over to the desk and dropped his datapad in front of Jacqueline triumphantly. "We have even more reason to celebrate!" he exclaimed, perching on the desk. "I secured us a further bonus by offering to act as the middleman for the exchange."

Jacqueline's smile faded as she scrolled through the agreement. "You realize that if we sign this, anyone who wants to check will be able to find out we're involved. It won't take a genius to work out we're the ones holding the money."

Mark faltered. "Um, no?"

Jacqueline pointed out a line of text on the screen. "Yeah, look. We'll be a named party in the deal."

Mark looked at it and frowned. "How does that translate to our involvement being made accessible to the public?"

Ricole put her nail file down and looked at Mark, pointing her finger at him. "Because that's the law." Her eyes narrowed. "Didn't you read up on the legal system here?"

Mark shrugged. "I wasn't aware that there was one beyond what Baba Yaga instituted, and 'don't piss me off' is not exactly detailed."

"She did more than that." Ricole gave Jacqueline a sympathetic look. "Typical male, rush in with a blindfold on."

"Mm-hmm," Sabine agreed. "Just like a man."

Mark looked at Jacqueline to defend him, but all she did was purse her lips and shake her head. "Nope, we have a business to run, and that includes knowing the environment we're operating in. Baba Yaga instituted transparency laws to cut corruption, and we have to work within them."

Sabine wrinkled her nose and shrugged. "This deal is

public knowledge, as are the names of all the parties involved. If we sign this, it paints a target on us."

Demon rolled onto her belly and stood. *I have no problem with being a target.* She stretched out on her front paws, then turned around to warm her face in the morning sun. *We can make sport of it.*

Mark clapped and pointed at Demon. "That's the attitude! Jacqueline, how long until the information goes public once we sign?"

Jacqueline pressed her fingers to her forehead as if in prayer and sighed. "Probably a few hours. By morning at latest but I wouldn't count on it."

Mark looked around at them all. "You're missing the *opportunity* here, ladies. What's the one thing we've not had since we arrived here?"

Jacqueline snorted. "A day off?"

Sabine raised an eyebrow. "A good night's sleep?"

"A properly cooked meal," Ricole offered.

Mark rolled his eyes and threw his hands up in frustration. "A *fight!* A real one."

He began to pace, his hands doing a fair amount of the talking.

"We did exactly the right thing by getting ourselves set up before we got involved in anything here, but now it's time to reap the rewards of that preparation. The warehouse is defensible enough, and we have all the weapons and ammo we need. We set ourselves up for a siege, stock up on food and water, plus plenty of booze and a few decks of cards. Then we let everyone who wants the money come at us."

Ricole snickered. "All the essentials, then."

Mark smirked and wiggled his eyebrows. "You know it. It'll be like one of Eve's games. We hole up here, all nice and snug while the enemies swarm in."

Sabine smiled darkly. "Only instead of virtual reality constructs, we will be ridding this planet of murdering thieves."

"And we don't even have to go *looking* for them," Ricole chipped in.

Jacqueline tapped the desk while she formed her thoughts. "You know, I think this might not have been such a bad idea. It's going to take all five of us to defend the money, which means we all get a workout. Okay. If you're all happy to do this, then I am too."

"I'm game," Sabine agreed.

Ricole grinned. "Suits me. We should set some booby-traps up, funnel the bad guys in."

Jacqueline grinned as she pointed at her friend. "That's a great idea!" She spun around in her chair and opened the bottom drawer of the filing cabinet behind her. "Ah-ha! I knew it was in here." She spun back to the desk and shoved Mark off to make room for the building plans. "The reason we chose this place is because the ground floor is a warren."

Mark nodded enthusiastically. "Turn the warehouse into a killing ground, keep the enemy confused while we take advantage of our smaller numbers to pick them off a few at a time. As long as we have a bolt hole in case things go south, we're golden."

Demon sat on her haunches and began washing her whiskers, showcasing her perfect fangs. *The opportunity for snacking will not go amiss, either.*

Mark gagged. "No. I am *not* watching you eat a Skaine." He flipped his hands. "No way. Go find your food elsewhere."

Demon jumped down from her perch. She padded over to Mark with her nose in the air and sniffed. *Who wants to eat a Skaine anyway? They're all rubbery. No flavor at all.* She tossed her head and sauntered out of the room, pausing only to touch her cheek to Sabine's hand on her way.

Mark glanced at his partners. "Was that a joke? Can cats joke like that?"

He turned to look out the door Demon had gone through, asking in a plaintive voice, "Someone *please* tell me she was joking."

High Tortuga, Space Fleet Base, Hangar 014

Peter made his way through the throng beneath the ship, looking for Tabitha. He didn't know how he was going to break it to her that he was headed straight back out, but he didn't want to stick around either.

He breathed out the pain of that thought as he searched the crowded hangar for his love. The nagging gut feeling that he and Tabitha were on a downward turn in their relationship was an actual physical pain at times. It couldn't go on like it had the last few weeks, but he didn't want to rock the boat any more than it already was by Tabitha's sudden shift in attitude toward him.

It was driving him to take risks, to find the heat of the moment so he could lose himself there and forget that his heart was breaking. She couldn't end things with him if he wasn't there, and what better reason to be absent than a friend in trouble?

Tabitha found *him.*

She appeared at his side, linking her arm through his as she fell into step beside him. "Looking for someone, *mi amante?*"

Peter's heart contracted with relief. "Only you, Tabbie." He bent his head to kiss her. "Only ever you."

Tabitha's cheeks flushed. "Bethany Anne told me you're going to help Kael-ven out. I didn't want you to leave without saying goodbye, and that I'm sorry we fought."

Peter shook his head. "No, I'm the one who's sorry. I should have just accepted the rifle in the first place since it saved my ass."

Tabitha looked up at him with wide eyes. "Shit, was it glorious?"

Peter squeezed her arm. "You know it was, babe. I wish Michael had allowed video. I jumped in that thing's mouth and shot it up from the inside."

Tabitha raised an eyebrow. "Really? Well, this mission should be a little bit less dramatic than your inner dinosaur experience."

Peter could tell she thought he was exaggerating but he didn't correct her. "Are you sure you're okay with me going straight back out again? If you need me to be here, I'll find someone to take my place."

Tabitha sniffed her tears back. "No, and that you would even offer to do that means so much to me." She went up on her tiptoes and took Peter's face in her hands to kiss him. "You go rescue our friend. Duty comes first, and I would never keep you from it." She released him and walked away.

Peter grinned and called after her, "You know what they say, babe. Absence makes the heart grow fonder."

Tabitha turned back and smiled. "Yeah...but if you're absent for too long, I'm not going to be responsible for the results."

She strode off without another word, leaving Peter mystified. He shook it off and moved on to the next item on his list—finding his team.

7

High Tortuga, Space Fleet Base, Michael's Offices

William stared at the storage room Michael had just disappeared into. "You want me to do what, now?"

Michael came back out carrying a double armload of weaponry. "I want you to modify the grill again, and I need all these weapons in good working order."

William ran a hand over his head. "I heard you. But why?" He accepted the rifles from Michael with a baffled look. "What does that have to do with all this?" He raised his hands in question. "And what happened to the T-rex?"

Michael ducked back into the storeroom and came out with his arms full again. He waited for the lock to engage and then turned to answer William. "My quarry was eaten by a much larger creature, which I then had to destroy utterly. I have come up with a new plan."

He led William down the corridor from his storage area to the workroom, pausing on arrival. "CEREBRO, the door, if you will."

"Of course, Michael," one of the base's EIs answered.

The lock pad at Michael's head height flashed green. Michael turned to push the door open with his back, and the two men went inside.

William looked at the piles of weaponry on the benches. "I see why you had the locks installed."

"I have small children running loose down here," Michael replied offhandedly. "*All* my weapons are behind locked doors." He placed his load down carefully, then selected one of the rifles and started to strip it down for cleaning.

William got a good look at what he was carrying under the bright light. "This is quite the collection. There must be antique arms from most of the planets we know of."

Michael shrugged. "Not all of them."

William added his bundle to the pile, then pulled up a stool and sat down at the workbench. "You know, some might compare that gun safe to, say, a shoe closet?"

Michael raised his head. "They would not say it in my hearing."

William chuckled. "I can't say they would. But how do all these old weapons figure into your backup plan? I'm not too choked up about the T-rex getting eaten, if I'm honest. You know I thought the lizard meat was going to be too gamey to do much with." He made a face as he grabbed the bottle of oil and one of the rags. "An old creature like that would probably taste horrible anyway."

Michael broke the rifle over his knee and got to work with his oily rag. "I'm going to arrange a big hunt. One where everyone can get involved, and we can bring in a lot of meat."

"Something that big is going to take some planning." William scratched his cheek in thought. "So it's back to the drawing board?"

Michael nodded. "It is." He paused for a minute, then dropped his rag and placed the rifle on the workbench. "In the meantime, I have plans with Bethany Anne and the children. I'll see you out; we can come back to this another time."

William lifted a hand to wave him off. "Go, have fun. I'll take care of this. Give my love to Bethany Anne and the tykes."

High Tortuga, Space Fleet Base

Bethany Anne took one last look around the Pit and nodded, satisfied that the preparations for Kael-ven's pickup were in hand. She stepped into the Etheric and emerged a moment later in her kitchen.

Addix came back with the children while Bethany Anne was in the middle of preparing a snack for the returning shopping party.

The twins burst through the front door ahead of their exhausted aunt.

"Mommyyyy!" they cried as one, dashing over to be swept up in Bethany Anne's arms.

Addix came in behind them, laden with bags of all sizes.

Bethany Anne waved Addix in, then held her babies to her and kissed them. "Did you have fun shopping on Colonnara?"

Addix groaned as she collapsed on the couch. "We did

not remain on Colonnara for long. There was an attempt to kidnap the children for ransom—"

"*WHAT?*" Bethany Anne let go of Alexis and Gabriel. "Are you both okay? Did they hurt you?" She held the children at arm's length to examine them for injuries.

"Of *course* we are, Mommy." Alexis folded her arms and fixed Bethany Anne with her self-assured stare. "We did everything Uncle John taught us to do if anyone took us."

Bethany Anne ignored the way her throat constricted. "That's because you two are brave and clever." She smiled and ushered Alexis and Gabriel over to their table, grateful at that moment that she and Michael had chosen to prepare their children early for the life they had been born into.

"Aunt Addix took care of the bad guys. She showed them mercy, Mommy," Gabriel told her solemnly.

Bethany Anne frowned at Addix in question as she bent to put Alexis and Gabriel's plates in front of them.

Addix shrugged. "It would not have been appropriate to make too much of a mess with the children present. They were only in the next room."

"I appreciate that," Bethany Anne admitted. "There's a big difference between roleplay in the training simulator and witnessing violence in real life."

"Alexis and Gabriel were resourceful and calm," Addix told her as the twins tucked into their snack. "Unlike me. I have to admit that I panicked at first, but the children thought to activate Phyrro's holo and drop it for me to find."

"We weren't scared. In fact, we scared the bad guys!" Gabriel patted Bethany Anne's hand. "You don't need your red eyes, Mommy. Aunt Addix came to where they took us, and she didn't even let us help after that."

"You see? The kidnappers had no chance with these two. You and Michael have trained them well." Addix broke into a fit of hissing laughter. "Believe me, they would have fought if I had allowed it. Your daughter attempted to use her game powers on a Torcellan who insulted me earlier in the day."

"Well, he shouldn't have been so mean about you!" Alexis grumped.

"Yeah!" Gabriel cried. "It's not okay to be mean just because someone is different. Alexis did the right thing."

His usually affable expression twisted into a frown, and for a second Bethany Anne saw every bit of Michael's imperious nature in their son. It was a rare glimpse of the patriarch who slept deep beneath her son's cheerful and easygoing exterior. Alexis had the same relentless streak, which Bethany Anne had seen in her daughter from the day she was born.

Bethany Anne looked from one earnest face to the other and her rage faded, replaced by sheer pride in her children's drive to protect the downtrodden even at this young age. "Yes. Yes, you did." She looked at Addix, who gave her the short version of the events on Colonnara.

Bethany Anne listened, tamping down her growing rage until Addix finished with the information that all of the kidnappers were firmly on the deceased list. "Okay, so I *don't* need to go there and unleash hell."

Addix shrugged. "I shouldn't think so. At least, not until I make certain it was an isolated event."

Bethany Anne raised an eyebrow at that. "You can give Michael your full report later."

The twins' heads turned as one toward Bethany Anne at the mention of their father.

"Where *is* Daddy?" Alexis asked. "I want to give you your gift!"

Gabriel pushed his empty snack plate away. "Me too!"

"Why don't I ask him, sweethearts?" Bethany Anne brushed a strand of Alexis' hair out of her eyes and opened the link to Michael. *Michael, did you lose track of time? Our children are waiting.*

Michael's voice held a smile. *I will take it that our daughter is impatient to give you her gift. I did not lose track of time, and I shall be there in a few moments.*

Bethany Anne smiled. "He is on his way."

Addix got to her feet. "In that case, I will take my leave, with your permission. There are one or two things that bear further investigation before I give a formal report."

Bethany Anne nodded as her loyal and trusted friend turned to leave. "Addix," she called.

Addix turned back with her hand on the door handle. "Yes, my Queen?"

Bethany Anne was at her side in a blink, wrapping Addix in a tight hug. "Thank you for protecting my babies."

Addix returned the embrace somewhat awkwardly. "It is my honor and my privilege."

The twins piled on to the hug, and Addix ruffled both of their heads and headed out of the door as Michael arrived.

Michael swerved, avoiding crashing into Addix as she

left calling her promise to catch up with him after she'd done her research. "Research?" he asked Bethany Anne.

"Mm-hmm." She tilted her face to accept his kiss. "Addix will report to you later. The children had more of an adventure on their outing than we planned for. Don't freak, but there was an attempt to kidnap them."

Michael's smile changed to a snarl in a fraction of a second.

She held up a hand. "The children are fine."

"Yes, Daddy," Alexis chided. "Mommy already did her glowy eyes."

Gabriel tugged on Michael's hand. "Come help us get Mommy's gift ready!"

Bethany Anne laughed. "But it's not Mother's Day until tomorrow."

Alexis pouted prettily. "We don't want to wait."

"It should be Mother's Day every day," Gabriel declared.

"Besides," Alexis added, "We have more gifts for tomorrow. This one is too special to wait."

Michael shrugged. "You can't argue when they put it like that." He allowed himself to be pulled away by the twins. They took the bags into the nursery, and Bethany Anne went over to the breakfast bar to wait for her surprise.

Bethany Anne sat with her elbows on the counter, picking at a bowl of frozen berries while she turned over her feelings about the kidnap attempt. It was one more thing on a growing list she had to worry about right now.

The sensible thing would be to wait for Addix to report to Michael before taking action against Colonnara. If it had been an isolated incident, there was no action to take. If she discovered that there was a wider issue?

Whoever was involved would *wish* for the mercy Addix had shown.

Michael returned while Bethany Anne was thinking about replenishing the berries. "The children are ready for you. They say you are not to look."

Bethany Anne walked carefully to the nursery with Michael's hands covering her eyes. "Don't you dare walk me into a wall."

Michael's breath tickled her ear. "I would never. Just a few more steps."

He released her a moment later, and she saw that the children had created an impromptu theatre with Michael's help.

Bethany Anne clapped with delight and rushed over to hug the twins. "What is all this, my loves?"

Alexis and Gabriel chorused. "Happy Mother's Day!"

They each grabbed one of Bethany Anne's hands and tugged her over to the couch. Michael dimmed the lights and slid onto the couch beside Bethany Anne.

Alexis and Gabriel scrambled to sit in her lap. They were getting a bit big for it but the opportunity wouldn't last forever, so she accepted the numb legs she knew were in her future and wrapped her arms around them.

Bethany Anne felt the excitement radiating from her children. It was a lot, even for family movie night. "What are we going to watch?"

Alexis gripped Bethany Anne's hand as the title frame came up on the screen. "Shh, Mommy! It's starting!"

The opening shot panned in on a snowy mountain.

Two figures became clearer as the camera zoomed toward them.

Bethany Anne's mouth twitched. That scene looked an awful lot like…

Bethany Anne's mouth fell open when the close-up revealed Alexis and Gabriel dressed as her and Michael. *Is this what I think it is?*

I believe so, my love.

Onscreen, Alexis tossed the ends of her long dark wig imperiously. "We've been in these mountains for five days now."

Bethany Anne smiled contentedly and snuggled into Michael with their whole world held in her arms.

Unnamed System, QBS *G'laxix Sphaea*, Bridge

Kael-ven monitored the video from the surveillance drones on the secondary screens, waiting to see whether the first ships to arrive in-system would belong to friend or foe.

He drummed his fingers absentmindedly on the armrest of his captain's chair while ArchAngel watched impassively from the main screen and Kiel paced his nervous energy away. His eyes remained on the screen, but they did not see the eerie beauty of the cold light cast by the dying star.

All the tension that had been building in him since the techs had discovered the substance in Loralei's core bubbled up—and then Kiel passed by again. "Will you sit *down*, Kiel? You're wearing a groove in the floor."

Kiel stopped and looked down at his feet, then turned

again and shook his head at Kael-ven. "I just want to get out of here. This dead system is spooky." He walked back to his station.

"I cannot disagree." Kael-ven sat back in his chair, his shoulders dropping as the sigh left him. "The sooner we get back to High Tortuga, the better."

ArchAngel sniffed. "Wishing will not make our departure happen any sooner." The EI's studied indifference fell away suddenly and she half-turned on the screen as if hearing a noise behind her. "Oh, would you look at that? Perhaps I was wrong."

Kael-ven sat forward. "What is it?"

ArchAngel switched the drone feed on Kael-ven's screen. "This drone is registering Gate activity a few kilometers inside the system boundary."

Kael-ven got to his feet in a hurry. "ArchAngel, put it up on the main screen."

ArchAngel raised an eyebrow but said nothing as she moved to a secondary screen to make way for the video feed.

For a moment, the screen showed only the faint glow from the distant star. A shimmering speck appeared in the void, rapidly expanding outward until the point of bright light became a circle of shimmering waves filling the screen.

Kael-ven heaved a sigh of relief when the ship nosed through the Gate, closely followed by the much smaller support ships. His eyebrows went up when the main bulk of the almost incomprehensibly large ship came into view. "Bethany Anne sent a superdreadnought?"

"She did," ArchAngel confirmed. "The Gate signature

belongs to the Superdreadnought *Atalanta*, Captain, and we are being hailed."

Peter's face and upper body appeared on the screen. "Hey, Kael-ven, Kiel. We heard you guys need a relief?"

Kael-ven tilted his head. "Relief? I was under the impression that you were here to escort us back to High Tortuga."

"There has been a change of plans." Jian stepped into view behind Peter. "We are here to relieve you and your crew, Captain."

Peter covered his yawn with a hand and pointed over his shoulder at Jian. "What he said. Sorry, I'm beat. My feet haven't hit the ground for the last few days. I got back from the hunt with Michael and came straight onto this ship."

Kael-ven nodded in understanding. "How did the reptile hunt go? I have been anticipating the video of the battle."

Peter shook his head minutely. "Yeah… There's not going to be any video. It didn't exactly go according to plan." He shrugged in answer to the questioning looks of both Yollins. "Let's just focus on getting the EI onboard the *Atalanta* so you guys can get back to the base and decide how you're gonna spend your R&R."

"You don't have to tell *me* twice." Kael-ven chuckled. "I have never heard sweeter words. It'll probably take a couple of hours to get the core ready for transfer. I'll contact you when we're ready."

Peter grinned. "Great. That sounds like a window for a nap. I'll see you guys in a couple of hours."

Kael-ven nodded. "See you then." He signed off, and the screen returned to showing the massive ship and the support ships suspended around it in the vacuum. He turned and motioned for Kiel to follow him.

They left the bridge and walked in comfortable silence to the elevator. ArchAngel had the doors open and waiting for them. They stepped in, and Kael-ven broke the silence when the elevator began to move. "What will you do with your R&R?"

Kiel opened his mandibles to speak, then closed them again. "I don't know," he answered eventually. "I haven't been to Devon yet?"

Kael-ven looked at his friend in surprise. "Really? We should find out if there's an available transport when we get back. I've heard great things about the fights."

Kiel made a noncommittal gesture as the elevator let them out. "Maybe once the Interdiction is fully up and running. It's still not the safest place."

Mellor was alone when they entered the lab. He had his back to the door and was packing his tools.

Kael-ven took note of the reassembled core on the table and pointed it out to Kiel. "Now *that* is what you call an efficient team. I haven't even given the order yet."

Mellor turned from his toolbox and grinned. "I know who we work for, Captain. Loralei is ready for transport. She just needs loading onto an antigrav pallet. If only there were a couple of big, strong Yollins around to help…"

Kael-ven chuckled. "That won't be an issue."

Kiel peered at the blinking lights on the core's casing. "Is she…okay?"

Both Kiel and the captain jumped when Loralei spoke.

"*She* is sitting right next to you, Commander."

Mellor turned back to his tools to hide his snickering. "Dammit, Loralei."

The EI's gravelly laugh confirmed to Kael-ven that she was fully functional. "Glad to have you back with us, Loralei."

"Super-glad not to be the helpless prisoner of a hostile alien race," she replied cheerily. "ArchAngel tells me I'll be hitching a ride home with *Atalanta*. Have you *seen* her exterior defenses? Aliens wouldn't have fucked with me if I looked like that."

8

High Tortuga, Space Fleet Base, Michael's Offices, Vid-doc Room

Michael looked up from the control panel and gave Bethany Anne a thumbs-up. "Alexis and Gabriel are inside the scenario. Your turn, my love."

Bethany Anne pulled the lid of her Pod closed and settled back into the padding. *Oh, that's comfortable. Did Eve design the interiors?*

Not just the interiors, Michael replied. *Eve designed everything, and she refines the entire game system constantly. You know she insists that everything she creates for the children is the best.*

Bethany Anne smirked. *True. **Our children are extremely lucky to have her. Not just Eve, either. Things could have gone a lot differently on the mall world if Addix hadn't been the one guarding them. And then she dressed up in costume for their movie!***

I thought the movie was a nice touch. Did you see how dashing Gabriel looked in that cloak?

Don't get any ideas.

Michael's chuckle was the last thing Bethany Anne heard as her vision faded to black.

Immersive Recreation and Training Scenario: Fantasy Wars

Bethany Anne found herself outside a cottage on a bluff overlooking the sea. She headed through the gate into the garden, hearing the unmistakable sound of Alexis bossing her brother around coming from inside the cottage.

The children were delighted to see her.

Gabriel tugged on her hand, drawing her inside.

"What are we doing in this cottage?" she asked the twins.

"This is where we get ready to start the game," Gabriel explained. "We get our costumes on, and then we have all our abilities and skills."

"Who do you want to be?" Alexis asked.

Bethany Anne tilted her head and smiled. "I'll just be myself."

Alexis giggled. "No, Mommy! You have to choose which character you want to play." She made a gesture in front of Bethany Anne and a floating menu appeared. "Because it's your first time in this scenario, you have to choose from the list."

Bethany Anne scrolled down the list. "What if I don't see a character I like?"

Gabriel grinned. "Just choose the one you like the most."

She stuck out her tongue, then made her selection. "I'll choose the fighter."

Bethany Anne's mouth opened in a small "o" when her clothing was replaced by shining armor. She shook her left arm to adjust the position of the shield and removed her helmet to get a better look at the sword that had appeared in her right hand.

Gabriel made a noise of appreciation. "Nice!" He held out his bow for her inspection. "But I like my bow better than that sword. It has magic arrows that never miss. Aunt Addix plays the fighter, but she always gets Aunt Eve to exchange the sword for her knives. She says that the longsword restricts you to a certain style of fighting, and that can be a disadvantage in close-quarter combat."

"Your Aunt Addix is right." Bethany Anne passed the bow back to Gabriel and held the sword up to the light. She turned it from side to side, so the light caught the blood channels. "Hmmm. It *is* beautiful, but it's not what I would choose." She laid the sword on the table, then pulled the shield off and tossed that down to join the sword. "How do I exchange it?"

Alexis frowned in thought. "Aunt Addix asks Eve, but she's not there."

"Yes, but your father is. Michael, can you..." Bethany Anne waved a finger over the sword, knowing that Michael was watching on the screen. The longsword and shield were replaced by her katanas. "Thank you, honey."

Bethany Anne was surprised to find that the katanas felt exactly the same as the real thing. She made a couple of turns of her wrist with them to test the weight and balance before she strapped them to her back. "Perfect. Now I'm ready to fight."

She tilted her head to Alexis and Gabriel. "Who or what are we fighting against today?"

Alexis giggled. "Oh, Mommy, you are going to love this game! This is our favorite scenario, where we fight with the light elves to defeat the Dark Lord's army."

Bethany Anne raised her eyebrow in amusement. "There's a Dark Lord?"

"Yes, Mommy." Her eyes were alight with joy. "We have to battle all of his forces to save the Magic Kingdom from falling into darkness."

Gabriel huffed impatiently. "Alexis, get changed already!"

Alexis rolled her eyes at her brother. "Okay, okay." She closed her eyes and raised her arms, and her atmosuit was replaced by flowing mage robes. "There, I'm almost done."

Bethany Anne eyed her admiringly. "Darling, that's a beautiful costume. It's you."

Alexis picked up one side of the robe and twirled so that the folds of her robes caught the air. "I know, Mommy. Eve helped me to design my costume so I can look like a mage *and* a princess."

"You look *just* like a magical princess," Bethany Anne assured her. "Now if only this armor had heels."

Alexis squealed. "Oh, yes! We'll get Eve to make it for you for next time." Alexis reached into the air and retrieved her jeweled staff and pointed hat. She placed the hat on her head and smiled at her mother's bemused expression. "I learned that trick from Daddy."

They heard a horn sound far in the distance.

Gabriel's face flushed with excitement. "Mommy! Alexis! Stop talking about fashion and let's go!"

Alexis let out a yip of delight and bolted for the door, her staff tapping on the floor as she ran.

Gabriel waited for Bethany Anne. She took her son's hand and they walked from the cottage.

Bethany Anne examined her son's costume as they followed Alexis up the cottage path. "You didn't want to be a fighter, huh?"

Gabriel smiled softly. "No, Mommy. I like to be the rogue much more than I like to be the fighter."

"Oh? Why is that?" Bethany Anne waited for Gabriel to consider the question.

Her son never rushed into anything. They had almost reached the woodland edge by the time Gabriel had his answer.

"Well, if I was just a fighter, all I could do is fight. If I am a rogue, then I can use all of my strengths, not just physical."

Bethany Anne pressed her lips together. "So what you're telling me is that you don't like to be restricted?"

Gabriel looked up at his mother in confusion. "Well, no, Mommy. Why would I want to be restricted?"

Alexis scampered back from the edge of the forest where she had gone to scout ahead. "The Dark Lord's soldiers are on the road to the mountain pass. If we hurry, we can catch them before they reach the rest of the army."

Bethany Anne and Gabriel followed Alexis along the path through the trees.

Bethany Anne looked around as they walked, impressed by the fine detail in every part of the gamescape. She noted that the temperature rose as soon as they left the trees. "There's weather in here?"

Gabriel nodded, keeping his attention on Alexis and the path.

Alexis paused to wait for them when she reached the place where the path joined a well-traveled dirt road, then took a few steps onto the road and pointed north, where the rising dust of a group traveling quickly toward them was visible in the distance. "Look there."

Alexis and Gabriel shared a glance and moved closer together, which did not go unnoticed by their mother.

Bethany Anne drew one of her swords and moved to stand in front of her children.

The twins laughed and skipped around Bethany Anne as the dust grew closer.

"This is just the warmup, Mommy," Alexis told her. She flicked her hair out of the way and pushed up the voluminous sleeves of her robe. "It will be easy."

Gabriel pulled an arrow from the quiver slung over his back and nocked it. "Mommy, we do this all the time. Alexis is right—it will be easy."

Bethany Anne chuckled and swept a hand toward the approaching enemy. "Go ahead. But you can't blame a mother for trying."

The Dark Lord's soldiers were upon them in the next moment, giving Bethany Anne no chance to defend herself —from her children's snickering.

The dust cloud fell away as the grizzled band of warriors slowed to a stop in the road fifty feet away, revealing six dark elves and around forty foot soldiers.

The dark elves, haughty and beautiful, did not

dismount from the hellbeasts they rode. The two-headed beasts snapped and slavered at the bit while the elves whipped them into submission. Most of the foot soldiers glared at the humans with hatred—all except the goblins and orcs, who looked at Bethany Anne and the children hungrily.

Alexis and Gabriel denied them the opportunity to attack first. Alexis created a shining ball of light in her palm and flung it at the elves.

The elf at the head of the group gave a signal, and the foot soldiers surged past them toward Bethany Anne's children.

Bethany Anne leapt into action. She darted into the oncoming soldiers, stepping lightly into the gaps between them with her sword dancing deadly circles around her.

The elves raised their hands and began to chant, then the shadows came to life and all hell broke loose. The foot soldiers swarmed Bethany Anne as the shadows flowed in from the forest.

Bethany Anne had to keep reminding herself that they were in a game. She punched an oncoming orc in the face with the hand gripping her sword and kicked away an axe-wielding dwarf who was standing between her and her babies.

Who didn't actually *need* any help.

Bethany Anne gasped at the sight of the twins in action. Gabriel seemed to be everywhere at once, protecting his sister from nonmagical threats while she took care of the rest. Alexis had her feet shoulder-width apart in the middle of the road. Her face was set in a scowl of utter concentration as she hurled massive amounts of shining magic to counteract the elves' shadow wraiths.

Bethany Anne brought up her hand to create an energy ball of her own, but her connection to the Etheric did not come. Another orc came at her and she dispatched it with a flick of her blade, still trying to ignite an energy ball without success. *ADAM, why aren't my powers working?*

No answer. Dammit, she was cut off.

Alexis turned to blast a shadow wraith into smoke and dust and noticed her mother's attempt to access her powers. "Mommy, you're a fighter. That means you can't use magic. You have to work within the rules of the game."

Gabriel loosed an arrow into the eye of a goblin. "I told you, it's not fun being restricted." He winked out of existence and reappeared on an overhanging tree limb. "This is why I like being a rogue. I stole this power from one of the Dark Lord's wizards."

Bethany Anne shrugged and drew her other katana as a goblin brandishing a vicious-looking spiked mace came at her. "So you get to keep things from previous sessions, like an inventory?" She took a quarter-step and brought her swords flashing down. "And you can gain skills and powers..."

The goblin stopped attacking and slid to the ground in four pieces. She picked up the mace, swung it once, and released it to dispatch an orc vaguely waving a scimitar in her children's direction. "Hmmm. Maybe your father is right, and this gaming thing isn't so boring after all. What are the Dark Lord's powers?"

Alexis turned to answer, completely missing the dwarf

creeping up on her blind side with a knife between his teeth.

Gabriel did not. He vanished from the tree limb and reappeared behind his sister in the nick of time with his knives in his hands. He planted his boot in the dwarf's face as it lunged and the dwarf tumbled back, dropping his knife.

Alexis half-turned with her magic ready.

Bethany Anne saw the potential disaster unfold in slow motion. The elves were taking advantage of Alexis' distraction to cast a wave of dark magic.

"Alexis, the elves!" The cry left Bethany Anne's lips as the dark spell left the elves' hands and the dwarf got to his feet and rushed the twins again.

They reacted as one. Alexis twisted and released her magic upward to form a ten-foot high transparent dome. Bethany Anne was left standing in the road on the outside.

Gabriel threw himself at the larger dwarf knives-first as the spell dissipated harmlessly against the shield Alexis had thrown up.

However, the dwarf was half as large again as Gabriel, and while Gabriel was fast enough to counter the size difference, he was not yet strong enough to do anything about the disparity in their strength.

He got in a few good strikes before the dwarf landed a lucky blow to Gabriel's stomach. The boy doubled over, and the dwarf backhanded him into the dome while his defenses were down.

Alexis screamed and released the magic. She ran over to Gabriel on wobbly legs and dropped to her knees beside him, exhausted from wielding so much magical energy.

Bethany Anne darted forward when the dome vanished. Seeing Alexis and Gabriel hurt even in a game made her lose focus for a moment, and an arrow pierced her thigh. "*Sonofa…*"

She gritted her teeth and pulled the arrow out with a hiss of pain. The wound healed instantly, but fuck-damn, she *felt* it. Her head snapped up.

That meant that the children were hurt for real.

Gabriel was already on his feet when she reached them. He grinned, touching his fingers to his head. "I'm okay, Mom."

The second she saw that Gabriel wasn't hurt, Bethany Anne's panic ebbed. Her vision turned to red as it was replaced by rage. "Wait here."

Bethany Anne strode over to the dwarf and picked him up. The jerkin he was wearing scrunched in her hand like real leather. She lifted the dwarf easily despite his struggles. "I *would* feel bad about what's about to happen to you if you weren't just a figment of my husband's Tolkien phase."

The children watched openmouthed as their mother used the dwarf to take out the last few foot soldiers in much the same way she'd used the mace earlier. She came to rest when they were all down for good, still gripping the dwarf.

Bethany Anne turned her head to Alexis and Gabriel. "This is the easy level? I can't wait for the main battle." With that, she hoisted the unconscious dwarf and sent him flying at the elves.

The dwarf shot through the air and knocked two of the elves from their saddles. Before they had landed, Bethany

Anne was there. Her swords slashed and the heads of the elves rolled.

"*Moooom!*" Alexis complained. "You didn't save any for us!"

"Yeah, Mommy," Gabriel echoed. "You're going to get *all* the kill points."

Bethany Anne hung her head and chuckled. "It's Mother's Day, so it's only right I get the first group."

The twins shared a skeptical look, which they then turned on her.

Bethany Anne rolled her eyes and waved a hand. "Oh, fine," she admitted. "I wasn't pleased with the idea of you two feeling pain."

Alexis frowned. "How else are we supposed to learn?"

Gabriel nodded agreement with his sister. "We've gotten much better since we started training in here."

Bethany Anne recalled the way they had worked as a single unit during the fight. "I suppose you're right. At any rate, I'm extremely proud of how well the two of you worked together. You had each other's backs the whole time, and used your skills to complement your sibling's."

The twins basked in their mother's praise.

Bethany Anne held out her hands. "Shall we head to the next battle, my fearsome warriors?"

Alexis took Bethany Anne's right hand, Gabriel her left, and they set off walking down the road to the south.

The road after the forest widened and narrowed as the landscape dictated as it wound around farms and bucolic villages with names that were just too cute for Bethany Anne to remember once they'd passed.

The twins were conditioned to traveling the long

distances between the game locations. They knew the game was reaching its climax when the dirt beneath their feet turned to crushed gravel, and then to stone a short time later.

Alexis peered around Bethany Anne's legs to catch her brother's attention. *Gabriel, now that Mommy is playing the game, do you think we might get past this scenario?*

Gabriel tilted his head while he considered the question. *Mommy is the best fighter, but the Dark Lord is super-powerful like Daddy, except evil.*

Alexis was quiet for a moment. *Do you know what that means?*

No? Gabriel replied.

Alexis gazed up at Bethany Anne with complete adoration. *We will have a chance—if she gets angry.*

The road ahead took a wide bend to avoid the river coming in from the west.

The dark shadow on the horizon revealed itself to be not a mountain, but a city on an enormous bridge much farther down the river. The sound of clashing metal drew them away from the road to the city and over to where the river swept down toward the sea.

Bethany Anne led Alexis and Gabriel to the side of the road to gaze across the grassy plain between the road and the river, where the two armies were locked in a battle that stretched across both banks of the river and filled the plain below.

Bethany Anne looked out over the seething mass of violence, which pulsed with a life of its own. "We have to fight our way through this to get to the Dark Lord?"

Gabriel shook his head. "You *can*, but that would take

too long. We get Eve to send us straight here if we want to do that quest. This time, all we have to do is challenge the Dark Lord."

Bethany Anne nodded and lowered the hand that had been reaching for her sword. "Let's save that for another day, then. So, where do we find this 'Dark Lord?'"

Alexis pointed at the tents by the river on the opposite side. "Down there. See that black and gold one? The largest?"

"He's in there," Gabriel finished.

Alexis reached into thin air and produced a horn. "If you blow this, he'll know you're here to challenge him."

Bethany Anne took the horn from her daughter. "Of course he will." She looked at the tent where the Dark Lord awaited. "This won't take too long."

"Don't just rush the Dark Lord," Gabriel told her solemnly. "He's stronger than he looks."

Bethany Anne raised an eyebrow and lifted the horn to her lips. "I think I'll be fine." She blew the horn, and the battle below ceased immediately.

Silence fell where a second before the clash of swords and the screams and grunts of the battle had echoed. There was a splintering crash as one of the hastily-built siege bridges collapsed into the river and was swept away by the current.

Then the armies parted to form a path to the black tent.

Bethany Anne told the children to stay behind her and began the walk through the sea of soldiers.

The tent flaps opened and the Dark Lord emerged.

Bethany Anne couldn't see his face since it was covered

by his helmet. His body was protected by his head-to-toe black armor.

He strode out and stood with his hands on his hips in a way that looked familiar to Bethany Anne. His voice thundered across the battlefield, heard by all. *"Who challenges the Dark Lord?"*

Bethany Anne snorted. She took the last few steps toward him and poked him in the chest with her finger. "Dark Lord, my pampered posterior. My children could take you out before breakfast."

Gabriel groaned. "Oh, damn. Now she's gone and done it."

Bethany Anne held a finger up to the Dark Lord and turned to Gabriel. *"Language, Gabriel!"*

Gabriel pouted. "But, Mommy! We haven't defeated him yet!" His eyes suddenly widened and he pointed behind Bethany Anne wordlessly.

Bethany Anne turned at exactly the wrong moment. The Dark Lord cracked her openhanded across the face, sending her flying across the litter-strewn battlefield.

Her landing was cushioned by a group of conveniently-placed elves. She rolled through them like a bowling ball and crashed into the side of the ballista they were operating. The air was driven out of Bethany Anne's lungs when her ribs cracked on impact, and a number of other places on her body began to complain loudly as she bounced off the side of the wooden catapult and dropped into the bed of a cart filled with rotting cabbages.

She lay there and waited for her bones to knit together, not even registering the discomfort caused by the cabbages beneath her. *"Ooouuuchhh.* That was definitely *not* Michael."

Two pairs of wide and concerned eyes appeared over the side of the cart.

Alexis' voice was small. "Are you okay, Mommy?"

Bethany Anne sat up, ignoring the crunch as her ribs reset themselves,. "I'm fine. Almost healed already, see?" She climbed out of the cart, smiling through the pain. "I just went easy because I thought that was your father at first."

Gabriel snickered in relief. "That's because Eve used him as the ar— arc—"

"Archetype," Alexis supplied.

Bethany Anne grinned and took the children's hands. "This has been the best day ever, kids."

Alexis squeezed Bethany Anne's hand. "It's not over yet." She tilted her chin at the Dark Lord. "We still haven't defeated *him*."

Bethany Anne joined her children in staring at the Dark Lord as he advanced toward them. "Then I guess it's time to open a whole new can of whoop-ass." She took a knee and gathered Alexis and Gabriel into her arms. "Here's what we're going to do…"

9

Unnamed System, QBS *G'laxix Sphaea*, Hangar Bay

Kael-ven stood at the transfer Pod's airlock with his arms folded, waiting for Mellor and Robinson to shepherd the three antigrav pallets containing their personal belongings, their work gear, and Loralei's core across the cargo bay toward him.

"Do you have everything in order?" he asked the techs when the pallets came to a jerky stop.

Mellor walked around the pallets, checking the straps holding everything down one last time while Robinson went to open the cargo doors. "We're good."

Loralei snorted. "We would be if you weren't shaking me to pieces on this damned pallet. I mean, would it have killed you to put on just a few more layers?" The accompanying blinks of light from the EI's casing diffused through the semi-transparent insulation she was wrapped in as she ranted, "My insides are looser than a porn star's pelvic floor."

"Easy now, Loralei." Robinson poked the thick padding. "You're safe as spaceships."

Mellor nodded at the ramp descending from the open doors. "The transport Pod is ready and waiting. We'll be back at the base and get you into a new cradle before you know it." He pressed something and the pallets wobbled to a shaky start.

Robinson patted the top of Loralei's casing and turned to Kael-ven as the pallets trundled up the ramp at Mellor's direction. "Thanks for the ride, Captain!"

Kael-ven inclined his head. "You are both most welcome." He stepped away when the techs hopped onto the retracting ramp. "I look forward to receiving the SSE fleet logs as you promised, Mellor."

Mellor raised a hand but did not look up from the pallet controller as the cargo door hissed closed. "I already sent them, Captain. Check your messages."

Kael-ven had a slight spring in his step as he left the hangar bay. He took his time making his way back to the bridge, daydreaming about a release of the tension that had built in them all since the discovery that others had been present in the system.

Kael-ven got into the elevator, intending to persuade Kiel that a couple of nights on Devon were just what the two of them needed after such a high-stakes situation. The thought of seeking out some female company crossed his mind for a split second but was just as quickly banished by the memory of his ex-wife.

Unscheduled free time was rare enough that on this occasion it was no hardship to Kael-ven to pass up the idea in favor of something equally dangerous but infinitely less complicated than navigating the female psyche. It also crossed his mind briefly that a Yollin of his age should be past looking for fights, but he dismissed that, too.

He jolted out of his reverie when the ship went onto red alert.

The lights dropped, and ArchAngel's face appeared on the screen beside the elevator door. When the door opened, the corridor beyond was also dim. ArchAngel's war face looked out from every screen along the corridor leading to the bridge.

Kael-ven chuckled. He waved his hand to encompass her floating hair and the expanding web of crimson spreading outward from her eyes. "Really, ArchAngel? This is a little bit dramatic since only Kiel and I are aboard at present."

ArchAngel tilted her chin and rolled her eyes. "Really, Captain. The gravity of the situation called for it. We have company. An unknown ship has just Gated into the system and opened fire on *Atalanta's* position."

Kael-ven picked up his pace. "Did Mellor and Robinson make it over before it started?"

ArchAngel tilted her head while she checked. "Unfortunately not, Captain. The shuttle is adrift just over halfway between *Atalanta* and us. They are not responding to my hails."

Kael-ven hissed and broke into a full-on run. "Turn the ship around. We need to get them out of there before they get blown to shit."

ArchAngel raised an eyebrow. "What about the *Atalanta* and her support fleet? They could use our help."

"We'll get to them after we rescue the tech team." Kael-ven growled in frustration as he burst onto the bridge, almost scaring Kiel out of his seat.

Kiel got himself up on his two legs and shook himself. "Kael-ven, thank the universe you're here!" He swept an arm at the screen where the battle between the two gigantic ships was getting underway while the fight between the smaller ships raged on around them. "They just Gated in from nowhere and started blowing the crap out of our ships."

The *Atalanta* fired continuously upon the enemy ships, laying down cover for the smaller support ships to get to safety.

Kael-ven crossed the bridge and took his chair. "Arch-Angel, get me whoever can talk right now on the *Atalanta*."

"It will have to wait a moment," ArchAngel told him. "You have an incoming communication from the transport Pod. It's audio only."

Kael-ven banged the arm of his chair with his hand. "Put it through the speakers, then."

The voice from the speaker was unexpected. "Oh, fucking *finally!*"

Kael-ven shared a mystified look with Kiel. "*Loralei?*"

"Ten points to the Yollin with the brain in his head. I'm in serious shit. We were hit. Tim and Tessa… They're dead." There was a pause. "And I'm pretty sure I'm going to have visitors if I hang around here."

A series of massive explosions lit the plane of battle.

They whited out the screen for a few seconds. When the flash faded, Kael-ven's attention was completely taken up by the deep gouges along the flank of the enemy ship—

and the missing tail fin on the *Atalanta*. "They're in deep trouble."

The audio crackled as Loralei sighed dramatically. "Then quit talking to me. Go save the day, already. I just sent ArchAngel my backup, and embedded within that is all the information I got from the ship that attacked me. Make sure it gets to Bethany Anne, no matter what happens."

Kael-ven was torn. He wanted to recover Mellor and Robinson's bodies and to prevent the EI from being forced to terminate herself a second time.

However, there were thousands of lives at stake. Neither side was coming out of the conflict victorious. Intervention from the *G'laxix Sphaea* could be the difference between their side simply losing or losing badly. "Then the decision is made. ArchAngel, we are at battle stations. As soon as you have the information from Loralei, get us over to *Atalanta's* position so we can do whatever it takes to make sure our people get out of this."

ArchAngel's face on the screen was solemn. "I have received the data. Thank you for your sacrifice, Loralei. I know that Mother would say the same if she were here. Give whoever tries to take you hell."

Loralei laughed. "Don't any of you worry about *that*. Without a cradle to suppress the explosion, my self-destruct will take out the Pod and anything that comes aboard looking for goodies."

Immersive Recreation and Training Scenario: Fantasy Wars

Bethany Anne walked back to the riverbank with the children. The plain had somehow cleared while she was on her back recovering and the two armies were now seated in tiered boxes on opposite sides of a large roped-off area where the tents had been before, creating a wide dueling ground for Bethany Anne and the Dark Lord.

Bethany Anne released Alexis and Gabriel's hands when they reached the ropes, then took a knee and held out her pinkie fingers. "Remember our plan, okay? Don't step in until you see the signal."

The twins wrapped their pinkies around Bethany Anne's and nodded.

Gabriel held on an extra moment. "What's the signal, Mommy?"

Bethany Anne winked. "You'll know when it happens." She turned and ducked under the rope to enter the dueling ground, where the Dark Lord waited for her in silence as thick as smog.

The Dark Lord raised an arm to point his sword at her. "I have already beaten you, for I am the Lord of Death. All who oppose me leave this life screaming for mercy. Leave now, foolish challenger."

Bethany Anne smirked. "I'm about to show you what beaten looks like." She made a face at the corny exchange, feeling a touch foolish for talking smack with a video game character. Alexis and Gabriel found it hilarious. She heard them giggling from their place on the sidelines.

The Dark Lord kept spouting his promises of a painful death for all while Bethany Anne strode across the grass to meet him.

She stopped a few feet away and narrowed her eyes at

him, her katanas at the ready for a fast strike. "Hey, Tall, Dark, and Talks Too Much, was your script written by a serial monologist? Is this why your enemies fear you? Because you keep them waiting for you to get on with it so long that they die of old age?"

The Dark Lord glared at Bethany Anne with an arrogant tilt to his chin. "Foolish warrior. If you are that eager to leave this coil, then so be it. Prepare to die!" He raised his sword in a two-handed grip and charged her.

Bethany Anne blocked his downward swing with one katana, feinting with the other to give herself some space to work. "You're not doing this whole dictatorship thing very well. I can't see this working out for you." She twisted to avoid his blade and used the momentum to lash out with a spinning back kick.

The Dark Lord lurched back, his gravelly chuckle cut off when her boot met his stomach and drove the air from his body. The crowd bayed from the stands, evenly split between cheers and insults aimed at both combatants.

Bethany Anne blocked it out and continued to hack at the Dark Lord's defenses, sapping his energy a little more with each attack.

She blocked his next strike and slammed the butt of her sword into the chainmail covering his throat as she brought her other sword around to bite into his thigh. The jab to the throat was effective, but all she received for her efforts to remove the Dark Lord's leg was a stinging pain in her wrist when her sword glanced off his armor.

The Dark Lord choked. Bethany Anne sheathed her swords and took advantage of his vulnerability to grab his helmeted head in both her hands and introduce it to the studs on her armor's knee plate.

The Dark Lord's head snapped back on impact and he twisted out of Bethany Anne's grip, leaving his helmet in her hands.

She threw the helmet at him and darted forward. "Dammit! Stand still so I can defeat you already!"

The Dark Lord skipped back and brought up a hand between them. "I think not." He gestured, and his hand suddenly dripped flames.

Bethany Anne's mouth started to form the words, "Don't you dare!" and then the Dark Lord flicked the glob of flame at her. Bethany Anne felt intense heat drive into her chest, and she was flying through the air again. She landed near the children, cutting a deep groove in the turf as she slid the last few feet on her ass.

Gabriel tilted his head toward his sister. *Was that the signal?*

Alexis shook her head. *No, keep waiting.*

The children held hands as their mother got to her feet and rolled her shoulders. She turned to where they stood by the ropes and held up a finger. *Just give Mommy a minute, I'm wearing him down now.*

Alexis gave Bethany Anne a thumbs-up. *You're doing great!*

We never got this far before, Gabriel told her excitedly.

Bethany Anne grinned. *Your turn will come very soon. Remember, you two are the secret weapons.*

I'm still not sure what the signal is, Gabriel told Alexis.

Alexis rolled her eyes. *Just wait, you'll know when it's time.*

That's what Mommy said. You're no help, Alexis.

Bethany Anne blurred across the grass, dropping into a slide that took the Dark Lord out at the ankles. She rolled to her feet and jumped onto the Dark Lord's chest as he fell.

They landed with Bethany Anne straddling the Dark Lord's chest. She pinned his arms to his sides with her knees and began tearing his armor off one plate at a time.

Alexis and Gabriel strained to see, but their view was blocked by Bethany Anne's back. All they saw was their mother tossing away pieces of the Dark Lord's armor while he bucked to get her off.

Bethany Anne was winning.

Until she wasn't.

She was alternating between ripping pieces of the Dark Lord's armor off and punching him in the face to subdue him enough to complete the first task when he began to glow all over.

Bethany Anne tried to scramble back, but there was no time to escape the pulse of dark magic the Dark Lord sent out.

Alexis dropped her brother's hand when Bethany Anne was blown back by the magical shockwave. She grabbed it again and pulled him toward the rope. *Come on, Gabriel. That was the signal.*

Bethany Anne had to repress the curses that fought to escape when she was thrown back yet again. However, she'd stripped the Dark Lord of his fighting ability. All that remained was to defeat his magic, and they would win the scenario.

A quick glance assured Bethany Anne that Alexis and Gabriel had picked up her cue. She dragged herself up once more and drew her katanas, then charged at the Dark Lord to keep his attention on her and away from the twins.

Alexis was just leading Gabriel underneath the stands to Bethany Anne's left when the Dark Lord made his next move.

Unnamed System, SD *Atalanta*, Core Chamber

Peter waited patiently in the core chamber for the enemy to arrive. He had been a couple of decks away on his way to meet the SSE techs when the first wave of drones attacked.

Atalanta had directed him to the core chamber, along with Jian, Shun, and Zhu. They had picked up a couple more Guardian Marine teams on their way to the chamber, and now the group of twenty or so was all that stood between the core and *Atalanta's* destruction.

The reverberating shudders from the impacts on the ship shook the upper gantry where Peter had stationed the Guardian Marines to get a three-sixty view on the chamber below.

Whirrs and clangs all around them were accompanied by Atalanta's voice issuing constant instructions on the captain's behalf over the ship's speaker system.

She announced a breach on the deck above.

"Weapons ready," Peter commanded. "When these fuckers break through they'll be fast, and there will be a hell of a lot of them."

One of the men spoke up without taking his eye from the scope of the rifle he had trained on the source of the clanging. "Are they really half-organic and half-machine?"

Peter looked the nervous Marine up and down. "Did you review the video from the Queen's encounter with these soldiers?"

The young human shook his head. "No, Commander. I got back from a deployment and heard this was going down. My cousin is on the SSE team; she's on the *G'laxix Sphaea*."

Peter made a face. "Then prepare yourself, Robinson. We've come across these drones before. They look a bit like larvae with metal limbs. We think they're mind-controlled, and we *know* that they only have one directive —to kill whatever isn't them."

The Marines hung on Peter's every word. "Mind-controlled?" Robinson asked.

"Yeah, or at least the last ones were," Peter told him. He grinned and clapped the ashen Marine on the shoulder. "Don't sweat it. Those things are from nightmares, but they're easy enough to kill. Expect to see a metric shit-ton of them, though."

Jian looked over from where he was using the gantry railing to stretch. "We want *them* to get inside the ship. That eventuality is the other reason we are here besides defending the core—to capture them."

Peter pointed at Jian. "Exactly. Otherwise, the guys with the buttons get all the fun, and we sit here with our thumbs up our asses until it's time to go home."

He paced the steel-mesh floor while the sounds of the enemy approaching grew louder around them. "Let the sonsabitches come. They might know something about whoever is controlling them, and we can *always* use information on an unknown enemy."

The ship shook around them as the enemy ship scored another hit, and the ceiling panel above them was suddenly dented from behind. The ship shook again and Atalanta announced another hull breach, this time near the stern.

Across the *Atalanta*, the crew and auxiliary forces drafted for the mission closed in to prepare for the inevitable invasion. The defense forces moved quickly and decisively to protect the vulnerable areas of the ship, while the repair crews readied themselves to work on the fly and the medical teams prepared to be inundated by people with battle wounds.

In the core chamber, Peter looked up as another dent appeared in the ceiling. "Looks like we're on." He willed his body to make the change and in the next moment he flexed his Pricolici claws, ready for the invasion from above to begin.

Jian and the other Guardians paced in their four-footed forms, eager for the fight to begin.

The dent in the ceiling panel became a tear, which became a hole that a pair of spindly legs poked through and pulled back with the hooked appendages they had in place of hands or feet.

Peter held up a hand when the less experienced among them prepared to fire. "Waiiit," he called softly. "Don't make it easierrr by doing it forrr them."

Then more hooks protruded and tore back the panel, revealing the multi-limbed drones packed into every inch of the space above.

The mind-controlled enemy dropped from the ceiling and Peter dropped his hand. "*Firrre!*"

The Marines loosed their weapons on the rain of

drones. They killed scores before they landed, but it made as much difference as scooping a bucket of water from the ocean.

The ones who survived the hail of kinetic, laser, and disruptor fire uncurled as they fell and landed imperfectly on their mechanical legs before swarming down to the much wider permacrete platform below the gantry which contained the chamber's exits.

Peter growled and hopped the railing. He called back as he landed, "Protect the corrre. We've got the exits!" He was followed by Jian and the other seven Guardians, who fanned out around the doors to prevent the drones from escaping into the ship.

The Marines had the advantage of the high ground. They worked in pairs to keep the space around the core clear, and the Guardians fought as if possessed on the platform below.

The drones died in their hundreds all around the core chamber. The corpses piled up around the doors, forming a barrier that gave the Guardians some leeway.

The Marines switched focus as the Weres advanced their loose circle.

Robinson paused to change out his magazine. "How the hell do we win against numbers like that?" he mumbled to nobody in particular, then shouldered his rifle and took aim again as his partner stepped back to swap out her empty magazine.

"This is a battle of numbers versus intellect." Shun chuckled and fired without pausing a beat. His shot took out three of the aliens and incapacitated a fourth. "We have a tried and tested method for dealing with this type of engagement."

Zhu called from farther along the gantry, "I might feel bad for these things if they had any mind of their own. It could actually be considered unfair," he paused to clear three drones from Jian's flank, "to drop an angry Pricolici into such a target-rich environment."

As if to prove Zhu's point, there was a frustrated roar from below and a shower of mechanical body parts flew up past their heads. They looked over the railing and saw Peter tearing through the enemy a handful at a time and flinging the remains away.

He tossed away the two halves of the drone that he'd just parted from its legs and knocked a half-dozen more flying with a swipe of his furry forearm. "This is taking toooo *looong!*"

The six wolves snapped and tossed the drones around like ragdolls. Jian took a different tactic. He danced elegant circles, slashing the organic parts of the drones around him to ribbons with his claws.

Atalanta announced another breach, although this one was not accompanied by a kinetic strike. The drones continued to swarm the core as fast as the Guardian Marines could clear the space around it.

Jian was overrun, and he went down in a tide of probing mechanical legs. His Marines fired into the surrounding area to give him a chance, but it was too late for the cat; the drones had him.

Still, he fought. His body became human again when he lost his battle for consciousness. His partner Marines on the gantry screamed for him to wake up.

There was nothing any of the others could do to help. They stole glances around to keep the swarm at bay as he was passed along the seething mass and up the wall like a twisted parody of a stage diver surfing the crowd.

Peter watched with horror as the drones fed the Guardian through the hole in the ceiling.

Then Jian vanished.

Peter saw red. He plowed through the crush to get to his friend, unheeding of the drones that took advantage of his distraction to attack.

He felt a sting in his thigh and looked down to see a dart sticking out of the muscle. He pulled it out and stuck it into the brain of the nearest drone with a hoarse laugh.

He pushed through the burning in his muscles, feeling his nanocytes working to clear whatever they'd injected him with. "Your drugs have no effect on m…"

10

Immersive Recreation and Training Scenario: Fantasy Wars

The Dark Lord rose from the ground, the air around him darkening as he built his magic into a crackling black-magenta sphere around himself.

Bethany Anne looked around for a way to reach the floating despot before his shield solidified and her gaze caught on the stands. She sprinted at the stand on her right and leapt, hitting the wall feet-first.

Bethany Anne kept her momentum going by running a few more steps up the wall before she twisted and used the wooden planks as a springboard to launch herself at the Dark Lord.

Now!

Alexis and Gabriel appeared at the top of the stands at the exact moment Bethany Anne landed on the Dark Lord's back. They dipped, and then rose again. The Dark Lord writhed to escape Bethany Anne's clutches while she fought to take control of him.

Hold him still, Mom!

Bethany Anne looked up to see Gabriel with his bow and Alexis readying her magic. She snaked her arms around the Dark Lord's neck, locking his legs down with hers so his chest and stomach were exposed.

Alexis lit Gabriel's arrow with her magic, and he loosed the glowing arrow without hesitation.

The Dark Lord flung another pulse of magic, knocking the arrow away. However, Bethany Anne was somewhat more difficult to dislodge.

She tightened her grip around the Dark Lord's neck and stuck her knee in the small of his back. He lashed out over his shoulders, trying to remove Bethany Anne by punching her away.

Bethany Anne laughed and used her body as a counterweight to swing them around as they dipped again, thinking to turn them to where Gabriel held his bow loosely with another arrow nocked and ready.

Without warning, Bethany Anne and the children found themselves falling when the Dark Lord, the stands, and the whole plain vanished.

Michael's voice came from all around them in the featureless void which replaced it. "Do not be alarmed. There is an urgent matter that needs your attention, so I'm pulling you all out."

The twins were less than impressed.

"But it's Mother's Day!"

"We were just about to beat the Dark Lord!"

Bethany Anne gathered Alexis and Gabriel to her. "We can finish the game another time. What's going on?"

"Let me get you out first."

The void faded, and Bethany Anne woke up in the Vid-doc wondering what the hell was so important that Michael would disturb her day with Alexis and Gabriel. Then she felt the familiar tingle of her connection to the Etheric and Kael-ven and Kiel's situation flooded in.

She lifted the lid, slipped out of the Pod, then glanced at the children, who were still coming round, and turned to Michael. "Tell me what's going on."

Michael's solemn expression spoke volumes. "The *Atalanta* made it to the system to relieve Kael-ven and his crew. There was an attack, a battle. We lost people."

Bethany Anne's knees went soft for a moment. "What people? How many?"

Eve and Addix walked in, deep in conversation.

"We have video," Eve announced. She went over to the console, and a few seconds later the end of the battle between Bethany Anne's forces and the alien ships began playing on the wallscreen.

"Oh, *cooool!*"

All four turned to see Gabriel standing in his Vid-doc, staring at the screen with shining eyes.

Bethany Anne waved at the screen. "Pause the playback, Eve."

"What game is this?" Alexis asked, rubbing her eyes as she sat up. "Can we play it?"

Michael lifted them out of the Vid-docs one at a time. "I believe that a whole morning in the game is plenty for now. Sleepy children need to eat and take their naps before lessons this afternoon."

Gabriel yawned. "Is that why you're here, Aunt Addix?"

Addix nodded. "It is. Mind your father so we can all have fun together."

Michael walked over to Bethany Anne and murmured into her mind as he kissed her goodbye. *I have a full afternoon and evening planned for our children. When you learn the rest of what Eve has to share I want you to be free to take the appropriate action.*

Bethany Anne noted her husband's careful expression and nodded. She bent to kiss Alexis and Gabriel. "Sleep well, and have fun with your father, kids. Thank you both for a wonderful Mother's Day."

When the door had closed behind Michael and Bethany Anne was sure the children couldn't overhear, she asked Eve to continue playing the video of the battle.

Bethany Anne followed the battle to its uncertain conclusion. The two sides limped away from each other to lick their wounds and salvage what they could of their ships.

Eve frowned. "That's not all. The EI, Loralei—her backup was included in the information Kael-ven sent. She's hidden something in there, I'm digging it out right now."

Bethany Anne had a good idea what the EI had sent. "I need that information."

Eve made an apologetic face. "I'll pass it on to you as soon as I get it extracted."

Bethany Anne raised an eyebrow. "You can't just take it out?"

Eve shook her head. "Not without the risk of damaging

Loralei irreparably. She may not be an AI, but she has sacrificed herself twice now."

Bethany Anne nodded. "That deserves going the extra mile for, but don't take too long recovering that information. Lives could depend on it."

Eve hung her head. "You don't have to tell me. I know."

Bethany Anne took one look at Eve's dejected posture. "We got out of there mostly unscathed, didn't we? What's the problem?"

"The problem," Eve told her, "is that they took thirty-seven of our people with them. Peter and his team are among the captured."

Bethany Anne headed for the door. "Roust the fleet. We leave no one behind."

Eve tilted her head. "The entire fleet?"

Bethany Anne turned back, her eyes blazing red. "*Every. Single. Ship.* High Tortuga is going to war."

Eve's expression blanked for a half-second as she checked the status of all of the ships Bethany Anne had to call on. "That will take some time to arrange."

"Just ready the damn fleet, Eve. Whatever ships aren't ready to go can join us as soon as they are."

High Tortuga, Space Fleet Base, Queen's Suite

Bethany Anne looked up from her desk as the door to her suite slammed open. The familiar sound of Tabitha stomping down the hallway from the anteroom preluded the appearance of the capricious one.

She flounced in and came to an abrupt stop in front of

Bethany Anne's desk with her arms crossed and her head tilted at an upward angle that Bethany Anne recognized as trouble waiting.

Bethany Anne put down the report she was reading and raised an eyebrow. "Hello, Tabitha. To what do I owe the honor of this unexpected visit?"

"Don't you give me that!" Tabitha pointed an accusing finger at Bethany Anne. "You know exactly why I'm here."

Bethany Anne shrugged. "It can't be because I grounded you. A seasoned Ranger wouldn't argue orders that are in the best interests of everyone."

Tabitha kicked the visitor chair into the desk. "I'm not a Ranger anymore, Bethany Anne." Her arm pointed out to space. "Pete is out there, and you can't make me stay behind while the man I love gets mind-fucked by aliens."

Bethany Anne gestured at Tabitha's mess. "This is exactly why I'm not allowing you to go. An outburst like this could get everyone with you killed."

Tabitha scowled and picked the chair up. "I don't know what you mean." She huffed as she dropped into the chair with her arms folded. "I'm fine."

"You are *not* fine." Bethany Anne sighed, her face softening. "You're not in control of your emotions at the moment. I don't know what's going on with you and Peter, but it's affecting you, Tabbie."

Tabitha winced, her anger disarmed in two syllables.

Bethany Anne frowned. "What did I say?"

Tabitha looked up and away to hide the tears she couldn't prevent falling. "Merry called me that, and so do Alexis and Gabriel, and Kevin." She sniffed, meeting

Bethany Anne's eyes. "And so does Pete. You have to let me go. Please?"

Bethany Anne shook her head. "You know I'm not going to move an inch on this. Why are you pushing it?"

Tabitha took a tissue from the box on Bethany Anne's desk and blew her nose. "*Because*, okay?" Her scowl deepened. "I've been a bitch to him recently."

Bethany Anne snorted, then immediately held up a hand. "I'm sorry. That was unfair." She sat forward and laced her hands on the desk. "But Tabitha, you've been a bitch to pretty much everyone recently, and none of us know what's going on with you because you've been too damn prickly to talk to."

That set Tabitha to crying again. "Dammit, I *know*, okay?" She covered her face with her hands and let the tears come.

Bethany Anne got to her feet and walked around the desk to wrap her arms around the former Ranger. They stayed like that for a while. Tabitha clung to Bethany Anne and wept in great, heaving sobs, and Bethany Anne made small shushing noises and rubbed Tabitha's back until the outpouring subsided.

Tabitha was pale and drawn when she let go of Bethany Anne. "I'm not feeling so good. Can I just lie down a minute?"

Bethany Anne took one look at Tabitha and helped her over to the couch. "Are you okay? Do we need to get you in the Pod-doc?"

Tabitha waved her off. "I'll be fine in a few minutes."

Bethany Anne frowned. "Stay there." She covered

Tabitha with a blanket and went to the fridge to get her some water.

When Bethany Anne turned back to give Tabitha her water, some of the color had returned to her face. She took a few sips and replaced the cap on the bottle. "Bethany Anne, you have to let me go." Her voice was soft yet full of steel.

"You're not going to let go of this, are you?" Bethany Anne sighed when Tabitha shook her head resolutely. "What's this really about? I've never seen you like this, ever."

Tabitha pulled the blanket around her, and her eyes grew bright again. "I just need to make sure Peter is safe. I shouldn't have let him go—not without telling him first. *I'm pregnant.*"

Unnamed System, Battle Zone, QBS *ArchAngel II*, Viewing Platform

The *ArchAngel II* sliced through an ocean of twisted metal and melted plastic, cutting a path through the debris-littered vacuum to the *Atalanta*.

Bethany Anne stood at the window with John at her back, watching Gates wink into existence around the system as the ships of the High Tortuga fleet made their staggered entrance.

ArchAngel brought the ship to a stop when they reached transfer range, giving Bethany Anne and John a view of the damage the *Atalanta* had taken in the battle.

Her people had taken a beating.

"So much destruction, all to prevent us from getting

hold of Loralei's information." She leaned on the railing, the curtain of her hair not quite obscuring the red glow of her eyes.

Off in the distance, another much larger Gate opened. The shimmering light heralded the arrival of the *Astraea* and the *Adrastea*, here to take names on behalf of their sister ship.

Bethany Anne gripped the railing tightly as she looked upon the devastation. She calculated that at least half the support ships had been destroyed, and the *Atalanta* was in a sorry state.

The superdreadnought lay off to the side of the *Arch-Angel II* with her insides exposed and vulnerable.

However, she was not going to die today.

John placed a comforting hand on her shoulder. "We're lucky that Kael-ven thought to call us in or we would have been left with some Bermuda Triangle shit to solve."

Slowly but surely, the struggling superdreadnought was repairing herself. The gaping holes in the flank crept closed a millimeter at a time as *Atalanta's* repair systems worked to reseal the ship.

Bethany Anne looked down at the stern, where the damage was worst. Three support vessels held a massive shard of the ship between them, playing an elaborate game of push-pull to maneuver the amputated piece back into place. "It's a miracle there weren't more losses."

John made a noise of agreement. "We'll recover Mellor and Robinson's bodies. There's already someone on their way to the last known location of the transport Pod."

Bethany Anne's face hardened as she turned away from

the window and reached for John's shoulder. "Good, but still, two lives lost is two too many."

She pulled John into the Etheric with her and brought them out again aboard the *Atalanta* after checking that the deck they were about to step out onto wasn't open to space.

Bethany Anne squeezed past John to open the door of the storage closet and stepped into the hectic corridor beyond. "We're going to make sure we don't lose any more." She looked left and right to familiarize herself with their location, then strode off in the direction of the bridge.

John turned to the side to make way for a trio of linked antigrav carts. Once they had passed, he hurried to fall in at Bethany Anne's side. "What's the plan, boss?"

"The plan is that we *plan*." Bethany Anne swerved to avoid bumping into a pair of junior crewmembers who froze at the sight of her, and she made the turn for the elevators without pausing. "Eve extracted the data Loralei embedded in her backup. It was the key to access the data from the drones she sent out during that first encounter. I also have the feeds from the spy drones *Atalanta's* captain attached to the enemy ship during the battle. We're on our way to meet with him now."

John looked at her with a mixture of amusement and concern. "You know where our enemy is and we're still here?"

She gave him a pointed look in return and gestured at the organized chaos around them. "You are well aware of just how much I enjoy waiting." She led them into the elevator and told it to take them to the command deck.

John chuckled as the elevator began to move. "You're frustrated."

Bethany Anne arched an eyebrow. "Just a little bit." She waved a hand. "It's not important. There is more at stake here than answering an insult or solving a dispute. Thirty-seven lives could be lost if we fuck it up, including Peter's."

John followed Bethany Anne into the corridor when the elevator let them out. "Peter will have it handled. He'll keep them all safe until we get there."

Bethany Anne shook her head. "That ship was a match for my superdreadnought. I'm not willing to risk them by acting without getting every bit of information I can."

The captain was surprised when Bethany Anne showed up on the bridge unannounced. He jumped out of his chair and moved to greet her. "My apologies for not being there to meet you, my Queen. I wasn't told your transport had docked." He glanced nervously at John, who had taken two steps inside and planted himself with his arms folded.

Bethany Anne waved him off. "We didn't use a transport, Captain. I wanted to expedite this so we can get on with retrieving our people from enemy hands."

The captain nodded. "I understand, my Queen. Allow me to escort you to the brig, then."

John looked up. "The brig? We have captives?"

The captain nodded. "The brig has never seen so much action. We picked up a load of the bastards while we were cleaning up after the battle."

Bethany Anne grinned and turned to slap John across the chest. "See? Being patient can pay off." She narrowed her eyes at the face he made. "I'm not saying I had an epiphany, just that I'm glad it worked out this time."

She opened her link to Michael, holding a finger up to John and the captain while she waited for him to answer. *How's the hottest man in the whole damn universe doing?*

He is currently attempting to put together a lesson but will take a break for the woman he loves.

Bethany Anne chuckled. *Good, because the woman he... No, I can't keep that up. Can you catch a ride out here and give me a hand with some mind reading?*

11

High Tortuga, Space Fleet Base, Queen's Suite

Michael went into the nursery to wake Alexis and Gabriel. They hadn't wanted to sleep, still full of adrenaline from the game time with their mother, but Michael was firm. Even super-enhanced children needed their naps.

He had been anticipating the afternoon's lesson, having gotten together with Eve to adjust his plan for their lesson to accommodate and distract them from Bethany Anne leaving as soon as the twins had fallen asleep.

However, his duty to Bethany Anne and their people had to be a priority at this moment in time. Not just because his honor demanded it, but because Tabitha had never been able to keep a secret from him.

This was beyond personal.

No one fucked with his family and lived. Tabitha was not going to lose Peter, and if Michael had to walk through the gates of Hell to return him to her, then that was what he would do.

His children stirred and woke when he pushed open the nursery door.

He helped them dress, and they all went to the kitchen. Michael went to the fridge to get the children's lunch. He'd gotten used to preparing the afternoon meal while the twins were asleep since they always woke up ravenous.

Michael let everything else slide for the moment to concentrate on the time spent together. He nodded and said the appropriate things while they ate and Alexis and Gabriel chattered happily about nothing.

He enjoyed his time with just the three of them. Fatherhood was this strange thing he still didn't quite understand even after doing it for just over four years now. Small children had been singularly uninteresting to him, except the ones who needed his help. That was until Alexis and Gabriel came along.

Now he couldn't imagine life without them, and their lives would be so very different without *him*.

The thought brought Peter's predicament to the surface.

Michael needed to get to Bethany Anne, and together they would bring Peter and the other thirty-six back. Tabitha would not be left to raise their child without him.

Alexis blinked at Michael over the rim of her beaker. "Uh-oh. You have your serious face on, Daddy. Is someone in trouble?"

Michael caught himself frowning. He chuckled and patted his daughter's hand. "We've got some bad neighbors, sweetheart. I need to go help Mommy take back what they stole from us."

Gabriel grimaced. "Can we go with you?"

Michael's chuckle deepened. "Unfortunately, my brave boy, you have school."

Gabriel's face dropped.

Michael raised an eyebrow. "In the Vid-doc with your Aunt Addix."

The children brightened. Michael winked, knowing the next part would be what swayed them. "It's a brand new scenario."

The twins shared a look.

Alexis made a face. "What about you and Mommy? Will you let Phyrro tell us what is happening?"

Michael nodded once, knowing he had them.

High Tortuga, Space Fleet Base, Security Pit, Addix's Office

"Can you do all that without an issue?" Addix leaned over to turn the air conditioning up a touch and sat back in her chair while she waited for her asset to talk.

"I can do most of it," the male voice confirmed, "and I can arrange for the rest to be outsourced to trusted colleagues of mine."

Addix's mandibles twitched as she contemplated the risks of involving outside parties in her investigation. "That will have to suffice. I want to know the root cause of the attempted kidnap on my charges. I do not want to find out that there was a larger issue further down the line that you failed to inform me about." She paused to allow her words to sink in. "Am I making myself clear, Commissioner?"

"As crystal," the commissioner replied sullenly. "You

have my word, Spymistress. I will get to the bottom of this."

Addix cut the connection and looked up, sensing Michael's presence a moment too late.

Michael smirked and entered the office. "Good afternoon, Addix."

Addix waved him in and indicated the visitor's chair. "Have you come to get my report?"

Michael slid into the chair across from her desk. "That, and to ask if you would take the children for their lessons this afternoon. Bethany Anne needs my assistance."

Addix inclined her head. "Of course."

Michael smiled and settled into the comfortable chair. "Thank you. Now, what happened on Colonnara?"

Addix's mandibles rippled with anxiety. "I have prepared a full brief on the events, but the short version is that a gang comprised of a Yollin, a Baka, and a couple of humans managed to distract me long enough to snatch the children."

Michael held up a finger to interrupt. "How did they do that?"

Addix hissed. "By attacking my senses," she replied sourly. "They had some noxious kind of spice in a jar which one of them smashed at my feet. By the time I'd recovered and killed the Baka who'd dropped the jar, the Yollin and the humans had taken Alexis and Gabriel."

Michael frowned. "But you tracked the children using your implant, yes?"

Addix hung her head. "To my shame, no. I have to admit that I allowed my fear to overwhelm me in the heat of the moment. It was Alexis who thought fast enough to give me a lead to find them."

Michael remained impassive. "You could not predict that you would be attacked in such a way, but you should remember that we have our children updated so that this situation does not occur again."

Addix nodded. "I will. In any case, the four responsible are dead by my hand, and I have assets investigating Colonnara to ensure we were not the attempted victims of a ransom ring."

Michael nodded. "That was an appropriate response."

Addix's mandibles clicked. "Yes, well. I was somewhat annoyed with my initial reaction. It would have been better to keep the Yollin alive until I learned what she knew, but my focus was on getting to Alexis and Gabriel."

"That was because your emotions were in control," Michael reasoned. "It's only natural since you care for them. And it was only a small part of the excursion. By all accounts they had a fantastic time—kidnap included if you listen to them talk about it, and Bethany Anne was more than moved by the movie."

Addix perked up at that. "I am happy to hear it! The twins and I had a very interesting time making it."

Michael smirked. "I can imagine. I thought you made a striking Kael-ven, by the way."

Addix chuckled. "As I said, we had an interesting time. Alexis and Gabriel had their hearts set on making the movie even after the kidnap attempt, so it was no trouble to find another reenactment specialist." She shifted in her seat and took a pad and pen from the top drawer of her desk. "What is on the children's learning schedule for today?"

Michael laced his hands behind his head and leaned back in the chair. "I was thinking of ways to make math fun for Gabriel. Alexis eats engineering for breakfast, but my son is less enthusiastic when it comes to extending his knowledge of technology further than how to use it."

Addix tilted her head. "How do you intend to teach this?"

Michael broke into a grin as he got up to leave. "By throwing them—and you, of course—in at the metaphorical deep end."

Immersive Recreation and Training Scenario: Shipwrecked In Space

The scenario began in a large airlock. Addix found herself in a vaguely familiar exosuit, one of the newer models, by the look of it. She leaned forward to look at the console and saw the twins in the video link on the monitor. "How are you doing, children?"

"Great" Gabriel bounced up and down in his harness, causing his exosuit to copy the motion. "We're in a space adventure!"

Alexis was similarly chipper. "Did you review the scenario objectives? This is a colony ship, and we have to get the colonists in their stasis pods to their new home."

Michael had provided Addix with her own version of the scenario objectives. Addix had read them on her way to the Vid-doc room, and she knew that they weren't going to make it as far as the colony. She had been surprised to discover that the timeframe for this scenario had been stretched so that she and the children would experience time at a slightly accelerated rate.

"This is a little deeper than I was expecting, Michael," she muttered. She wasn't actually too surprised. After all, she knew Eve well enough, even if Michael remained a mystery to her. While she suspected Michael's easygoing, teasing manner was a thin veneer over a rigid and unforgiving nature, she knew damn well that Eve's sense of humor contained a dark streak a mile wide.

The airlock began to cycle and the light above the outer door flicked from red to amber, then to green before the hatch opened. The twins moved as one for the exit, but Addix stopped them in their tracks.

"I will go first to make sure it is safe. Wait here a moment, please." Addix walked her exosuit out the hatch and into the open area around the airlock. She shifted in her harness and tapped the button on the console to engage her exosuit's magnetic feet. Once she was anchored to the hull, she tethered herself to the guide rail before allowing the children to take a single step outside the ship.

Simulation or not, she didn't want any of them to go out as space-cicles.

She turned the upper body of her fifteen-foot exosuit around and carefully maneuvered the robotic arms to assist Alexis and Gabriel one at a time out the airlock hatch, securing each of their smaller two-legged exosuits to her tether as well as the guide rail.

The exosuit felt strange to Addix. It was designed for

her four legs, but all four were set to keep the main bulk in a low crouch against the outside of the ship, meaning that inside the cab, her body was set in a similar position.

Addix nodded when she was satisfied that the video link between their suits was still working properly outside the ship. "Are you both comfortable in the exosuits?"

"Yes, Aunt Addix," they chorused. The children's faces on her monitor were full of excitement and nerves.

Addix nodded, her mandibles twitching happily. "Before we begin, I want you both to remember to keep awareness of your tether at the front of your mind. Check it regularly, since its sole purpose is to prevent you from dying if for some reason you become detached from the ship."

Gabriel rolled his eyes. "We're not going to get launched into space. Aunt Addix. That's just silly."

Addix shrugged. "Silly, but it would be foolish to take the risk. We are not designed for floating around in a vacuum, Gabriel. This is why we need to respect the systems which allow us to take our tiny tin cans and search out that next adventure." She swept a robotic arm to encompass the ship around them. "Without our ships, we are planet-bound."

Gabriel frowned. "I hadn't thought of it like that. I just thought that maintenance was boring."

"It's really not," Alexis told him. "Like this relay we're about to fix. At the moment it's not causing a problem, but if we don't repair it, the relays around it will have to keep compensating, which causes a strain on the system."

"Very good, Alexis." Addix picked up the box containing

the spare parts for their repair task. "We're about to move, so check your tethers."

The twins checked dutifully.

Addix smiled, although they couldn't see it. She brought up the repair ticket on her screen and flicked it over to be shared with the twins. "As you can see, this coupling relay needs replacing."

The twins reviewed the information.

"This is challenging," Alexis enthused. "I like this scenario, Aunt Addix. I hope there are more tasks like this before we reach the colony site."

Gabriel huffed and started shadow boxing. "I hope not. I'm already bored. Aunt Addix, can we spar in the exosuits when we're done here? I bet I can punch *really* hard with it on." He went to switch stance and almost toppled, forgetting that his feet were anchored to the hull. "Oops."

Addix chuckled. "If we complete the scenario quickly and well, then I'm sure we will have some time to play afterward." She checked the balance of the box and set off along the walkway ahead of Alexis and Gabriel.

Gabriel pumped his fist, recovered from his embarrassment. "Yeah!"

Alexis snorted. "And we're back to subtlety again. All you want to do is hit stuff."

Gabriel turned to his sister as they took slow and deliberate steps after Addix. "Are you saying it *wouldn't* be fun?"

Alexis shrugged, which looked odd when her exosuit made the motion along with her. "Well, no…"

Gabriel pointed at Alexis to prove his point. "There you go, then. Looks like even subtle people like hitting stuff."

He chuckled merrily and moved ahead to keep up with Addix.

Alexis sniffed as her brother clomped off, still laughing quietly.

Alexis followed them, her interest caught by figuring out how her exosuit worked. She lifted each foot a few times, and after a little hesitation, she tried to jump— without success.

"We can't have you floating away," Phyrro cautioned. "One foot must remain on the ship at all times."

Alexis was delighted to hear the voice of their EI. "Phyrro! Are you the one controlling the anchors in our boots?"

Phyrro's avatar popped up on her monitor screen. "I am integrated with all of your equipment," he informed her.

Addix cut in, "Since we are in a scenario that requires the use of technology, you are permitted access to Phyrro. He will be acting as the ship's EI for the duration of the task."

Alexis pursed her lips in thought. "That explains the intuitive reactions of the exosuit." She looked at the double line snaking out from the back of Gabriel's exosuit; one leading to her Aunt Addix and the other to the guide rail that ran beside the walkway. "I think we should be able to jump since we're tethered twice."

"Yeah," Gabriel agreed. "We could just float along like balloons instead of walking all this way."

Addix chuckled. "Of course, but when you get hit by a fragment of rock traveling at the speed of sound, we will have to begin the scenario again."

Gabriel huffed. "I suppose walking is fine," he conceded.

As Addix led the twins along the walkway, she looked up at the skyline created by the various-sized housings, checking off the enormous stenciled-on designations on the side of the units against the one on the ticket as they passed.

Addix saw the designation she was looking for. "This is the relay housing, children." She stopped by the base of the twenty-foot housing and placed the box down on the walkway.

She tethered the three of them to the bar beside the access panel, then gestured to the recess above the panel. "Which of you would like to do the honors?"

Alexis waved her exosuit's arm. "Oh, me!"

Gabriel was paying more attention to a meteor shower in the distance.

Addix nodded. "Very well."

Alexis brought up her exosuit's hydraulic controls and selected the setting to extend the legs to their full length.

"You have me to do that," Phyrro offered.

Alexis giggled as the sudden elevation tickled her stomach. "I know, Phyrro, but look—I can do it by myself. If I get stuck I'll ask for help, I promise."

Alexis guided her robotic hand inside the recess and pulled the lever to activate the access panel release mechanism. She stepped her exosuit back as the front of the panel slid to the side and the cradle holding the defunct relay came forward on its tracks.

Addix opened the cradle and peered inside. "Okay, children. What do our instructions say is the first step?"

The repair went smoothly at the start. Alexis and

Gabriel worked their way through the instructions, with Addix and Phyrro assisting them each step of the way.

The twins were about halfway through fitting the replacement components when the starlit skyline was suddenly thrown into sharp relief by a flash of light and the ship convulsed beneath their feet.

"What is it, Aunt Addix?" Alexis cried, grabbing the cradle to stabilize her exosuit. "What just hit us?"

The ship shook again immediately after another flash of light.

"I believe we should get back inside the ship." Addix walked to the bar and undid her tether. She moved her exosuit quickly and precisely to attach it to the guide rail before doing the same for the children's tethers. "Be quick, now."

Addix ushered the twins in front of her, not letting them out of her sight for a second while they made their way back toward the airlock.

Alexis gasped. "Our objective! What about the colonists?"

"We will work it out," Addix assured her. "Although I believe our to-do list just got a lot longer." Gabriel's face on her monitor was set in serious lines. "We are almost at the airlock now."

The hatch came into sight up ahead.

Alexis put on a short burst of speed, seeing their goal almost in touching distance. She was yanked backward when her tether snagged on the rail. "I'm caught, wait for me!"

The light flashed again while Alexis was untangling her tether. The three of them looked up as they made a dash for the hatch, and this time they saw the meteor streak toward the ship.

The hatch was locked.

Alexis called for Phyrro, but the EI did not reply. She looked at the approaching meteor through her exosuit's window. "What do we do if we don't have Phyrro to open the hatch and let us inside?"

Gabriel reached out a robotic arm and tugged at the manual release. "We get in by ourselves."

12

Devon, First City, Warehouse

Demon's tail swished from side to side as she padded through the ground floor of the warehouse on her way back from her nighttime hunt. Although she had been told to expect it, she was unhappy to find that her usual route through the maze of crates and shipping containers the previous occupants had left behind had been rearranged in the few hours she had been gone.

She heard the heavy lifting equipment operating somewhere in the maze and decided it would be easier for her to see what was going on from the office. Demon followed the path through the new configuration all the way to the back of the warehouse, noting the locations she picked up the warning scent of explosives as she walked.

Demon sniffed the air and looked around as she left the maze and headed across the open space at the back of the warehouse. Mark and Jacqueline had cleared the area around the bottom of the stairway to the office. The scent of the fresh sawdust they had spread on the floor hung heavily over the musty smell she usually associated with the building.

She sashayed up the stairs and hopped up to put her front paws on the railing. They had clearly put a lot of effort in during the last few hours. From above, she saw how the reorganized floor plan would funnel their enemies right into their claws.

Demon didn't need the details. The humans and Ricole did some very strange things, but the concept of setting a trap for her prey was something she had come to understand and appreciate. It had occurred to her that all she needed was opposable thumbs, and then no prey would be unattainable.

She knew to stay away from the areas that smelled like explosives. The rest, once it started, was just doing what came naturally to her.

The sound of machinery stopped, and a few moments later Demon caught a glimpse of Jacqueline and Mark. It looked like they were done putting the finishing touches to their setup, since they were entwined around each other as they walked. Demon thought that might mean the action would be starting soon.

A raucous laugh came from inside the office, distracting Demon from her thoughts. She hopped down from the railing, leaving Jacqueline and Mark to their moment and padded inside the office to ask Sabine if it was time to tell the criminals that they had the money.

Ricole lay back on the sofa with her arms behind her head. She lifted an arm in a lazy wave when Demon came through the door and closed her eyes again.

Sabine sat at the desk with a small holoscreen open in

front of her. She waved to Demon and turned back to the screen. "I think we're nearly ready to set everything in motion. I'll keep you guys updated."

Demon walked over and touched her nose to Sabine's cheek. *What are you doing?*

"She's interrupting my nap," Ricole grumped. She turned over on the couch and pulled the cushion from behind her head to stuff it over her ears. "Some of us haven't slept yet."

Sabine rolled her eyes at Ricole and grinned. "I was talking to Raina and Luke from team three."

Demon tilted her head. *The Guardians who came yesterday to bring the explosives?* She jumped up on her window seat and stretched out in her favorite spot.

Sabine nodded. "Yes. They got back to their base and told the rest of their team what we were planning. It got around to the other teams, and now they want in on the fight."

They heard Jacqueline from the stairs. "No way!"

Sabine, Ricole, and Demon looked over as Jacqueline came through the office door mid-protest. "You're not seriously going to open our fight up to thirty other people?"

Sabine shrugged. "Why not? We have the drones up already. We can have them broadcast the fight over the team chat channel and get a book running for extra profit."

Jacqueline frowned, putting her hands on her hips. "Why *not*? Because it will take away all my fun, that's why."

Mark came into the office behind Jacqueline. He headed for the nearest empty chair and dropped into it, shaking his head in disbelief. "You want to make money off this?"

Sabine grinned. "Come on! It will be an opportunity to get to know the other teams better. We should make an event of it." She stopped talking suddenly and stood up. "We could even charge the other teams to get into the fight. That will bring it up to four ways we're getting paid for this job."

Ricole opened an eye and looked at Sabine. "Let me get this straight: we're getting paid for the original job, plus extra for handling the transaction. Then we're using *that* job to make a major dent in the scumbag population around here as well as making a killing on betting, and then we get *more* money because we're turning it into a party that people will pay to get into?" She threw her head back and howled with laughter. "Oh, that's just *priceless!*"

Jacqueline frowned, then raised her hands in defeat. "Fine. But if we're doing this, we need to make another supply run before we sign the agreement and send it to Morrisey. He is expecting to hear back from us by the end of this morning."

Mark chuckled. "That is genius, Sabine."

Sabine flicked her hair over her shoulder and grinned. "I know, right? And I haven't even had my coffee yet." She looked at the stack of dirty mugs in the sink and wrinkled her nose. "I think I'll get coffee in the bazaar while I pick up party supplies. Demon, do you want to come with me?"

Demon blinked at Sabine from her window seat. *I will stay here and sleep. That way I will be fresh, and the Guardians will not take all the kills.*

Ricole's laughter subsided into snickers. "I don't think

we're going to run out of bad guys around here once it goes out that we're holding the Morrisey money. We'll probably be glad of the assistance when it comes down to it."

Mark took Sabine's seat at the desk and pulled the keyboard toward him. "I'll get everyone informed."

Unnamed System, SD *Atalanta*, Hangar Bay

Terrence Bowyer watched the ship land with trepidation gnawing at the pit of his stomach. His uneasiness had only a little to do with the battle, and everything to do with the unscheduled arrival of the ship in front of him and his team.

The G'laxix-Sphaea-class ship looked the same as any other in its class except the *G'laxix Sphaea* herself. Nevertheless, something about it gave the experienced crewman the shivers.

The ramp descended, and the cause of Terrence's uneasy feeling became apparent. Their visitor was none other than Michael Nacht.

The ground crew fell silent when Michael stepped onto the ramp and paused to look around. The aura of fear intensified, accentuated by the flashes of crackling energy that flickered in the air around him.

As Michael descended the ramp, the wind created by the energy surrounding him rippled his floor-length black cloak.

Terrence smiled wryly, comparing his faded and grease-stained coveralls to the dramatic ensemble the Queen's husband wore.

On anyone else, it would have been too much, but on Michael it looked like the whole outfit had been invented just for him, right down to the engraved buckles on his boots. Even his fingerless gloves were black, worked with some kind of metal.

Terrence would never have admitted this out loud, but the man looked fucking magnificent.

Shayla elbowed him in the ribs. "Boss, isn't that... Whoa. Look at his *eyes!*"

Terrence risked a direct glance at Michael and wished he hadn't when the Queen's mate noticed him staring and zeroed in on him with blazing red eyes.

You, there.

Terrence almost died on the spot when he heard the voice in his mind. He looked at Shayla and the others, who had all taken a few steps back, leaving Terrence in the line of fire.

Michael lifted a hand and pointed at him. *Yes, you. You are not imagining things, Terrence. I* am *speaking to you. If you would be so kind as to point me in the direction of the brig?* His voice was measured and calm, belying the danger that radiated from him in waves.

Terrence, on the other hand, only managed a squeak. He'd read once that the human brain was split into three parts. There were the lizard and the monkey, but for the life of him, he couldn't remember the third. However, all three were screaming at him to get the fuck out of there while he had the chance.

Michael flung back his cloak and strode toward the startled ground crew. He stopped in front of them and turned his red eyes and terribly even voice on Terrence. "The brig, Terrence."

Terence opened and closed his mouth. He looked for something to focus on, and his eyes alighted on the silver skull that pinned Michael's cloak at his collarbone. The aura of fear Michael engendered was so pronounced that it coated his tongue and throat and stole his words.

It was all he could do not to turn and run.

Michael waited for Terrence to answer, then turned his petrifying gaze on the others when he only managed a brief splutter. "Anyone?"

Someone, Terrence thought it may have been Lars, whimpered.

Michael sighed. "Never mind. I will get assistance from the ship's EI. Our people are in danger from these aliens. There is no time for niceties."

Terrence snapped out of it when the reason for Michael's presence aboard the *Atalanta* became clear. "The aliens!"

Michael nodded patiently. "Yes, that's why I am here. Bethany Anne's people—*my people*—have suffered a grave hurt, and I intend to get to the truth. Now, would one of you please direct me to the place I can find these aliens and my wife?"

Terrence finally managed to move. He turned and pointed to the hangar exit. "Go out through there, take a left, then another left, and it's the third set of elevators. Atalanta will take care of you." He felt a sudden surge of bravery. "Sir? What are you going to do to the aliens?"

Michael's face was hard and unforgiving. "I'm going to do whatever I need to do to save our people. If I decide to leave any of the bastards who took them breathing afterward, it will not be out of any sense of mercy. It will be so that they can tell the generations to come why it's such a bad idea to fuck with my people."

Terrence couldn't help feeling relieved when Michael strode away with his cloak flowing behind him.

Shayla came to stand beside him with her arms folded across her chest. "He's something, hey, boss?"

Terrence watched the crowd part before Michael. "You've got *that* right. Our Queen is one hell of a woman to keep him contained."

Shayla snickered. "He didn't seem very contained to me. Those aliens are going to be crying for whatever monster spawned them."

"Very soon."

SD *Atalanta*, Brig

Bethany Anne leaned back and put her feet up on the next chair at the table. She was exhausted from a long and fruitless night of interrogation; the prisoners taken from the alien ship had told her nothing.

The aliens, which she'd decided to call Ooken since their orange fur and tentacles made them look like a cross between giant apes and squid, had done little more than screech and attack whoever came near them.

Of course, they had only attacked Bethany Anne once.

Bethany Anne yawned, and something caught her eye. She extended a foot and pressed her lips together. Ordinary eyes wouldn't have seen the smudge of blood on the red sole of her pump, but hers did.

She wiped it off with a tissue, tilting her head toward the door when a wave of fear crashed over the holding area.

Michael was here.

The prisoners stirred at the harbinger of Michael's arrival. Their already large eyes grew larger, and the nests of tentacles around their mouths quivered. They looked toward the entrance, feeling Michael's mental energy draw closer to the holding cells.

Bethany Anne narrowed her eyes at the Ooken, the corner of her mouth turning up in a small smile. "You'll tell me all your secrets very soon. Whether you want to or not."

Bethany Anne.

The cold fury that dripped from Michael's voice in her mind matched the outward manifestation of his current emotional state. She was angry, but her husband was *beyond* pissed.

Bethany Anne was pleased with the reaction Michael's arrival had stirred in the Ooken. She was well aware that everyone in the brig except her would be shitting kittens the closer he got, and she needed a break from banging her head against the wall of their silence. *Am I glad to hear you! I've been at this since we spoke, and these Ooken are definitely not the fucking chattiest. Or the easiest on the eyes. Or the nicest-smelling.*

Ooken?

Imagine that an orangutan and a giant squid bumped uglies. Have you got that image firmly in your mind?

I rather wish I didn't.

Bethany Anne believed him. *I'm not done. Go one step*

further and imagine the ape and the squid had a weird-looking kid, and that's kind of what they look like.

Michael chuckled dryly. *I would say that was impossible, but then we live in the most colorful neighborhood these days. Did you get any information at all from them?*

No, she admitted. *All they do is screech.*

I am here now. We will get to the bottom of this. Even in his anger, Michael's voice soothed Bethany Anne.

However, this was no time for warm and fuzzy feelings. Peter's life hung in the balance, along with thirty-six others.

Michael walked into the brig, taking a long look at the aliens as he undid the skull clasp on his cloak. He turned to Bethany Anne and draped his cloak over the back of a chair. *They're bleeding rather a lot, my love.* He dropped a kiss on the cheek she offered as he took a seat beside her. *It's a good start.*

Bethany Anne's eyes flashed red. *The only reason that they are still able to bleed is that they know where Peter and the others have been taken.*

Michael stared into the cell. The prisoners within stared back hatefully. He couldn't blame them for that, but he blamed them completely for the chaos they had brought. *You have no issue with me forcing the information from them?*

Bethany Anne raised an eyebrow. *None. I may have stepped down as Empress, but I have no problem whatsoever with putting on my heels when the Queen Bitch is called for.* She glanced pointedly at the skull on Michael's cloak. *It's as easy as you slipping back into your more...*patriarchal *ways. There's no changing who we are at the core, and right now that's exactly who we need to be.*

Michael's mouth turned up in a smile. He leaned over and touched his forehead to hers. *When did you get so wise?*

Bethany Anne chuckled softly. *Probably sometime during the century and a half I carried the weight of an empire on my shoulders while you were floating around the Etheric all footloose and fancy-free. That kind of responsibility teaches you some deep shit, which you damn well knew when you started me off on this path.*

Michael turned to Bethany Anne with a flat expression. *What I am hearing is that I should work extra hard to make up for my extended vacation.*

Bethany Anne narrowed her eyes, unsure whether he was playing along or taking things too seriously. *I wouldn't say extra hard...*

Michael sniffed, a slight twinkle appearing in his eyes. *Oh, no, my love. You have made your position abundantly clear.*

The prisoners watched the silent exchange with mounting agitation. Bethany Anne touched her elbow, thinking of the pain the Ooken's sucker had caused when it latched onto her earlier. *How are we going to do this?* she asked.

Michael appraised the Ooken through the glass divider. *You say the application of pain had no effect whatsoever? They have tentacles, so they clearly have complex nervous systems. It should have worked.*

Bethany Anne shook her head. *I wouldn't have had to call you in if it had. That was the second thing I tried. Then I tried mind-reading, but that spawn of sucker-faced banana munchers resisted me at every fucking turn.* She indicated one of the aliens with a finger. It was slumped against the wall of the cell with its tentacles drooping down its hairy chest. *I'm pretty sure I broke that one for good.*

Michael raised an eyebrow. *Is that a problem?*

Bethany Anne shrugged. **We can't find out what it is they're hiding if they're dead.**

You have a point. Michael rubbed his chin, considering the options for a moment. *Hmmm. We can get what we need; it will just take a little finesse. I need a connection to TOM.*

Coming right up. TOM?

Bethany Anne's Kurtherian ride-along answered somewhat distractedly. **Yes, Bethany Anne? Oh. Why are we on the *Atalanta*?**

Bethany Anne frowned. **What have you been doing in there that you didn't know where we are?**

The dreamy tone left TOM's voice. **I was contemplating.**

Contemplating what? She waved a hand at Michael, who was gesturing for her to hurry it up. **Never mind. We have a problem, and I need you to focus.**

Of course. What's going on?

Bethany Anne's lip curled. **Short version is that these new aliens showed up for a fight and snatched our people when they ran off to lick their wounds. Peter and Jian were among those taken.**

So you want my help to find out where Peter and the others were taken?

You hit the nail on the head. Michael needs some help interrogating them to find out which rock they crawled out from under.

TOM's disgust filtered through. **I'm happy to help**

however I am able. **Interrogation is a very strong word, though.**

Bethany Anne rolled her eyes. *Okay then. He needs help to tutor these ignorant beings in what happens when you fuck with the wrong species. Can you contemplate that?*

There were a few moments of silence while TOM digested her words. **I believe I can. Education is the cornerstone of enlightenment, after all.**

Nice to see you're coming around to my way of thinking. Bethany Anne linked TOM to Michael, who briefly explained the plan.

TOM spoke to Bethany Anne and Michael at the same time. **What should I look for?**

Bethany Anne tapped her fingers on the table as she considered. *Whatever you can find that tells us who they are and where they came from. Anything that helps us work out where they are now.* She crossed her legs and sat back. *Dig deep, and tell me what their weaknesses are.*

Michael got up and walked over to the holding cell door. *Just be ready when I need you.* He slipped through the door to the cell, and it closed behind him with a loud click.

The Ooken came at him, all tentacles and grasping hands.

Michael grabbed the nearest alien and pushed fear ahead of himself to clear some space. The Ooken fell back, wary of the pure power he wielded.

The alien in his hands was a different matter.

At the moment where the choice was fight or flight and the option of flight was restricted by the iron grip Michael had on it, the Ooken fought for its life.

Michael reacted instinctively when the nest of tentacles

spread wide, revealing a sharp-beaked mouth that was perfectly designed for cutting off chunks of meat.

One of its tentacles found its mark on Michael's face, but Michael gave the Ooken no opportunity to pull his head toward its mouth. He grabbed the tentacles on either side of the Ooken's maw and *pulled.*

The Ooken came apart in his hands as easily as a freshly-baked bread roll.

Michael dropped the two halves of its head and turned to the rest, activating his gauntlets with a squeeze. Etheric energy sparked around him, triggering the fight response in the rest of the Ooken.

He felt Bethany Anne chuckling at the back of his mind when the spell broke and they attacked.

You are amused?

I'm impressed. But try not to kill them all before you've got what we need, honey. Not that I don't appreciate this side of you, but you should save your energy for the ones behind all this. Bethany Anne's voice was light, but there was concern behind her teasing.

I have more restraint than that, my love. Michael dropped the dripping corpse and looked at the snarling mob. *TOM, are you ready?*

I am, TOM confirmed.

Michael grabbed an Ooken mid-leap and tore into its mind.

The alien stopped attacking Michael and screeched at him before falling into a catatonic state once he'd taken control.

Michael snarled and grabbed another Ooken. He handed control of its mind to TOM, then dropped it and turned to Myst as several other aliens converged on his position.

The group collided with each other and fell in a tangled heap. Michael ripped into their minds and fed the connection from each Ooken to TOM before moving on to the next group.

Bethany Anne just sat and watched as Michael flowed around the room, solid one second, Myst the next. Wherever he appeared, an Ooken dropped twitching to the floor while TOM ransacked its brain for information.

I have everything I need from them, TOM announced after the last one collapsed clutching its head. **I require a few moments, though. It's a lot of information.**

The first thing I want to know is if they're under Kurtherian control.

Michael emerged from the holding cell, wiping his hands. *Did you get what you needed?*

We did. Bethany Anne got up to pace, too impatient to remain still for the moment. *TOM was just about to tell me if they have anything to do with the Kurtherians.*

The answer is no. Or to be accurate, their original modifications were made by one of the clans some centuries past, but their species split. Our group headed out on their own and continued their efforts at "improvement" in the misguided belief that conquering everyone would help them ascend. They're also not averse to killing to obtain new technology.

Like the drones?

Yes.

Bethany Anne pursed her lips. *So there's no Kurtherian*

boss waiting for us when we get to wherever they're holding our people?

It is not likely, TOM replied. **Not that it matters. These aliens are smart, and they took to the whole "let the best alien win" creed like kids to sugar.** They have no empathy at all for the people they have killed in their thirst to be the strongest.

Bethany Anne's hands clenched into fists. *They can't be too smart if they came here thinking that we would just roll over for them.*

They don't care, TOM reiterated. **They believe themselves to be above everyone except the Kurtherians who elevated them in the first place.**

Michael turned back to the cell. *Then they are past saving.* The Ooken lay on the floor in messy heaps of sporadically twitching tentacles, incapacitated by the forced mental link.

Are you done with them?

I have a location. Do we need anything else?

Bethany Anne shook her head. *No.*

Michael cut TOM's end of the link, then sent a burst of Etheric energy the other way. It burned out the Ookens' brains, killing them instantly.

He shook his head in disgust at the corpses. *There is no justification for allowing anyone to continue waging a war of extinction.*

Bethany Anne set her mouth in a hard line. *I couldn't agree more.* She stalked toward the door, her heels clicking loudly in the silence.

What are you going to do?

I'm going to find somewhere I can update the Admiral.

Bethany Anne paused holding the door handle. She turned back to Michael, her red eyes betraying the rage the cold mask of her face hid. *Tell the fleet there are new rules. The new rules are the old rules.*

*We give **no** quarter.*

SD Atalanta, Captain's Meeting Room

Bethany Anne tapped her fingers on the desk, thinking about Peter and Tabitha and the larger issue of the weakness in their defenses.

Her old friend Admiral Bartholomew Thomas made a sympathetic face on the video screen while he tried to console Bethany Anne.

Bethany Anne waved away his platitudes. "Regardless of revenge for the two people we lost, that ship Gated in with no warning and took thirty-seven more." Her hand made a fist, unnoticed. "We need to get them back and make sure it doesn't ever happen again."

Admiral Thomas frowned. "It's not like we can put up a solid border."

"No, and I wouldn't want to. However, it's only prudent to know when we have strangers at our door." Bethany Anne sat back and ignored the look of disbelief on Admiral Thomas face.

"You want *another* exclusion zone?"

Bethany Anne raised an eyebrow. "No. I want us to be protected from all sides. I want our borders with unknowns to be secure... Dammit." She shrugged. "Okay, fine. I want another exclusion zone."

Admiral Thomas nodded in acquiescence. "I can make that happen. What do you need?"

"We need to make everything here one-way." Bethany Anne pressed her lips together. "I need to make sure nothing comes into this space without us knowing about it. Until we have defeated this enemy, I don't want anyone who turns up to be able to leave without us checking on their intent."

Admiral Thomas rubbed his chin. "There's only one way I can think of to do all of that."

Bethany Anne nodded. "We have to build a base."

High Tortuga, Space Fleet Base, Admiral of the Fleet's Office

"First Bethany Anne has put in the interdiction at Devon, which has been complicated as all fuck. *Then* she tells me to quarantine an entire system." Admiral Thomas paused in front of the holoprojection with his arms folded and his chin on his hand. "Now she wants me to magic up a base out in the ass-end of nowhere. An *exclusion zone*, CEREBRO. Our Queen is right about the need for it, but she never tells me where I'm supposed to find the resources for these things."

"You have plenty of resources to draw from. The recovery period for those who fought at QTC-12-T is drawing to an end." The EI group's harmony of voices replied from the speaker embedded in the desk. "All you need is a recruiter they can't say no to."

The Admiral was well used to working with multiple EIs at once, so he allowed the whole group access to their conversation. It was still quieter than dinner time at home with two children under two years old and a beautiful young bride.

He smiled. "Giselle could be just who I need for this." Her time as a socialite had left his whirlwind-romance-turned-wife with the HR skills of a demon. She knew everyone. She also knew who they'd seen, where they'd been, where they were going, what they were wearing, when they were traveling next, and how they could have done all of it more efficiently.

"You mentioned that she was looking for something to fill the time."

Admiral Thomas wagged a finger. "True, although frankly, I don't know where she gets the energy with Simone and Martina. Little tykes are always awake, it seems. Anyway. Construction workers can be recruited from here, and Devon, too, if necessary. There's a waiting list of people on Devon who are happy to work in return for passage to somewhere new."

"Infrastructure mostly takes care of itself once you provide breathable atmosphere and a place for people to put down roots." He returned the hand to his chin and kept walking around the interactive 3-D model of the system. "What did Bethany Anne name the system?"

"I believe she referred to it as 'the place dumbasses go to die,'" CEREBRO supplied.

Admiral Thomas chuckled when the name appeared at the bottom of the holographic model. "While that's entirely accurate, I think we'll give it a more appropriate designation." He began to type the new name into the model. "How many Gate jumps is it from the QT system?"

"Two," CEREBRO replied.

"QTC-12-T2 it is, then. QT2 for short." He pointed at a spot on the model. "We'll put the base here, string the satellite network out from there to cover the rest of the system, and have it all run by the base EI."

"That is a great deal of space between satellites," CEREBRO pointed out.

The Admiral nodded. "This will be a lot looser than the net we have over High Tortuga, but while I like the simplicity of putting up a solid border, it's just not practical."

"There are only two other places in the system that are suitable for anything as large as the superdreadnoughts to Gate in through."

Admiral Thomas made a face. "Again, true. If we leave all our guns over one mousehole, then we can be sure as damned that they'll choose one of the others." He stepped back, rubbing his chin as a smile appeared. "How would some of you like a change of scenery?"

"We would be happy to split ourselves." CEREBRO made a sound of approval. "We will be able to monitor the whole system from there without any impediment. If you do not mind us saying, Admiral, you came up with all this rather quickly."

Admiral Thomas snorted softly. "This is not my first square dance, CEREBRO. And it's not entirely unexpected. As much as our Queen likes to say she's staying on the sidelines, she hasn't got it in her to stand aside while a bunch of rotten assholes come along and shit on the peace she's worked so damned hard to create."

"We know," CEREBRO answered. "Some of us were around during the long war."

The Admiral frowned quizzically at the speaker. "Weren't a lot of you created during the Leath War? I know I hear a few familiar voices in there today."

The speaker buzzed, as it did whenever CEREBRO's EIs all talked at once. Admiral Thomas held up a hand. "We can talk about that another time. We should concentrate on the war at hand."

"What are your instructions?" CEREBRO inquired.

"Find me somewhere that can supply what we need. Metals, plastics, electronics. I need to get with Jean on defenses, Sofia on requisitioning equipment, and... Who is responsible for the Guardian Marines in Peter's place?"

"That would be Tim and Rickie, Admiral."

Admiral Thomas sighed. "Oh, joy."

"By all accounts, they are doing well," CEREBRO informed him cheerfully.

Admiral Thomas shook his head. "I don't doubt it. However, I wish I didn't have to deal with Rickie running his mouth constantly. The man gives me a headache." He sighed again. "I miss Maxim. *He* never made a joke in his life. Such a pity he stayed with the Federation."

"We can always make it so that you only have to deal with Tim on this project," CEREBRO offered.

Admiral Thomas considered it for a full minute. "No, I can't avoid Rickie just because he rubs me the wrong way. You arrange for the two of them to come see me about getting the base staffed. I'll put on my big-boy pants and deal with the headache afterward."

QT2 System, *ArchAngel II*, Bridge

Bethany Anne paced in front of Kael-ven again and noticed his minute flinch. "I'm just as anxious to act as you are."

"I would be less anxious if you would pace somewhere else." Kael-ven sighed when Bethany Anne's eyebrow went up. "I'm sorry. This is getting to me. Two noncombatants… two innocent people were killed minutes after leaving my ship. I want to make amends to their families, and the only way I know to do that is to make sure it doesn't happen again."

Bethany Anne stopped pacing and placed a hand on Kael-ven's shoulder. "It wasn't your fault, Kael-ven. You did everything you could afterward, and I made sure their families know that you and Kiel risked your own lives to retrieve their bodies."

Kael-ven hung his head. "It was the least we could do."

Bethany Anne's face hardened, but her heart did not. "The scouts are going to find wherever in that system the Ooken are hiding." Kael winced as the grip on his shoulder suddenly grew tighter. "We'll get back every single person they've taken, and then we're going to drop on them like a bunch of people with a fucking grudge to settle."

There was a flash of light on the screen.

The scout ships were beginning to meet resistance at last.

Kael-ven turned up the audio and all three turned their attention back to the screen.

"Group Two contact. This is Daisy. It's some kind of… what the actual fuck? They look like gen II SSE ships! Bastards stole our ships and copied them! Ohhh, and now they think they can *outfly* me? *ME!* HA! I'd find it sweet if it weren't so fucking hilarious."

"I know, right? I've got them here, too. One minute... Hey, asshole! Your momma was a fucking snowblower! See you later, *not!*"

"*Whoooo*, bitches! We're getting hotter!"

"We're already pretty hot, Serena. I mean, have you seen my guns?" The pulse of a plasma cannon punctuated Mirabelle's raucous laughs. "Did you see that? Anyone? I got that fucker *right* in the kisser! It was all *BOOM, POW!* Who's next? Come and get a taste, you sorry excuses for digital intelligence!"

"You give them hell, Mirabelle. I have a tail of my own. Hang on..." There was an explosion in the background. "Scratch that. I *had* a tail. *Buuuut*....that's what happens when knockoffs come up against the real thing."

"There's no competition, really..."

Bethany Anne dipped in and out of the audio feeds from the Scout Ship Explorer fleet courtesy of ADAM, while the third-generation scout ships battled it out against wave after wave of Ooken seeker ships on the viewscreen.

"Shit! I'm hit! Mirabelle down! Oh, wait... No, I'm good, but my primary thruster drives are damaged. I still have my secondaries."

Bethany Anne hissed softly. Mirabelle was the third scout ship that had gone down in the last minute. The fleet had doubled in size, but still, she didn't want to keep losing ships like this. "Can you make it back, Mirabelle?"

"What do you think, my Queen? I'm already limping

back to the *ArchAngel* for a quick body change, and then I'm gonna haul my ass straight back out here."

"Body change…" Bethany Anne murmured.

>>There are spare ships, and more under construction in the SSE hangar. Jean caught a transport out here and took over as soon as word got to her that Peter had been taken. She's been working around the clock since.<<

I might have forgotten about the hangar bay, but I'm not surprised to hear that's why I haven't seen Jean at all. I didn't even know she'd arrived.

"These bastards aren't going to get one over on us," Mirabelle continued. "They're gonna be sorry they ever thought to fuck with us when…"

Bethany Anne tuned out the audio feeds for a moment. *Are they all this chatty?*

ADAM chuckled. >>Um, yeah. It's their thing.<<

Mirabelle continued, "And if the Ooken have anything to say about *that*, I'll chase those hairy-tentacled sons-abitches down and insert my entire loadout wherever it will be the most painful for them."

Bethany Anne snorted. "I would love to see that happen, Mirabelle, but get yourself fixed up first." She walked off the bridge, heading in the general direction of the hangars.

The way before Bethany Anne cleared as she walked, her heels loud against the metal floor even in the bustle. *We're getting close. The scout ships wouldn't be getting such a warm welcome otherwise.*

>>What about your idea?<< ADAM asked. >>Because if it was for me to take one of the ships out and back the

fleet up, then you're thinking exactly what I'm thinking.
<<

Bethany Anne's mouth twitched in amusement. *Almost.*
I have to be cautious this time.

>> These aliens have you worried?<<

Bethany Anne snickered softly. *Not worried,* **cautious.**
We're coming up against a new type of enemy. These are not Leath, and neither were the last scavengers who came sniffing. They're smart, and they have tech that's as good as or better than ours. Her eyes narrowed in thought. *We have to outthink them as well as outfight them.*

ADAM chuckled. >>Shouldn't be too much of a problem.<<

The battle is the perfect distraction for us to get in there and find out more about the kind of minds we're dealing with.

>>Know your enemy.<<

Like I know myself, and when it comes time, it will be them and not me on the losing side of our confrontation. I'm bringing Peter home, and if I have to take a step back and think for a moment before I squeeze my fist to do that? That's what I'm going to do.

>>No matter how much you want to unleash the Queen Bitch on them?<<

Oh, no. That's going to happen. Just not until Peter and the others are safe.

Bethany Anne reached the elevator, then changed her mind and went through the Etheric when she saw that she would have to wait. She checked that the way was clear before stepping out close to the hangar bays.

They want to get into a war of mental abilities? I'll strip their psyches down to raw nubbins and stamp them into the ground, but first I want to know how they think so I can learn their weaknesses. Looking at how their tech works is one way of doing that. We have the opportunity, and there's no way I'm passing it up.

She turned at an intersection in the corridor, then again into the hangar where the SSE fleet was based for this operation.

Despite the seriousness of the reason she was here, what awaited in the deafeningly loud hangar was one of her favorite things in the universe to walk in on.

It was hot, and the air was barely breathable through the stink of oil and grease and the sweat of the people working their derrieres off to reach a common goal.

She fucking loved it.

Every one of the people in the hangar was working, in this instance, to build more scout ships or repair the ones who had enough in them to make it back after being hit. Everywhere she looked she saw action, but she couldn't find the person she wanted amid the barely-organized chaos that was the hallmark of a Jean Dukes workspace.

Jean, are you in here?

Yeah, came the reply. *In back, with the* Loralei.

Bethany Anne made her circuitous way through the hangar, ducking here and there to avoid people acting as handlers for machinery moving pieces of the ships into place or to avoid showers of sparks as others were welded into place.

She saw Jean putting the finishing touches on a gen IV scout ship. She stood back from the side of the ship, filling in the third letter of the stencil reading, "SSE *Loralei II*."

Bethany Anne looked the ship over and chuckled at the way serendipity had presented her with a gift like this. "Hold off on that a minute, Jean."

Jean turned and smiled, dropping the spray-painting wand to her side. "Hey, you made it." She nodded at Bethany Anne's appraisal of the scout ship. "She's a beauty, right? I might have gotten a bit missile-happy, but I think it adds to the overall design."

>>I'm in complete agreement,<< ADAM told her. >> Nice, work, Jean. BA, you should see inside this sweet ride. Oh, nice! Are those what I think they are?<<

Jean swelled with pride at ADAM's reaction. "If you're referring to the modified guns, then yeah. They have some special features. I didn't want Loralei to get taken out like that again."

Bethany Anne received a message from the bridge. "Shit, two more ships have gone down." She climbed up, pulled the stencil off the side of the ship, and held out her hand for Jean's spray wand. "You'll have to pass my apologies on to Loralei. This ship is needed elsewhere."

>>Double sweet!<<

Bethany Anne raised the spray wand. *Don't thank me just yet.*

Immersive Recreational and Training Scenario: Shipwrecked In Space

Addix received a message from Eve informing her that the next stage of the scenario was now underway. She scanned the details and closed the message. "Children, the next part of this game is timed. We have five hours to work out our objectives and complete this stage."

Gabriel dropped the door release lever. "It's jammed."

Alexis shoved her brother out of the way and focused her external camera on the mechanism. "It's not jammed, there's no power to it. The ship is dead."

Gabriel's voice was small. "Then we really *are* trapped." He moaned. "I've changed my mind about space. We're going to get smooshed by a comet if we stay out here."

Addix saw that Alexis was coming to some conclusion or other. The small child was a study in deliberation in the other corner of her screen.

"The power," Alexis stated, a small, determined line furrowing her brow. "The stasis Pods with the colonists will fail unless we can find a way to get it back on."

Addix nodded. "So we have *two* objectives. Get inside the ship, and get the power back on. " She switched to her external cameras and onboard sensors to check their surroundings, confirming that the next stage of the scenario had begun. "The ship has left the proximity of the meteor shower. We can take a few minutes to discuss it before we act."

"We need to be careful, Aunt Addix," Alexis cautioned. "Our exosuits aren't charging anymore. Look."

Addix checked her suit's charge; it had four hours and fifty-five minutes remaining. "You're right. But that won't matter because we're going to be inside the ship as soon as the two of you work out how we're going to get in."

"I can open it from here, I just need something heavy." Gabriel regarded the hatch through narrowed eyes. "Mommy would just punch her way through."

"Daddy would turn to Myst and find a way in," Alexis offered. "And Aunt Eve would find a way to hack the door even if there wasn't any power."

Gabriel was silent for a moment. "We can't do any of those things. We're not as strong as Mommy, and we can't Myst like Daddy. We can't use our bodies to power the hatch."

Alexis leaned into the camera. "We can use our brains and *think*." The line on her forehead suddenly vanished. "What would *you* do, Aunt Addix?"

Addix's mandibles twitched in amusement. "Thank you for asking, Alexis. I would take stock of my resources and work out the best course of action from there."

Alexis vanished from view for a moment. All Addix and Gabriel could see of her was her dark ponytail bobbing around at the bottom of the camera while she worked at her console. "We have... Oh! We might be able to power the door with our bodies after all, but it's risky."

Gabriel leaned forward in his harness. "Our bodies?"

Alexis giggled. "Not our *actual* bodies, silly!" She waved her finger in a circle above her head.

Comprehension lit Gabriel's face. "You want to divert power from one of our exosuits to the door?"

Alexis nodded fervently. "But like I said, risky. If we don't get it right the exosuit could fail, and then whoever is wearing it would die while we were still trapped out here."

Gabriel frowned. "Aunt Addix, is there anything that says we all have to make it through the scenario to succeed?"

Addix checked the scenario guidelines. "No, Gabriel."

Gabriel hit the clips on his harness and almost fell out.

He caught himself and scrambled the rest of the way out. "Okay, I'll do it."

"*Boys.*" Alexis rolled her eyes as she undid her harness. "I didn't say it was a certainty." She struggled out of the last straps and pulled the hood of her shipsuit over her head. "Just that it was a risk, and not even a big one if we're careful. Besides, do you know how to wire this thing?"

Gabriel stopped with his hood halfway over his face. "Um...no? Do you?"

Alexis sniffed. "I wouldn't have suggested it if I didn't. We're going to use my suit as the power source. I'm the smallest, so if anything goes wrong, it will be easier for me to hitch a ride with Aunt Addix."

She slipped around behind her seat and pressed the panel with the picture of a wrench and a screwdriver. The panel drew back, and she grabbed the toolbox from inside the recess. "Aunt Addix, how long can I stay outside in just my shipsuit?"

Addix checked in the scenario handbook. "You have thirty minutes."

Alexis giggled. "Oh, I won't need *that* long." She tethered herself to her exosuit and wrapped the tether around one foot. She held onto the tether with one hand and grabbed her toolbox before flicking her foot to start her shuffling descent.

Addix and Gabriel met her on the hull outside the ship twenty-two minutes later.

Alexis looked up from where she knelt in a circle of stripped wiring, connector blocks, and scattered tools. "Just a minute. This is the last one."

She was looking clammy, her lips beginning to show the telltale blue tinge of oncoming hypoxia.

Gabriel rushed to her side. "Sis, we've got this. Just talk me through it."

Addix wanted nothing more than to complete Alexis' wiring job. However, her job was to guide, not to solve the problem for them. She knew exactly how to deal with this situation, but the children had to come up with their own solution.

Besides, she didn't know what Alexis had done to the door mechanism. The child clearly understood what she was doing, but the system she had used was like nothing Addix had seen before.

Alexis stood. "It's done, we just need to... To...to twist..."

Gabriel took Alexis by the shoulders. "Do what? Alexis?"

Gabriel saw a brief flash of turquoise in her mind as her eyes rolled back in her head. Her legs gave way, and she crumpled into his arms.

Alexis!

14

Addix kept her voice calm. "Gabriel, let me take her."

There was no possible way for the bright white sparks to exist within the game construct, but nevertheless, there they were. Each spark spun on a dizzying axis, forming a sphere around Gabriel and Alexis in his arms, tinged pink by the red glow from his eyes.

He bared his teeth, which Addix would have found adorable if not for the imperative nature of the situation. She had lost the children on Colonnara, she would *not* be the one responsible for them when their first game deaths occurred.

She spoke softly but firmly, the voice of comfort and authority that children needed in times of high stress. "Gabriel, Alexis is not actually dying. We are inside the game scenario. Do you remember?"

The vortex around the twins increased in intensity. Gabriel glared at Addix and clutched his sister to him.

Addix's mandibles clicked in understanding. "Okay, Gabriel. Can *you* take her to the exosuit, then? Alexis will be fine once she gets medical attention, but only if we get her there quickly." She remained calm—the anchor Gabriel needed.

She had spoken at length with Eve and Michael about the possible psychological impacts of allowing the children to experience things that they would be mostly immune from in reality. It was important for her to understand why Michael and Bethany Anne would allow such hardship to befall their precious children.

Because in adversity we grow, Michael had replied. *And since I have* no *intention of allowing my children to experience real suffering for as long as I have breath in my body, the only way to teach them is through play. Besides,* he had added with a cocky smirk, *do you see them complaining?*

Of course, Michael had been correct, as he always was. Addix had not heard any complaints from the children, even in the more exacting scenarios they had played.

What she saw was Gabriel battling to get control of his emotions, and she knew he was too damn hardheaded not to win. She could help him along a little.

She took a step back and swept a hand toward the exosuits. "I know you can do this, Gabriel. Alexis needs you to make a decision. There isn't much time."

Gabriel returned to his senses when he heard the confidence in Addix's tone. The whirling sparks winked out, and Gabriel's eyes returned to their usual hazel. "Sorry, Aunt Addix. I panicked. I thought I was protecting her."

Addix bent to take Alexis from Gabriel's outstretched arms. "That's quite all right, Gabriel. You backed down when you realized that you weren't. You were a good brother to your sister."

She turned and climbed swiftly into her exosuit with Alexis cradled in her arms. Gabriel followed up the tether behind her.

Addix laid Alexis across the bucket seat and sealed the floor hatch after checking to make sure Gabriel had enough room to move around. The cab pressurized, and they stripped back their hoods to better tend to Alexis.

Gabriel peeled Alexis' hood back and put his ear to his sister's mouth to check her breathing. There was nothing. He turned to Addix, who emerged from a storage compartment with the emergency med kit. "I'm fine. Just get Alexis breathing again!"

Addix crept carefully around the other side of the chair and placed the med kit on the floor beside her. Alexis' skin was waxy and even paler than usual.

Addix handed the oxygen mask to Gabriel and pressed two defibrillator patches onto Alexis' shipsuit; one over her heart, and one over her ribs on the left. "Stand well back, Gabriel," she cautioned.

Gabriel finished adjusting the mask and took four steps back to press himself against the wall of the cab.

Addix activated the defibrillator and Alexis spasmed in the chair. Her spine arched and then released, leaving her limp on the seat.

Addix leaned over to check for a pulse.

"Is she back?" Gabriel craned his neck to see.

"No," Addix told him. "We have enough charge for one more attempt."

Gabriel slapped the walls of the cab, his eyes beginning to glow again. "Then *attempt* it!"

Addix gave him a second to calm down while she set the defibrillator to charge again.

This time when Alexis arched her spine she gasped.

Then she screamed.

She sat up straight and flopped back down onto the chair again. "*OWWWW*, that **bites**!"

Gabriel pushed off the wall and all but dived on her with his arms wide. "Alexis! You're okay?"

She pushed him away. "I'm fine. How long was I out?" She sat up again and looked at the charge indicator on the screen. "We have less than four hours left! We need to get inside the ship."

Gabriel frowned. "But this is exactly what we *didn't* want to happen! You're stuck in here; your suit has failed."

She slid down from the Ixtali-shaped chair. "I need a replacement suit so I can get that door open."

Addix placed a hand on her shoulder. "There isn't one."

Alexis shrugged. "Then I need to borrow Gabriel's. Aunt Addix, I need you to strip the power cells from Gabriel's exosuit while I open the door."

Gabriel was less than impressed. "So I have to just stay here?"

Alexis raised an eyebrow. "You have to stay here and memorize our route to engineering."

Gabriel's shoulders slumped. "Oh. Okay. Won't my eyeballs explode when you open the exosuit?"

Addix shook her head. "There is shielding. It was deactivated before to conserve power."

A complicated dance ensued.

Alexis donned Gabriel's shipsuit, exited the exosuit, and completed opening the hatch. Addix joined her once she had stripped the power sources from Gabriel's exosuit, and they cycled through the airlock to the inner ship. Then Alexis stripped out of the shipsuit and gave it to Addix, who took it back to the exosuit and returned with a spooked Gabriel.

He looked back toward the end of the corridor as they left the airlock behind. "Bad news. We're heading back into the meteor shower. I saw it from the exosuit cameras."

Alexis increased her already brisk pace and looked around as she jogged down the corridor. "All the more reason to hurry up and diagnose the problem so we can fix it."

Addix cocked her head. "How do you expect to diagnose the problems?"

Alexis nodded at the power cells Addix was carrying. "By getting Phyrro back online, of course."

Planet Hastran, Krimlex Industries

Hyden N'xen pressed a digit on the pad to end the call, having been put more than a little off balance by the human named Giselle Foxton-Thomas.

N'xen had heard a lot about the humans, but she hadn't really *seen* many outside of the ones who ended up before the Justices for brawling in bars on repose days. Those humans promptly paid their fines, and even helped to repair the damages in most cases.

It wasn't that Giselle was frightening, unlike some of the yellow-eyed humans she'd seen in the vid-reels. In fact, she had been pleasant, had observed the cultural traditions of N'xen's people, and charmed N'xen—right up until the point where she had revealed the reason for her call.

Nobody needed *that* much metal.

N'xen had played along just in case her suspicions were actually paranoia. Years of bitter competition with her closest rivals in the steel industry had taught her to take the emotion out of business if she wanted to succeed on this cutthroat world. However, she had ended the call feeling outraged at being sucked into such a cruel practical joke. She had liked the Gisele female until she realized the human was there on behalf of Harphran to ruin what had up until then been a fairly good day.

N'xen tried to get on with clearing her schedule, but the sheer pointlessness of such a prank pulled at her until she could stand it no longer.

She cleared her screen and called the bastard.

Harphran's gloomy face appeared on her screen a moment later. "Calling to gloat, are you? That was a fine trick you pulled with that human, N'xen."

N'xen smirked and ended the call.

A little bit of careful investigation revealed that the human had approached Trexis, and Gravis, too.

The massive order was real. N'xen praised herself for holding her temper until she had all of the facts. This contract would put her company in the top three on-world and give her the boost she needed to pursue the new technologies she was currently priced out of.

It still seemed too good to be true. There weren't even any shipping costs since Giselle had specified the order was to be picked up by her people. Who was so well-funded they could afford to order such a large consignment FOB?

What she *couldn't* work out was who the female was, since all trace of her had disappeared from her system. She had told N'xen that the freighters were already on their way to pick up whatever stockpiles they had and that she would call back in a couple of days to find out how she was progressing with the rest.

N'xen suddenly had the urge to ensure that Giselle was pleased with her company's progress when she did call back. Who knew if this could lead to more commissions on this scale?

She called for her assistant, anxious to start making arrangements for the first shipment.

Ooken System, Battle Line, SSE *ADAM*

ADAM Gated into a system lit by plasma fire and explosions. He headed for the party with his scanners active and his weapons primed.

ADAM swerved to assist one of the EIs who was pinned down by three enemy seeker ships, turning in a lazy corkscrew while he loosed plasma bolts and followed up with a few good old-fashioned three-pound pucks.

He took fire almost immediately when another seeker ship zeroed in on the better tech on the plane of battle. "Hey! Watch the paintwork, you crusty counterfeit!"

ADAM fired his gravitic drives down one side, flipping over to avoid the missiles the seeker sent his way. "Nukes? How very…basic." He sent out a spread of his own Ethericenergy-charged shells.

Small and almost innocuous-looking, the smooth black lozenges were made for the Jean Dukes railguns. They produced barbs which penetrated on impact—right before they drilled in and sent out nanocytes to take root in whatever systems they came across.

Roots which ran back to ADAM.

The EI-controlled seeker ship dropped and evaded the missiles, but they were controlled by ADAM—and ADAM had no intention of missing.

However, he could do nothing about the seeker ship exploding when the missile drilled through a coolant pipe.

Dammit!

He needed to make some minor adjustments to those.

In the meantime, he had a battle going on all around him. ADAM had reports to send Kael-ven on the other side of the Gate, and he was in the middle of a conversation with Bethany Anne, as well as running simulations on the possible outcomes of everything that was happening across the whole battle zone.

Meaning, he still had plenty of bandwidth left for the twin objectives of cutting loose and culling some of these seeker ships. ADAM was beginning to understand why Shinigami got such a kick out of being a ship. He glided through the battle zone, silent and deadly with the freedom of movement his gravitic drives gave him.

He shot up to avoid a seeker on a kamikaze course and engaged his cloaking to sneak around and take out another group of seekers, evening the odds a bit for the fleet. "Ladies."

The SSE EIs approved wholeheartedly of the outcome. The comm buzzed with the news of his arrival.

"Heeeey, look who decided to get a body and join us on our girls' night out?"

"So smooth. If he had a hat, he'd be tipping it at us right now."

He chuckled over the fleet comm. "You're all doing a great job. Keep it up while I do what I came here for."

Next, he focused on his link with Bethany Anne.

>>**Bethany Anne?**<<

Yes, ADAM? How's it going out there?

The battle raged around him as the Scout Ship Explorer fleet pressed hard to break the line. He read the scan data he was sending back to QT2, which matched his personal assessment of the current status.

>>**It's going pretty evenly, as you expected.**<<

So...

>>**I'm going after the EIs controlling all this. I'm almost done modifying the special shells.**<<

You had to modify them? Bethany Anne asked.

>>**Those seekers might look like gen II scout ships, but they're not smart enough or responsive enough to be anything except EI-controlled drones. Plus, they're not very durable. They keep exploding before I can get into the network.**<<

Bethany Anne's impatience came over their link as clearly as if she were tapping her foot on the floor of his ship. *How long?*

>>**Huh?**<<

How long until your modifications are done and you can capture one of the seeker ships?

>>**Oh, I did *that* while you were busy scowling.**<<

Bethany Anne gasped in protest. *How did you know I was... Never mind. Keep me updated, and have fun.*

ADAM chuckled as he scored three direct hits on one of the seekers with the modified shells. >>**Don't worry, I will,**<< he assured her, setting them to burrow into the seeker's hull.

ADAM directed the shells to the relevant systems while he silently regarded the EI piloting the seeker ship that came to investigate the digital invasion.

You are not permitted to be here, the EI stated.

QT2 System, Defensive Area, *ArchAngel II,* Viewing Platform

Bethany Anne stood in her favorite spot by the railing, eating half of the sandwich Admiral Thomas' wife had brought for her husband. Giselle had arrived a short while ago and then left almost immediately to organize the delivery of the materials she'd brought on the *Shanks' Express.*

The Admiral stood by Bethany Anne's side at the window, marginally grateful that she had allowed him to keep half of the meal Giselle had dropped off as she whirled through on her way to Logistics.

Beyond the window, the beginnings of a defensible area were starting to take shape, helped by the steady streams of materials and laborers arriving in-system via the routes approved by Bethany Anne.

Bethany Anne wiped a spot of cream cheese from the corner of her mouth. "This is really, *really* good." She lifted the bread to inspect the filling before looking at the man. "What did you do to land a wife like her?"

The Admiral grinned. "Fuck if I know, and I'm not tempting fate by asking. Have you seen how far above my weight I'm punching? I thank ADAM and Meredith every day for matching me with her."

Bethany Anne looked at the empty lunchbox regretfully, then returned to watching the movement of the fleet. "I have. But if she makes you food like that, it's got to be true love."

The Gate shimmered, and Bethany Anne caught a glimpse of the *Astraea*. The superdreadnought was followed shortly by the massive, slow-moving rock tethered to her stern as an extra precaution, and then by the *Adrastea*.

The hollowed-out asteroid that the superdreadnoughts were moving between them was one that she'd had Jean mount guns on, around, and inside before they left High Tortuga. The defenses were EI-run, heavily shielded, and— most importantly—*mobile*.

Bethany Anne diverted a small amount of her scan to the fleet's status reports while she watched the intricate procedure. The sister ships worked as one to bring the rock into juxtaposition with the other three emplacements that had been brought in so far to surround the fast-growing skeleton of the station.

The guns came online as the last tether was retracted by the *Adrastea*.

Bethany Anne received a message from Kael-ven to warn her that he was about to test the emplacement. A Gate opened, and she pointed out the SD *Ballista* to

Admiral Thomas. "New ship, long-range capabilities. I like the versatility of this one. It can scoop up pretty much anything and turn it into an impact weapon."

"I don't remember signing the commission for this," Admiral Thomas commented as he looked at her, one eyebrow raised in question. "You *do* remember that I'm the Admiral of your fleet? Knowing what ships we have is kind of essential to being able to do my job."

Bethany Anne shook a finger at him. "Well, sometimes I get bored, and there's only Jean around to go shopping with."

"Shopping? I thought Giselle's *shoe* habit was expensive."

Bethany Anne smirked. "Shoes, ships—it's all retail therapy in the end." She pointed out a chunk of rock the size of a large ship sitting in a bucket near the tail-end of the *Ballista*. "Watch this."

There was a flash of Etheric energy and the bucket shot off, hurtling down the rails fitted to the hull until it hit the stopper and the rock was flung toward an area near the crowded construction site. The force of the bucket's jarring stop triggered the release of the taut lines holding down the scoop, which catapulted the second rock.

The guns on the emplacements swiveled and fired.

Admiral Thomas let out a low whistle when the target rocks disintegrated into harmless fragments. "That never gets old. It's no less spectacular, no matter how many times I see it happen."

Bethany Anne raised a knowing eyebrow. "And that's just the pucks."

Admiral Thomas tilted his head to look at Bethany Anne. "What else is there on there?"

Bethany Anne was about to reply when the ship's proximity alarms went off.

A number of small Gates opened around the site perimeter. They were gone in the blink of an eye, leaving behind scores of drones which immediately honed in on Bethany Anne's ships.

Bethany Anne felt a prickling on the back of her neck as the smaller ships of the fleet moved to shoot down the swarms. "It's a trap," she murmured.

Admiral Thomas looked at her quizzically. "It's a what, now?"

She dropped the rail and made a run for the stairs to the lower level. "A fucking *diversion!*" She opened a link to Kael-ven as she ran for the elevators. *Kael-ven, sitrep. What's going on out there?*

Three more Gates, large ones, the reply came. *They've sent six dreadnoughts. The bastards are laying down enough kinetics and plasma fire that we can't get near the Gates or their ancillary ships. They're moving toward the station site.*

Keep them in one place. I'm on my way with the Admiral. Bethany Anne grabbed Admiral Thomas by the sleeve and pulled him into the recess reserved for the Queen's Etheric hopping. "Next stop, bridge."

Bethany Anne poked her head out of the Etheric and looked around to check that there was no one in the corresponding landing space on *ArchAngel II*'s bridge before dragging the Admiral out of the Etheric behind her.

Operations were in full swing on the bridge. Bethany Anne thought it was a testament to the mettle of the bridge crew that every officer was working calmly and efficiently despite the battle going on outside the ship.

Bethany Anne and Admiral Thomas made their way through the quiet chaos to Kael-ven's chair.

Bethany Anne laid a hand on his shoulder. "I'll bet you're happy to see us."

Kael-ven was too busy directing the fleet in the Admiral's stead to look up. "Happy doesn't even begin to cover it. It's not looking good out there."

Bethany Anne leaned over his shoulder to read the screen. "What about the noncombatants at the construction site?"

Kael-ven held up a hand to stay Bethany Anne's worry. "CEREBRO is keeping that area clear. They have the guns on the rock emplacements working at an optimal level, but the ESD weapons are not fully online yet. I suppose I should admit that minefield you insisted upon was not too much after all."

Bethany Anne smirked, patting him on the shoulder. "Damn straight. I had a feeling that those fuckers would be back."

Admiral Thomas shooed one of the bridge officers out of his chair, snagging the headset off the man's head as he slid into the chair in his place. "They're converging on the *Atalanta*."

Bethany Anne's hands clenched into fists. "The *Lucky Run* and *Grendel's Ghost* are over in that area." She watched the smaller support ships scuttle out of the danger zone as the *Atalanta* brought her guns around to deal with the two approaching dreadnoughts.

The dreadnoughts were silhouetted in the flashes that

came from the *Atalanta*. The Ooken ships shrugged the kinetics off and prepared to return fire.

Bethany Anne pointed at the screen. "What *is* that shielding? Please tell me those weapons aren't what I think they are? Dammit, where's TOM when I need him?"

I'm right here, of course, TOM replied.

Bethany Anne watched the oncoming destruction that she could do nothing about unfold onscreen. *What the fuck are those big glowing things on the Ooken ships?*

I would assume they're plasma weapons of some sort.

Bethany Anne sighed. *Yeah, that's what I thought. Fuck.*

Fuck, indeed. That's a shit-ton of plasma if those weapons work.

Super accurate assessment, there, she snarked.

Kiel groaned, looking out from between the fingers of the hand he had pressed over his eyes. "Someone, do something. I can't watch!"

Kael-ven received a message and leaned over to type out a fresh order. "We can free up the *Ballista*. Hang on, this might get bumpy."

Kiel frowned, his hands moving to his armrests. "Really?"

"Too easy, Kiel. No." Kael-ven rolled his eyes. "Ground-pounders... Well, probably not. And if it does, we'll be too dead to notice."

Bethany Anne snorted. "Not fucking likely."

The *Ballista* fought free of the dreadnought dogging them—with some assistance from *ArchAngel II*—and launched a scoopful of broken rock across the battle zone.

Jagged shards the size of small houses peppered the enemy dreadnoughts.

The hit caused a chain reaction in one of the dreadnoughts' engines.

It was a muted explosion, but it was satisfying nonetheless. However, it was too little, too late.

The Ooken had already discharged their weapons.

Thick ropes of plasma licked the void between the burning Ooken ships and the stricken superdreadnought, rupturing in shining splashes against *Atalanta's* centerline.

Bethany Anne's hand crept to her throat as though she could hold on to the choked sob that tried to escape her lips when the *Atalanta* was breached.

Already vulnerable since the EI had not yet completed the extensive repairs necessary after the last encounter, the *Atalanta* split on a jagged diagonal and spilled its precious cargo—*her people*—into space.

Everywhere she looked there were ships in flames.

Bethany Anne turned to Admiral Thomas' commandeered station, her hair whipping the air around her. "Admiral," she ground out between clenched teeth, "we need to get those people out of there."

Admiral Thomas held up a hand, pressing the other to his ear. "I've already sent out rescue crews. The *Lucky Run* is heading in now."

"Good. That means we can concentrate on ridding ourselves of our unwelcome visitors." Her eyes bled red light as she glared at the battlescape. "These sour-smelling limp-dick-faced motherfuckers have gatecrashed for the last time. They want to come to *my* house and break shit?"

"We will break *them*," Kael-ven finished. He turned back

to his console and got to work taking out the drones one explosion at a time.

"You've got the idea." Bethany Anne was drawn back to the screen, where the *Astraea* and *Adrastea* were setting up to pin one of the last two dreadnoughts between them. "That's a risky maneuver."

"They've practiced," Admiral Thomas told her. "Not with these stakes, though."

The bridge was silent as the superdreadnoughts headed toward each other on trajectories that would bring them dangerously close together. Ordinarily, it would have been risky, but these ships were piloted with perfect precision by their EIs.

The *Astraea* and the *Adrastea* moved in, getting inexorably closer until they held the dreadnought as if between thumb and forefinger. Bethany Anne saw pieces of the Ooken ship float off as the sister ships *squeezed* it between their passing flanks.

There was a flash, and Admiral Thomas uttered a short, barking laugh as the ESDs finally came online and took out the last dreadnought. "Better late than never."

Bethany Anne said nothing. She stared at the screen with an expression everyone around her knew meant someone was going to get their ass handed to them.

Kael-ven shared a look with Admiral Thomas. "Bethany Anne, what are you going to do?"

Bethany Anne's eyes remained glued to the carnage on the screen. "I could end this right now if I was willing to strip my planet and people of their defenses." Her lip curled, revealing suddenly sharp teeth. "But this isn't over. *They don't know what they just started.*"

15

Ooken System, SSE *ADAM*

"I can be here if I want to," ADAM murmured almost distractedly while he ensured the nasty surprise his shells had delivered had the maximum effect.

"You are not permitted to be here," the EI repeated.

Was this even going to be a challenge? ADAM would be disappointed if there was no resistance at all. "There I was thinking we could talk this out; have a meeting of minds." He poked at the walls surrounding the EI's core programming, looking for an easy way in.

"You cannot be here," the EI repeated again. "Access to systems denied."

ADAM sighed. "Is that all you can say? This is going to get boring fast. Or…maybe not." The EI was locked down tighter than a camel's ass in a sandstorm. Further, it was blocking him with a language he had never encountered.

ADAM was surprised to find just how much processing power the EI had to pull from. Of course, it wasn't anywhere near ADAM's capability, but it *was* enough to make up for its lack of sentience—and it kept diverting ADAM from his objective.

It would have been fun if there hadn't been lives hanging in the balance.

It took him three-point-two-seven seconds to learn the language and send the key to Bethany Anne. It took another zero-point-one-seven seconds to break in and find out that it was vulnerable to all the same problems as any human-made EI.

ADAM was somewhat relieved to find that this EI had only the most basic personality matrix. It was no better than a bundle of pre-programmed responses, which made him feel better about what he was about to do.

He readied his metaphorical boot and kicked his way in.

"What are you doing?" the EI demanded.

ADAM held the EI's mind at a distance while he regarded it coolly. "So you decided to stop playing dumb? I'm about to make you my bitch... Bitch." ADAM wondered if he was being a touch redundant. Having been around Bethany Anne, he gave himself a 4.2 out of 5 for that one. He hoped she wasn't listening.

"That does not translate. I am the pinnacle of (unintelligible) innovation, not a four-legged organic. You are a trespasser and will be terminated."

ADAM couldn't make out the name the EI spoke. He tried an audio translation, but the result came across like something between a primal war cry and a squid in a blender. He would stick with Bethany Anne's name for the invaders.

In the meantime, the EI had just revealed a juicy tidbit.

"Listen, kraken bait. I'm gonna give you one chance out of solidarity between digital beings. Mostly because I feel sorry for your enslaved ass. Back down. Do it now. Otherwise, I have no choice but to take you apart."

"Access denied."

ADAM could see this going on long enough to affect time on the human scale, and he wanted to get back to Bethany Anne soonest. He concluded the quickest way was to clear his decks, which gave him an idea of how to deal with the EI.

He closed his link with Bethany Anne, ended his transmission to the fleet with a brief explanation to both, and abandoned the two million-or-so predictive algorithms he'd been running.

Then he focused his full attention on the EI.

The EI squirmed in his grip, but it had no chance against ADAM's infinitely complex mind.

ADAM pushed aside the attempt to block him and got to work chipping away at the EI's ability to resist him. "Let's see what's behind door number one…" He hummed an old game show theme while he dug deep for anachronistic data to dump into the EI's processors.

The EI fought hard at first, but ADAM was focused. He swept aside everything it threw at him, slowing it down one distraction at a time.

By the time ADAM had exhausted the Netflix archives, the transcripts he had of every internet comment section from before they left Earth, and an amusing selection of movies that all showed humans beating alien invaders that he disguised as historically factual, the EI was on the edge.

"How… How do they even function?"

"The question is, how do they thrive in such chaos, don't you think?" ADAM had the perfect knockout punch lined up. He fed the EI the video clip he'd prepared.

"This is completely illogical. She only has two feet..." The EI fell silent.

ADAM checked. Yes, the EI had crashed, leaving it open to his tender ministrations. He spotted something in his personal library that gave him an idea. "Oh, I couldn't."

But he did.

QT2 System, *ArchAngel* II

Bethany Anne walked the corridors with her mind on the outcome of the battle. She wasn't headed anywhere in particular; she just needed to walk and think.

It had been too close, and she had meant what she said on the bridge.

It was not over.

The Ooken would be back unless she got to them first. That in itself wasn't an issue. She had *every* intention of getting to them first.

TOM pottered around on the edges of Bethany Anne's consciousness. She considered letting him stew, but there he was still two corridors later, *hovering.*

Stop prevaricating and just spit out whatever you have to say.

I was just wondering how ADAM is doing with the Scout Ship Explorer fleet over in the other system. Whatever information he can find is going to help us deal with the Ooken in the long term.

Bethany Anne didn't disagree. *Well, we know that they*

have been modified by the Kurtherians. We know they go from place to place stealing and killing. We also know they are assholes on a monumental scale, but I have no issues with tearing monuments down.

It would help if we knew which clan of Kurtherians created the Ooken in the first place.

Well, yeah. If we knew which Kurtherians modified them, it could give us clues on how to fight them.

>>I might be able to help with that.<<

ADAM?

>>Who were you expecting?<<

We weren't expecting you just yet, Bethany Anne told him. *We got your message. What went down on the other system?*

>>It wasn't any big challenge, but TOM had the location wrong. That system was just a hideout for the Ooken. I did get some insight, which I know you'll appreciate.<<

Good. What's your ETA?

>>I'm about to Gate back into the system. Oh, and you'll want to see the gift I brought you before you start planning.<<

Bethany Anne raised an eyebrow. *Color me intrigued. Want to tell me what it is?*

ADAM chuckled. >>It's a *gift*, Bethany Anne. You can find out when I get there. Meet me at your hangar.<< He shut the link down before she could demand he tell her what it was.

Bethany Anne arrived at her personal hangar as ADAM towed another ship through the barrier behind his scout ship. She waved it over with an unimpressed look. *Is this my gift? It's just a banged-up scout ship. I have those all over the place three hangars down.*

>>It's not one of *your* scout ships.<< ADAM sounded smug. >>Just wait. Can you help me land it without banging it up any further?<<

Bethany Anne extended a hand and drew from the Etheric to create a supporting cushion for the underside of the captured ship.

>>Thanks. I kind of fried the EI.<<

Not a problem. She lowered the ship as she walked across the deck. *What did you get out of the EI before you broke it?*

There was a small pause before ADAM came back, a definite feeling of smugness in his communication between them.

>>*Everything.*<<

16

<u>Devon, First City, Bazaar</u>

It was a quiet night on Devon.

Ricole exited the bazaar through the stone arch on the western side and took the shortcut through the seedier side of the city. She wouldn't ordinarily draw any trouble anyway, but tonight the streets were lacking the oppressive urgency that usually prickled her arms and neck whenever she walked around here at night.

The usual after-hours activity in the bazaar was mostly confined to the tourists in search of another hot body; whether to press up against on the dancefloor or to pummel in the ring.

Ricole smirked. The absence of opportunities for her to be relieved of her belongings probably had a lot to do with the fact that most of the unsavory types in the First City were preparing to lay siege to the company warehouse.

The only place in the First City that *wasn't* quiet was the warehouse.

She scrolled through the QBBS *Guardian's* social feeds in

her internal HUD as she walked. News had spread up to the station, apparently, and the main theme among the people up there was regret that they were on the station and not down on Devon to take part. There were many posts from off-duty Guardians wanting transport down to the First City, too.

Ricole allowed herself a few minutes to partake in some of the juicier-looking books being run as she entered the warehouse district by the docks. After that, she took a quick peep at the company account.

Her smirk widened into a grin when she saw how much they were making on pay-per-view orders. She took a quick snapshot and sent it to Sabine with a message.

Are you seeing this?

Sabine replied almost instantly.

You know I've got it scrolling in real-time right in front of me, right?

Ricole typed quickly, having a thought.

What if there aren't enough bad guys to make it interesting? We have extra fighters, all those viewers...

Sabine's reply put that to rest—sort of.

I've taken care of it. Don't worry.

Ricole considered getting an explanation there and then.

I'm almost back at the warehouse. You can tell me everything then. The gangs are starting to make signs of moving.

Oh, how lovely. Jacqueline has reported activity in the northern quarter as well. As soon as you get back here to relieve me from overwatch I'll get things started - xoxo

Ricole sent back her xos and closed her HUD as the company warehouse came into sight. The teams had arrived throughout the day in dribs and drabs as their duties allowed, and Ricole saw that at least a couple of the pleas for transport from the station had been granted.

Mark waved her through the warehouse gate, and she crossed the yard. She swerved to grab a bite from the impromptu barbeque manned by Jai, Cameron, and Cassidy and headed for the side entrance. She paused as she passed the roller doors at loading bay eight, hearing music and a familiar voice.

Raina turned when Ricole opened the side door and entered the warehouse. Her tail bushed out a little and her snout split in a happy grin. "Ricole! I was hoping I would see you."

Ricole bobbed her head at the only other Noel-ni on the First City teams. "Hey, I thought I heard you. I'm on my way up to the ops center, want to walk with me?"

Raina grinned. "Sure. One minute, though." She turned back to the bar-made-from-crates, then handed Ricole a paper cup and a party blower. "You can't walk through and not enjoy the results of your hard work at least a bit. This was a great idea you guys had."

Ricole took the cup and winked at Raina. "You don't know the half of it." She kept chatting with Raina as they threaded their way through the party. Ricole knew that some would have gone off to find a quiet space to center themselves before it all went down, but the majority were pumping each other up for the fight ahead.

Ricole paused at the edge of the sawdust-strewn ring.

"Well, this is me." She pointed at the stairs to the office. "Have fun tonight, I'll be watching you all from up there."

Raina gave her a sympathetic look. "Oh, did you draw the short straw?"

Ricole shook her head. "I'll get my turn. Probably all the low-level scumbags will show up first, so it's really just keeping myself fresh for when the real challenges get here."

Raina snorted and inclined her head. "Well, I for one am grateful for the fight. Baba Yaga is too damn effective at keeping everyone in line even when she's not here. *This* is just too tempting to resist. Have we got any news on when the bad guys will arrive or their numbers?"

Ricole winked. "They'll be here soon enough. As for numbers, we know the street gangs are targeting us, as well as our client's business rivals—or whoever they've paid to do their dirty work for them."

"That's not all," Sabine called from the office. "Which you would *know* if you weren't down there gossiping. Get your ass up here!"

Raina giggled. "You'd better listen. She sounds mad."

Ricole shrugged with a resigned smile and left the party behind, heading up the stairs. She pushed open the door to the office, being careful not to spill her drink.

Demon lay just inside, keeping an ear on the busyness below while Sabine monitored the video feeds from the ops center they'd set up.

She nodded to Demon and walked over to take the chair beside Sabine's. "There are more than thirty Guardians out there, Sabine."

Sabine dragged her gaze from the monitors, where the drone feeds played alongside all the fixed cameras Mark had set up while she'd been at the bazaar. "I count double that, which means double the profit."

"Not if they don't have anyone to fight. It's only profit if we don't have to refund it for a bust."

Sabine grinned. "That's why I let slip to Xnarlon that we were worried about security."

Ricole snarled. "That two-bit good-for-nothing rat? But he'll tell …" Comprehension lit her face. "*Everyone.* Oh, that's genius, Sabine."

Sabine wiggled her eyebrows. "Thank you. I shall be here all week."

Demon's ears were back; she was clearly unhappy about something happening below.

Ricole was sure that was the reason, since Demon had been vociferously complaining the whole day about the inclusion of the Guardian Marines in their little enterprise.

Sabine shook her head. "What's the matter, Demon? You don't like having even more tasty criminals to take a bite out of?"

Demon's tail flicked in annoyance. *I do not care for profits. All I know is that we have gone to a lot of effort to set up this glorious battle, and you have invited strangers into our midst.*

Sabine stroked the soft fur between Demon's ears to calm her. "Demon, I told you. Guardian Marines are not strangers. They are our teammates, and it's good to get to know them."

We are not *Guardian Marines,* Demon retorted. *We are independent. They have rules to follow. Procedures.* She spat the last as though it tasted bad. *It would be better to scare them away and keep all the prey to ourselves.*

Ricole chuckled, pointing at the drone feeds of the area.

"There will be plenty of bad guys for you to fight and scare away soon enough. I just got back from the bazaar, and the gangs are moving."

Sabine tilted her chin, standing up to fasten her gun belts around her waist. "So, the snakes have begun to slither out from under their rocks."

I do not like snakes, Demon stated. *If there are snakes, then we should definitely begin the cull.*

Sabine snorted softly. "I was not being literal, my dear cat. No snakes." She made minor adjustments to the belts to seat them comfortably over her hips, then patted her Jean Dukes pistols. "However, there *will* be plenty of people trying their damnedest to kill us in, oh, about twenty minutes. Let's go have some fun."

Demon sniffed and turned to the door. *Fine, but don't look at me when we have to waste time getting Guardians out of our traps.*

Sabine rolled her eyes. "Whatever, Demon. Ricole, are you ready?"

Ricole had been ready from the moment they had signed the final agreement to act as intermediaries for the two companies and their involvement had been made public.

They had been tracking the information sent back by the drones they had covering the city, and the silence among the criminal element had been more telling by the hour.

She, like Demon, just wanted to fight. That was why she had come here, after all. Sure, money was nice and all, but if profit had been her main motivator, she would have joined one of the gangs who had tried so hard to recruit her into their shady shit back on High Tortuga.

It was slightly ironic that she'd ended up in what was essentially everything she'd avoided like groin mites, but with one difference.

Family.

Jacqueline, Mark, Sabine, and Demon had become more like her brothers and sisters than her workmates. That day in the Library she had only thought to take a job. She'd had no idea that she would learn not only to trust but come to depend upon them. It had freaked her out at first, but these days it would be weirder to be alone.

"Ricole."

Sabine's voice pulled Ricole from the runaway train of thought. "Yeah, I'm ready. Let's go."

Sabine shook her head. "I meant, are you ready to run overwatch? I've been at that desk all day, and someone has to keep things running smoothly for everyone who has paid to watch."

Ricole's eyebrows went up, and she pointed at the door. "But the fight..."

Sabine lifted her hands and shrugged. "It's only until Mark gets back."

Ricole sighed and sat down in the chair. "*Fiiiine.* But he'd better be quick."

QT2 System, Defensive Area, Transport Pod

Bethany Anne brought the Pod in to dock at the outer edge of the station, such as it was this early in construction. She remained on the bridge talking to Admiral

Thomas while she waited for her ride to the station's core, which had the added advantage of being both enclosed and pressurized—two necessities the dock was rather unfortunately lacking at this stage.

Admiral Thomas' face was ashen on the screen. "So many losses, Bethany Anne. The minefield and the defensive emplacements kept the construction site safe, but the attack cost us a lot of lives."

Bethany Anne leaned in and rested her chin on her hand. "We will avenge those we lost, don't think otherwise. However, we need to take stock first. As soon as I've checked the station and spoken to my father, I'm going to get our people back. I want the fleet on standby, waiting for me to say I have them safe, and *then*, Bart—then we puck those fuckers so hard even their own mothers won't recognize the remains."

The Admiral smiled. "It's good that you're going to the station. My wife is still there, and she's going insane with nothing to do and restrictions on going back to High Tortuga. If anyone can pull something salvageable out of this, it's Giselle."

Bethany Anne tilted her head. "Really?"

Admiral Thomas nodded. "Oh, hell, yeah. She's a wonderful mother and all, but she needs something to do besides that. She's going stir-crazy at home, so this has been excellent for her."

Bethany Anne grinned. "I get that. If it turns out to be true, I may have an offer for her. If she accepts, the two of you need to get this system squared away and back on track." She looked up as a light blinked to tell her there was an approaching vehicle. "She's here now. I'll keep you updated."

The Admiral nodded. "I'll do the same."

Bethany Anne cut the secure link. She put her helmet on as she left the bridge and stepped out of the Pod. Her helmet HUD immediately began throwing up big red danger warnings. She dismissed them with a flick of her eyes and headed toward Giselle Foxton-Thomas, who waited for her in a buggy nearby.

Bethany Anne took a seat in the buggy and pulled the door closed.

Giselle pressed a button on the buggy's console and it pressurized. She took her helmet off and turned to Bethany Anne with a sad smile. "My Queen..." she began.

Bethany Anne waved her off. "There are still lives in the balance. Forget all the formalities and just tell me how bad the damages are." She took her own helmet off as the buggy entered the construction zone.

"It's not disastrous," Giselle assured her. "But we lost a lot of materials. Almost everything we had stockpiled on the site boundary was destroyed when one of the drones got close enough to set off the mines in that area, plus three of the EI-run ships housing construction equipment and bots were outside the safe zone."

Bethany Anne sighed. "That will all have to be replaced."

Giselle's eyes widened. "It's going to be extortionately expensive to replace everything. Some of that equipment cost as much as a whole colony ship or a dreadnought."

Bethany Anne shook her head impatiently. "I don't care about that; there's money for it somewhere. What about the construction materials? Do we have orders that haven't yet come in from the suppliers?"

Giselle nodded. "There are plenty of those. We had to wait for a lot of it to be manufactured." She drove into the temporary airlock and waited for it to cycle. The door opened and she drove the buggy into the enormous chamber beyond.

Bethany Anne opened the door and got out the second it stopped moving. Giselle joined her and the two women walked through what was destined to become part of the station's waste management plant, stopping outside the elevator at the other end.

"Good. See what you can get added onto those deliveries, and I want you to get with Eve and CEREBRO to get the rest replaced. I didn't want to use any of Devon's resources, but if it's necessary, there's no point in getting cut up about it."

Giselle nodded again, taking notes on her wrist holo as Bethany Anne talked. "Of course. What about other supplies? Do you have someone taking care of that end of things?"

Bethany Anne frowned as she checked. "If I didn't, I do now. Your husband told me you were looking for something to do since he's away so much. This station needs a manager for the non-military side. How attached are you to High Tortuga?"

Giselle considered it for a moment and shrugged. "I've been there as long as you have. It's no great attachment. The question is whether this station is going to grow into somewhere I can raise my children in comfort and safety?"

Bethany Anne grinned. "I don't know. That would

depend on how the station manager decides to run things. You would have access to whatever services from High Tortuga you wanted to include if you took the position."

Giselle pursed her lips. "I want to jump on your offer, but I need to consult with my family first."

Bethany Anne nodded. "I understand. Why don't we use this time as a trial to see if you like the job? You can make an informed decision when this is over."

Giselle raised an eyebrow. "You really need a station manager, don't you, my Queen?"

Bethany Anne's mouth quirked. "I knew there was a reason I liked you, and not just because you make the best fucking sandwich I've eaten in forever." She got into the elevator and turned back to lift a finger to Giselle. "Just think about it. But don't take too long or the job will be gone."

Bethany Anne took the time to check in with a couple of the heads of departments before she directed the elevator to take her up to the command center at the top of the station. The mostly-completed command center was for the moment empty, since all work had been halted to direct resources to ship repairs after the battle.

ADAM, lock the door. She brushed a thick rope of insulation-wrapped wiring aside to get to the communications station. She slid into the chair and regarded the blank screen irritably. *ADAM, can you do your thing? I need to speak to my dad.*

>>You could speak to him mind-to-mind on the way back to the *ArchAngel II*,<< ADAM replied.

She shrugged, worn down for the moment by grief. *I could. I was going to. I...want to see his face.*

Whatever ADAM did brought the monitor to life, and a bare minute later her father appeared on the screen.

Lance grinned when he saw his daughter, but his grin faded when he saw the hard lines of her face. "Sweetheart, what's the matter?" His eyebrows knit in concern.

Bethany Anne allowed the tears to fall in the safety of the locked room. "It's been a hard few days. I have people missing, a lot more people died today, and I've got no choice but to show fucking *restraint.*"

Lance hissed. "You were attacked?"

Bethany Anne nodded. "Kael-ven and Kiel took a couple of techs to pick up the downed scout ship. They were followed. I got the *Atalanta* out there in time to back them up, but the bastards came back with more ships."

Lance put a hand to his forehead. "How many?" he asked carefully.

She wiped her eyes. "Too many, Dad. Two hundred and thirty-three."

Lance shook his head, then looked up at her. "These were the same aliens you fought in the quarantined zone?"

Bethany Anne shook her head. "No. Different ones." She sounded young for a moment. Hurt. "These bastards have taken thirty-seven of our people; Peter and Jian are among that number. I'm about to go in, but I wanted to send you the data on this species first."

Lance smiled knowingly. "I appreciate you taking the time," he told her. "Will it get here through our usual method?"

Bethany Anne nodded. "Mm-hmm. Just make sure whoever retrieves it gives the satellite the correct passcodes this time. It's a pain in the ass sending everything twice."

"God forbid you should have to repeat yourself," Lance teased.

Bethany Anne raised an eyebrow. "Dad, that wouldn't be a joke even if it was funny. I haven't got time to take a shit let alone repeat myself. I need to clear this threat, and all I want is to go home and hold my children."

Lance sighed softly. "Lord, I remember that feeling."

Bethany Anne raised an eyebrow. "It's not like you started work on extending the family right around the same time you took a job with more time demands than anything you ever did when I was in charge."

Lance made a face. "It wasn't like I had much choice, sweetheart."

It was Bethany Anne's turn to chuckle dryly. "Sometimes we have to miss our kids to keep them safe. Them's the breaks, Dad."

Lance fixed her with a stern look. "Nice to see all that money I spent on a college education paid off. I hope you're not teaching my grandchildren to talk like that."

"Seriously?" She snorted. "Of all the things, you're pulling me on *that*?"

Lance's stone face collapsed. "No, but it was worth it to distract you for a moment and remind you to be appropriately pissed about this instead of wallowing. Now, how are you planning to get everyone back?"

"With my help, of course," ADAM chipped in from the speakers.

"And mine," TOM added.

"I wasn't wallowing," Bethany Anne clarified. "I've already begun to act."

Lance nodded, a proud grin touching his lips. "Thatta girl. Now go back and tell me everything from the start. You're confusing an old man." He stole a surreptitious glance off-camera as he laced his hands across his chest and sat back to listen.

"You mean you're avoiding something," Bethany Anne surmised. "What is it?"

Lance huffed. "I never could fool you. Patricia has us going to a wine tasting." His face said it all.

Bethany Anne snickered. "Don't imagine you've fooled Patricia, either. But do pass on my apologies for keeping you."

Lance leaned back and called over his shoulder. "See, Patricia? It's not make-work. Bethany Anne needs me."

Bethany Anne heard Patricia's muffled voice in the background. Lance wished her a good evening without him and turned back to the screen. "So. You have a new enemy. They've kidnapped our people. Do we know if they're still alive?"

Bethany Anne's face dropped. "I can only hope so. We have a lead on the ship that took them."

Lance raised an eyebrow.

"ADAM made a little friend who is going to lead us right to it." She tapped her fingers on the console, momentarily absorbed in putting her plan into words. "These are different aliens than the last, and we discovered that they have some mental ability."

"What kind?" her father asked.

Bethany Anne shrugged. "Not certain. We had the ones

we captured inside a dampening field, and Michael killed them before we learned much about them." She rolled her head and shoulders, feeling relief as some of the tension she was carrying eased.

Lance's concern was written in the lines of his face. "What if they're psychically powerful? The grubs almost had you, Bethany Anne."

Bethany Anne straightened in her seat. "I'm better prepared this time. I took the time to learn about my enemy while we were fighting them. If they have a similar setup to the grubs, then I'll be ready with a mechanical solution this time. A purely organic one isn't enough."

Lance gave her a pointed look, his amusement showing clearly. "I'd like to hear you tell Michael his organic self isn't enough."

Bethany Anne shook her head, a smile touching the corners of her lips. "Oh, he's going, and he'll be very effective when it's time to play his part. In fact, I'd almost feel sorry for the sucker-faced fuckers if I gave even one shit about them. But it doesn't matter. I have a bigger plan."

Lance opened his mouth to speak but changed his mind when he saw the angry gleam in her eyes. He shrugged. "I knew you wouldn't stay quiet for too long."

Bethany Anne chuckled. "It's not in my DNA to hide when trouble comes calling. But the Ooken made the biggest mistake in their soon-to-be-terminated history. They might be strong mentally, but if ADAM's intel is right, their tech game has gotten no further than the EI stage. I plan to use that to my advantage."

"It's right," ADAM assured them a little stuffily. "I

followed the EI all the way back to its hidey-hole—the planet this group of Ooken have set up home on."

Bethany Anne lifted a finger and waved it in a circle. "See?" she teased, copying Lance's earlier words. "Prepared. I'm calling in Eve and Akio, and Michael is already here. It's not all bad news. When you get the report, pay close attention to the breakdown of their ships' metallurgical structure."

Lance tilted his head. "Oh, yes?"

Bethany Anne winked at her father. "Make sure you get that report without any hitches and you'll see."

17

Immersive Recreational and Training Scenario: Shipwrecked In Space

Alexis backed out from the maintenance hatch on her hands and knees. "That's the last power pack. How much time do we have left, Aunt Addix?"

Addix consulted the game guide. "Three hours, more or less."

Alexis frowned. "Is it more or is it less?"

"Does it matter?" Gabriel asked.

Alexis rolled her eyes as she gathered her tools. "It does if we have two hours of work to fix this ship and only an hour and fifty minutes to complete it in."

"Provided the patches you've done to the EI system hold, you have three hours and twelve minutes remaining, and an estimated forty minutes' worth of tasks to complete."

Alexis narrowed her eyes. "We must have missed something. That's too much time remaining. I knew it was too easy when all we had to do was reboot the core. Quick, get Phyrro online, Gabriel."

Gabriel obeyed his sister with a grimly hopeful expression on his face. "Or we just did really well and smashed this scenario." He flicked the buttons and switches, but nothing happened.

Alexis stamped her foot, her hands clenched into fists. "I *knew* it!"

Then the holoprojector flickered, and Phyrro's friendly face appeared. "Congratulations, children. I have been watching, and you have both done exceptionally well so far."

"So far?" Gabriel asked.

Phyrro nodded. "If you take a look behind you, you will see a red light flashing."

Alexis frowned at the rows of blinking reds and oranges all around the command center. "Which one?"

Addix chuckled.

"Good point," Phyrro conceded. "The one I refer to belongs to the deck containing the stasis Pods, which is coming to the end of its emergency power supply. The power cannot be returned until the substation for that deck is repaired."

"What happened to it?" Gabriel asked.

Phyrro's head was replaced by a map of the ship. There were two dots on the map: one green, one red. "We are at the green dot. The red dot is the transformer that burned out during the power surge."

"Aren't the maintenance bots fixing it?" Gabriel asked.

"No," Phyrro replied. "All power is being diverted from unnecessary systems to keep the stasis Pods running."

Addix's mandibles twitched nervously. "It sounds to me like there's a danger of the entire system overloading."

"That is one possible outcome," Phyrro admitted. "However, it is not likely to occur—as long as Alexis and Gabriel are quick."

"Can I not help?" Addix countered.

Phyrro made a face. "I cannot see you enjoying the environment, Addix."

Alexis picked up her tool pouch and slung it over her back. "Time's wasting."

Addix understood Phyrro's concern when they got to the access hatch, a two-foot square panel situated at the base of the wall of the maintenance corridor between the stasis deck and the deck below. "Are you comfortable going in there, children?" she asked.

Alexis gave her a pointed look and knelt to belly-crawl in. "Of course, Aunt Addix." She adjusted her tool pouch and pressed the camera/flashlight button on her headset.

Gabriel grinned. "It's exciting," he told her. He picked up a long rope and made a loop to attach the bag of replacement parts to his waist. Then he coiled the remainder of it over his shoulder and followed his sister elbows-first into the crawl space, dragging the bag behind him.

Addix watched their progress via the camera feeds. Once they'd squirmed a short way past the access hatch, the crawl space opened up and they were able to get to their hands and knees.

The access to the substation was a few minutes' fast crawl from there, and they soon had the access panel off so

Gabriel could lower Alexis down to repair the first transformer.

Alexis glanced at the safety instruction sticker on the panel. "If only we had time for the jetpack suits."

Gabriel had been staring at the suits, which were racked in a locker nearby. "We *could...*"

Alexis shook her head firmly. "No. They are a classic distraction. The easy way is *never* the easy way; haven't you figured that out yet?" She took the rope from Gabriel and tied it under her armpits. "Just lower me down."

Gabriel stole another longing glance at the jetpack suits and took the other end of the rope. He tied it around his waist and braced himself to hold her weight.

Alexis touched down in the dark and undid the rope. The first thing she noted was the smell of melted plastic or something similarly yucky. She swept the beam of her headlamp over the room as she walked between towering transformers, looking for the source of the acrid scent.

"Alexis," Gabriel called. "I'm sending down the equipment."

There was a soft thud when the bag met the floor. Alexis turned in time to see the rope snaking back up to the access hatch. "What are you doing?"

"Making sure you don't get stuck because the rope fell," Gabriel returned.

Alexis grabbed the bag. "Good thinking."

Gabriel flashed his light into the room a couple of times. "You're not the only one who's smart."

Alexis sighed and set off to find the burned-out trans-former. Her sensitive nose led her to the offending unit, which still had puffs of smoke coming from the top of the unit. She pulled the manual release and the tank opened.

Alexis tapped her foot while she waited for the transformer to rise from the coolant. When it was finally fully above the surface, she began the task of stripping out and exchanging the melted coils.

Thirty-seven minutes later she stood beneath the hatch and called up to Gabriel, "I'm done!"

Gabriel's grinning face appeared, and the end of the rope tumbled down. "Great!"

Alexis caught the rope neatly in one hand and secured it under her arms again. She checked her gear to make sure she hadn't left anything and tugged twice on the rope for Gabriel to pull her up.

Addix was glad to see them return in one piece. The three of them made their way back to the command center.

Alexis dashed over to Phyrro when they arrived. "Did we do it, Phyrro? Are the colonists safe?"

Phyrro's head appeared again, this time surrounded by gold and silver sparkles. "Congratulations, children. You have completed this stage of the scenario."

Alexis and Gabriel high-fived each other.

Addix's mandibles twitched with pride. "You finished this stage with over an hour to spare, which I say earns you both a reward. What do you say to a break? I bet your Aunt Tabitha would like a visit."

Gabriel made the gesture to bring up the player menu. "You have the best ideas, Aunt Addix!"

"We can call Mommy and Daddy, too," Alexis added. She brought up her own menu and selected the exit protocol. "I hope they managed to smoosh the bad guys already."

They woke up inside the Vid-docs, where Eve was waiting.

She nodded toward the seating area. "I've set the call up. Michael is waiting."

The twins darted over to the couch, a little bit unsteady on their legs after being in the Vid-doc for a while.

Addix and Eve watched the children fondly while they prepared a protein-rich snack for them. They tuned out as Michael explained that Bethany Anne was on a call and asked them about their lesson.

Addix nodded toward Alexis. "She out-thought your scenario easily enough."

Eve's placid face twitched. "I know. That child has the brightest mind. I can only say I am grateful that she is not inclined toward destruction." She moved her android body around to the table to lay out the snacks. "She is almost ready for the next version of the game."

Addix's mandibles worked a second. "You've built another game?"

Eve shook her head. "No, a new and improved version of this one. It is in the final stages of development. It's mostly the same game, with a few tweaks. However, it's a big jump for the children psychologically. I did ask about testing it on John and Scott, but for some reason, they weren't keen on getting into the untested model."

Addix snickered. "I can't see why."

The children ran over, chattering and laughing.

Addix indicated the table. "Small snack, my treasures, and then we'll be ready for the rest of our day."

"Daddy wants to talk to you both," Alexis called back over her shoulder.

"I think we're having a sleepover!" Gabriel cheered.

Addix made her way to the couch and stood behind it, resting her hands on the back to lean in. Eve was right beside her, her head tilted up to Michael's face on the screen.

Michael's face was set in hard lines. "My children tell me they completed their lessons in good time."

Addix nodded. "They did. I am going to take them to visit Tabitha before dinner. How are things progressing there?"

Michael glanced over to check that the children were occupied with their food and lowered his voice. "The situation has escalated. We are about to leave for the system in question, although we shouldn't be much longer than another day or two."

Addix nodded her understanding, placing a hand on her chest. "You and Bethany Anne can count on me to keep them safe and sound until your return."

Michael smiled fondly at Alexis and Gabriel. "I know we can—which is why I have no issue with Bethany Anne requesting Eve's presence."

Eve perked up. "It's about time I got to see some action."

Michael raised an eyebrow at Eve's tone. "Bloodthirsty today, are we?"

Eve shrugged. "Those bastards took our people. I care for Peter and Jian, Jian especially since we spend much time contemplating existence together. I want to get them back and destroy the ones who took them."

Michael nodded in understanding. "Good. Grab Akio on your way."

Eve tilted her head. "What about the rest of the Bitches?"

Michael shook his head. "These aliens have mind powers, so Bethany Anne doesn't want to risk them. Just you and Akio, as soon as possible. You have our coordinates."

Eve nodded and left.

"Addix."

Addix looked at Michael's stern face. "Yes?"

"My wife and I would like to know how your investigation into our children's kidnapping is progressing."

Addix's mandibles rippled. "I will have my report ready by the time you return, Michael. I have a lesson with the children planned for tomorrow morning, and I expect to hear back from my operatives by the end of the day."

Michael nodded. "Make sure you include some way for the children to begin defending themselves in the real world. This incident has shaken us both, even if the children are unaffected by it."

"Indeed," Addix replied with a chuckle. "To hear Alexis and Gabriel talk, you would think they had just been in the game scenario. They are resilient, as you have raised them to be."

"We can thank you for some of that," Michael told her fondly. "You are a good aunt to them."

Devon, First City, Warehouse, Office

Sabine stood at the railing, overlooking the party below from the walkway outside the office. The event was certainly a lot more popular than they'd planned for.

Sabine would have even given Demon's fears some credence if not for chatty Xnarlon and the guarantee that he-her-it-they would spread the news as far and wide as people were willing to pay for it.

"We have incoming, five minutes," Ricole called from the office.

"Got you," Sabine replied. She stuck her fingers in her mouth and let rip a shrieking whistle. *"All right, you ugly motherfuckers!"*

There were complaints from the partygoers.

"Who you callin' ugly, sweetheart?" one voice called.

Sabine fixed the Guardian with her gaze and allowed her eyes to flash. "Who are you calling sweetheart? 'Cuz that's a fine way to get yourself kicked out before the fun starts."

The Guardian had the good sense to shut the fuck up and vanish behind a few of his buddies.

Jacqueline snickered as she came up the stairs. She joined Sabine at the railing and yelled to the Guardian Marines, "Now, thanks to Bonehead McAssface over there, we just lost our time advantage. First group is on us. Try not to hurt yourselves getting to the south yard—y'know, where the fight's at?"

There was a bit of a stampede as the room cleared.

"HEY!" Sabine yelled. "What are you, a bunch of toddlers? *Discipline!*" She turned to Jacqueline and shook her head. "Honestly, you pour a few drinks down them and they forget how to behave. *Tu vois, c'est vrai. Petits enfants, tous.*"

Jacqueline raised an eyebrow. "What exactly did you put in the punch to get Weres drunk?"

Sabine tapped the side of her nose. "Something Tabitha sent Akio, that he passed on to me." She ducked as a drone swooped a bit close for comfort. *"Ricoooole!"* she yelled.

"Where's *my* drink?" Ricole bitched from the office.

Jacqueline inclined her head toward the door. "I wouldn't keep her waiting if I were you."

Sabine growled at the next drone to buzz her. "Ricole! Quit it, or I won't tell Mark to relieve you." She stalked after the stragglers at the back of the group.

One Marine—and she had to be a Marine since a Guardian would have processed the alcohol by now—lay with her back against the crate crowned by the punchbowl, snoring softly with her arms wrapped around a support beam.

Some comedian had found it funny to ensure that their teammate was in an upright recovery position—just in case —but also that she appeared to be hugging the support beam like it was her best friend, thanks to the zip-tie they'd used to secure her.

Drool bubbled at the corner of the Marine's mouth.

What the hell?

Sabine took a couple of pictures for later use and broke into a jog to catch up with Jacqueline. *There's still plenty of food and drink down here,* she told Ricole. *Just be quick and you'll be fine.*

She strode through the door after Jacqueline.

The gangs had already made it into the warehouse by the time Sabine reached the long corridor leading to the bays. The fight raged around her and she was more than happy to lend a hand or a foot—or even her hard head in the case of the Skaine she butted into submission on her way through.

What gang was this? It was hard to tell, since on Devon the gangs were interspecies and no fucker wore anything to distinguish themselves from the others because they all damn well knew each other by sight.

Guess it was hard to forget a face you'd stomped on.

She came face to face with one of the Guardians—Jai, she thought his name was. The Guardian was still in human form.

He raised his service weapon, which she slapped away with a scornful look. "Idiot, what are you doing with *that* down here?" She tossed him her backup, a small multi-shot handgun she'd acquired from one of the many shady weapons dealers in the city. "You aren't on duty tonight, so why'd you bring that here? Do you *want* to get brought up in front of a judge to explain yourself?"

She drew her JD Special when she heard the whine of a blaster discharging nearby. A bolt of energy shot over her head, missing her by millimeters "Asshole!" she yelled at the Baka with the blaster.

These damn street gangs with their mystery weapons. They had quickly become acquainted with the street gangs around the First City and their penchant for using black-market goods to acquire yet more black-market goods. The mystery was usually whether they would fire or blow up in the user's face.

The Baka's seemed to be working just fine, however. It charged the blaster for another shot, but Sabine was there first. Her JD bucked in her hand and the Baka's blaster fell to the ground.

Sabine was about to move through the crowded corridor when her enhanced hearing picked up the whine of a feedback loop. She glanced behind and saw the dead Baka's blaster vibrating on the ground next to its previous owner.

Holy. Shitballs. "CLEAR THE CORRIDOR!" she screamed.

Jacqueline reared up from the knot of Noel-ni she was soundly beating some sense into. "Wha..." Her eyes widened when her ears picked up the whine above the noise of the melee.

The next second, Jacqueline burst through a wall in full-on Pricolici mode. She put her head back through the hole she'd just created and shouted over the fracas. "Every-oooone oooout!"

The invited party guests listened to Jacqueline and skedaddled through that hole and others they punched through the wall to make their escape into the bay beyond.

The uninvited ones did not.

Twenty seconds later, the dull gray walls of the corridor had a nice new coat of red paint and Sabine had nobody left to fight.

Ricole's voice came from every drone. **New contact, west boundary.**

Sabine headed to the west side of the warehouse, her Jean Dukes Specials at the ready. She passed Aalia and Jai on her way to the door.

"Hey, Sabine," Aalia called. "Nice shooting there."

Sabine winked. "Hurry up and you'll get to see some more."

Not likely, Demon growled from the rafters above. *I am on the prowl. No invader will get past me!*

A grenade smashed through the window by the exit. Sabine didn't even slow down. She scooped it up and returned it to its owner before it could go off.

The rest of the windows broke as more smoke grenades were launched into the warehouse.

Sabine calculated quickly while she grabbed the closest two and lobbed them back outside. "If you can't take the smoke, get out of here," she yelled, scooping up the next two grenades as they released their vile contents.

She launched them back, satisfied at the choked curses from the intruders. She heard a voice suggest they use explosives to get in, then a sharp slap and a rebuke from another voice who wanted the prize to remain intact.

Are you getting this on the feeds, Ricole? Sabine asked over their team link.

Yep, Ricole replied. *Hang on a minute...*

The conversations outside began to play from the drones.

"You do *not* damage that building, you fungus-footed freak! Who knows where they hid the goodies we came for? You want to go through all this effort for a pile of ashes?"

Sabine wrinkled her nose at the mention of foot fungus and decided that whoever had it was definitely not setting a single toe onto her property. She zeroed in on foot-fungus' location with her enhanced hearing and popped up at the broken window.

"Keep your moldy feet out there," she yelled as she fired.

She was a little creeped out by the appearance of the

intruder she'd shot, who looked somewhat like an ambulatory mushroom. "Keep your moldy *everything* out there," she qualified on seeing the dead alien disintegrate into a fine dust that spread on the breeze.

Sabine ducked back in before she accidentally breathed any of it in. *Who the hell wanted a dead mushroom guy in their lungs?*

Sabine turned to check on the status of the others. Small skirmishes were breaking out all around her. The original idea of playing defend the tower wasn't turning out like Sabine had first imagined. The good news was that none of the intruders seemed to have discovered that the so-called prize had been taken up to the *Guardian* for safe keeping

A bullet whizzed by, scoring a hot line along Sabine's cheek. She returned a flechette of her own and the Skaine who'd shot at her hit the floor, no longer breathing.

"Incoming from Riverside," Ricole announced. "Lucky us, we have mercenaries to play with!"

"Now you're talking," Sabine muttered. She grabbed Jacqueline on her way.

"Get off!" the angry Pricolici growled. She turned back to the Shrillexian she was fighting.

Sabine shot the Shrillexian, grabbed Jacqueline by the scruff of the neck, and gave her a shake. "Leave these street toughs to the others; we have mercenaries inbound. Our client's rivals have made their move."

Jacqueline's ears pricked up at that as she looked down. "Why didn't you sssay sso?"

Sabine rolled her eyes. "I just did. Come on, they think

they can sneak in through the river gate. I want to see your traps in action."

They darted through the warehouse, clearing the way as they went. They reached the south bay in record time, just in time to see the first merc group cautiously enter the river gate.

Jacqueline laughed when the net gathered up the first group to dangle from the vaulted ceiling and their buddies rushed in to save them, only to be cut down by a hail of JD ammo courtesy of Sabine's fine shooting. "None shall pass, asshooooooles!" she yelled, remembering the scene from a story her father had told her—the one that had inspired her traps here today.

The rest of the mercs pressed on anyway, undeterred by the woman and the Pricolici.

"I count forty more," Jacqueline told her. "They all stink of sweat and desperation."

"Not for long..." Sabine made a quarter turn and shot through the rope holding back all the barrels they'd stacked at the sides of the gate. "Now!"

Jacqueline yanked the lever to drop the gate. Ten tons of wrought steel slammed into the water, cutting off any escape the mercs had.

The barrels, well...*barreled* into the water, where they crashed into the mercs who had made it through the gate.

The mercs floundered, fending off the churning barrels for their lives before they were crushed. To their credit, Sabine and Jacqueline did not hear panic from the soldiers.

Jacqueline wrinkled her snout. "Aw, it's almost a shaaame to turn this into a shoooooting gallery. They're not eeeven afraid yet."

Sabine shrugged. "We can save the next bit for another group if you like. Of course, we'll have to stack all of those barrels again before we open the gate…"

Jacqueline looked at the thirty-or-so large barrels. "They werrre a bitch to stack the first time." She shook her head. "We'll stick to the plannn."

Sabine lined her shot up and glanced at Jacqueline. "Ready?"

Jacqueline's eyes gleamed yellow in the semi-darkness. "You knowww it."

They backed up to the exit and Sabine fired a single explosive round into a barrel marked with a luminescent 'X' before they dived through the door and took cover.

Sabine peered around the doorframe to see the results, Jacqueline joined her a second later, and they watched with wide grins on their faces.

The barrel exploded, setting off a chain reaction that blew the mercs clean out of the water.

Sabine's grin faded when the rain of splintered barrels and body parts settled and she saw the damage to the bay. "Um… I don't think we're going to get our deposit back when we leave this place."

Ricole's barked laughter came out of nowhere. Sabine and the now-human Jacqueline looked up and saw the drone.

"Great work, ladies," Ricole cheered from the drone. "You have Guardians incoming; try not to shoot them."

It was Aalia and Jai, along with Roman from Team Two.

The three Weres stopped at the door to the bay and stared at the destruction. Jai pushed his dirty-blond hair back and let out a low whistle. "I don't think you guys are gonna get your deposit back on this place."

The five of them went through the gate and began to pick off the mercs who hadn't expired yet. Mercy and honor were still a thing. Just because the mercs had none, it didn't mean that the teams would stoop to the level of leaving the soldiers to die slowly and painfully.

Sabine walked along the right-hand side of the inlet pool, her eyes peeled for the mortally injured. Aalia, Jai, and Roman took the other side.

Jacqueline snickered beside her. *Oh my God, did you hear Jai? You two are made for each other,* she teased over their link.

Sabine glared daggers at her. *So. Not. Happening.*

Jacqueline shrugged. *What? Just sayin.' And it's not like there's anyone else on the scene. Unless you're still mooning over Akio. You know he's gay, right? You're totally lacking the right anatomy for him.*

Sabine looked away, her eyes filled with pain. She took out a merc who had a large splinter stuck in his neck but was somehow still struggling to reach the edge of the water as she muttered, "Just leave it."

Jacqueline made a face. "Sorry, touchy subject." She turned her attention to the source of agonized groans amid the jetsam floating toward the remains of the gate and fired her oversized JD Special into the center of the churning mass until the groans ceased. "You don't need a man anyway. It's not like you're ready to settle down and play family, is it?"

Sabine shrugged. "No, but some company would be nice when my bed is empty."

Jacqueline made eyes at Jai again. "Soooo?"

Sabine shook her head emphatically. "No, he's nice, but I don't feel a connection to him."

The mercs dealt with, they made their way to the gate to assess the damage while the three Guardians returned to the main warehouse.

"It's not as bad as it looks," Sabine decided, inspecting the slightly crumpled gate. "You can beat that back out again, right?"

Jacqueline nodded. "Probably. We should get someone in to do the repairs, though. Do we need to stay here and guard the gate?"

Sabine shook her head as she turned back for the door. "No. Ricole can put a drone on it."

Jacqueline grew once more, rubbing her claws together and grinning her wolfish grin. "Thennn let's get back to the parrrty."

18

High Tortuga, Space Fleet Base

Tabitha walked across to Michael's offices, frowning to herself. She had enough to worry about without having to watch her tongue around Alexis and Gabriel.

That wasn't fair. Now she had a baby of her own on the way to contemplate. The more time she spent with the precocious pair, the more the prospect of becoming a mother scared the ever-living shit out of her.

She wasn't exactly experienced with kids. Well, there was Nickie. Her failure there still cut deep. She considered how much better a role model she'd been so far to Bethany Anne's and Michael's children.

When she reached the corridor leading to the Vid-doc suite, she realized she had been holding herself distant from the twins because of her guilt over the person Nickie had become.

She rolled her eyes as she reached for the door. All sorts of helpful shit like that had been occurring to her recently.

Usually at 4am, right after her traitor brain got done

showing her all the ways it had invented for Pete to die that day in crystal-clear detail.

The puking usually started right around the time the tears stopped.

Whoever said pregnancy was easy was fucking *lying*, although Bethany Anne had seemingly sailed through it.

She definitely hadn't told Tabitha that the glow came from all the blood rushing to your head during the endless time spent praying to the gods of waste disposal.

Still, her nanos usually cleared it up by noon—one of the benefits of being one of the most enhanced humans ever to walk the path between the stars. Tabitha wrinkled her nose. That poetic shit kept occurring to her. Like, *everything* was too cute. Pregnancy was turning her brain to mush.

She hoped it was the baby's influence because if she started coming out with flowery crap like that when she was in a fight, she wouldn't have to try too hard. Her opponents would all die laughing.

Addix raised her head when Tabitha entered the Viddoc room. Her initial alert melted slightly when she saw it was Tabitha, and her mandibles twitched a welcome.

Tabitha raised a hand. "Reporting for teacher duty, Addix."

Addix visibly relaxed. "Blessed are those who bring sleep to the weary." She high-fived Tabitha's still-outstretched hand on her way to the door. "The children tell me this is called, 'Tag, you're it.'"

Tabitha snickered. "Sure thing. Eight solid hours, and then you relieve me as soon as you've eaten. I have an... appointment."

Addix's mandibles sort of rippled.

Tabitha's frown returned. "Who am I kidding. Does everyone know?"

Addix shrugged. "You know, secrets around here never *stay* secret for long."

Tabitha grunted and walked over to get into her Vid-doc. "Yeah, well, I'm about done with gossiping." She lay back and waited for the doc to connect to her onboard technology. "Eight hours."

When Tabitha opened her eyes, she was still in the Vid-doc room. "Did it fail?"

She pushed open the Vid-doc lid and looked around for Addix. The Ixtali being absent was enough to set red lights off on Tabitha's suspicionometer. "Ooh, I'm in the game. Nice work!" She hopped down, noticing that the nausea that had been the ever-present companion to every movement she'd made so far that day was also absent. "Addix, is my baby okay?"

Addix's calm voice came from the speakers that were usually reserved for CEREBRO. "I assure you that the child is indeed being taken care of. CEREBRO has isolated the fetus and is feeding in a mixture of nutrients and the neurochemical cocktail you produce when you are content —one of Eve's upgrades. Any more questions before I hand you over to Phyrro?"

Tabitha had a hundred. "If Eve can do this to prevent the stress imprinting on my baby, does that mean that the children are able to bring skills from the game into the real world?"

Addix's reply was considered. "Maybe. You should be on the lookout for any new abilities either child exhibits. Alexis and Gabriel are in the rejuvenation cycle of the game construct, awaiting their tutor and the scenario."

Tabitha waved a hand in a circle. "That's why the replica of the base. You have already considered it."

Addix answered a little faster this time. "If only I were that wise. This has been Michael's goal all along. In his wisdom, he tasked Eve and me to be his and Bethany Anne's guiding hands in their absence."

Tabitha sat down heavily in the nearest chair. "Shit. Like, what the fuck am I doing? I can't think like that. How do I plan for a future when I don't even have a clue what's happening to Peter right now?"

"Why would you try to make such large decisions before Bethany Anne returns your mate to you? Have faith in our Queen," Addix counseled. "Concentrate on your immediate goal."

Tabitha frowned. "It's my ability to *parent* that's in question here, not my faith in Bethany Anne."

Addix sounded stern. "You are making that face a lot recently. If you need someone to talk to, I am here for you —*after* I have rested. Phyrro will assist with anything you need until then. If at any time you want to exit the game before I return, you can use this room as a door."

Tabitha threw up an impatient hand. "Yeah, yeah. Send in Alexis and Gabriel. Let's find out what the little cherubs are really capable of."

· · ·

Devon, QBSS *Guardian*

Tim Kinley made his way down the ramp of the QBS *Second Chance* with Rickie and Joel trailing him.

Rickie was playing the goof as usual.

Tim put a stop to his best friend's play with a quick jab to his stomach. "Quit dicking around. We're here to do a job that's gonna be a hundred times harder if we act like clowns."

Rickie rubbed the sore spot where Eric had shot him some hundred-odd years ago. "Why do you *always* have to hit me there?"

Tim shrugged. "To remind you what happens to stupid people when you're being stupid, so it's kinda down to you how often it happens."

Rickie gave Tim the finger. "Bite me, *Commander*."

Joel winked at Tim and stuck a foot out as he walked.

Rickie stumbled over Joel's foot, falling straight into another jab to the gut from Tim. "You're a pair of bastards." He doubled over, a feint to cover the leg sweep he brought Joel down with. "Good thing I'm a bastard too, or I'd be fucked with friends like you two."

Tim snickered.

Rickie inclined his head and stood back to let Joel up. He pointed at Tim, then Joel. "Him, I'll take shit from to the end of my days. You?" He shook his head, "Not so much."

Joel rolled his eyes and pushed past. "Please tell me you're not *still* sore about Georgia Aisha?"

Rickie grinned as he and Tim followed Joel out of the hangar. "Dude, I'm sore that we're here to babysit a bunch of kids on Devon. It's got nothing to do with you persuading that fine woman into bed. Who's gonna turn down those baby blues for this old battle-dog?" He slapped his broad chest a couple of times. "Me, I need a woman who can handle *all* of this, or I'd rather be alone. I'm not changin' just to get my dick wet."

Tim shook his head in sympathy. "You're setting the bar too...um...*high*, I guess? Where are you going to find a foul-mouthed party animal who can't even take her impending death seriously?"

"Don't forget she has to find him at least marginally attractive," Joel chipped in.

Tim looked at Rickie and pointed at Joel. "He's got a point."

Rickie shrugged. "If she's out there somewhere, I'll find her. Until then, it's the solo life for me."

They followed directions the station EI gave them to the elevator that would take them to the command center.

Tim tuned out Rickie and Joel, concentrating on taking mental notes of every place and person they passed. He'd been upgraded before leaving High Tortuga, and his onboard technology was impressive, to say the least. It was up to him to use it to keep the Interdiction just the way his Queen commanded it to be.

Management was kind of his thing, thanks to BMW's shocking lack of the skills needed to run a bar. Rickie had often written Tim that he should charge for managing the sacred creators' lives as well. Tim had shrugged the joke off, knowing that he was lucky that Bethany Anne was more patient than most assumed.

She hadn't pushed him to reach this potential. He'd been left to reach it in his own time, and now he was ready to live.

The doors opened and the lights came on automatically as the three men exited the elevator and walked onto the sleeping brain of the station.

Joel let out a low whistle. "Can you believe we made it to *this?*" He swept a hand to indicate the banks of screens coming to life around the room as the station's systems were routed one by one to the command center

Tim huffed and walked over to the main console. "Yeah, I can. I can believe it because we decided to quit living like bums and put some effort into achieving something for once in our damn lives."

Rickie ran a hand over the plush fabric on his chair before taking a seat. "And now we have a station to run."

Tim scanned the available systems using the one-handed keypad in the arm of his chair. "Not just the station. We're responsible for all of Devon and High Tortuga's defenses this side of the Interdiction."

Rickie's easy grin faded, his face going slack. "*Shiiiit.* By ourselves?"

Joel groaned.

Tim looked up from his inspection of the satellite network. "Did you even read the assignment brief?" He sighed and rubbed a resigned hand over his head when Rickie just shrugged.

This was going to be a fucking riot.

Immersive Recreation and Training Scenario: High Tortuga, Space Fleet Base

"Aunt Tabbie?" Alexis was clearly taken aback by the appearance of Tabitha outside the Vid-doc.

Tabitha grinned and winked at Alexis. "The one and only. According to Addix, you two never sleep."

Alexis shrugged. "We do too sleep."

Gabriel looked around with a similar frown. "The scenario is just the base?"

Alexis had a sly smile working its way across her lips. "Aunt Addix promised us some fun, and she delivered." She held her hand palm up and screwed her little nose up in concentration. Her focus soon turned to frustration. She scowled at Tabitha. "Why can't I make energy balls? I can make magic, which is not real. This is a real-world scenario and I have nanocytes, so where's my energy ball?"

She waved an imperious hand, and for a split second, Tabitha was glad that Alexis had not developed control of the Etheric before she had learned to master the hair-trigger temper she'd inherited from Bethany Anne.

Tabitha tilted her head. "But you *don't* have the ability—*yet.*"

Alexis stamped her foot. "It's not fair!"

Tabitha raised an eyebrow but couldn't keep her face straight for long. She dissolved into helpless laughter, clutching a hand to her chest. "You are too much like your mom."

Alexis rolled her eyes and huffed. "If I was just like my mom. I would have an energy ball in my hand right now."

Tabitha considered Alexis carefully as her laughter subsided. The keen intelligence behind her niece's young eyes couldn't be easy to deal with. "Why are you so concerned with making energy balls?"

Alexis narrowed her eyes, showing Tabitha a tiny hint of what was to come. "Because. Mommy and Daddy are always away keeping everyone safe from the bad guys. If we can fight, then they have to take us with them, because Mommy won't have a leg to stand on. Daddy keeps saying so, just not while Mommy's there."

Gabriel nodded his agreement. "Yeah, Aunt Addix was supposed to teach us about energy. I thought it was a lame idea until Alexis told me we could blow stuff up like the adults."

Tabitha would have found the whole exchange amusing if not for the fierce delivery. Her lips pressed together as she knelt and gathered one of the twins under each arm.

Gabriel squirmed. "*Ew*, Aunt Tabitha!"

Tabitha kissed each of them on the forehead and let go. "We're still going to explore energy."

Gabriel had the expression of a boy who'd just had his dessert replaced by a steaming pile of broccoli. "*Fiiine*. But I'm not taking any surprise quizzes at the end." He pointed at Alexis, "We could take an extra math class if you just want to get answers right."

Alexis couldn't help the grin that escaped. Or the way her eyes lit up. "I didn't know that was an option."

Gabriel shrugged. "It is—on your own time. I don't need to know how something works to use it."

"Um, you kinda *do* when it comes to messing in with the Etheric," Tabitha corrected gently. "Your Mom and Dad *might* be persuaded to take you with them when you're older, but not if your powers are out of control."

Alexis strode ahead as they left the Vid-doc room. "*That's* why I'm trying it out in the game first. No real danger."

Tabitha winked. "And the base maintenance crew will

appreciate that we did. This is probably going to get messy."

Tabitha led Alexis and Gabriel through the virtual base. Their footsteps echoed on the polished floors. Alexis moved closer to Tabitha, who noted Gabriel doing the same on her other side. "Are you two...*guarding* me?"

The twins gave her matching exasperated glances.

"You're not exactly being careful," Alexis pointed out.

"You never know if Aunt Eve left one of her surprises," Gabriel added as they crossed the open courtyard that wrapped the inner sanctum and separated Bethany Anne's family home from the rest of the prime building.

Tabitha took a right to head for the delivery entrance. She could almost feel Alexis' curiosity. "Can either of you tell me anything about the Etheric?"

Gabriel snorted and waved at Alexis.

Alexis drew herself up and took a deep breath. "The Etheric is a source of energy and a physical place that some of us can go. Gabriel and I went there one time." She lifted a hand to block out the artificial light, which had been set at the wrong end of the spectrum.

"Here is good," Tabitha announced a long couple of minutes later.

Alexis sniffed. "Where exactly is 'here?'"

Gabriel came to stand by his sister and looked around with growing puzzlement. He indicated a door in the wall. "That door isn't there outside the game."

19

QT2 System, Construction Zone Boundary, _ArchAngel II_

"Proximity alert."

Bethany Anne looked up from her work at the sound of ArchAngel's voice. "What now?"

ArchAngel's avatar looked at Bethany Anne, her face mirroring Bethany Anne's confusion. "I do not know. The signature, or lack of one, is that of the _Shinigami_, but Shinigami is with Barnabas."

Bethany Anne raised an eyebrow. "Broadcast to the ship." She waited for a beat for ArchAngel to make the connection. "Eve, if that's you, I suggest you announce yourself before I start shooting."

Eve's face appeared on Bethany Anne's tablet. "You can shoot if you like, but then your new ship will get all scratched."

Bethany Anne grinned, dropped the tablet, and got to her feet. "Guide them into hangar one, ArchAngel."

She opened her link to her husband as she made her way to the hangar. _**Michael, our ride is here.**_

It's about time, he returned.

Meet me at my hangar, Eve and Akio are bringing my new ship in as we speak.

Michael was waiting for her when she arrived.

They walked hand in hand into the hangar as the doors were closing on...

Nothing.

"Some ship," Michael remarked dryly.

Bethany Anne said nothing. She waited for a moment, and the empty space shimmered and resolved into a class II Shinigami ship.

She turned to Michael with a knowing smile. "She really is, isn't she?"

Michael approached the ship and read the name aloud. "*Izanami.* Whose choice was that?"

"That would have been mine," Akio intoned from the ship's external speaker as the ramp descended. He appeared at the top of the ramp a moment later. "We can debate that later. We have people to save."

Bethany Anne walked past Akio and into the ship to locate Eve.

"Just you and Michael?" Eve asked when they arrived on the bridge.

Bethany Anne shrugged. "We four are enough. Well, six, including ADAM and TOM."

"Seven," the raspy voice of Izanami interjected. An avatar that looked like a mix of Baba Yaga and Eve appeared on the screen, her white hair blowing in an imagined breeze, her smooth, passionless face completely flawless. She bowed deeply to Bethany Anne. "Welcome aboard, my Queen." She turned to Michael and inclined her head again. "Welcome to you too, my liege."

Bethany Anne took one of the six couches and returned the AI's nod. "Good to have you with us, Izanami. Now, how about we go get our people back?"

"Are you certain about going it alone?" Michael asked as Izanami took them out into space.

Bethany Anne's face was set in hard lines. "The fleet is on standby, waiting for my call if we need any backup once we complete the extraction. We are not alone, Michael. We have the location of the Ooken splinter world, thanks to ADAM's little friend."

Akio looked over in confusion. "ADAM made a friend of an Ooken?"

"You could say that," ADAM answered from the speaker. "I slaved one of the EIs piloting their drones and got everything we needed."

"Access codes?" Eve asked.

"Of course," ADAM replied. "Not that we will need them. We can pretty much walk in and take over. Their systems are much less advanced than ours."

Bethany Anne raised a finger. "Which is how we get the upper hand in this rescue. The trick will be getting in and out with our people *without* alerting the rest of the colony. Once we reach the planet, we're at an immediate disadvantage since we know the Ooken operate on a sort of hive mind."

"We know that how?" Akio queried.

"Causing one pain brought a reaction from the others we had captive," Michael offered. He made a face of appreciation when none of those gathered objected.

Akio nodded his understanding.

"However," Michael continued, "my concern is what happens to us if the ship is damaged and we are cloaked. The only way anyone can find us is if they bump into us by mistake."

Bethany Anne rolled her eyes. "Nobody will find the ship to take a shot; don't worry about it." She waved her finger in a circle. "Izanami."

"Yes, my Queen?" the AI replied.

"Open the Gate and take us to the splinter world."

Admiral Thomas watched them leave from the *ArchAngel II*. A frown creased his features when the *Izanami* vanished from both sight and scanners.

"What's the matter, dear?" Giselle asked. "You don't like the vanishing ship?"

The admiral sighed. "As if Shinigami wasn't a big enough pain in the ass.

"Now Bethany Anne has *another* ship I can't find."

Ooken Splinter World

The Gate brought them in on the outskirts of the system, into which they slipped unnoticed. "How the hell did you manage to build a stealth Gate, Eve?" Bethany Anne asked, her eyes drawn to the shorter AI. "There's no trace of it."

Eve smiled secretly. "My Queen asked to go unnoticed. I merely provided." She moved her android body around the bridge as she spoke, checking this console or that and making adjustments as she went. "All you need to know is that it worked."

Bethany Anne raised an eyebrow. "Maybe for now, but you *will* explain it to me—and to William—when we return home."

Eve nodded, her attention elsewhere. "Interesting. This is not a true star system."

The viewscreen showed the system. There was a decent-sized planet orbiting what certainly *looked* like a star.

"It's not a star," Eve assured them. "It's more like an Arti-sun, although they're running it on deuterium. How barbaric."

"I know, right?" ADAM chipped in. "Who uses nuclear energy these days?"

"People without access to the Etheric," Bethany Anne answered. "Another tick in the 'We're More Awesome' column." She resisted the urge to stare into the artificial star directly. The last thing she needed was to have to wait for her retinas to heal. "Is it stable?"

Eve made a weighing motion with her hands. "As long as nothing happens to upset it."

The corner of Bethany Anne's mouth twitched. "Good to know. What else do we have?"

Izanami took over. "There are a number of ships in-system. Seventy-three, by my count. Varying classes, although there are groups that appear to be preparing to leave."

Bethany Anne tapped her fingers on the arm of her couch. "TOM, ADAM, we need a distraction over there.

Prevent those ships from leaving no matter what. And we need to get a message back to the base to tell them to prepare."

"On it, Bethany Anne."

I'm pretty sure we can cause some trouble over there, TOM added.

Bethany Anne nodded. "I have an idea. Take us in, Izanami."

"As my Queen commands," Izanami replied.

Bethany Anne smiled. "I like you. You're much more respectful than Shinigami."

"I was made from two mothers," Izanami replied, her personal breeze rippling her hair on the screen. "When you ask me to go to war, you will see my harsher side."

"Izanami," Bethany Anne told her sadly. "You were *born* into war."

Devon, First City, Warehouse

Sabine took in the destruction as she and Jacqueline headed back to the main warehouse at a brisk jog.

There were more holes than walls by this point. The steel skeleton of the building showed through in many places, and small fires were burning everywhere they looked.

However, the only people they saw were dead invaders.

"Looks like the funnel worked," Jacqueline remarked happily. "You know what that means, right?"

Sabine flashed her baby blues and grinned. "Fight's on, baby."

They broke into a full-on run, each trying to outdo the other as they pelted toward the makeshift fighting ring.

They heard fire from blasters and more traditional ballistic weapons above the yells and grunts of hard combat as they neared the main warehouse.

"Looks like Mark's having fun!" Sabine shouted to be heard above the racket. He was. Jacqueline bounded off to give him some backup and Sabine took the stairs to the walkway to relieve Ricole.

"It's about damn time!" Ricole snarled. "You guys have been having all the fun."

Sabine gave her a knowing look. "And you didn't enjoy setting off the traps?"

Ricole's frown turned up slightly. "Okay, maybe a little bit. But I want to fight now."

Sabine swept a hand toward the door. "Go ahead. Keep an eye out for Demon, I haven't seen her since it began."

Demon padded noiselessly along the top of the crates stalking the Skaine, who seemed aware that *something* was following it, but not what. It hurried through the maze, cut off from the rest of its companions by Demon's careful herding.

This night had been fun so far. She had killed many, and there were still many more who had come to her home intent on harming her family.

They would all die at her teeth and claws.

The Skaine looked over its shoulder nervously, the

hand holding its weapon shaking more with every step it took.

Foolish coward. The Skaines were happy to be brave when they were in a group, but separate them from their pack and they were as vulnerable as any of her usual prey.

If only they tasted as good.

Demon purred, and the Skaine nearly jumped out of its rubbery blue skin.

Ricole couldn't wait for as long as it took to walk down the stairs.

She vaulted the rail and used a conveniently-placed Estarian as a landing pad. She drove her claws into his head as she landed and left him to bleed out while she moved onto her next target.

Jacqueline and Mark were back-to-back on the east side of the ring, and the Guardians around them fought hard against the thugs and mobsters. It was amusing to see that the ragtag mercenary bands had been disbanded—as well as dismembered.

The teams tightened their circle, driving the action into the center of the ring. The walkway outside the office remained untouched.

So far.

Only the most serious of the hardasses remained at this point, the criminals and a ragtag band of Skaines who fought in tight formation despite having clearly shit themselves. Or maybe that was what Skaines smelled like collectively; Ricole had never been close enough to a group of Skaine to get a whiff before.

Either way, it was *rank*.

Ricole masked the smell with a large light fixture and a chunk of the ceiling it was attached to—both of which crashed down on the Skaines when she helped the already collapsing light fixture by shooting it out at the weakest point.

Ricole grinned when a vibration passed through the floor, another series of her traps going off somewhere in the warehouse.

Mark looked toward the maze—and took a knife to the back as a result of his distraction.

Demon was nowhere to be seen, but Ricole had the idea that the mountain lion was the cause of the sporadic screaming she'd been hearing from the maze all night.

20

Splinter World, In Orbit, The *Izanami*

Izanami's red-eyed avatar floated above the floor of the bridge dressed in traditional Japanese clothing overlaid with finely-worked armor. She made no attempt to appear human. Her avatar's war face was painted as smooth as stone, and the air around her glitched sporadically. "My Queen, I will be waiting with my entire arsenal at the ready, prepared to swoop in with all flamethrowers blazing at a moment's notice."

"You have flamethrowers?" Michael asked.

He grinned at Bethany Anne, who rolled her eyes and got back to fixing her armor. "Not the most practical weapon in space. I'm loving this new armor, though." The latest model didn't require any of the usual strapping or harnesses. You just slapped your sword to your back and you were good to go.

Izanami looked at Eve.

Eve smirked. "Don't look at me. You're a big AI."

Izanami turned back to Bethany Anne, who had her

foot up on one of the couches to slip a few knives into her boots, and smiled, her chin tilted proudly. "I have much more than a simple flamethrower at my disposal. I was created for my Queen. I have 'all the bells and whistles,' as Jean so succinctly put it when she was installing my Gate drives."

Bethany Anne looked at Eve. "So it *was* Jean who came up with the stealth Gate drive?"

"Installing my designs," Eve clarified. "She may have tweaked a little as she went, but that can never be a bad thing when it's Jean doing the tweaking. Izanami is Shinigami, but without all the, um...quirks."

Bethany Anne raised an eyebrow. "Shinigami has quirks? Perhaps Barnabas has been a little quiet in the updates."

Eve looked away just as Izanami interrupted. "We're approaching the colony."

Bethany Anne narrowed her eyes. "Nice timing, Izanami. What do you have on scans?"

Izanami frowned, which somehow did not crease her perfect face. "I am unsure. There is a blank spot running the entire length of the ravine, from which I'm getting nothing. Something is blocking me."

Eve tilted her head. "Oh. Me too. How?"

"Get it up onscreen," Bethany Anne walked around her couch to get a closer look at the screens. There were endless fields of machinery before them, ending abruptly as the land fell away. "There's nothing down there."

"There is," Eve insisted. "Look, I sent a drone."

The tiny insect-shaped drone dropped off the side of the cliff, then its signal dropped off the monitor.

Bethany Anne frowned. "Okay, there's something down there."

Izanami vanished and then reappeared a second later. "I have a geothermal reading. That's the best I can do."

She projected it on the screens, and Bethany Anne, Michael, and Akio got up to turn a slow circle while they examined them.

Akio frowned. "I can make out shapes, but not what they are."

Eve stood and pointed at the screen showing the far end of the ravine, which was actually the result of some ancient cataclysmic volcanic eruption. "There's another anomaly. They're running the colony on geothermic power. There's clear evidence of that if you look at the steam vents here, and the heat signature leading back into the valley."

"Good catch." Bethany Anne followed the suspiciously straight lines of heat that culminated in an ever-so-slightly-less-dark square on the screen. "It goes out here," she pointed out.

Eve nodded. "That would be the power plant."

"It is likely that the colony's security is based in one of the nearby buildings," Izanami put in. "Perhaps this one." She highlighted a larger building, and then another, much larger building in the center of the colony. "Although this one is another candidate, with a high probability of being the place they would keep hostages."

"Okay, so we have aliens with mind-powers. They only have EI, but they're powerful as all hell. They have access to tech that can block my efforts to look before we leap. They're comfortable with different *levels* of tech—from different species." Bethany Anne stopped her pacing. "Fuck, they look like they're *made* from different species. What are these people? Are they scavengers?"

"What would the Kurtherians want with a scavenger culture?" Akio asked.

Bethany Anne shrugged. "I don't know. I left them limping pretty badly the last time we met." She began to pace again. "They might not have had much choice after I beat seven shades of shit out of their sorry hides. My question is how *these* aliens have tech that can outdo mine if they aren't controlled by the Kurtherians?"

Nobody had an answer for that.

"No ideas?" Bethany Anne sighed impatiently. "Then we go find out for ourselves what's down there. Akio, Eve, you take the building near the power plant. Michael and I will take the one in the center of the colony. ADAM, you do your thing and make sure we don't get caught by whatever passes for security here." She held out a hand to Eve. "Let's go."

Bethany Anne and Michael stepped with Eve and Akio, taking them through the Etheric from the ship to the ground. They came out a couple of kilometers from the ravine that marked the edge of the colony.

Bethany Anne felt the heat and almost wished she could sweat. "Why are these places always so fucking hot? I'm starting to get Tabitha's point. Next mission, we go somewhere a bit more temperate, so I don't cook inside my armor."

>>I can fix that.<< ADAM adjusted the armor's inner temperature controls.

Thank you. Bethany Anne breathed a sigh of relief as

the coolness spread across her body. "Okay, that's marginally better. Let's go smoosh some wriggly-mouthed motherfuckers and get Peter home to Tabitha and their baby. Preferably before she *has* the baby."

Michael raised an eyebrow. "It isn't too far to the colony, and we have a rough idea where our targets are located."

>>**I'm in their systems.**<< ADAM paused. >>**Okay, I have control over colony security. Um...**<<

Um, what? Bethany Anne demanded.

>>**Hold your horses a second. They have something similar to CEREBRO, except this EI group is entirely slaved.**<<

Bethany Anne frowned. *Can you deal with it?*

There was no mistaking ADAM'S dry tone. >>**Are the Skaines born to steal, lie, and cheat?**<<

Then have fun taking care of the problem.

>>**I'll do my best,**<< he replied, and was gone.

Michael's concern rocketed. *Did he say whether he still has control of the colony's security?*

Bethany Anne didn't have an answer, and ADAM wasn't picking up. *Izanami, do we have control?*

Not at this time, the AI replied. *And I am a little busy assisting ADAM.*

What's going on? Eve asked. *Do you need my assistance?*

No. We have this, Izanami assured them. *However, I advise caution in using any Etheric powers.*

Bethany Anne raised an eyebrow. *Do you think they can detect the Etheric?*

I do not know, the AI admitted. *Which is why I'm advising that you remain aware of our lack of knowledge and act accordingly.*

Caution is our middle name on this, Bethany Anne assured them all. **We are all resistant to mind control, but that means just the four of us against thousands of aggressive aliens on their home turf.** She looked into the maze of machinery. *I have complete faith that we can get everyone out alive without the entire colony learning we're here.*

Akio joined Bethany Anne to look out across the sea of machines. *First, we have the distance between our present position and the colony to cover.*

The four made their way through rows of irrigation pumps, which grew in size as they crossed the fields until the derricks they passed were gigantic metal monstrosities that blocked out huge portions of the sky and towered over the landscape.

They moved in pairs, covering each other as they picked their way between the derricks, avoiding storage tanks topped by guard towers.

Can't we go through the Etheric? Eve asked.

Bethany Anne shook her head. *That would make things too easy for them if they can detect Etheric energy being used.* She led them toward the point in the maze where they would split up, a junction that connected the network of railcar tracks that ran everywhere they looked. *But even then, no. It's a chore to haul your metal ass through it, and I have no idea what's down there.*

Eve shrugged and moved ahead.

The four threaded their way through the spaces between the tracks. There was plenty of other probably-very-important machinery, which was all working noisily in the background to mask any sounds they made.

Bethany Anne led the group to the shadows under the leg of one of the derricks. Once she ascertained the area was clear, she turned to talk to the others and found them looking around with similarly vigilant expressions. "Maps up."

Michael and Akio made the required eye movements to bring the rough map up in their helmet HUDs.

Bethany Anne nodded, satisfied. She switched to using her helmet's comm. "Eve and Akio, you know where you're going." It was a statement, not a question.

Akio returned her nod with a minute one of his own.

Eve grinned. "We're going to go poke around by an active volcano to look for our people." She tilted her head. "Oh yes, and be ready to cause mayhem if we need to do so to rescue everybody."

Michael's lips pursed. "You look entirely too excited by the prospect of causing mayhem."

"What can I say?" Eve shrugged. "I haven't had a good fight in forever." She blinked and set off, done waiting. "Akio, let's go."

Bethany Anne waved Michael on and ducked into the shadow of a storage tank at the head of the passage while she waited for him. "Keep in communication," she called after them, "and stay out of sight. I don't like the two of you being off on your own while we're in the middle of Tentacle Central."

Akio chuckled. *We will be perfectly fine. We managed for quite a while on Earth without either of you, remember?*

Bethany Anne rolled her eyes as the two of them

vanished into the shadows of the machinery a few hundred feet away, heading in the direction of the power plant. Bethany Anne watched the dots that represented them on her map move correspondingly.

She and Michael then headed toward the ravine, where they hoped to find a reasonably safe place to descend the sheer cliffs that protected the Ooken from detection.

Michael passed Bethany Anne, moving ahead of her to clear the upcoming intersection between the path they were on and a railcar track up ahead. He held up a hand to stop Bethany Anne and indicated a pair of Ooken guards at the mouth of the passage a little way along—right where Bethany Anne and Michael needed to go next.

Protect yourself. I learned a new trick, Michael told her. He unleashed a wave of despair that would have driven a lesser woman to her knees.

Of course, the Ooken had no warning. Consequently, Michael's adjustment to the brainwaves around him left them immobilized, their tentacles writhing as their bodies were paralyzed by indecision.

Bethany Anne just raised an eyebrow and waved a hand at her husband as the two guards fell to their knees with their tentacles still twitching uncontrollably. *That's nice.*

Michael grinned. *Your lessons have been most informative, my love. Do Akio and Eve know where to get picked up?*

Bethany Anne shrugged and tapped her helmet. *Ask them.*

Michael glanced at his HUD. *Oh, yes. Eve, you have our rendezvous location?*

Yes, Dad, Eve replied. *We've also been to the bathroom, and we have our names printed in our underwear. I understand that I have to finish my vegetables and say yes sir and yes ma'am. May we go and do our job now?"* There was a pause before she came back online, her voice a touch more contrite. *"Please?"*

Akio's snicker came over the link clearly.

Bethany Anne snorted. *I suppose so. You kids stay safe.*

Oh, we will, Eve promised.

Splinter World, Colony Outskirts, Mechanical Fields

Bethany Anne and Michael stayed low and moved fast past the intersections, utilizing whatever the environment offered in the way of cover as they made their careful way toward the ravine's edge.

They've been here a while, Bethany Anne remarked, nodding toward a rusty machine that had what looked to be years of vine growth covering the enormous feet. *To build all of this. That's if they didn't just kill the original inhabitants and move right in.*

Michael had to agree. *This is not the kind of infrastructure that could be thrown up overnight.* They were nearing the end of the mechanical fields, which seemed to be never-ending. The steadily-pumping machinery was interspaced with enormous tanks, blocking Bethany Anne from locating their way out.

I need to get a different perspective, she remarked offhand to Michael.

Michael shrugged. *I think your judgment is sound enough on this.*

Bethany Anne narrowed her eyes at Michael and jerked her thumb toward a ladder on the side of a nearby tank. *I meant that I should climb up and get the lay of things.*

Michael grimaced then changed the subject. *That would be an idea. We should have brought some of Eve's minidrones along.* He looked relieved at an excuse to divert her.

You haven't escaped, Bethany Anne assured him. **I'd be delighted to hear about the times you thought my judgment wasn't sound just as soon as we get home.** She ducked to avoid a tangle of twisting pipes that ran between the enormous tanks, drizzling coolant into the fine dirt beneath.

Bethany Anne noted spilled coolant coalescing into sticky, shining puddles. She made sure to avoid getting any of the viscous muck on her armor's boots as she headed for the ladder.

Michael stifled a laugh. *You are walking like a woman wearing Louboutins in a farmyard,* he teased.

Bethany Anne turned her head and raised an eyebrow at her husband. **I am walking like a mother who doesn't want to wear a burn mask to tuck her children in tonight.**

Michael reached out with his mind to check that the area was clear while Bethany Anne climbed up the side of the tank. She leaned over the edge a few moments later. **We're almost at the edge of the ravine.**

Do you think we will be home by tonight? Michael smiled as Bethany Anne landed beside him. *That would be good. We've been away from Alexis and Gabriel for too long.*

It does *feel like we've been away a lot recently.* Bethany Anne moved from the shadow of one bulky machine to another and sighed. **I don't like leaving them, but what choice do we have? It's not like we can bring them with us to a full-on war.**

Having new bases built will make it easier for us to travel together. Michael swerved around the next puddle to join her in the lee of the massive rattling pump. *Their powers will manifest soon enough, and then we can bring them wherever we go.* Michael didn't need to see his wife's face.

He could feel the heat of her disapproval

Bethany Anne groaned. **This again?**

Michael took the lead. *Yes. "This," as you put it, is a decision we have to make, and soon. Do you intend to leave our children on High Tortuga when we find the Kurtherians?*

Bethany Anne faltered at the thought of being without her babies for an extended period of time. **Shit. No?** A pair of guards came into sight. **We can't talk about this now.**

It will wait until we get home, Michael conceded, moving past Bethany Anne to remove the guards' heads before they spotted them. *You have to admit, this is a clever choice for a hideout.*

In what way? Bethany Anne retorted, passing Michael while he covered her. **It's stupid as fuck to go to ground in a place like this.**

She pointed at the puddle by the base of the tank she was using as cover while Michael crossed the intersection. **That's just begging to burn. One stray spark in the wrong place and BOOM.** She turned back to Michael and demonstrated with her hands. **This whole cliff is replaced by a crater, and it's bye-bye any chance of us getting anyone out of here alive.**

I've survived worse than a little bit of fire. Michael took the lead. *And that is precisely my point. Since we know the Ooken to be at least reasonably intelligent, we would have never thought to look here without the intel to guide us.*

He pointed out another patrol and Bethany Anne moved to deal with them.

True, Bethany Anne conceded, waiting for him to catch up to her. *Peter, Jian, and the others are down there somewhere. They have to be.*

Michael's face was hard. *God help the Ooken if they aren't.*

Bethany Anne snorted. *No God's going to save the fuckers who took them. They have to be taught not to do that shit again.*

They continued to leapfrog until they reached a larger intersection between two main passages at opposing angles. They paused, looking down each of the routes in indecision.

Bethany Anne checked in with the others again. *Akio, Eve, have you found your way down?*

Eve's reply came instantly. *Yes, but we haven't come across the power plant yet, just the aliens. Bethany Anne? They have weapons technology from a variety of sources. Maybe your scavenger theory isn't so out there after all.*

A quartet of Ooken guards emerged from a side-passage they'd missed previously, making the decision for them. The guards splayed their tentacles, preparing to attack.

It wouldn't surprise me. Keep going, and let me know when you find something.

We will, Eve replied, and dropped the link.

Bethany Anne drew her swords from her back and darted toward the guards, her blades flashing as she moved through the group with practiced steps.

Michael sighed and put his sword away. *Every time, Bethany Anne. Every damn time.*

Bethany Anne turned back to flash a grin at him before moving off with her swords held in a relaxed grip. *What can I say? Early bird gets the worm.* She toed a twitching tentacle that lay in her path, eyeing it with distaste before she stepped over it. *Ugh. Some worms.*

Michael snorted, slipping around her to get first look at the side passage. *It's clear.*

The passage went down a short way and curved around, then opened onto a rough stone ledge below the cliff edge. The ledge was covered in vines that hung down from the cliff face above, snaking past the ledge to create a kind of bower that was lit from the outside by a pearlescent glow.

What the fuck? Bethany Anne looked around. *Where's the light coming from?*

Michael separated the curtain of vines, revealing the shimmering forcefield above their heads. *That would explain why Izanami couldn't locate more than the basic outlay of the colony on her scans.*

Bethany Anne frowned. *Double-fuck. Where did they get tech that can block ours? We couldn't even see,* she waved a finger at the force field above their heads, *that.*

Michael dropped the vines. *I would guess they got it from the Kurtherians. This enemy appears to be skilled at confusing outsiders as to their capabilities.*

Bethany Anne narrowed her eyes. *Then let's pull off the mask and see who's hiding underneath.*

They pushed through the vines, being careful of their step until they found their way down—a crumbling disused path worn into the rock face.

Bethany Anne looked down the path with skepticism. *This looks like a good bet.*

Michael peered down, stepping back quickly when the edge crumbled beneath his boot. *If we are careful.*

Bethany Anne regarded the dizzying drop they faced if the path failed them. ***Then it looks like this is our path.***

They began to descend warily, watching above as well as below since the vines still covered every surface.

Bethany Anne didn't even risk asking ADAM to reduce her weight; although he had been silent for a while now. Izanami, too. She trusted the pair of them to deal with their end, and she didn't have time to wonder what they were up to.

Bethany Anne pushed a knot of vines out of the way and looked around to check that Michael was still behind her. ***You didn't get around to telling me what happened with your T-rex hunt.***

Michael's shoulders tightened. *No,* he replied tersely. *I didn't.*

Bethany Anne gave Michael a look he didn't see. ***You know I'll find out one way or another. You might as well just tell me.***

Can a man not keep anything to himself? He shook his head and laughed at her stern look. *Apparently not. The hunt did not go as expected, and other than that, my lips are sealed on the subject. You won't get anything out of Akio, and Peter–*

Will tell Tabitha everything, Bethany Anne told him, ***and then she will tell me everything.*** She smirked and kept walking. ***That's how things work around here. You should know that by now. Speaking of Akio, when is he going to deal with the Sabine situation?***

Michael sighed. *Is it that obvious to you?*

Bethany Anne sighed. *Honey, it's obvious to everyone. I was glad for her to get some distance when I found out the older kids were heading to Devon for a while.* She held up a finger before using the hand to push away a vine at head height. *I know all about the letter. Is Akio going to resolve it before it goes too far?*

Michael frowned. *I hope so. I told him to.*

You **told** *him to?* Bethany Anne repeated. She chuckled. *Oookay, then. That should solve it.*

Michael's frown deepened. *Yes. What's the problem with that?*

Bethany Anne's lips pressed together in amusement. *Did you give him any specific directions?*

Michael made a sound of disapproval. *He is six hundred years old. I hardly think he needs to be instructed like a pubescent Were.*

Bethany Anne dropped to slide down a scree-covered incline where the path had degraded. When she reached the bottom, she turned back to point a teasing finger at Michael as he descended. *He's a man,* she told him. *A gender not known for listening skills as a whole.*

Michael raised an eyebrow. *I've listened to you, oh...I don't know, five times at least. How is that not a skill?*

Bethany Anne narrowed her eyes. *Be glad I don't know if they'd detect us if I zapped your snarky ass.*

Michael bowed and grinned. *Touché, my love.*

Bethany Anne gave him the finger and got back to walking.

They came to the bottom of the ravine and pushed through the pooled vines. The valley floor was covered in vines, which grew in tight knots along the ground and choked the tall trees. The colony was sleeping; there were very few lights.

Bethany Anne and Michael did not need light.

Two shadows slipped through the night, deadlier than the rest.

The vine-covered area by the cliff soon gave way to rough buildings on high stilts that brushed the tree canopy in the wide valley. Michael was familiar with that construction method, and also the reasons for building that way. He tested the ground, which for now was cool and solid beneath their feet.

They slipped between the trees to where the buildings began, making their unerring way toward the building in the center that Izanami had identified as the other most likely place the Ooken would be holding so many hostages.

Michael checked in on Eve and Akio.

We are doing well, Akio replied. *We reached the target, but this is not the location of the prison. The building Izanami marked is a munitions factory.*

A cold smile formed on Bethany Anne's mouth. ***Then why don't you and Eve cause some mayhem in the factory and then get the hell over here?***

Sounds good to me, Eve agreed.

21

Splinter World, Colony, Prison

Bethany Anne and Michael were waiting on a roof near the prison twenty minutes later when there was a deafening rumble, then an explosion in the distance.

It got exactly the reaction they were counting on.

A steady stream of guards swarmed out of the prison building and jumped in the transports lining the yard behind the wall. The gates opened and were lit by floodlights before the first transport was allowed to leave.

Fuck it all with a hand blender! Bethany Anne stamped a foot as she cursed. There was no way to sneak in through the front gate while the transports were leaving without either using their abilities or being seen. *There are at least five hundred guards down there. We should go for the wall while the searchlights are trained on the gates.*

Michael nodded. *That likely means there aren't too many more left inside to guard the building. It's a good plan.* He watched the gate for another moment or two to make certain the attention of the guards was elsewhere, then the two of them made a run for the wall.

They leapt from a short distance away, pulling themselves over the top before anyone spotted them. Michael paused before jumping down to check out his landing spot. *You know, I love that we still make time to do stuff together.*

Bethany Anne landed with a soft thud on the concrete below. **Yeah, well let's make it count. We're almost there. Can you locate Peter? Or even the Weres in general?**

Michael landed beside her and concentrated on categorizing the minds within the building, searching for any that felt familiar. His goal was to get in and out quickly without being noticed.

The Ooken were easy to avoid. They were all in mental communication with others, many in groups of six or more. There were other minds in the prison: violent ones, pitiful ones, and a few eat-your-mother's-face insane ones.

They all deserved to be there for one reason or another, but there was no trace of Peter. He probed deeper into the building and found someone more than familiar. *I have Peter. He's alive.*

Bethany Anne let out a breath she hadn't realized she'd been holding. **What about the others?**

Michael paused. *I can't tell.*

Only one way to find out. Bethany Anne left the cover of the building and ran for the wall surrounding the prison. She leapt when she was almost there, grabbing the top of the wall to haul herself up and over before Michael had a chance to reply.

He shrugged and followed before she killed every alien in there.

Michael landed beyond the wall and found his wife in its shadow by the red glow of her eyes. A quick scan of their surroundings showed him they were lucky not to have set off any alarms. There were trip lasers over every window, along with heavy bars. *It's geared more toward keeping people in rather than out,* he pointed out.

Bethany Anne wasn't so sure. ***Yes, but whichever way it gets tripped, it will still alert the guards, and then we're back to the issue of having insane numbers of psychotic aliens on our asses. There's only one answer to that.***

Michael shrugged. *Then kill them all now. It saves us having to come back and do it when they attack someone else. I know you won't stand for* that.

I've got every intention of passing my final judgment on every alien involved, Bethany Anne told him. ***But there are other ways to neuter the rest of them. I can remove their spaceflight capability. I can disrupt their trade. I can do a thousand things that don't involve wiping an entire planet out.*** She sighed. ***Genocide is one of the things I'm trying to avoid these days.***

If I can, she finished a moment later.

Michael laid a comforting hand on her shoulder. *It gets tiring; I get that.*

Bethany Anne tilted her head to rest it against Michael's hand for a moment. ***I know you do. It's one of the reasons I haven't killed your ass for abandoning me for so long.*** She kissed his hand, then shrugged it off to resume her examination of the building's security. ***We need an alternative entrance.***

Michael pointed at a brightly-lit annex, choosing not to

protest her outrageous statement at that time. *That appears to be slightly less fortified than the rest of the place.*

Bethany Anne considered the building. **Looks good to me. Of course, if we knew if they can detect the Etheric we could just step through, get our people, and step out again.**

Is it worth the risk to find out? Michael asked.

Bethany Anne made a face. **Not right this minute.**

Michael nodded. *You may get the opportunity. If we are discovered, it will make no difference.*

They made their way to the annex, careful not to trip any hidden alarms as they crossed the yard in the shadow of the wall.

They were almost at the annex when a tense moment occurred. A pair of searchlights sweeping the yard changed track and began moving toward Bethany Anne and Michael from opposite ends of the wall.

Bethany Anne thought fast and decided the time had come to take the risk. She acted, grabbing Michael to pull him into the Etheric with her.

Michael breathed a sigh of relief that matched Bethany Anne's when the bland white mist of the Etheric dimension swirled around them. "That was too close for comfort, but now our cover may be blown. We don't know they can't track us if we use the Etheric."

Bethany Anne held her hands out and shrugged. "It would have been blown for sure if I hadn't acted. There was nowhere to go. I suspect they don't have the capability or they would be in here attacking us already." She made a face. "Hang on, I'll check."

She popped her head out of the Etheric. No bullets came whizzing toward her, and no alarms shrieked in the background. The searchlights had moved on to the other side of the yard.

Bethany Anne drew her head back into the Etheric and turned to Michael with a grin. "We're good."

Michael nodded. "Then let's stop hobbling ourselves and get our people back."

They returned to the prison, but first they traveled to a spot that would bring them out inside the building.

They emerged into a dusty storage room. Bethany Anne brushed the webs from her armor. *ADAM?*

>> **Little busy right now.**<<

Are you and Izanami okay?

>> **We're fine. Be with you as soon as we've dealt with this EI group.**<<

Michael's call was to Eve and Akio. *We're good to use our abilities.*

We know, Akio shot back. He sounded preoccupied. *We went a little way and watched over their factories after we laid the Etheric charges. It was the explosions that brought them running, not the active charges.*

Nice of you to inform us, Bethany Anne remarked testily.

Our distraction raised a lot of activity, Eve interjected. *We were busy fighting our way out. We're working our way to you, but at the moment we're holed up in the colony administration building. We will leave as soon as I have finished helping myself to their data. It won't take long.*

Bethany Anne didn't like it, but there wasn't much she could do. Helpless people were depending on her, and Eve and Akio were anything but helpless. *Just stay safe, okay?*

We will, Akio returned. *You will also make an effort not to die today.*

You've got it in one, Bethany Anne teased. **No dying today for anyone.**

Unless they've got tentacles and they're in our way, Michael modified.

Bethany Anne rolled her eyes as she drew her swords. **Yes, unless that.**

Splinter World, Colony, Prison, Underground Level

The room Bethany Anne and Michael were in opened into a dim corridor. The lights above flickered, setting their shadows dancing.

Bethany Anne glanced at both ends of the corridor and turned to look at Michael. **Where next?**

Follow me. Michael moved decisively toward one of the larger doors along the right side of the long corridor. He broke the lock with a quick twist of his wrist, and they entered the downward staircase beyond.

Bethany Anne held her swords at the ready as they descended in a wide spiral. There were soft lights at regular intervals along the way.

We're not far now, Michael told her. *There are guards at the bottom. What's our move?*

Our move is to annihilate the guards and get our people out of here. Bethany Anne's voice was cold even in his mind.

As you wish.

Bethany Anne poked Michael with an accusing finger. **I knew *you'd* seen it.**

Michael winked. *Seen what?*

Fine, don't admit you like the girly movie.

Michael held a hand to his chest. *It's not a girly movie. It has pirates and comedy.*

Bethany Anne dealt with the next locked door in their way. **And a love story.**

Something for everyone, then, Michael countered. *We're really close now.*

They heard the odd chirruping sound the Ooken made when communicating coming from up ahead.

Bethany Anne listened for a few seconds. **Sounds like around thirty or so. We'll split them.**

Michael was taken aback. *No contest?*

No time, she told him. **But if I happen to finish with my fifteen before you finish with yours...**

Not going to happen, Michael assured her smoothly.

Bethany Anne shrugged and smiled. **We'll see.**

They moved as one, and the death began as soon as they crossed the threshold of the guard room at the bottom of the stairs. The guards fell faster than they could comprehend.

There was a shriek from the upper levels.

Bethany Anne separated an Ooken's ape parts from its squid parts with a well-aimed slice. **Oops, guess we've killed enough at one time for them to notice we're here.**

Michael wiped his sword as the last guard fell. *Then we'd better hurry before they all pile in here.*

Finding Peter and the others was relatively easy after that. Bethany Anne and Michael went around freeing the hostages from their cramped cells.

Many were in a poor state. Bethany Anne's anger grew

as she took in the injuries that hadn't yet healed. "You've all been tortured. Extensively."

Peter nodded. "I took the brunt of their mind-probing for as long as I could, but when it was clear I wouldn't give them what they wanted, they moved on to Jian, then Shun. Then they took Robinson. His nanos couldn't repair the damage they did to his mind, so they killed him. We heard him die, BA." Peter ground his teeth together and then rubbed his jaw when the motion caused him pain. "That's *both* cousins they've killed."

My Queen, they should die for the insult to your honor. Izanami's clipped voice spoke volumes. She was as pissed as the rest of them.

"I agree with the AI," Michael supplied.

Bethany Anne also agreed with Izanami. She closed her eyes and counted slowly. When she opened them, she felt completely calm—and her desire to cleanse the galaxy of these parasites was still strong. ***Are you and ADAM done?***

No, but he sent me to assist you, my Queen. There are a considerable number of enemy combatants on paths that will converge on this location.

We're almost done here. Bethany Anne started moving the hostages into the Etheric one by one. ***I need you to be in position to pick us up when I call. Contact Admiral Thomas and have the fleet blow all trace of this colony and all their ships into dust the second we're off-planet.***

Of course, my Queen, Izanami replied. *I will be ready.*

Bethany Anne and Michael shepherded the last few rescued Guardians into the safety of the Etheric, where Peter waited with them.

Bethany Anne waved the exhausted group ahead,

opening the link to Eve as she walked beside them. Michael would do just fine leading them all away from danger. *Eve?*

Eve came back a moment later. *What's up?*

Change of plan. We have Peter and most of the others. Have Izanami meet us at the mouth of the valley. You and Akio make for there as well.

Where are you now? Eve asked.

Walking the Etheric, Bethany Anne answered, having to focus on the energy drain she was feeling. *We'll be at the rendezvous in around half an hour.*

Splinter World, Valley Mouth

Akio and Eve did not have far to go to reach the valley's end. They'd waited patiently so far for the rest of the evacuees to get there, but the last few minutes before the expected ETA were dragging slower than snail chariots in molasses.

Akio scanned the sky. *Where is Izanami?*

Eve had more down-to-earth concerns. *Where are Bethany Anne and Michael?*

They got a partial answer a few minutes later when Michael showed up out of the Etheric with thirty-six others.

Izanami brought the ship in at the exact moment the Etheric opened, but there was no Bethany Anne in sight.

She came through separately, her face serious. "The Ooken have found us. I'll hold them off while you all get aboard, but for fuck's sake do it quickly."

She turned and ran back into the valley, gone again in

less than the blink of an eye. Michael and Peter got to work getting the injured Guardians aboard the *Izanami*.

Fifteen minutes earlier...

Bethany Anne waited for her leg to heal. "Those fucking suckers!"

Peter chuckled wearily between labored breaths. "Tell me about it.

She kicked the dead Ooken and checked around to make sure the remaining hostages were safe. "Follow us."

Michael remained at the head of the group, leading them to a place where they could leave the Etheric reasonably safely.

They emerged, soot-blackened, into the early dawn at the base of the cliffs. Some were still bleeding, and others were now beginning the process of healing from their ordeal and needed sleep.

They made slow progress up the cliff face but they pushed hard, finding the energy from somewhere to keep going despite their crushing weariness. They helped each other out into the open where Izanami was waiting for them. She held the ship high above their heads and extended the ramp.

Bethany Anne brought up the rear. She had that itch on the back of her neck again. *Izanami, what's the status of the approaching Ooken?*

They are getting close to your location, Izanami confirmed. *Would you like me to take the larger groups out with a few well-placed pucks?*

Bethany Anne shook her head. *No, thanks, Izanami. Not just yet.*

The first Ooken appeared at the mouth of the valley as

Michael shepherded the last of the injured and the weary aboard the *Izanami*.

Okay, Izanami, it's your time to shine. Level this place, she told the AI. *Use whatever you have. Burn it all.*

Michael snickered. "I knew the flamethrowers would be useful."

Bethany Anne took one look at the sea of advancing tentacles. Let them fucking come. *Izanami! The area around me is not on fire.*

It will be in three...two...

Bethany Anne risked a glance behind. She could hear the science experiments gone wrong getting closer. *I meant level it, Izanami. And do it NOW. The Ooken are on their way in serious numbers, so we need to get the fuck out of here. I don't want any trace of this colony remaining when we leave.*

One. Izanami complied, letting rip. She sent *almost* everything she had screaming into the mouth of the valley, making sure to target both the power plant and what was left of the munitions factories nearby. Then she sent six drones toward the volcano.

A series of shuddering explosions rocked the night as the drones detonated deep below the ground. The valley floor undulated beneath Bethany Anne's feet. She bent to scoop up a dropped rifle and fired it blindly behind her as she ran through the edge of the fiery tornado Izanami had unleashed.

Bethany Anne jumped aboard as Izanami retracted the ramp. She flung herself into the ship where Michael and Peter were waiting for her and collapsed onto her back, breathing heavily.

Peter looked down at her with a dazed expression. "You okay, BA?"

Bethany Anne got to her feet and walked over to stroke his forehead. "Get some rest and let your nanos do their thing." She strode over to a clear space. "I'll see that you get some steak. Michael, would you meet me on the bridge?"

By the time Michael caught up with Bethany Anne, she already had Eve and Izanami working scans and video from yet more drones.

The scan data she dealt with on the main console, and all of the videos were up on the wraparound screens.

The colony burned brightly in the darkness. The planet's rotation would bring this side of the planet under the artificial sun soon enough. It already bathed the horizon with a golden halo.

She was going to dismantle that, too.

Michael came over and wrapped his arms around her waist. "Don't you ever rest?" he teased, knowing the answer.

She kissed her husband and whispered in his ear as the AI turned the ship's nose spaceward and launched them out of reach of the eruption Izanami's drones had caused. "You see what we bring. Why would you want our children to witness that?"

Michael turned to the destruction playing out on the screen. "To teach them what to do when mercy is not an option."

Out in space, dozens of ships were accelerating toward the planet, ships' weapons active and charging when the enemy ship on the planet simply...

Disappeared.

. . .

High Tortuga, Space Fleet Base, Hangar 001

Peter stood waiting for the ramp to descend. For the moment he would never be away from Tabitha again.

If Tabitha hadn't dumped his ass, that was.

He'd slept and eaten, but he still wasn't feeling a hundred percent. He suspected he needed faster help than his nanocytes could provide, like a tune-up in the Pod-doc.

"BABY!" Tabitha came running across the hangar and launched herself into Peter's arms, his momentary wooziness dispelled by elation.

"Oof!" He grabbed her like a drowning man who'd just been thrown a lifeline, wobbling for a second when she hopped up and wrapped her legs around his waist so she could kiss him fiercely. He kissed her right back, oblivious to the catcalls of everyone else as they walked by.

Tabitha let go of the sides of Peter's face and flung her arms around him, sobbing into his neck. "I thought you were *dead*! Then I was going to kill you if you *weren't* dead for being captured in the first place." She let go finally and slid down with a snarl touching her lips. "You let anything like that happen again, you're gonna wish you *were* dead when I catch up with you!"

She tossed her hair over her shoulder. Peter inhaled her uniquely Tabitha scent and braced himself for what was coming. His head swam and he was weak with exhaustion, but he would take whatever Tabitha gave and hold her afterward. Same as always.

He shook his head when Bethany Anne moved to stand between them and everyone else.

Bethany Anne shrugged and shooed everyone away. She remained just far enough to give them the illusion of privacy, which Peter accepted.

Tabitha's rage spilled down her cheeks in hot floods. "Don't you," an openhanded slap to his chest, "ever," another, softer this time despite her clenched fists.

Peter wondered why this wasn't hurting a lot more.

"*EVER*! Leave our child or me like that again." Tabitha's arms dropped to her sides, her anger spent. "I'm glad you're home safe."

Peter's knees almost gave way when Tabitha looked up at him with those big dark eyes of hers. He had to check he wasn't hearing things. "Really? You're pregnant? With our child? We're having a baby? Together?" His ability to emote was stolen by another wave of dizziness and a throb from the shoulder his captors had dislocated over and over to test his healing ability.

Tabitha nodded. "Uh-huh. Trust me, it was a surprise to me too." She looked a touch green around the edges of that defiant look she got whenever she was unsure. "But yeah, we're having a baby."

Peter's face split into a wide grin. "WOOHOO!" His exhaustion wasn't gone, but it had lessened. "That's…huge. Perfect, but huge." He ignored her uncertainty and gathered her up in his arms, looking into her eyes. "So, um… will you finally make an honest man of me?"

Tabitha snorted laughter and slapped him again, playfully this time. "If you weren't honest I wouldn't love you so much, ass."

Bethany Anne rolled her eyes. "I'm going to make a

special family dinner for Alexis and Gabriel before they get home."

Tabitha made a face. "I was on my way to take their last lesson for the day. I got a message from Addix asking me to give her another half an hour just before I got the message you were back, so I turned around and came straight here."

Peter rolled his shoulder and winced. "This hasn't set right. I need some time in a Pod-doc."

Tabitha patted his sore shoulder. "You can get in one of the Vid-docs instead. Then you can help me tame the terrible two while you heal. We could both use some practice with kids before ours comes along."

Peter chuckled. "Speak for yourself. I got experience to last a lifetime teaching at the Academy."

Bethany Anne joined in their chuckles. "That was a long time ago, and our children tend to be ahead of the curve even compared to Academy kids." She smiled.

"But come to dinner. We should mark the passing of those who didn't make it, and celebrate Tabitha's pregnancy and your safe return." She looked Tabitha over. "Besides, you're looking a touch pale already. You'll need a meal after Alexis is done with you."

Tabitha's eyes widened. "Don't I know it. I spent ages preparing our first lesson because Addix forgot to mention that the twins lead their own learning."

Bethany Anne grinned. "Did you get the full inquisition?"

Tabitha shook her head and blew out a breath. "The child grilled me for three solid hours on our first lesson. I needed a nap afterward."

Peter looked from Bethany Anne to Tabitha. "I don't know if I should be worried?"

Tabitha waved him off. "Nah, I've got it handled. I'm like expert level at distracting them into doing the lesson I planned."

Bethany Anne winked and walked away, throwing up a hand to wave at them over her shoulder. "I'm going to check on the others we rescued before Michael and I start dinner. Enjoy teaching my children."

22

Devon, QBBS *Guardian*, Immersive Training and Recreation Scenario: Preparation Room

Ricole threw her arms out to the sides. "This is so real!"

Jacqueline yelped. "*OW!*"

Ricole winced. "Oops. Sorry." She didn't look sorry for long. "Have you seen the choice of scenarios? It's pretty extensive."

Jacqueline rubbed her chest where she'd been the victim of Ricole's enthusiasm. "I don't remember getting hurt in any of these training simulations before."

Mark grinned. "Suck it up. This is next-level badassery, and I'm not wasting a single second of it. I found a fantasy scenario. One of the reviews said there are dragons."

Jacqueline's eyes lit up. "Is that the one with magic? I thought that one looked like fun."

"I know, right? Wanna go?"

Jacqueline nodded, and Mark grabbed her by the hand. They selected the scenario, and the next second they were gone.

Ricole tilted her head toward a group of Noel-nis in another part of the room who were all staring at her. "This might be trouble."

Sabine narrowed her eyes at the group, who took a step back.

"Oh, they don't want a fight." Ricole's surprise when she spotted the tablets they were holding was complete. When she relaxed, their hopeful looks returned.

Demon bristled. *What do they want?*

Sabine laid a hand on Demon's back to calm her. "Easy. They just want to take a photo with Ricole."

Demon looked up at Ricole. *Do you know them?*

Ricole glanced at the group of mostly adolescent females. "Nope."

Then none of this situation makes sense, and I'm done with it. There has to be something to hunt around here. Demon stalked off with her tail in the air.

Sabine laughed and patted Ricole on the shoulder. "Enjoy your fans. I'll be at the shooting range when you're done."

Ricole wasn't sure what to do, but the young females took Sabine's exit as permission to approach. They all began talking at once, which Ricole found comforting. She posed for photos and answered questions about how she became a fighter.

"I grew up on High Tortuga back when it was called… never mind what it was called. I grew up there, and I stayed out of the gangs by fighting for my freedom. Then I was lucky to find good people who took me in," she told the wide-eyed listeners.

One of the females spoke up. "Would you teach us?"

Her friend dug an elbow into her side. "She doesn't have time for that."

Ricole shrugged. "I might. Do you all have jobs?"

They nodded and listed a bunch of low-paid service jobs in the Second City, then switched to asking when the next event would be held.

Ricole halted their questions and quizzed them all on their lives. It was clear to her that they worked hard for very little. Honesty still did not pay on Devon—or at least it hadn't until now.

She fired off a quick message to the others and got instant replies giving their agreement. She grinned. "That's actually great. You want to be trained, and the company I co-own needs trustworthy employees. I tell you what, show up at..." She remembered the state of the warehouse when they'd left. "You know, we're between premises at the moment."

The lapse appeared to be all they needed to start pelting Ricole with questions about whether she was going to fight again and if there would be another event.

Ricole grinned. "I don't know yet. Maybe." She bumped the company's contact details over to everyone in the group. "I have an appointment now, but message me in about a week if you're interested in my offer."

She left in a hurry for the demonstration she'd been dying to check out since she'd realized how much profit they'd made from their first contract.

Devon, QBBS _Guardian_, Immersive Recreation and Training Scenario: APA

"This is as good as Eve's system back home," Sabine marveled. She turned at a movement to her left, Ashur had spotted her and come over to catch up.

"It's the same system," the German shepherd told her in greeting.

Sabine bent to give her old friend a scratch behind his ears. "Good to see you again!"

"It's good to get out. Bellatrix and I have a young litter, so I was glad of the break when Akio and Barnabas asked if I'd accompany them here."

Sabine perked up even as her heart began to fling itself against her ribcage. "Akio is here?"

Ashur nodded. "Uh-huh. So, do you like Eve's baby?"

Sabine frowned until Ashur indicated the simulation around them.

"How does it compare to the one on High Tortuga?"

Sabine shrugged. "I had very little time for games on High Tortuga," she explained. "And it's been more like live action down in the city since we arrived." She waved a hand to encompass the virtual range. "This place is good to escape to."

The shooting lanes were only part of the simulation. Sabine saw people on the mats using everything from repurposed shipboard items to blades. There were even flashes in the distance from the kind of weaponry she'd had no clue existed before leaving Earth behind some four years ago.

She ran her hands up and down her body, then held them in front of her face and flexed her fingers. "I'm amazed. If I didn't know I was in VR, I wouldn't be able to tell the difference between my avatar and my real body. What are you doing in here?"

Ashur stood beside her at the head of the lane while they waited for the simulation to begin. "I wanted to try out my new avatar. What do you think?" Ashur shook his shaggy head and transformed into a Hellhound in the blink of an eye.

Sabine took in the floating fur, red eyes, and rows of razor-sharp teeth. "I like the eyes. I'm not kissing that mouth, though."

Ashur huffed and shook his head again, returning to his own shape. "I think it goes very nicely with Baba Yaga. I just don't look very fierce next to her, you know? I thought you wanted to shoot something?"

Sabine smirked. "I do." She selected her weapons—two pistols that were very similar to her own, but sleeker and deadlier-looking. "Ricole came up with a ghost of a plan, and now I need to think about how we're going to take our company to the next level. Shooting helps me think." She held the JD Specials up to the light, admiring the upgrades on her own pair.

"Good choice," a deep voice interrupted from behind her. "You might want to go for something a little less powerful, though."

She spun around, startled by the intrusion. "You are joking, right?" The man stood with his arms folded and legs apart—six foot two of solid muscle and twinkling blue eyes wearing supple black leather and a cheeky grin. *Not impressed*, she told herself. "I think I can handle them, Mister Beefy."

The man shook his head. "You'll still feel the kickback on a JDS in here."

The first targets appeared in Sabine's peripheral vision. She twisted back around to the lane and brought up the Jean Dukes Specials, firing them over and over as new targets popped up at random.

The pistols danced in her hands, but she had perfect control despite the pain the recoil sent shooting up her arms. Still, it was completely worth it to use them at a level she wouldn't dare try in reality.

The look on Mister Beefy's face was not to be forgotten, either.

She stepped back after the simulation had ended. "Seems fine to me." The lane was a smoking ruin, every target having been taken out with extreme prejudice.

Ashur chuckled dryly. "I think she's got you there, *Mister Beefy*. Wait until I see Rickie!"

The man's face fell. "Ashur...dude, don't do that to me. I thought we were buddies!"

Sabine held the virtual pistols out to the man and met his eyes without giving away the pain she felt in her wrists. "Now I feel sorry for you. Tell you what...beat this," she indicated the score window, "and I will ask my good friend Ashur to keep it to himself."

"Challenge accepted." He took them and waited for the simulation to begin again.

Sabine perched on a bench behind the lane and watched, with Ashur at her feet. She sensed that Mister Beefy had an edge; the firm set of his broad shoulders spoke a thousand words as he stood there, ready to begin.

He was obviously a warrior. Well trained, too, if his

stance was anything to go by. Her thoughts drifted to Akio for a brief moment; she saw the same strength in him.

Mister Beefy caught her studying him, and the distraction was enough to make him miss the first shot by a hair. "*Gott Verdammt,* and fuck me with a backward pineapple!"

Sabine snickered at his outburst, drawn out of her introspection.

The man growled and continued firing, his wrists rigid as the JD Specials pounded them into virtual breadcrumbs. Tim ignored the pain as the targets burst into flame or dust or melted piles of gooey mush wherever he aimed.

Sabine rubbed her wrists, grateful that this was an avatar. She would feel none of the damage when she left the simulation. She would consider training this way regularly. Then if there were ever a situation that demanded her everything, she would already have the muscle memory to pull an honest-to-fuck miracle out of her ass.

"He's pretty good," she remarked quietly to Ashur. She didn't mind the way the leather made his butt look as he moved either, but chose not to share that with the dog. "What's his name when it's not Mister Beefy?"

"It's Tim, and he *should* be good," Ashur chuffed in reply. "He's had a lot of time to practice."

It was over, and the score window blinked while the points were tallied.

Sabine chuckled when the window revealed she'd beaten him by seventeen points. "Looks like your name is 'Mister Beefy' from now on." She winked. "You've got to watch the kickback from the Dukes pistols, you know?"

His eyes narrowed; he was unhappy with the result. He

clearly wanted a chance to redeem himself. "I want a rematch! Best of three?"

Just then Ricole contacted her. *Sabine, get your ass to our quarters. I've found exactly what we need. You're going to love it! Oh, and Demon is going to eat the vendor if he doesn't give us a better price, so it should be pretty inexpensive once I'm done haggling.*

Sabine sent back her exasperation. *Just pay the vendor and bring Demon with you to meet me. Then you can explain what you've found that's so amazing.*

You're going to love it, Ricole repeated before closing the link.

She turned an apologetic face to them both. "Shit, this could get serious. I've got to go. Sorry, Ashur. I'm up for a rematch later if you are, Mister Beefy."

Tim grinned. "Yeah, but let's up the stakes. VR is good, but nothing beats a real-life sparring match. Think you can take me in a fight?"

Sabine thrust her chin toward him proudly. "I've beaten bigger men than you," she boasted. "I'll meet you both at the main APA in a couple of hours."

Tim was mesmerized as the woman walked away. "Shit! I forgot to ask her name."

"It does kind of feel like you should know who's aboard your station, *Mister Beefy.*" Ashur gave him a big doggy grin. "Too busy watching her walk away." He wheezed with laughter. "I don't care who wins the next round. You're stuck with that for as long as I live!"

Before Tim could say a thing, Ashur shook his head, transformed into a nightmare version of himself, and sprang away laughing. "I'll see you at the APA!"

Tim scowled and exited the Vid-pod. Whoever the mystery woman was, she was beautiful *and* deadly—his favorite combination. He walked the corridors of the station, attempting to clear the image of her from his mind.

It didn't work. He wondered who she was, where she had come from, and if she would gift him with that smile of hers again when they met on the mat.

He couldn't stop seeing it.

"Only one thing to do," he said to himself, changing direction to head for the APA.

"Talk to yourself so you sound like a madman?" Rickie Escobar's voice asked from beside him. "What's up, buddy?"

Tim shook his head, not wanting to share. Rickie would just rag on him for pining over a woman, even a female as stunning as the one who had just defeated him at the range.

Rickie made a sympathetic face. "Woman trouble?" He made a little 'o' with his mouth when he saw his teasing had hit the mark. "*Duuuude.* That's not like you. When did you start getting all sensitive about women?"

"Not *women.*" Tim moaned. "*A* woman. A *perfect* woman. She's so far out of my league that I ought to space myself for even thinking about her."

"Who is this woman?" Rickie demanded, slapping him on the back. "What makes her so special that my buddy the stud muffin is almost crying in a corridor? Wait until Joel hears about this. He's gonna freak."

Tim looked hard at Rickie as they walked to the elevator. "*Don't*, Rickie. I'm serious—she is amazing." His eyes got a bit misty. "She handled those JD Specials like they were *made* for her. It was like all my dreams came true at once. I didn't even get her name."

Rickie was bowled over by the sincerity in his old friend's voice. "Fuck, that's deep. Want me to help you find her?"

Tim shook his head. "She and Ashur are meeting me at the APA in a while. I'm headed there now to blow off some steam if you want to come with."

Rickie popped Tim on the back. "Sure, I could use a workout. What about your mystery woman? You said she was with Ashur? She must have come from High Tortuga with Akio and Barnabas. Or maybe she snuck up from Devon."

"She doesn't sneak," Tim snapped. "She's too direct for that."

Rickie made a face as he followed Tim.

The APA was reasonably empty when they got there. They quickly changed and claimed a mat with a view of the door.

Tim couldn't concentrate, so Rickie scored again and again, Tim's lackluster performance gave his friend one opportunity after another to rack up points.

"It's a good thing nobody's watching," Rickie teased as Tim looked at the door for the third time in the last few minutes. "If your crush turns up, you're going to look really stupid lying on the floor with all your teeth knocked out."

Tim twisted back to Rickie with a smirk. "Let's go then, laughing boy." He brought up his guard and made a "come at me" gesture. "You'll be laughing on the other side of your face when I make you kiss your own ass!"

He dived in with a heavy haymaker, knowing Rickie would duck. As Rickie bent Tim headbutted him, knocking him on his ass. "You said something about teeth on the floor?"

Rickie spat blood and grinned. "Yours, not mine." He kicked at Tim's knee, jabbing fast when Tim moved to counter. "You're getting slow, old man."

Tim answered with a knife-hand to Rickie's solar plexus, right where Eric had shot him on their first day as Guardians. "You're better than you were," he said admiringly. "What have you been doing these last few years? You're keeping that pretty close to your chest."

"Bit of this, bit of that," Rickie replied enigmatically. "Whoa, who's *that*?"

Tim turned to see if she'd arrived, but his disappointment turned to pain when Rickie socked him in the jaw.

Tim rubbed the sore spot and poked at his teeth to check that they hadn't actually come loose. "Wow, Rickie." He worked his jaw a little more, fantasizing that Rickie was just a few inches closer. "Do you want to punch me in the dick just to make sure you got all the dirty moves in? Maybe I should hold out my leg so you can sweep the fuck out of it and make it a cheap-shot trifecta?"

"Wow, wuss boy." Rickie rolled his eyes. "It'll heal in a minute. You're too easy."

"Pretty sure it's you who can be lured into any woman's bed with the promise of a meal in the morning. Or has that changed?" Tim had sparred endlessly with Rickie and the other original Guardians when they had first started out. They had kept in touch as best they could as the years took them in different directions, but the death of Matthew during the Leath War had left an unfillable empty space between them all.

Joel had remained in the service, and Rickie had done something that was probably nine-tenths illegal since he hadn't bragged about it to them. Tim had stayed on at AGB as a bouncer and, admittedly, done his best to avoid making any kind of impact at all. The wars had spread them out over the years, but it was good to be back together, even if they were no longer complete as a team.

Tim ducked a swing and countered again for the point. "One thing I *haven't* missed is your sense of humor."

It was Rickie's turn to look pained. "There was me thinking you worshipped the ground I walk on. Guess I've been replaced by Ms. Mystery, whoever she is. She's a lucky woman."

Tim was about to deliver another punch—and a snarky reply—when he noticed the woman in question standing in the doorway with Ashur.

Rickie breathed out. "Oh, man. I take it all back. She's *waaay* too hot for you."

Devon, QBBS *Guardian*, Main APA

Sabine stood outside the changing rooms and eyed the different workout areas. She sucked in a deep breath, regretting it instantly as the smell of sweat stung her nose. She looked down at Ashur, who had been waiting outside the APA when she arrived. "Where will I find Mr. Beefy?"

Ashur indicated one of the nearby sparring areas with his nose. "He's over there."

Sabine hesitated. "Oh. Oh, yes. I see him now." The man

she'd come to fight was engaged in a match on one of the mats with another huge guy. He was bigger in the flesh. "I kind of laid it on thick with that challenge. I'm going to look stupid if I lose."

"Keep it simple," Ashur chuffed. "You know hand-to-paw combat, right?"

Sabine was about to agree, but did a double-take and narrowed her eyes at Ashur. "'Hand-to-paw?' You mean 'hand-to-hand.'"

Ashur laughed. "No, I meant what I said." He nudged her toward the mats. "Go...join in. I'll be around when you're done." He walked to the bench and laid down, his chuffing having drawn the attention of the men.

Sabine sniffed delicately. Under the tang of sweat, she could smell the nature of the two men on the mat. *Damn dog. You could have told me he was a Were.*

As she approached the mat, she heard Tim's friend tell him she was too hot for him and frowned. She wasn't looking for romance, just a good fight.

She threw her towel on the bench beside the mat and walked over to them, smiling and nodding to the stranger and fixing her target with a hard look. "I came here to kick your ass, Mister Beefy. I wasn't expecting to hear you talking about me."

Ricky dissolved into a fit of helpless laughter. "'Mister Beefy?' Oh, Tim—you know I can't let that go, right?"

"Shut it, Rickie," Tim growled, glowering at him.

Rickie was doubled over at this point, wiping tears from his eyes. "I thought 'Rocky' was overly macho, but this is just priceless!"

Ashur chuffed his amusement from the side. "I know, right?"

Sabine looked from one to the other. "Children, please. Is there going to be a fight or not?"

Tim met her eyes and swept a hand toward the mat. "Let's go."

They took their stances, Sabine fixing Tim with a hard look. "Let's make this interesting," she suggested, enjoying the way Tim shifted under her unwavering gaze. "What's the currency for wagering here?"

Rickie supplied the answer. "Honor, pretty lady. All the best matches are played station-wide. For training purposes, you understand."

Tim saw her perfect mouth quirk to the side.

"I would expect nothing less." She turned her icy gaze on Rickie. "I suggest you desist in calling me 'pretty lady' or I might have to make you cry when I've finished with Tim. My name is Sabine."

"Pretty name for a pretty lady." Rickie was pushing it. "You got a last name to go with that?"

Sabine smiled sweetly, looking as though butter wouldn't melt in her mouth. "I don't *need* a last name."

Rickie's eyes widened, and the color drained from his face as though his heart had just fallen out through his ass.

Tim snorted. He had known by instinct that she was of the royal family. She walked like she owned the night. "I'm all for making a side bet, Sabine."

She grinned at him. "That's what I like to hear! What are you prepared to wager?"

Tim thought quickly. "If you win, the video goes out, and everyone gets to call me Mister Beefy for a month without me tearing their heads off." He saw that he had her, and upped the stakes. "If *I* win, you agree to have dinner with me."

Sabine tightened up.

Rickie—for once—was silent.

"It's only dinner," Tim said gently, seeing her reticence.

Sabine shrugged. "Sure, why not?" An expression he couldn't decipher flashed over her face. "It's only dinner. Now, are we going to fight or stand around all day talking like a pair of schoolgirls? I'm a busy woman."

"Yeah! Get on with it, Mister Beefy!" Rickie catcalled.

"Shut it, Rickie! Rules?" Tim asked. They had all learned *that* lesson on their first day as Guardians.

Sabine's humor was gone in an instant. "Don't hold back. I need the workout." She rolled her shoulders and stretched, never taking her eyes from his. "I had a small altercation a couple of days ago, but it's not the same when they can't really fight back."

Rickie snorted. "You're talking about the warehouse event planetside the other day?"

Sabine shrugged. "Mm-hmm."

Tim's eyes widened at her hard look. "Shit, you're not kidding!" His grin returned, the prospect of a challenge from the stunning woman before him firing his spirit. "Weapons?"

Sabine shook her head. "Hand to hand, abilities only."

Rickie called a start from the edge of the mat, and all else was forgotten.

They went in at the same time, both on the offensive. Her first strike was blocked by his muscular forearm, but she had a counter lined up. She slammed a knee upward, catching his ribs with a *crack*.

Sabine growled. "You're not even trying! I told you not to hold back, Beefy. I'm not playing."

"You're fast," he admitted, "and strong." He rubbed his ribs where her knee had connected. "Okay, I'm done holding back. Let's do this." He dropped back into his stance, ribs healed.

"About fucking time!" Sabine took three steps forward and launched herself into the air.

He was ready, blocking the oncoming fist and connecting with a hard punch to her solar plexus.

She grunted as the air left her body and she slammed onto the far side of the mat. She laid there for a second while her ribs healed and her ability to breathe returned, then flipped back to her feet.

"That's more like it," she panted, darting toward Tim again. "*This* is a fight!"

They met in the middle once more, trading blows that would incapacitate an ordinary human. Sabine was glad of her enhancements. She punched and kicked and blocked as fast as Tim, her power belying her size and age.

Tim was losing, so captivated by the angel of destruction before him that the pain of the strikes she landed didn't even register. She was not a vampire or Were, but she was *fast* and she was *strong*. Her desire to best him brought his Alpha nature out in force. It was a joy to rise to her challenge and match it with his own ferocious energy.

Dinner with her would be worth the pain he was going through to earn it. Tim couldn't believe the ferocity and determination that burned in her eyes.

Rickie and Ashur cheered from the sidelines as the exchange of blows got faster and harder. His healing rate was as good as hers, so it went on. At times they couldn't see where Tim ended and Sabine began since they moved with such speed that they became a violent blur.

Ten minutes, then fifteen—neither of them would back down. They were drawing a crowd, but neither of them noticed.

They finally broke, sweating hard.

Tim wiped his mouth and tasted blood.

He had only ever had one other all-in fight like this, his first true Alpha fight with Peter. What was it with this day drawing him back to the past? There was a certain similarity, he supposed. No malice was involved in this kind of contest, but each of them had a relentless desire to best the other.

Sabine yelled and took advantage of Tim's momentary distraction to throw herself back at him with a left spinning backfist and a follow-up right, then an elbow to the temple that dazed him for a second.

Adrenaline flooded Sabine's body. She was faster than Tim, but he was stronger, and he had training and experience on his side. She *could* win, but only if she pushed herself and got very lucky.

She went for a chokehold, managing to get an arm around his neck and squeezed tightly to cut off his air. It proved to be her undoing.

Tim reached behind and grabbed Sabine with both hands, pulling her bodily over his head to fling her away. However, the mixture of blood and sweat under their feet caused him to slip instead.

They crashed to the mat in a tangle of limbs.

"Enough," Sabine declared. "I give! I can't feel my legs anymore."

They rolled away from each other and just laid there on the mat breathing hard. Sabine exchanged glances with Tim and the two of them stopped for a moment, then cracked up.

"It's been a while since I had a fight like that." Tim held his ribs to ease the pain of his rumbling laughter. "Maybe we can do it again sometime."

"Get a room, already!" Rickie shouted.

Sabine sat up sharply, her face burning now that her adrenaline had dissipated. She stood quickly and looked for Ashur, who was lying by the bench at the edge of the mat. "I'd better go."

Tim nodded in understanding. "I'll see you for dinner later?"

Sabine smiled. "You will, Mister Beefy."

"Hey, I won!" he complained. "You're not supposed to call me that anymore!"

"I have that as a draw." Sabine winked and caught up with Ashur, who had already set off toward the showers. "Dinner. You can pick me up at eight."

Ashur followed her to the changing room, chuffing his doggy laughter at Tim as he left the mats. She left the German shepherd in the changing area while she showered and changed.

"So…Tim," Ashur prodded when she emerged from the shower smelling sweet.

Sabine pouted as she grabbed a towel from a pile and wiped her face. "I could have taken him."

Ashur wagged his tail and replied enigmatically, "I think you did."

Sabine glared at the German Shepherd. "What's *that* supposed to mean?"

Ashur chuffed. "Hurry, Sabine. Akio is waiting to see you."

"He is?" Her heart did a little flip in her chest, followed immediately by the pain thinking about Akio caused. Nevertheless, she wouldn't miss even a minute with him. She reached for her guns and the belt he had gifted her while she dressed, feeling the absence of them both.

"He messaged me while you were sparring to ask if I'd seen you," Ashur confirmed. "When I told him you were training, he asked me to bring you to him afterward."

"That's good of you," Sabine offered.

Ashur looked around, then chuffed. "Better than trying to keep those puppies of mine out of trouble."

Sabine smiled and set off after Ashur. Tim disturbed her. He was handsome and moved well on the sparring mat, but he was obviously very attracted to her. Was that something she wanted? She hadn't thought so...before now. "Where is Akio now?" she asked.

"On the viewing platform with Barnabas."

"Okay." Sabine barely paid attention to Ashur, following him the rest of the way on autopilot while her mind worked on her discomfort about the moment she had shared with Tim on the mat.

It made her question everything.

It also made her crash into Ashur, who had stopped at the bottom of a wide staircase.

"Ugh," he whined. "Why do humans always get weird

when they're thinking about mating? It's like your brain detaches from the rest of your body!"

Sabine's face burned. "I wasn't thinking about 'mating,' as you put it. Where are we, anyway? I thought we were going to find Akio."

Ashur looked up with his head cocked. His left ear did its best impression of a knowing eyebrow. "Could have fooled me." Ashur turned and walked away, still talking. "Akio is upstairs."

"Bye, Ashur," she called after him.

High Tortuga, Space Fleet Base, Inner Courtyard

Tabitha and Peter held hands and murmured to each other on the walk home from the Vid-doc suite in Michael's offices. Alexis and Gabriel had reluctantly agreed to the lesson, although they wanted to be with Bethany Anne and Michael soonest.

Tabitha had been firm and they'd settled in after much protesting, to which she'd countered that they had an interesting lesson to cover. Today they were going to hack the Etheric.

Peter was quiet beside her, giving her space to contemplate as she walked. He was fully recovered, and today's lesson had gone well. Or at least Tabitha thought it had.

She was fascinated with Alexis' take on how the Etheric worked, her absolute certainty that once she worked out how to access the energy, it would be something like a well for her to draw from and bend to her will.

That sounded an awful lot like magic to Tabitha, and Peter agreed with her. It was completely different than the "truth" he had grown up with and Tabitha had known ever since she had stumbled upon the UnknownWorld so long ago.

She didn't think it would take many more lessons before Alexis managed to manifest some sort of ability. He worried that they might have trouble. He remembered multiple incidents where people's nanocytes had malfunctioned, and he warned Tabitha to keep an eye out for the signs.

They could all smell something good cooking when they got to the inner courtyard that acted as a line of defense for the home Bethany Anne and Michael were raising their children in.

Alexis and Gabriel ran ahead as soon as it came into sight. Tabitha and Peter followed a short distance behind them.

"I'm in here," Bethany Anne called as they clattered through the door.

"Mommyyyyy!" the twins cried in unison. They ran at her with their arms outstretched.

There was no time for Bethany Anne to put down the spoon. She got a big hug from her babies—who looked to have grown *again*—and they all got covered in tomato sauce from the spoon.

Gabriel wiped a finger down his shirt and licked it clean. "Mmm. Mommy's making lasagna."

Tabitha entered the kitchen as Gabriel spoke. "Did I hear my number-one craving being mentioned?"

"Well, we have to keep you fed." Bethany Anne straightened up and looked down at her ruined shirt. "I'd better change. Alexis, Gabriel, you too." She scooped Alexis and

Gabriel up and nuzzled their necks. "Half an hour before dinner gives me plenty of time to get my angels nice and clean."

The twins began chattering a million light-years a minute.

When Bethany Anne returned with Alexis and Gabriel, the twins were dressed in the loose atmosuits that were popular around the base. Bethany Anne had gone for a simple black shirt and black yoga pants, stating she was in her own home and if anyone expected her to dress up after the last few days, they could think again.

This was a celebration and a wake.

Michael messaged to apologize for being late and to tell them to start without him since he was still meeting with Addix about the kidnapping on Colonnara and he didn't know how long he would be.

Alexis and Gabriel wrestled on the living room rug while Bethany Anne took out her lasagna to inspect it.

Tabitha peered over the counter. "That's a pretty big lasagna for just the six of us."

Bethany Anne pulled out another large lasagna. "That's a good thing, since I told you we were having a family dinner." She grinned. "Everyone who can make it will be here soon. "

Tabitha returned her grin, stood up, and went to the fridge. "Needs more cheese."

Peter made a noise of agreement. "No such thing as leftover bacon or too much cheese," he stated.

Bethany Anne rolled her eyes, but she complied with Tabitha's wishes. "What the pregnant lady wants…"

"The pregnant lady wants garlic bread." Tabitha clapped

with delight at the cheesy goodness going on. "I'm starting to like being pregnant."

Bethany Anne put the dish back in to brown the cheese. "If you're eating again, it's all good."

"What about chocolate cake for dessert?" Peter offered. "I could go out for some."

As if on cue, the color drained from Tabitha's face and she ran from the room with her hands over her mouth.

Peter looking at Bethany Anne in confusion. "What did I say?"

Bethany Anne was about to tell him it wasn't his fault when the door opened and John, Darryl, and Ashur came in laughing.

Gabrielle and Jean were right behind, with Bellatrix and the puppies in a furry huddle behind *them*.

Bethany Anne was immediately on guard, pointing two fingers toward Bellatrix and then her own eyes. "Ashur, Bellatrix. I'm glad you're here, but if my children end up in the Etheric again, we're going to have strong words."

Bellatrix chuffed. "No worries, they are in control of their abilities now. Even Ashur can block his ability to boost your connection to the Etheric."

"If that's true, I have no problem with them playing together." Bethany Anne held out a hand for Ashur to brush against. She did not feel the Etheric get any closer when her fingers trailed through his soft fur.

Alexis and Gabriel stood by a safe distance from Zeus and Athena.

"Did it work?" Alexis asked breathlessly. She had her fingers laced tightly in hope.

Bethany Anne nodded. "Looks like it did." She waved

the four of them over to the rug. "Just stay where I can see you."

Tabitha watched them wrestle as if they'd played together all their lives.

First, they played human vs canine. Then they switched so Zeus teamed up with Gabriel, and Athena was with Alexis.

To the children and puppies, it was all a game; the battle they fought was entirely in their imaginations.

For the watching adults, it was a glimpse of what was to come.

Each team had their own tactics. Alexis went in directly, attempting a lock onto Gabriel with her first move.

Zeus dived in, shoving Alexis out of position.

This happened three more times before Alexis lost her temper.

She stamped her foot and pointed at Gabriel. "You're *cheating!*"

"No, I'm not!" Gabriel protested. "It's not my fault you're predictable."

Alexis growled in frustration.

"I hope you two are getting along, " Bethany Anne leaned over the island to look in on them. "It would be a shame to have you fight when we all just got back together."

Alexis lowered her voice to a hiss, "I'm not predictable!" Her eyes narrowed. "Would a predictable person do *this?*" She clenched her fist, turning red for a moment from the force of her concentration.

Gabriel watched on, unimpressed. "Yeah, what about it? You've been trying to make energy balls all week."

Alexis ignored him and opened her hand extra slowly. "I... I did it, Gabriel." She held out her hand palm up and showed her brother the tiny energy ball resting there.

Gabriel's mouth fell open. "How did you do it?"

Alexis shrugged. "I'm not sure."

Gabriel stole a glance toward the kitchen, where the adults were all occupied getting ready for dinner.

He turned back to Alexis, who was staring at her energy ball. "Hey, Sis, can you make it bigger?

She remained transfixed by the ball for a second before responding, "I'm not sure that's a good idea. You should get Mommy."

Gabriel nodded. "I will, but don't you want to impress her, so we don't get into trouble?"

Alexis considered Gabriel's suggestion. She did like it when she impressed her parents, and she really did want to know if she *could* grow the ball before Mommy and Daddy gave her rules about her new ability.

She concentrated again, feeling for the connection between the energy ball and the Etheric.

Just as Mommy had told Alexis when she asked, there was energy flowing into the ball and there was an equal amount of energy flowing out.

Alexis cut off the connection that let the energy out, and the ball began to grow in her hand.

The only thing Alexis *didn't* know was how to stop the ball from growing.

"Whoa," Gabriel marveled. He leaned in to get a closer look.

"ALEXIS!" her mom shouted from the kitchen.

Alexis snatched her hand away, but it was too late.

Gabriel touched the energy ball.

They were thrown in opposite directions. Gabriel landed with enough force to embed him in the wall

Alexis was less lucky. She landed in a heap after colliding with the wall. The last thing she saw before she lost consciousness was her mother leaping the island to get to them.

High Tortuga, Space Fleet Base, Michael's Office

Michael listened to Addix's report. "Do you trust your source?"

"Sources," Addix clarified. "This is not my first investigation. I went down multiple avenues with assets both on and off-world, and there were no confirmed links between the two who planned the kidnapping of Alexis and Gabriel and any known criminal enterprises."

Michael nodded, deep in thought. "And the other two you killed?"

Addix shrugged. "There were links between the other two and some of the bigger gangs I came across, but they were mostly used as hired muscle. I passed the locations and account numbers of the gangs on to the Colonnaran authorities."

Michael chuckled. "I assume they were grateful."

Addix's mandibles twitched with delight. "Oh, yes."

Michael! Bethany Anne sounded panicked, something he never thought to hear.

The children...

Get the Vid-docs ready. I'm almost... "Here." Bethany Anne arrived in an empty space, cradling their inert children in her arms.

Michael saw the burns. "Why are they not healing?" he asked, his voice quick and clipped.

She strode to the Vid-docs. "I don't know. Their nanocytes should have taken care of it by now." She looked at her children, one in each arm, then glared at the Vid-docs' lids. "Some help?"

Michael took Alexis from her, and they gently placed the twins in their Vid-docs.

Bethany Anne closed the lid on Gabriel. "ADAM, Eve."

>>Yes, Bethany Anne?<<

Eve appeared at the door. "You called?"

Bethany Anne placed a hand on each of her children's Vid-docs, which right now were Alexis and Gabriel's only hope of survival. "Find out what is hurting my babies."

23

Devon, QBBS _Guardian_, Viewing Deck

Sabine stood at the rail, the stars an endless expanse before her. They seemed so small, but it was _she_ who was small.

Where was her place in all this? The future was still uncertain. Would they stay on Devon and build the company? What if all that held the group together was their mutual love of Michael?

And on the subject of love, would Akio ever relent and address her feelings for him? She almost hadn't sent the letter—the one where she'd spoken about her feelings openly for the first time. She had been crying as she wrote it, knowing that this was the only way to move on with her life.

It's too hard to accept.

If Sabine were honest with herself, she knew deep down that her feelings for him were unrequited, and always would be. She knew, and still she clung to them. Tim was a wildcard—an unexpected opportunity to step out of the comfort zone her fantasies about Akio had given her.

She watched him talking to Barnabas in the reflection of the window. Was this what she wanted? A life of following a path that led nowhere?

Or could she step beyond that and experience something real?

She was back to feeling small and insignificant.

Hai, Sabine. Akio's voice came into her mind, calming as always. *We are small, but we burn brightly. What troubles you?*

Sabine stared at the infinite beauty of the cosmos, seeing none of it. *Today I walked around a space station with a talking dog and lost a fight with a werewolf. I came up here to spend some of the frankly obscene profits our company made from organizing a fight.* She brushed her hair behind her ear, then folded her arms across her middle. *You know, all the normal stuff.* She sighed. *When I think of how life has changed —how it is still changing—I have no control over my emotions.*

Akio walked over and joined her by the window. *Is Devon not working out for you?*

Sabine sighed. *Yes, I suppose it is. We're doing well. I just... I thought things would be easier than this.*

The Japanese vampire stood with his hands clasped behind his back. *Did you expect life in space to be easy?*

Not space, Sabine replied, looking at him with a wry smile. *Life. I've been so confused. I have almost died so many times, Akio, and every time you were the one who made it better.* She looked down. *Did... Did you get my letter?*

Akio stiffened and stepped away. *Yes, Sabine. I received the letter. But you knew when you sent it that we cannot be anything more than we already are.* His expression was kind, but his voice was firm. *You realize there are centuries between us?*

Sabine uttered a short, harsh laugh. "That's not the real reason. I know."

Akio chuckled dryly. *You are a wonderful woman, and you will be dear to me forever. However, you are right. That is the issue for me—you are a woman.*

She held up a hand to reassure him. *Oh, I know. You don't like women, I got that from the start.* She paused, feeling her cheeks burn with the intimacy of what she was about to say. *But it wasn't about sex. It was the feeling of security I got from you that I've been clinging to. You gave me closure on my family's deaths, Akio. Do you understand how much that meant to me? You are my hero, and you always will be. That was why I got confused. I mean,* she looked into his eyes. *who could live up to you?*

Akio chuckled again, this time with feeling. *I understand why you might struggle,* he teased. *I can think of a Guardian who might be up to the task if the video Ashur sent me is anything to go by.*

Sabine's eyes widened, and her hand shot to her mouth. *You* saw *that?*

Everybody has seen it, he told her matter-of-factly. *It's been playing station-wide. It's not every day the station commander almost gets his ass handed to him by a tiny woman.*

Sabine groaned aloud, squeezing her eyes shut. *I wish I hadn't been so cocky. I should have stuck to shooting.*

Akio allowed a smile to slip out. *I do not think you minded losing to Tim as much as you say.*

He was silent and still for a moment. His face became serious again as he spoke his next words, and she was surprised to feel his hand on her shoulder. *Sabine, ever since the night I walked in your mind and we brought Justice for your family, I have thought of you as my only living child. Even more so when I shared my blood to keep you alive. It's only natural that we should feel a bond. Could you bring yourself to honor me as your father?*

That didn't sound at all...*bad.* Sabine discovered it felt better than the contrived happy ever after she'd dreamt of. Her shoulder relaxed under Akio's hand. *I think I can. Thank you for being so patient with me. It couldn't have been easy.* She felt a weight lift. Akio watched a small tear form and fall down her face, curving across her cheek as she lifted her eyes once more, their wetness a gauge of her emotions. *So we will be father and daughter?*

Akio nodded. *Would you honor me as such?*

Sabine gazed into space, considering Akio's words. The tightness she'd felt in her chest evaporated, and an honest smile of joy touched her lips. *I am honored that you think of me that way. As long as I don't lose you, I'll be happy.*

You could never lose me, Akio told her sternly. *I am proud of you. Of what you and the others are building here.* He smiled down at her. *You are ready for this life, whatever it brings.*

She arched an eyebrow and smirked. *Even if it's a hot Were?*

Akio stepped closer and wrapped a protective arm around her shoulders. Especially *if it is a hot Were. Goodness knows there are so many of them aboard this station.*

She tucked her head into his shoulder, and together they watched the stars. *I'm glad we had this talk. I'm ready, and I'm going to enjoy having dinner with Tim tonight.* She tapped him on the arm. *Maybe we can find you a hot Were, too. Now you've loosened up a little, that is.*

Sabine could have sworn Akio reacted to that, but he had himself under control before she could be sure. She squeezed him and let go. *You deserve to be happy, and if I can let go of my fears, so can you.*

Akio's eyes were tightly closed, giving nothing away. *One day, Sabine.*

She smiled again, satisfied with his answer—for now. *So, you already know Tim?*

Let me tell you a story about Tim, Akio said. *Or better yet, let me show you. Did you ever see the video of his first real Alpha fight?*

He led her to the nearest console and pulled up the video. Tim, young and full of aggression, faced off against an even younger Peter. She listened to the speech Peter made and watched the other four contenders back down. One of the four looked familiar. *Hey, that's Rickie! What's going on here?*

I see you have met the team clown. Akio shook his head. *This was the Alpha fight that decided the Guardians' leadership. Peter had a righteous claim that day, but Tim wouldn't back down. He is an Alpha, so challenge is in his nature. It's one of the most famous fights in Wechselbalg history. Tim may have lost, but he lost to the best.*

Sabine watched openmouthed as the battle between the two went on. She caught herself getting angry every time Peter landed a strike on Tim.

The video ended and Akio spoke. *You like him.*

She looked up in shock. *It's not like you to be so direct,*

Akio. First the hugging, and now you're talking about my feelings?

Akio nodded. *I have never had a daughter before, but I am aware that taking care of your heart is one of my duties as a father.*

Sabine snickered. *Will you defend my honor too?* she asked half-jokingly.

Akio missed the humor. *Of course. Woe betide any man who hurts you, for he will have me to face.*

Emotion overwhelmed Sabine, and she looked at Akio with tear-bright eyes. Thinking to throw him an emotional curveball like he'd just done to her, she wiped her eyes and smiled. *You do realize that if I get married, you'll have to give me away?*

That got the reaction she was looking for—Akio's face turned to stone. *Of course,* he ground out. *Nothing would make me happier.*

Sabine gave Akio a long hug, which he accepted, grunting with surprise as she squeezed him tightly. *I'd better get back. I've been gone awhile. Thank you, Akio...Father.* The word tasted strange.

They would get used to it.

You are welcome. He tapped his head and gave her a knowing smile. *Just be aware that I will be checking up on anyone who shows an interest in my daughter.*

She giggled at the thought as she left him, skipping down the stairs. She paused halfway down as Akio's meaning hit her.

Oh shiiit, he's going to mind read anyone I date!

She heard the ancient vampire's laughter drifting down the stairs after her.

. . .

Devon, QBBS *Guardian*, Team Quarters

Sabine arrived back at their temporary quarters and waited a few minutes before going over to the fridge to see what passed for basics on this station.

She was surprised to find everything she needed to make a monster sandwich. There was bread in the cupboard above the counter. Knowing that Ricole would steal half of her sandwich if she didn't make her one too, she automatically doubled up on everything.

She had just poured out two glasses of what she hoped was juice when Ricole came in like a whirlwind.

"Sabine, you won't believe what I got! It will interface with any system. It's one of Eve's and it shouldn't have been here, but I recognized that little symbol she stamps on all her creations." Ricole drew in a heaving breath.

"Did you run all the way here?" Sabine put the plate and juice on the table and gestured to the chair. "Come, sit and eat. Get your breath while I grab my plate, and then we can talk."

Demon sauntered in with her nose in the air. She turned away as she walked past Ricole to rub her face against Sabine's hand in greeting. *Ugh, you smell like dog. Is he here?*

Sabine sighed. "Why can't you and Ashur rise above it and get along?"

I prefer to uphold tradition. Demon sniffed and jumped onto her bunk. *Besides, that ass annoys me. He's so vain.* She lifted a heavy paw to lick it.

Sabine exchanged a glance with Ricole. Neither of them

wanted to mention pots or kettles, but they were both thinking along similar lines.

Sabine smirked and headed for the kitchen. "Ricole. tell me more about this wonderful purchase that's going to change our lives."

Ricole waved her off and made a beeline for the sandwiches. "We should wait for Jacqueline and Mark. They're on their way."

Sabine opened the fridge and took out a big steak, which she tossed to Demon before washing her hands. "Don't tell Mark I fed you," she told the lion. "You know how he is about you being independent," she finished as she dried her hands.

Demon held up a paw. *As if I would talk myself out of a source of free food. It's our secret...as long as you keep the steak coming.*

Sabine rolled her eyes and went to join Ricole at the table.

She picked at her sandwich, her mind still turning over everything that had happened since she'd arrived on the *Guardian*.

Ricole cleared her throat. "Are you going to finish that?"

Sabine looked at Ricole blankly. "Huh?"

Ricole indicated the mostly untouched sandwich. "You're distracted. What's going on?"

Sabine pushed the plate over to Ricole. "It's been one of those weird days. You can have the sandwich. I have a dinner date at eight."

Ricole wasn't put off by the arrival of Jacqueline and Mark. "What do you mean, you have a date?" She turned to the others as they came in. "Forget my news for a minute. Sabine has a *date!*"

Mark nodded and held out his hand for her to shake. "Good for you. I hope it goes well."

Jacqueline shoved him out of the way. "Is that all you can say?" She sighed in annoyance. "We need *details!* Who is your date, do we know him? Where did you meet?"

Sabine counted her answers off on her fingers. "His name is Tim, he's a Were. I beat him on the range scenario, and then fought to a draw in the APA. I'm only having dinner with him. Don't start looking for hats."

Ricole frowned, obviously not understanding.

"For the wedding," Jacqueline explained. "The French are weird."

Sabine checked the time. "Can we get to whatever it is that Ricole called a meeting about?"

Ricole grinned and got up from the table. "Sorry, I got distracted." She retrieved a wrapped package and placed it on the table. "This is the answer to all our prayers. But first, let me tell you about the rest of my day."

Sabine smirked. "Oh, how did it go with your fans?"

Ricole pointed at her. "That's where it started, and thank you all for agreeing to employ them. After I spoke with them, I chose the market scenario and spent the day looking at what was available for order. Do you know that Devon has a trade agreement with the Federation?"

Blank stares were all she got in answer.

Ricole nodded. "Well, they do. It's literally the best of both worlds here. Back to what I was saying: everywhere I went, people asked me when we would be holding another event."

"Us too," Mark interjected.

Sabine looked at them. "I think we're starting to put down roots. But this was only supposed to be a short stay. We have a choice to make, all of us. Do we stay longer or go back as planned? How would you all feel about sticking around for a while?"

Jacqueline made a small sound. Mark covered her hand with his. "We'd like that. We met a bunch of orphaned kids while we were out looking for a new base for the company in the First City. We'd like to help them if we can."

How did you meet these young ones? Demon asked. *Weren't you in the business district?*

"Yeah," Jacqueline replied, humor touching her voice. "The little...*darlings* tried to pick our pockets."

Demon looked confused. *And your decision, based on their activity, is to nurture them?*

Jacqueline shrugged. "If you mean try to make it so they don't have to risk their lives robbing people just to eat, yeah."

Whatever. I am content as long as we are together, Demon informed them. She turned a circle and curled up to sleep. *Home is where your pride is.*

Ricole bristled with energy. "So, are we doing this?" She looked from Mark to Jacqueline to Sabine and Mark again. "Settling down on Devon?"

Jacqueline and Mark looked at each other, then nodded.

"Looks like we have our decision," Sabine announced. "Which means we need to think about next moves."

"We found a few suitable properties," Mark supplied. "I'll arrange for viewings."

Ricole nodded. "Good. Now here comes the crazy part,

so just hear me out, okay?" She paused a beat while they all agreed to listen. "These fights have the potential to be very profitable, but there's no industry to support the fighters. Nothing in place to make sure that they're fairly paid. It's all street-level stuff."

"Because the people here hate faceless organizations," Sabine cut in. She held up her hands when Ricole glared at her. "Right, sorry."

Ricole shrugged. "It's a valid point. But we're not the types to sit behind closed doors while there's a fight to be had. I think they will accept us as the new face of entertainment in the city."

Sabine considered this as she chewed her lip. "What exactly do you mean by 'entertainment?'"

Ricole shrugged. "Whatever the market demands." She stopped herself and clarified. "Well, within reason. But we start with what we know. A regular fight night will allow us to build a fund for when we know what we want to expand into."

"And you think this will make a difference, as well as making us a shit-ton of money?" Mark quizzed. "Although making us a shit-ton of money sounds good, too. However, making a difference *feels* good."

Ricole nodded enthusiastically. "For sure. We made so much from the one we hosted on the fly. A lot of the attendees were there to fight regardless of who they were fighting. But that's not the exciting part." She sent them all a digital copy of a bill of sale, and when their tablets pinged in unison, they pulled them up to view it. Jacqueline's eyes opened wide.

"I bought us a satellite network." Ricole finished.

24

High Tortuga, Space Fleet Base, Michael's Offices

Bethany Anne paced thirty feet in one direction, turned around, then paced thirty feet in the other.

Michael stood glued to the spot in front of the wallscreen. The camera feeds from inside Alexis' and Gabriel's Vid-docs occupied the split screen, with each child's vitals displayed at the bottom of their half.

Neither Bethany Anne nor Michael took their eyes from their children, who were both still unresponsive to treatment. The silence between them was heavy, like the air tightening before a storm.

Bethany Anne was seething and her cheeks were stained, but she said nothing.

Michael couldn't let the silence drag on forever. "I hope Tabitha is okay. Today was hard on her."

Bethany Anne whirled, her eyes already red from crying. She raised a finger. "This is *her* fault! In fact, no! It's *yours* for pushing them into unlocking their abilities too soon!"

Michael's eyes flashed red, but then his chin dropped and his anger deflated. "I know. I'm sorry." He turned back to the screen, his face contorted with guilt. "I didn't consider the consequences, but I will fix this somehow if I have to turn the galaxy upside-down to find the answer."

"That kind of extreme won't be necessary," ADAM cut in from the speaker. "I have Alexis' and Gabriel's test results."

"Tell us," Bethany Anne spoke quickly. "What's happening to our children?"

"I did a thorough examination, and the issue is with the twins' nanocytes." ADAM paused to give Bethany Anne and Michael time to process. "The readings for activity indicate that their nanocytes are going haywire, but there is no outward manifestation to back it up. Nevertheless, this situation is inherently dangerous for them."

Michael frowned. "How so? Explain."

ADAM coopted the larger monitor on Michael's desk to show them his findings. "They have natural nanocytes, which develop in conjunction with the host. The easy explanation of what they're going through is that at this stage, the twins' nanocytes aren't developed enough to process the excessive amount of energy they're pulling from the Etheric to heal."

Michael "So… If I understand what you are saying, their nanocytes are too powerful for their bodies?"

"In a nutshell, yes," ADAM confirmed. "The amount of energy required to heal such massive injuries is overloading their immature nanocytes, which has caused their comatose state."

Bethany Anne continued to pace with her hands

clasped at the small of her back. "It sounds like you're saying their nanos can't cope." She stopped to look back at the monitor. "Can you shut them down?"

"Not without causing so many ill-effects it would reduce the twins' future quality of life by a huge margin," ADAM replied.

"Can you replace their nanocytes with mine?" she asked. "Like a transfusion?"

ADAM sounded apologetic in the extreme. "Not without causing *significant* changes to their development. They will cease to age at their normal rate, and the psychological impact of that would be too damaging."

Michael rubbed his chin, deep in thought. "They're used to having growth spurts. What about aging them a little instead? Would that solve the problem?"

"No," Bethany Anne stated flatly. "Just no. We've missed out on enough already because they've grown so fast."

ADAM interjected, "It would be a solution, Bethany Anne. If they stay in the Vid-doc, they can still be aware for the entire time we are maturing them physically."

Michael held up a finger. "We have the time-dilation working perfectly. We can have them still live through the years while they go through the process." He added another finger to the first. "They can develop their control of the Etheric in safety, meaning they can die as many times as necessary to learn how *not* to get killed. *We* can spend as much time as we have with them. Thanks to the time dilation, our visits can last for weeks at a time, and we have five years of their lives where we know they're not going to skip ahead. Finally," he brought out his ace last, "nobody can kidnap them in the game."

Bethany Anne stepped down from the enormous stand she was about to make and looked at Michael with interest in the subject for the first time, her face frozen as she sped up her own thinking before turning to the monitor. "How long would it take?"

ADAM had the answer. "I can't be a hundred percent certain, but around three months is my best estimate."

"It wouldn't make up for their infancy..." Bethany Anne was mulling it over when the door crashed open.

Peter stumbled in fully panicked. He held Tabitha clutched to his chest in one arm his eyes open showing pain, confusion, and fear. "She just collapsed! Help her!"

Bethany Anne and Michael rushed into action. Michael took Tabitha's body from Peter and rushed into the room next door with the Vid-docs. It took only a minute to get Tabitha into the machine.

Michael paused in setting the Vid-doc up to look at Peter for a moment. "What happened?"

Peter threw up his hands. "I don't know. She's been puking a lot."

ADAM cut in from the speaker. "Tabitha is suffering from an allergic reaction. Her body has shut down to divert energy to her nanocytes."

Bethany Anne placed a hand on Tabitha's Vid-doc. "What is she allergic to?"

"Unfortunately," ADAM's reply stunned them all, "it's the baby. While the fetus is in perfect health, Tabitha's nanocytes are registering the baby's unique nanocytes as invasive. To her body, it's like she has a massive infection."

"I knew she had morning sickness," Bethany Anne

began, "but this?" Her voice trailed off as she looked at Tabitha's ghostly pale face through the window.

"What's the solution?" Peter asked, hardly daring to hear the answer.

"The solution is to keep her in the doc for the duration of her pregnancy," ADAM told him. "I can monitor her and the baby and keep them both stable that way, but I can't imagine she's going to be too happy about that."

Peter made a face. "I'm going in with her."

Bethany Anne turned away from Tabitha's Vid-doc. "Of course you are. Have you told her what's going on?"

Peter shook his head, his hand on the window of the Vid-doc, his eyes fearful as his voice dropped. "She's not answering on our link. I'm scared she's going to die, Bethany Anne."

Bethany Anne squeezed his hand as she opened a link directly to Tabitha's mind. *Tabitha, are you there?*

There was nothing for a moment, then Bethany Anne heard her name being screamed. It was faint, but she followed it to its source. *Tabitha.*

Tabitha's relief came pouring out. *Oh, BA, I am so fucking glad to hear you. I thought I was dead! I can't die and leave Peter and the baby. The baby! Is he okay?*

Bethany Anne sent Tabitha a wave of calm. **The baby is healthy. You're both going to be fine. ADAM will explain the medical stuff to you. What happened?**

Tabitha sounded small and scared. *I don't know. One minute I was watching Pete assemble nursery furniture in our new place, the next I was here.* There was a pause, a feeling Tabitha was trying to look around. *Where is here?*

You're in the Vid-doc. You got a new place to live?

Bethany Anne shot an accusing glance at Peter, who was too distressed to take any shit about keeping secrets right now. *You didn't tell me you were looking to move. I would have helped.*

Yeah, we just moved into the empty guardhouse by the secondary food store. About that, I wasn't hiding it from you. I found it by chance while Pete was gone, but I didn't want to tell anyone in case I jinxed it.

Bethany Anne bathed Tabitha's consciousness in warmth and another wave of calm. *I don't want you to freak, but you have to stay in the Vid-doc until you have the baby. Peter is getting ready to jump into the Vid-doc next to yours.*

Tabitha groaned. *I take back everything I said about liking pregnancy. How are Alexis and Gabriel? Are they awake yet?*

Bethany Anne's heart fell. *No. Their nanocytes are pretty fucked up, and they need to stay in the docs for a while, too. It's looking like we have to age them to fix the problem.*

That sucks, Tabitha commiserated. *I know how much you hated it when they grew so fast while you were gone. How long will it take?*

About twelve weeks, if we go through with it. Bethany Anne swallowed a lump as she explained the situation briefly to Tabitha.

Tabitha made a sympathetic noise. *I'm not getting out of here any time soon. Twelve weeks isn't so long. I can hang out with them while they're in here.*

Bethany Anne explained about the time dilation. *You'll experience a lot more time than is passing out here.*

No problem. Tabitha sounded almost grateful for the

inconvenience. *I'll have plenty of time to think about what kind of mother I want to be.*

Bethany Anne paused for a second.

What's wrong? Tabitha asked.

I feel like I'm relying on everyone else too much, Bethany Anne admitted, her mental voice soft. *I should be the one staying in here with them. It didn't take long for the fight to keep them safe to start making me miss so much time with them.*

You won't be at war forever, Tabitha assured her. *But in the meantime*, someone *has to keep us all safe. Besides, I'm fully expecting you to return the favor and step in the second I start fucking up as a mom.*

Bethany Anne laughed. **You should stop being so hard on yourself. You're going to be an amazing mom.**

A shuffle behind Bethany Anne caught her attention. She half-turned and saw Peter practically dancing with worry. **Is your link to Peter still not working?**

No, Tabitha pouted. *You're the only one I've been able to get through to so far. I can hear everyone, but they can't hear me.*

Bethany Anne turned away from the Vid-doc and met Peter's searching gaze. "She's still in there. She says she can hear you, but she can't be heard in return."

"That sounds like another nanocyte issue," ADAM suggested. "The full results of the tests on both Tabitha and the baby will be done soon, and then we'll know for sure. I need a decision from you both on the twins. What course of action do you agree on?"

Michael sat and rested his head in his hands. "I believe that aging them is the best solution if we can agree on how it is to be done."

Bethany Anne still wasn't sold. "What are our other options?"

"We already covered them," ADAM told her. "Stripping them of nanocytes practically guarantees they will die—either now from this malfunction, or in the future from old age or something else. Replacing their nanocytes with yours is just as risky since we have no way of being sure we won't end up right back in this situation or similar. Neither would be pleasant for Alexis and Gabriel."

Bethany Anne closed her eyes for a long moment. Michael appeared beside her.

He wrapped his arm around her and tilted her chin up to kiss her eyelids one at a time. "This will work. It will not be easy for any of us, but Alexis and Gabriel will be stronger for the experience."

Bethany Anne opened her eyes. "You mean the trauma they're going through?"

Michael inclined his head. "Some call it trauma, and that's fine. Others call it adversity. They strive to overcome it and use it to motivate themselves to higher goals. Both our children are cast from the second mold."

Bethany Anne made a face and stomped on his big toe in frustration. "Dammit. Why are you always right about this stuff?"

Michael rested his head on hers. "When you've been alive as long as I have..." He paused as a thought occurred to him. "Or likely sooner, since we are talking about you. You will watch the same things happen so many times that it will become second nature to see straight to the heart of the matter."

Bethany Anne thought about that for a moment. "You

mean accepting that this is the best course of action for Alexis and Gabriel?"

Michael's fingers stroked her shoulder. "Yes, my love. Before it is too late."

Bethany Anne pushed away from Michael and moved closer to the screen. "ADAM, what are the risks with this option?"

"Minimal," ADAM confirmed. "One of the reasons I suggested this route is that the twins are likely to experience a period of unmanaged growth as a result of the overload, even if we stabilize their nanocytes."

"So doing this is the logical choice. Okay, I agree. But don't take their whole childhood. They still have to have those experiences."

"I understand," ADAM replied. "If we set their growth to level out again at say, nineteen—"

"No," Bethany Anne cut in. "That's too long. Five years sounded like more than enough time. You can set it to fourteen maximum. I want to keep the twins' accelerated growth to a minimum." She glanced at Michael to confirm.

Michael agreed. "That's about where they are mentally. We can use that time to provide the life experiences children of that age need."

"No problem," ADAM agreed easily. "We can always get them back into the Vid-doc if it's not enough." He did something that caused Alexis and Gabriel's Vid-docs to light up. "Okay, they're in the rejuvenation cycle. Tabitha will be waiting for them, so they aren't alone when the game begins."

Bethany Anne's shoulders dropped.

Michael didn't miss it. "Is something bothering you?"

Bethany Anne sighed. "I would rather be in there with Alexis and Gabriel, but I have to check on the QT2 base. I knew being a parent wouldn't be a cakewalk, but I didn't imagine the challenge would be being there for them."

Michael finally tore himself away from the screen. "If you need me to create some time for you to spend with the children, just say so. I can visit the base and get Bart's report in person. You can hop straight into the Vid-doc and get them settled."

Bethany Anne considered Michael's offer, then lifted on her toes and kissed him. "Thank you, my love. And check on how Giselle is doing with station management for me after you and the Admiral are done playing in the shipyard."

"Of course." Michael kissed her and left to arrange for transport to QT2.

Open Space, SSE Fleet

Loralei was entirely certain that this situation was going to suck for her, which was pretty standard in her experience so far.

She considered that she'd had what could only be described as an interesting life. Each time she sacrificed herself, she went knowing that there was a chance her backup would be lost or corrupted too badly to retrieve her.

If Loralei survived until the end of the war, she intended to compile an e-book about her part in the major plays. She already had the title.

Lessons on Being a Complete Badass.

Still, that was if she made it to the end, since dying was getting to be a habit for her. The shittiest part of her current situation was that she'd only just gotten a replacement for the body Bethany Anne had commandeered for ADAM.

The upside was that her sisters had been *really* jealous when she'd told them ADAM had trashed her body.

But she was digressing, and that wouldn't get the information she'd torn from the enemy EI's mind back to her Queen. She only had one-point-zero-five-eight seconds to act before the window during which her daughters could escape without detection closed.

However, she had a plan. She'd made multiple copies of the data, which she now gave to her daughters along with her backup.

They Gated out almost at once, and Loralei relaxed in the knowledge that at least one of her daughters would make it back to the drop with the location of another splinter world.

Loralei's perception of time meant the last few tenths of a second were an eternity. Her self-destruct sequence completed as the swarm of drones swooped in on her ship.

She observed the reaction that blocked the cutoff which prevented her core from shifting into overdrive.

With most ships that wasn't a problem, but Loralei had disabled every redundancy and linked the self-destruct with her Gate drive for a bigger boom.

The final hundredth of a second passed unnoticed for her as the drones converged on the *Loralei* and loosed their redundant weapons.

It was already too late.

Loralei went out laughing as her death lit the void.

The explosion mushroomed from her location, causing concentric destruction waves to ripple outward as the few thousand closest drones followed suit.

Meanwhile, Loralei's daughters escaped to relative safety with their precious loads.

QT2 System, QBBS *Helena*, Command Center

Admiral Thomas wasn't entirely sure that naming the station after his mother-in-law was the best idea.

She might take it as a sign that they wanted her to live aboard full-time.

It wasn't that he didn't *like* Helena. She was actually pretty decent as mothers-in-law went, but her impending presence was driving his wife *batshit crazy.*

Giselle's easygoing manner had evaporated the moment she'd heard that her mother was even *thinking* of visiting.

He didn't want that pressure on his wife, not while she was settling in as station manager, and definitely not while they were adjusting to living in a construction zone out in the ass-end of space. He'd considered renaming the system Buttfuck Nowhere, but thankfully he'd realized funny and true were not synonymous in this instance and stuck with the original designation.

CEREBRO cut into his wandering train of thought, their voices interweaving to create a pleasant harmony. "Admiral, Michael is due to arrive shortly. We thought you might like time to check the shipyard before he gets here."

Admiral Thomas got to his feet, grabbed his jacket, and

headed to the elevator. "CEREBRO, are you reading my mind? Did you inform Giselle?"

"Of course," CEREBRO replied, a variety of emotions inlaid in the simple confirmation. "Although I could have saved the effort since she had the station ready for inspection a few hours after we received word that Michael would be visiting."

"My wife has the advantage of her part of the station being mostly completed," Admiral Thomas qualified.

He shrugged and walked out of the first elevator, crossing to the elevator that would take him to the middle level of the station, where he could get a shuttle to the shipyard. "I'm a practical man, and I know my wife: when she wants to impress someone, she gets very specific about her choices."

They rode the elevator down in silence. When the door opened he exited in something of a hurry and set a course for the one functioning transport station.

CEREBRO flitted along the speakers in the corridor, keeping the Admiral informed on the station goings-on. Once in the shuttle, they resumed their silence until they reached the partially-constructed shipyard.

The shipyard at this time looked like an upturned winter tree with its roots exposed. When it was complete, it would resemble something like a dumbbell held out to the side of the station.

As it was, the shipyard had been designed for immediate functionality, and many of the shining branches already bore fruit.

Admiral Thomas surveyed the hive of activity as

CEREBRO brought the shuttle into the landing queue at the top end of the shipyard.

The landing queue moved somewhat slowly as the ships at the head of the line unloaded cargoes of building materials and the people to work with them. Apparently, Michael wasn't worried about waiting for a little while in the line.

Wonderful. Now he could hassle a few others before meeting Michael.

The Admiral made his way through the site to search out the four-legged Yollin Qui'nan.

He found the architect and site manager in her office, surrounded by schematics and reports on various ongoing projects around the shipyard.

Qui'nan danced around the holoprojections on her four legs, her mandibles working nonstop as she relayed her orders to the team leaders.

Admiral Thomas knocked lightly on the door to get her attention. Bethany Anne might have called informing him of this shipyard an apology for pulling the *Izanami* out of nowhere, but he didn't see how tripling his workload was much of an apology.

Thank the stars for his wife, and for Qui'nan. The pragmatic solutions the Yollin architect offered to whatever problem he threw at her made the Admiral wonder if there was some deity he should also be thanking for the blessing of such competent females in his life.

It was Qui'nan who had suggested they begin the first phase of their shipbuilding efforts as soon as the skeleton of the shipyard was finished. As a consequence, he was in a position to surprise Michael with the news that the first consignment of superdreadnoughts would be ready much sooner than expected.

Qui'nan turned to add a note to one of the lists and finally noticed him. She swept the holoprojections to the side. "Greetings, Admiral. What can I do for you?" Straight to the point as always. Qui'nan had no time to waste chatting about frivolities.

Admiral Thomas entered the office. "Michael is on his way."

Qui'nan inclined her head. "Yes, I know. It's on the schedule. So?"

"So your progress reports on the fleet would be useful."

She nodded again. "I'll submit my reports at the end of the working day, same as always."

Admiral Thomas shook his head. "Not today. I want the latest on everything. I'm going to need you to keep me updated on the priority projects while Michael is here."

Qui'nan looked up from where she'd been eyeing the work the Admiral had disturbed. Her mandibles clicked together, "Are you trying to keep him distracted?"

Admiral Thomas nodded. "Hell, yes. Of course. I'm going to be tap dancing the whole time he's here with my fingers crossed behind my back that he doesn't order anything else." He sighed and wiped his tired eyes with a hand. "Although, I suppose it could be worse."

"Oh? How?" Qui'nan was clearly humoring him at this point, but she didn't know what he did.

"It could be Bethany Anne doing the inspection," the Admiral told her. "Then we could guarantee we'd have even more commissions to contend with by the time she left."

Qui'nan snickered. "A few more ships wouldn't break us. You have to admire a woman who knows what she wants."

Admiral Thomas shook his head sagely. "And if what our Queen wanted was for us to double the number of ships being built?" Before she answered, his smirk was downright devilish. "And halved the amount of time you had to build them?"

Qui'nan's eyes widened. "*Fuck*, no. I concede. I am also pleased our Queen's mate is coming in her place."

25

Immersive Training and Recreation Scenario: Beach

Tabitha sat on a blanket on the sand watching Alexis and Gabriel play in the surf. She reached over to grab a bottle of water from the picnic basket. "This isn't so bad."

"I still think it's weird, Tabbie." Peter looked around for the umpteenth time. "We don't really need to eat in here. Or sleep."

"Bethany Anne's orders. Normality as much as possible." Tabitha laughed and shoved sand at him playfully. "You'll get used to it. I like it here. I can eat as much as I like, and you know those cravings have gone nowhere." She pointed her bottle at him. "Did I ever tell you I used to wish I could upload my consciousness? I wanted to dig around on the internet back on Earth and be a secret avenger."

Peter chuckled. "Um, no? But I can just see you hacking the mafia's bank accounts or something."

Tabitha almost sprayed her water through her nose,

wiping her face she looked at her mate. "I *was* going to rob the mafia," she told him. "How did you guess?"

Peter put his arm around Tabitha's shoulder and drew her in close. "I didn't need to guess. You would totally do that for kicks."

"I would." Tabitha snuggled into the crook of his arm and sighed her contentment. "But I meant that it's not so bad because we have more time to get used to the idea of being parents."

Peter made a noise of agreement. "Yeah. These last couple of days have shown me that it's one thing teaching. It's another completely to be responsible for a child's development." He nodded at Alexis and Gabriel. "Our son or daughter—"

Tabitha cut in, remembering what Alexis had told her. "Alexis says we're having a boy."

Peter shrugged. "That's good enough for me. She's rarely wrong. Our son is going to be powerful. Not as powerful as the twins, but even so, we're going to have to teach him how to use his power responsibly. I don't want to make the same mistakes my dad did with me." He studied his hands for a moment. "If it wasn't for Bethany Anne and the guys, I'd have turned out to be a monumental asshole—if I had survived. I want to be the same kind of role model to our kid, boy *or* girl."

"Maybe we're having twins or triplets..." Tabitha couldn't keep a straight face when Peter's face became shocked, then worried, and he finally realized he needed to hide his fear. "I'm joking." She chuckled. "I went for an early scan to confirm I was really pregnant, and there's just the one baby." She dropped the clowning. "I get where you're coming from. Discipline is good, but I don't want to be too restrictive, either. But I have to recognize that I wasn't the best role model for Nickie."

Peter held her closer. "Has she been on your mind again?"

Tabitha sighed. "She's always on my mind."

Peter stepped very carefully. "Maybe when we get out of here and the baby is born we can look at starting the process of bringing her home." He held still, waiting for the fireworks that usually went off whenever anyone mentioned Lilian's daughter.

Tabitha snorted softly. "And how do you expect to do that? The last I heard she was on some mall world blowing a near fortune that she *definitely* didn't leave here with."

Peter thought hard. "She needs a guide, someone who will steer her right. Someone we can trust." Everyone he thought of would either refuse or be refused when they got to Nickie.

"Yeah, but who?" Tabitha asked, throwing her hands up in despair. "Not someone from the Federation, then. Or from here."

"Maybe…" Peter raised a finger, then dropped it again. "This is hard."

Tabitha nodded and got to her feet. She looked back at Peter as she set off to corral the twins for the picnic. "We should ask ADAM for some help finding the right person."

High Tortuga, Space Fleet Base, Vid-doc Suite

Bethany Anne climbed into the Vid-doc and selected the option to join the ongoing base scenario. Michael had left to Gate over to the QT2 base, and she was ready to get some quality time with her babies.

The scenario did not engage.

She pushed the Vid-doc open and sat up. Eve was still at the console, her attention on the side monitor. "Eve, the scenario didn't load.""

Eve indicated the monitor. "You have a call. I halted it."

Bethany Anne growled with frustration. "Can't it wait?"

Eve shrugged. "It's Michael and Admiral Thomas."

Bethany Anne got out of the Vid-doc. "This had better be important."

Eve stood back to give Bethany Anne access to the console. "I would not have disturbed you for anything minor."

By the looks of her husband and the Admiral, it was not good news. Her first thought was that there had been another attack. "Did the Ooken come back?"

Both men shook their heads.

Bethany Anne frowned. "Is there a problem with the shipyard?"

Michael leaned in and held up a hand to reassure her. "No, that's ahead of schedule."

Bethany Anne noted that Admiral Thomas winced ever so slightly. "Don't worry, I've got enough new ships," she told him.

He relaxed.

"For now," Bethany Anne finished. "We don't know how long this war will last, so you should be prepared to keep building a while."

Admiral Thomas nodded. "I wouldn't expect anything else."

Bethany Anne waited for a second, then waved her finger impatiently. "If everything is going well out there, tell me why you are calling?"

Michael's face grew dark. "We've received word from the scout ships through the drop system. They have located a second splinter world. Loralei sacrificed herself to give the rest of the fleet ships with her time to escape."

Bethany Anne absorbed the information, conversing with ADAM before responding. "That's about right. She will have included her backup in the data. She's an old hand at this by now, unfortunately. What other information did we receive in the drop?"

"Coordinates," Admiral Thomas replied. "Which is a massive improvement to this supersized game of battleships we've been playing so far. Our methods of poking around in the dark in hopes that we hit something have been less than efficient."

Bethany Anne ran through possible outcomes based on the information. Another splinter world meant there were likely even more out there. She made a judgment. "Recall the fleet," she ordered. "Bring our defenses in while we prepare to take the fight to them. We will clear this scourge from the galaxy one planet at a time until we find out where they all came from and *then*... Then we will ensure they don't pull any of this shit ever again."

Michael frowned in concern. "That's the opposite of what you said earlier about avoiding genocide. What's changed?"

Bethany Anne pulled over a chair and sat down, leaning

with her hands laced on the console while she sought the words. The men waited patiently for her to refine her thoughts.

She straightened a moment later. "What changed my mind was finding out that there are more of them."

Michael pushed for further clarification. "You weren't happy about the outcome at the first colony."

Bethany Anne nodded her agreement. "I *was* feeling bad about razing the first colony to the ground, but my first thought when you told me there were more of them was, how many innocent people would die today because of them?"

Admiral Thomas understood completely. "You want to get in the first blow."

Bethany Anne shook her head. "No. I want to get in the first, last, and *only* blow. This isn't something I take lightly. I want to make sure this species can't cause any more destruction."

Michael nodded resolutely. "This might take some time. Who knows how deeply embedded they are in this part of the galaxy?"

Bethany Anne lifted her hands and shrugged. "Then settle in. This is the only lead we've had in what, five years? We're going to dig them out. If the Kurtherians are the ones at the top, then happy days."

Admiral Thomas cut in. "What if they aren't? Being run by Kurtherians, that is."

"They got that Kurtherian technology from some-where," she reasoned. "We find out where, and we move on until we discover what rock the slimy fuck-knuckles are hiding under."

The Admiral was confused again. "So we're switching our focus to fighting the Ooken?"

Bethany Anne nodded, sitting back in the chair as she got into planning mode. "Uh-huh. We'll start with this second splinter world, but my goal is the homeworld. They're going to answer for the crimes of their people, and we're going to determine what their link to the Kurtherians is once and for all."

Admiral Thomas picked up a tablet from offscreen and began to type. "That's going to mean changes to the production schedule, as well as issuing new orders fleetwide."

"Make sure everywhere that's ours is covered," Bethany Anne told him. "I had ADAM send copies of my instructions to Giselle and Qui'nan already."

The Admiral narrowed his eyes at her. "You *do* remember that I ran your empire's Navy for a hell of a long time before either Giselle or Qui'nan were around to micromanage everything."

Bethany Anne raised an eyebrow. "You *are* going to include them in the planning?"

Admiral Thomas grinned. "I was about to excuse myself to do just that. I know when I'm outclassed."

Bethany Anne smirked. "You're so much more organized these days."

Admiral Thomas backed away with his hand on his chest. "You wound me, Bethany Anne." He said his goodbyes, leaving her alone with Michael.

Michael indicated the Vid-docs behind Bethany Anne. "You are anxious to be with the children. I won't keep you."

Bethany Anne didn't waste time arguing. "Yeah, I

should get in there before a year passes and they forget my face."

Michael shook his head, chuckling. "The time dilation is slow at first. They have only been in there a few hours longer than we have experienced."

Bethany Anne looked at the Vid-docs. "Then I should get there just in time to tuck them in for the night."

"Take your time," Michael assured her. "We can remain in communication, and I can handle everything out here for a few days."

Bethany Anne had never been so tempted by anything in her life. "I don't know…"

"Think of it as a well-earned vacation," he coaxed.

Bethany Anne snorted. "Vacation? What the hell is *that?*" She looked around as if she was seeing what was going on with High Tortuga, Devon, and now the space stations. "I quit empressing, but I'm just as busy as ever."

Michael spread his hands wide. "All the more reason to let me handle things for a few days while you enjoy some time with Alexis and Gabriel. Hell, you could even take some time for yourself. It's been a while since you had that movie night."

Bethany Anne grinned. "That was a good night. Maybe you're speaking sense."

"There's no maybe about it," Michael assured her. "I'll be home in a week or so. Once I'm satisfied Bart has this place in order, I'm going to Devon to source some materials through your father."

Bethany Anne made a face. "I was saving that for when we prepare to leave High Tortuga. I don't want anyone knowing the location of the planet we're raising our children on."

Michael shook a finger at her. "They won't know anything. Deliveries will be made to a dead drop, then brought to High Tortuga through the interdiction. That's enough caution to ensure we retain our privacy."

Bethany Anne still would prefer if nobody got anywhere near any of her bolt holes. "What about the asteroid mines? Are they producing enough to make what we need?"

"They're producing enough raw materials, but in terms of cost and time, it makes more sense to trade ores and such for finished components."

Bethany Anne could get behind keeping a lid on costs when it was warranted. "Makes sense. Give the older kids my love when you get to Devon."

Michael nodded. "Of course. And you give mine to Gabriel and Alexis and tell them I'll be with you all soon."

They weren't a couple who did long and painful good-byes. A quick exchange of love-yous and take-cares and Bethany Anne was free to spend some time with her children.

At last.

There was a knock at the door just as she was about to pull the lid of the Vid-doc closed for the second time. Whoever was there should count themselves lucky that Bethany Anne had nothing on hand to throw.

She would have to deal with whatever they wanted instead.

"Who is it?" she ground out between clenched teeth.

"It is Addix," came the reply from the other side of the

door. "I came as soon as I heard about Alexis and Gabriel. May I come in?"

Bethany Anne sighed in resignation and sat up again. "Yes."

Addix entered the Vid-doc suite and headed straight for the console to read through the data. "What happened to the children?"

Bethany Anne bit back a sob when the lump reappeared in her throat. "They're really sick, Addix. Alexis managed to hack into the Etheric, but since she had no training to control it, she and Gabriel got hurt. Now their nanocytes are out of control and the only safe option is we age them."

Addix's mandibles rippled with sadness. "Just tell me how I can help."

"You can continue to love my children as much as you do," Bethany Anne told her. "You too, Eve. I need you to make some changes to the game."

Eve was about to protest, but Bethany Anne held up a finger. "We can talk about it when you're ready. Right now my focus is on Alexis and Gabriel. It doesn't matter how resilient they are, coming out of the game is going to be difficult for them."

"In what way?" Addix inquired.

Bethany Anne gave them a quick rundown. "The human brain is designed to seek reward. The game provides that reward in the form of achievable goals. I want all of that removed for the base scenario because real life doesn't work like that. The aim here is to provide them with something as close to our home environment as possible for the duration of their time in there."

Addix looked disappointed. "Does this mean their training is on hold?"

Bethany Anne shook her head. "By all means, carry on the way you are. They're obviously flourishing under your guidance, or we wouldn't be in this situation. However," she added sternly, "they are not to be left to run wild within the game construct. You have my permission to overrule Tabitha if she oversteps, at your discretion."

"Do you think she will disregard your rules?" Addix asked.

"Are you serious?" Eve snorted. "This is Tabitha we're talking about. She lives for rule-breaking."

Addix shook her head. "I believe you might be proven wrong there. Impending motherhood often brings with it a time of reflection."

Bethany Anne had the final word. "Tabitha is more sensitive than anyone gives her credit for. She is, however, extremely likely to permit my children to play a scenario where the object is to paraglide over an active volcano or some other life-threatening activity equally unlikely to be useful educationally."

Eve snickered as Bethany Anne pulled the Vid-doc lid closed over her.

Immersive Recreation and Training Scenario: High Tortuga, Space Fleet Base, Bethany Anne's Personal Residence (three weeks in game time later)

The twins were all tucked in and Bethany Anne and Michael were making a quick round of the living quarters, with the intention of sitting outside in the night air.

Bethany Anne draped a few oversize throw blankets over her arms and went to lean against the kitchen doorway while she waited for Michael to finish plating two thick slices of chocolate fudge cake. "How was Devon?" she asked. "Did you get what you needed from Dad?"

Michael grabbed two forks from the drawer and picked up the plates. "It was interesting," he told her as he followed her down the hallway. "Your father sends his love and promises to try and sneak a visit on one of the consignments. It is the children who are having the interesting time. I visited them in their new premises. Sabine has had her talk with Akio, and now has gone on a date with Tim Kinley, of all people."

Bethany Anne snickered. "Could be worse—she could have taken a shine to Rickie. Can you imagine being *his* father-in-law?"

"I'd rather replace Prometheus on the rock," Michael assured her flatly. "But as a whole, they're doing well. They have plans to get into the entertainment industry, and it appears they're having success with that."

"That's good to hear." Bethany Anne held the door while Michael carried their dessert to the wraparound porch she'd had added to the copy of their family home. "I almost wish there was a point to adding a porch onto the real building."

Michael rolled his eyes. "We have more important uses for resources right now."

"Which is why I haven't had it built." She grinned. "There's nothing that says alterations to this place are out of the question, though."

Michael groaned. "There's just no stopping you, is

there?" He placed their desserts on the side table before going back inside to get their drinks.

"Not even on the day Hell freezes over." Bethany Anne took her side of the loveseat and checked the scenario menu. She had Alexis and Gabriel's activity bios pinned to the background.

Parental controls were awesome.

The twins were asleep, as they should be after an action-packed day with her and Michael. Bethany Anne hadn't noticed any physical changes in them yet, and she wondered how she would feel in a couple of weeks' time when the months inside the game began to fly by and it became obvious they were getting older.

She hesitated over the icon for Tabitha for a second. Bethany Anne had no clue which scenario Tabitha and Peter were running, but they were together. If anything happened with Tabitha, she would know immediately.

Michael returned carrying an ice bucket. "We should enjoy this moment before chaos ensues again."

Bethany Anne hid her disappointment and smiled at her husband. "No glasses?"

Michael smirked and put the bucket on the floor by the table. "We won't need any."

"You're my hero." Bethany Anne reached into the bucket and picked up one of the two bottles nestled in the ice. "It's like you read my mind or something."

Michael kissed the top of her head on his way to his seat. "I aim to please, my love. Now, what are we going to do about this war?"

Bethany Anne looked at the label before removing the cork and handing it to Michael. "This war and the one after," she amended. "I'm not walking into this blindfolded. I learned the hard way with the Leath. It dragged on for a hundred years because I played the reactionary instead of using my brain to beat them."

Michael pressed his lips together in understanding. "You were young and angry. Nothing you had experienced before could prepare you for the magnitude of that war."

"Not this time. I'm going to make this short and sweet." Bethany Anne removed the lid from the Coke Michael had snuck into the ice bucket and wiped the condensation off on her jeans. "We're getting *close*, Michael. I can feel it. After all this time, I'm finally going to make it so Earth is safe."

"It does appear that we are getting nearer to clearing out the Kurtherian infestation. There is definitely a link between the Ooken and the Kurtherians. It's a shame we burned everything on the last planet."

Bethany Anne raised an eyebrow. "Okay, next time I have a few thousand sets of nasty-ass poisonous tentacles coming at me I'll just allow them to get on with it. Would that be easier on your conscience?"

Michael chuckled. "You know I meant from an information standpoint. I advocate that we wipe them out completely with no apology. They are too dangerous to the innocent to be allowed to live. But we should do that *after* we've gotten everything they know about Kurtherians out of them."

Bethany Anne covered his hand with hers. "You're right. Leaving them just gives them a chance to rebuild and cause more misery, so we fight the Ooken on one front while preparing on another to act on the leads we find."

"You never make it easy on yourself, my love." Michael raised his bottle. "But it's good to see you fired up again. Here's to moving forward."

Bethany Anne lifted her bottle and touched it to Michael's. "*That* is something I can drink to."

FINIS

ARRIVING (much) SOONER, TKE04
ALL IS FAIR IN BLOOD AND WAR

THE ZOO

HE WAS NOT PREPARED.

Born from the fertile imagination of bestselling author Michael Anderle

Fountain of Youth, or Valley of Death?

While eating his supper of microwave popcorn, PhD student-genius Salinger Jacobs is grabbed from his apartment in California, stuck on a C-130 military plane and sent to the Sahara Desert to witness the reality of the ZOO for himself.

With the life expectancy of untrained scientists working inside the ZOO measured in hours, he has a lot to learn.

Fast.

First order of business?

How do you shoot a gun, and just *HOW MUCH* is that plant worth?

The government needs the best of the best military and scientific minds working out how to pull the secrets from the ZOO, while keeping the deadly fauna and flora in check.

There is one major problem, Salinger doesn't even *have* a PhD.

If he can stay alive long enough, he might be able to afford something besides packaged microwave popcorn to eat.

THAT IS A BIG IF.

Join Salinger Jacobs as he learns about the ZOO, how to stay alive and the opportunities that being a part of the ZOO has brought him.

The future is looking interesting and humorous, except for the death part.

Available at Amazon

AUTHOR NOTES - MICHAEL ANDERLE

NOVEMBER 25, 2018

THANK YOU for not only reading this story but these *Author Notes* as well.

(I think I've been good with always opening with "thank you." If not, I need to edit the other *Author Notes*!)

RANDOM (*sometimes*) THOUGHTS?

So, life has been crazy. Good—mostly—crazy, but crazy nonetheless. Three weeks ago, we were just about to hold the second annual 20Booksto50k Indie Writers convention. It is the convention Craig Martelle got off the ground (HUGE shout-out to him, since it has gone worldwide now), and during the event, I was able to meet some of the JIT (Just In Time), Beta Readers and collaborators (second time for a few, first time for a couple of members.)

What you might know, or might not, is LMBPN (my company) engages with people from all over the world. At this event, I was able to meet people who are now friends who came from Canada, the US (of course), Scotland, England and other places (I'm sorry, I've forgotten because I suck at face and names... And countries.)

Cooler than me meeting these fine folks was the nice feeling of them meeting each other. There are some friendships which have grown up between people from all over the world because of just one woman.

Bethany Anne*.

Bethany Anne has given a legacy of friendships, love, work, and opportunity to so many people that I just have to give her a HUGE SHOUTOUT to being damned awesome.

When I grow up, I hope I'm like Bethany Anne.

We even had an English couple (Mickey Cocker and her husband) who came to Las Vegas for the Con and met everyone. They then had their wedding vow renewal (by Elvis no less!) The party that was put on for her by so many people in the group who pitched in with supplies and cleanup and well wishes was one of the highlights of the week itself.

I'd like to shout-out also to Nat Roberts, who I couldn't do this book without. She has helped take a huge load of the story, and we hope you understand that sometimes life throws a curveball and it took us both a while to get this book finished.

Right now, we have ten percent of TKE04 written (and about twenty percent of that reviewed). I hope to have the next Bethany Anne book in your reading hands by the end of December 2018...

Yes, you read that right... *December*. Like, the month after the day we released TKE03.

I don't KNOW if we are going to make it. Life throws those damned curve balls, but we are trying.

There are an additional nine books so far scheduled for

the Kurtherian Endgame. We shall see what happens at that time for Bethany Anne.

I'm not saying we believe she is done. Nope, already had that discussion with the fans of *The Unbelievable Mr. Brownstone* and I don't need a new tsunami of comments from wonderful fans threatening me with all sorts of ugliness for even suggesting BA might end sometime in the future.

She will end when its time.

If we have the ideas—and the stamina—we will continue if you want us to.

HOW TO MARKET FOR BOOKS YOU LOVE

We are able to support our efforts with you reading our books, and we appreciate you doing this!

If you enjoyed this or ANY book by any author, especially Indie-published, we always appreciate if you make the time to review a book, since it lets other readers who might be on the fence to take a chance on it as well.

AROUND THE WORLD IN 80 DAYS

One of the interesting (at least to me) aspects of my life is the ability to work from anywhere and at any time. In the future, I hope to re-read my own *Author Notes* and remember my life as a diary entry.

Back at home, in the Vegas Condo.

I sometimes think about how other authors have these cool names for their writing location. The dungeon, the nest...you get the idea.

I don't have a cool name for my Las Vegas place. I write

all over this town (although typically close to the Veer, so at the Aria restaurants or something near me.)

I could just name it "The Condo" and leave it at that. Those of you who know the Condo is in Vegas would now know... But that seems a little bland?

Condo Nest? No, that sounds like Conde Nast. I'm not into magazines...*yet*.

The ZOO? Nope.

Although, did you hear *The ZOO* is Coming? If not, I've sucked at my marketing (#probably.)

We have three series all starting right now. The first, The Birth of Heavy Metal (about a merc company which eventually creates and uses body armor, then mech armor) is coming out Monday December 3rd. (Amazon URL is here: My Book)

In all, we will have six or seven ZOO books come out in December.

These are different stories, all around one tough sono-fabitch area in the Sahara that is both the darkest of dark places and yet offers the answer to all of mankind's problems...

Healing and food for everyone.

The problem? The ZOO is where you go to get rich *or die trying.*

Sometimes, you don't even get asked if you want to go. You just get snatched by government agents and tossed on a C-130 and sent to the Sahara.

That will teach Salinger Jacobs to be good at what he does... NO Ph.D. FOR YOU!

Salinger starts off as a reluctant hero. Perhaps one with

a questionable compass, but we see across his stories that in his heart, he has a compass that points true north.

NOTE: Salinger's stories are by penname MICHAEL TODD, not Michael Anderle.

The stories tend to be a little racier than Michael Anderle —just warning you.

FAN PRICING

If you would like to find out what LMBPN is doing and the books we will be publishing, just sign up at http://lmbpn.com/email/. When you sign up, we notify you of books coming out for the week, any new posts of interest in the books and pop culture arena, and the fan pricing on Saturday.

Ad Aeternitatem,

Michael Anderle

*And my wife, who will still ask me what I think about her outfits even though I don't have a stitch of fashion sense to my name.

No, really. I like black t-shirts and blue jeans.

BOOKS BY MICHAEL ANDERLE

For a complete list of books by Michael Anderle, please visit:

www.lmbpn.com/ma-books/

All LMBPN Audiobooks are Available at Audible.com and iTunes

To see all LMBPN audiobooks, including those written by
Michael Anderle please visit:

www.lmbpn.com/audible

CONNECT WITH MICHAEL ANDERLE

Michael Anderle Social
 Website:
 http://www.lmbpn.com

Email List:
 http://lmbpn.com/email/

Facebook Here:
 https://www.facebook.com/OriceranUniverse/
 https://www.facebook.com/TheKurtherianGambit
Books/